By Steve Perry

The Tularemia Gambit
Civil War Secret Agent
The Man Who Never Missed
Matadora
The Machiavelli Interface
The 97th Step
The Albino Knife
Black Steel
Brother Death
Conan the Fearless
Conan the Defiant
Conan the Indomitable
Conan the Free Lance
Conan the Formidable
Aliens: Earth Hive
Aliens: Nightmare Asylum
Aliens: The Female War
(with Stephani Danelle Perry)
Aliens vs. Predator: Prey
(with Stephani Danelle Perry)
Spindoc
The Forever Drug
Stellar Rangers
Stellar Rangers: Lone Star
The Mask
Men in Black
Leonard Nimoy's Primortals
Star Wars: Shadows of the Empire
The Trinity Vector
The Digital Effect
Windowpane
Tribes: Einstein's Hammer
The Musashi Flex
Titan AE (with Dal Perry)
Isaac Asimov's I-Bots: Time Was
(with Gary Braunbeck)

By Steve Perry with Tom Clancy & Steve Pieczenik

Net Force
Net Force: Hidden Agendas
Net Force: Night Moves
Net Force: Breaking Point
Net Force: Point of Impact
Net Force: CyberNation
Net Force: State of War
(also with Larry Segriff)
Net Force: Changing of the Guard
(also with Larry Segriff)

By Michael Reaves

The Burning Realm
The Shattered World
Darkworld Detective
I, Alien
Street Magic
Night Hunter
Voodoo Child
Star Wars: Darth Maul: Shadow Hunter
Dragonworld
(with Byron Preiss)
Hell On Earth
Mr. Twilight
(with Maya Kaathryn Bohnhoff)
Batman: Fear, Itself
(with Steven-Elliot Altman)
InterWorld (with Neil Gaiman)

Anthologies

Shadows Over Baker Street
(co-edited with John Pelan)
The Night People (short stories)

By Michael Reaves & Steve Perry

Sword of the Samurai
Hellstar
Dome
The Omega Cage
Thong the Barbarian Meets the Cycle Sluts of Saturn
Star Wars: MedStar I: Battle Surgeons
Star Wars: MedStar II: Jedi Healer
Star Wars: Death Star

Death Star

DEATH STAR

Michael Reaves

and

Steve Perry

BALLANTINE BOOKS
NEW YORK

Star Wars: Death Star is a work of fiction. Names, places, and incidents either are products of the authors' imagination or are used fictitiously.

Published in the United States by Del Rey Books,
an imprint of The Random House Publishing Group,
a division of Random House, Inc., New York.

DEL REY is a registered trademark and the Del Rey colophon is a trademark of Random House, Inc.

LIBRARY OF CONGRESS CATALOGING-IN-PUBLICATION DATA

Reaves, Michael.
Star wars : Death Star / Michael Reaves & Steve Perry.
p. cm.
ISBN 978-0-345-47742-2 (hardcover : alk. paper)
1. Star Wars films—Miscellanea. I. Perry, Steve. II. Title.
PN1995. 9. S695R43 2007
791. 43'75—dc22 2007018664

Printed in the United States of America

www.delreybooks.com

2 4 6 8 9 7 5 3 1

First Edition

Book design by Katie Shaw

For Deborah
—MR

For Dianne, as always,
and for the new grandkid, Nate
—SP

Acknowledgments

We'd like to thank the usual crew for aiding and abetting: Shelly Shapiro, Keith Clayton, Betsy Mitchell, Sue Rostoni, Leland Chee, Steve Sansweet, and all the folks at Del Rey and Lucasfilm. And especially George Lucas, who made up this wonderful world and allowed us to play in it again.

Dramatis Personae

Atour Riten; Imperial Navy commander, Chief Librarian (human male)

Celot Ratua Dil; convicted smuggler (Zelosian male)

Conan Antonio Motti; Imperial Navy admiral (human male)

Daala; Imperial Navy admiral (human female)

Darth Vader; Dark Lord of the Sith (human male)

Kornell "Uli" Divini; Imperial Surgical Corps captain (human male)

Memah Roothes; pub tender (Twi'lek female)

Nova Stihl; Imperial Marines guard sergeant (human male)

Rodo; bouncer (Ragithian human male)

Teela Kaarz; architect, convict (Mirialan female)

Tenn Graneet; Imperial Navy master chief gunnery officer (human male)

Villian Dance; Imperial Navy lieutenant (human male)

Wilhuff Tarkin; Imperial Navy Grand Moff (human male)

"That's no moon. It's a space station."

—Obi-Wan Kenobi

PART ONE

CONSTRUCTION

1

FLIGHT DECK, *IMPERIAL*-CLASS STAR DESTROYER *STEEL TALON,*
POLAR ORBIT, PLANET DESPAYRE, HORUZ SYSTEM, ATRIVIS SECTOR,
OUTER RIM TERRITORIES

The alert siren screamed, a piercing wail that couldn't be ignored by any being on board with ears and a pulse. It had one thing to say, and it said it loud and clear:

Scramble!

Lieutenant Commander Villian "Vil" Dance came out of a deep sleep at the blaring alarm, sat up, and leapt from his rack to the expanded metal deck of the Ready Room quarters. Save for the helmet, he already wore his space suit, one of the first things an on-call TIE pilot learned to do was sleep in full battle gear. He ran for the door, half a step ahead of the next pilot to awaken. He grabbed his headgear, darted into the hall and turned to the right, then sprinted for the launching bay.

It could be a drill; there had been plenty of those lately to keep the pilots on their toes. But maybe this time it wasn't. One could always hope.

Vil ran into the assembly area. A-grav on the flight deck was kept at slightly below one g, so that the pilots, all of whom were human or humanoid, could move a little faster and get to their stations a little sooner. The smell of launch lube was acrid in the cold air, and the pulsing lights painted the area in bright, primary flashes. Techs scrambled, getting the TIE fighters to final-set for takeoff, while pilots ran toward the craft. Vil noticed that it was just his squad being scrambled. Must not be a big problem, whatever it was.

Command always said it didn't matter which unit you got. TIE fighters were all the same, down to the last nut and bolt, but even so, every pilot had his or her favorite ship. You weren't supposed to personalize them, of course, but there were ways to tell—a scratch here, a scuff mark there . . . after a while, you got to where you knew which fighter was which. And no matter what Command said, some were better than others—a little faster, a little tighter in the turns, the laser cannons a hair quicker to fire when you touched the stud. Vil happened to know that his assigned ship this rotation was Black-11, one of his favorites. Maybe it was pure superstition, but he breathed just a little easier, knowing that particular craft had his name on it this time around.

The command officer on deck, Captain Rax Exeter, waved Vil over.

"Cap, what's up? Another drill?"

"Negative, Lieutenant. A group of prisoners somehow managed to take over one of the new *Lambda*-class shuttles. They're trying to get far enough away to make the jump to hyperspace. That isn't going to happen on my watch. The ID codes and tracking will be in your fighter's computer. Don't let 'em get away, son."

"No, sir. What about the crew?" Vil knew the new shuttles carried only a pilot and copilot.

"Assumed dead. These are bad guys doing this, Dance—traitors and murderers. That's reason enough to cook them, but we do *not* want them getting away to tell anybody what the Empire is doing out here, do we?"

"No, *sir*!"

"Go, Lieutenant, go!"

Vil nodded, not bothering to salute, then turned and ran. As he did, he put his helmet on and locked it into place. The hiss of air into his face was metallic and cool as the suit's system went online. It felt very comforting. The vac suit's extreme-temp-resistant weave of durasteel and plastoid, along with the polarizing densecris helmet, were the only things that would protect him from hard vacuum. Suit failure could make a strong man lose consciousness in under ten seconds, and die in under a minute. He'd seen it happen.

TIE fighters, in order to save mass, had no defensive shield generators, no hyperdrive capability, and no emergency life-support systems. They were thus fragile, but fast, and that was fine with Vil. He'd rather dodge enemy fire than hope it would bounce off. There was no skill in piloting some lumbering chunk of durasteel; might as well be sitting with your feet up at a turbolaser console back on the ship. Where was the fun in that?

The TIE tech had the hatch up on Black-11 as Vil arrived at the gantry above the ship. It was the work of an instant to clamber down and into the fighter's snug cockpit.

The hatch came down and hissed shut. Vil touched the power-up stud, and the inside of the TIE—named for the twin ion engines that drove it—lit up. He scanned the controls with a quick and experienced eye. All systems were green.

The tech raised his hand in question. Vil waved back. "Go!"

"Copy that, ST-One-One. Prepare for insertion."

Vil felt his lips twitch in annoyance. The Empire was determined to erase all signs of individuality in its pilots, on the absurd theory that nameless, faceless operators were somehow more effective. Thus the classification numbers, the anonymous flight suits and helmets, and the random rotation of spacecraft. The standardizing approach had worked reasonably well in the Clone Wars, but there was one important difference here: neither Vil nor any other TIE pilot that he knew of was a clone. None of the members of Alpha Squad had any intention of being reduced to automata. If that was what the Empire really wanted, let them use droid pilots and see how well that worked.

His musing was interrupted by the small jolt of the cycling rack below the gantry kicking on. Vil's ship began to move toward the launching bay door. He saw the tech slip his own helmet on and lock it down.

Already the bay pumps were working full blast, depressurizing the area. By the time the launch doors were open, the air would be cycled. Vil took a deep breath, readying himself for the heavy hand of g-force that would push him back into the seat when the engines hurled him forward.

Launch Control's voice crackled in his headphones. "Alpha Squad Leader, stand by for launch."

"Copy," Vil said. The launch doors pulled back with tantalizing slowness, the hydraulic *thrum* of their movement made audible by conduction through the floor and Black-11's frame.

"You are go for launch in five, four, three, two . . . *go!*"

Outside the confines of the Star Destroyer, the vastness of space enveloped Lieutenant Vil Dance as the ion engines pushed the TIE past the last stray wisps of frozen air and into the infinite dark. He grinned. He always did. He couldn't help it.

Back where I belong . . .

The flat blackness of space surrounded him. Behind him, he knew, the *Steel Talon* was seemingly shrinking as they pulled away from it. "Down" and to port was the curvature of the prison planet. Though they were in polar orbit, Despayre's axial tilt showed more of the night side than day. The dark hemisphere was mostly unrelieved blackness, with a few lonely lights here and there.

Vil flicked his comm—though it came on automatically at launch, a good pilot always toggled it, just to be sure. "Alpha Squad, pyramid formation on me as soon as you are clear," he said. "Go to tactical channel five, that's tac-fiver, and log in."

Vil switched his own comm channel to five. It was a lower-powered band with a shorter range, but that was the point—you didn't want the enemy overhearing you. And in some cases, it wasn't a good idea for the comm officer monitoring you back on the base ship to be privy to conversations, either. They tended to be a bit more informal than the Empire liked.

There came a chorus of "Copy, Alpha Leader!" from the other eleven pilots in his squad as they switched over to the new channel.

It took only a few seconds for the last fighter to launch, and only a few more for the squad to form behind Vil.

"What's the drill, Vil?" That from Benjo, aka ST-1-2, his second in command and right panelman.

"Alpha Squadron, we have a *Lambda*-class shuttle captured by prisoners. They are running for hyper. Either they give up and come back, or we dust 'em."

"*Lambda*-class? That's one of the new ones, right? They have any guns?"

Vil sighed. That was Raar Anyell, a Corellian like Vil himself, but not somebody you'd want to hold up as a prime example of the human species. "Don't you bother to read the boards at all, Anyell?"

"I was just about to do that, sir, when the alarm went off. Was looking right at 'em. Had the latest notices right in my hand. Sir."

The other pilots laughed, and even Vil had to grin. Anyell was a foul-up everywhere except in the cockpit, but he was a good enough pilot that Vil was willing to give him some slice.

His sensor screen pinged, giving him an image of their quarry. He altered course to intercept.

"Anybody else behind on his homework, listen up," he said. "The *Lambda*-class shuttle is twenty meters long, has a top speed of fourteen hundred g, a Class-One hyperdrive, and can carry twenty troops in full battle gear—probably a couple more convicts in civvies.

"The ship carries three double-blaster cannons and two double-laser cannons. It can't accelerate worth a wheep and it turns slower than a comet, but if you get in its sights, it *can* blow you to itty-bitty pieces. It would be embarrassing to have to inform your family you got shot apart by a shuttle, so stay alert."

There came another chorus of acknowledgments:

"Copy, sir."

"Yes, sir!"

"No sweat."

"Anyell, I didn't hear *your* response."

"Oh, sorry, sir, I was taking a little nap. What was the question?"

Before the squad commander could reply, the shuttle suddenly loomed ahead. It was running as silently as possible, with no lights, but as its orbit brought it across the terminator and out of Despayre's night side, the sunlight struck rays from its hull.

"There is our target, four kilometers dead ahead. I want a fast flyby so they can see us, and then I want a fountain pattern dispersal and loop, two klicks minimum distance and bracket, one, four, four, and two, you know who you are. I'll move in close and have a word with whoever they have flying the stolen spacecraft."

Benjo: "Aw, Lieutenant, come on, let us have a shot, too."

"Negative. If you had a clue about the vessel, I might, but since you're just as likely to shoot each other as the quarry, you'll hold the bracket."

More acknowledgments, but without much enthusiasm. He couldn't blame his squad—they hadn't had any action except drills since they'd been assigned to this project—but his secondary goal was to bring all his men back alive. The primary, of course, was to accomplish their mission. He didn't need a squad for this; any fighter pilot worth his spit should be able to deal with a lumbering shuttle, even one with the new-vehicle smell still in it. The Lambda's delta vee wasn't all that efficient, but with constant drive it could get above the solar plane and far enough out of the planet's gravity well to engage its hyperdrive fairly soon—and once it was in the chute, they'd never find it.

But that wasn't going to happen.

The pyramid-shaped formation zipped past the fleeing shuttle, close enough for Vil to see the pilot sitting in the command seat. He didn't look surprised, of course—he would have seen them coming on the sensors. But he couldn't outrun them, couldn't dodge, and no way could he take out a full squad of TIE fighters even if he was the best gunner who'd ever lived, not in that boat. And anyway, Vil wasn't going to give him the opportunity to try.

The squad flowered into the dispersal maneuver as ordered, looping out and away to their assigned positions, angled pressor beams in their arrays providing maneuverability. Vil pulled a high-g tight turn and came around to parallel the shuttle a few hundred meters away, slightly above it. He watched the wing turrets closely. As soon as they started to track him, he jinked to port, then to starboard, slowed, then sped up. They tried to keep up with him, but they were a hair too slow.

Vil toggled to a wide-band channel. They'd hear this back in the Destroyer, he knew.

"Attention, shuttle RLH-One. Turn the craft around and proceed immediately to Star Destroyer *Steel Talon*'s tractor beam range."

There was no answer; nothing but the slight hiss of the carrier.

"Shuttle craft, do you copy my transmission?"

Another pause. Then: "Yeah, we hear you, rocketjock. We aren't of a mind to do that."

Vil looked at his control panel. They were two minutes away from Minimum Safe Distance—the point far enough from Despayre where they could safely attempt the jump to lightspeed. Jump too close to a planet's gravity well and the shift would tear the vessel apart. If the guy he was talking to had enough skill to fly the shuttle, he'd know that. His control panel would tell him when he reached MSD, and then it would be over. Lieutenant Dance would have failed a mission, for the first time.

Never happen, he thought. "Turn it around, or we *will* fire," he said.

"You'd do that? Just blow us apart? Essentially murder fifteen men—and two women? One of them is old enough to be your granny. You can live with that?"

He was stalling for time, Vil knew. The beings on that shuttle were bad enough to have been sent to the galaxy's number one prison planet, and the Imperial courts didn't bother to do that with petty thieves or traffic violators. His granny hadn't robbed any banks or killed anybody. Not that he knew of, anyway.

"Shuttle pilot, I say again—"

Vil saw the port turret on the shuttle open up. He cut across the craft's flight path, angling away aft as the starboard gun began firing. He hit his thrusters full, coming up in a half loop and twist away from the incoming laserfire.

Even a good gunner couldn't have spiked him at this angle, and these guys weren't anywhere close to good enough. Still, the pulsed incandescent beams came close.

"Lieutenant—!" That from Benjo.

"Hold your position, Alpha Squad, there's no problem here." Cool and calm. Like discussing what they might be having for dinner.

He zipped Black-11 out of range.

The clock was running down. Less than a minute to MSD.

"Last chance, shuttle. Turn it around. *Now.*"

In answer, the pilot pulled the shuttle topward so his gunners could get a better angle. They started shooting again.

The shots were wild, but there was always a chance a stray beam could hit you, even by accident. And wouldn't that be a glorious end to an unblemished career? To be killed by a convict on a milking shuttle?

Enough of this. Vil hit the drive controls and damped the thrust to zero. Then he pushed the throttles to full, angled to port and topside, did a roll and loop, and came around, driving at the shuttle amidships.

He pressed the fire-control button.

Black-11 spat twin laser bolts from the low-temp tips—*blip-blip, blip-blip, blip-blip*—

Vil Dance was a better-than-average shooter. The bolts ripped into the shuttle, chewed it up, and as he overflew and peeled away to starboard-downside, the *Lambda* blew apart, shattering into at least half a dozen large pieces and hundreds of smaller ones amid a cloud of flash-frozen air, liquid, and debris.

And pinwheeling bodies.

Vil switched back to tac-five. "Anyell, Lude, move in and check for survivors." He kept his voice calm, emotionless, no big deal. His pulse was racing, but they didn't have to know that. Let them think his heart pumped liquid oxy.

"None of 'em were wearing suits, Lieutenant," Lude said a moment later. "No survivors. Too bad about that brand-new ship."

"Good hit, Vil," Benjo said. "Congratulations."

Vil felt a warm glow of satisfaction. It had been a good hit. And they had been firing at him, so it wasn't like shooting yorks in a canister. It had been a righteous response.

He switched back to the main op-chan. "Fighter Control, this is ST-One-One, Lieutenant Vil Dance of TIE fighter Alpha Squadron. Mission accomplished. You might want to send out a recovery vessel to pick up the pieces."

"Copy, ST-One-One," said Captain Exeter. "Good job."

"Thank you, sir. Let's return to base, Alpha Squad."

Vil smiled as he waited for his team to form up again. This was the best job in the galaxy, being a fighter pilot. He couldn't imagine a better one. He was young, not even twenty-five yet, and already a legend among his peers—and among the ladies as well. Life was good.

As they started for the Destroyer, Vil saw in the distance the frame of the gigantic battle station that was being built in planetary orbit. They were a hundred kilometers away from the structure, and it was still skeletal, its interior construction only just begun, but even so, it looked impossibly huge at this distance. It was to be the size of a small moon when it was finished, dwarfing the largest Star Destroyer.

Incredible to think about. And if he kept racking up missions like the one just completed, there was a very good chance that he would be assigned as unit commander on board the new station.

He led his squad back to the equatorial launching bay. Looking at the awe-inspiring base, he felt a surge of pride in the Empire, and a feeling of gratitude at being a part of the Tarkin Doctrine's glorious mission. There was no official appellation or designation, other than *battle station,* that he knew of for the Grand Moff's vision, but there was a name for it that everybody he knew, officers and enlisted alike, used.

They called it the Death Star.

2

LQ FLAGSHIP *HAVELON,* IN GEOSYNCHRONOUS ORBIT ABOVE PLANET DESPAYRE

Wilhuff Tarkin—now Grand Moff Tarkin, with that exalted promotion being due to this very project—stood before the deck-to-ceiling transparisteel viewport on the observation deck, looked out at his creation, and found it good.

He was building a world.

True, as worlds went, what was taking form three hundred kilometers from his flagship would not be quite as imposing as Imperial Center, say, or Alderaan. But when finished, it would be larger than two of the satellites of his own planet Eriadu, and it would be home to well over a million beings.

More to the point, it would hold countless worlds under its—*his*—thrall.

It had been nearly three decades since Raith Sienar had first made Tarkin privy to the concept of the "battle station planetoid," and it had taken almost a decade to get the idea through the snarls of red tape and bring the Geonosians on board to improve and implement the designs. The project had been known by various code names—such as *the Great Weapon*—and the original plans had been much improved by the Geonosian leader Poggle the Lesser. But it had taken years for the concept to be stewarded through the tortuous maze of government bureaucracy before construction was finally ordered to begin. There were still flaws in the original plans, but many of them had been addressed during the building of the proof-of-concept prototype in the Maw Installation, and others were being corrected as they were uncovered. The greatest minds in the galaxy had been recruited or drafted to lend their expertise to the building of this ultimate weapon. The brilliant Dr. Ohran Keldor, the mad weapons master Umak Leth, the young but nevertheless laser-sharp Omwati prodigy Qwi Xux, the Twi'lek administrator Tol Sivron—they, and many, many others of like stripe, had been investigated and approved by Tarkin himself. All were as good as the Empire could provide, willing or unwilling.

In addition, he had conscripted a veritable army of enslaved Wookiees, plus tens of thousands of convicts from the steaming jungles of the prison planet Despayre, and a plethora of construction droids, the latter the largest such collection of automata ever assembled. All of them, organic and artificial, now worked around the chrono, with but one goal in mind: the culmination of his vision.

The project code-named Death Star.

Tarkin pursed his lips slightly. There was a taint of melodrama to the name that he didn't care for, but no matter. The words, along with the reality of the battle station itself, would amply convey its terrifying purpose.

The Horuz system had been scavenged for raw material; asteroids and comets were being harvested from both the inner and outer belts and broken into components of oxygen, hydrogen, iron, nickel, and other elements; enormous bulk transports, ore haulers, tankers, and cargo craft had been gutted and reconfigured as orbiting laboratories, factories, and housing, all filled with workers producing fiber optics, electronics, and thousands of other technological instruments and construction materials. After nearly two decades of frustration, of false starts, union disputes, administrative procedure, and political maneuvering, the construction of the Empire's doomsday device was at last irrevocably under way.

Certainly there had been problems. Tarkin had been surprised and annoyed to find that Raith Sienar's original designs—the very same ones he himself had presented to Palpatine, and which the Emperor had rejected more than ten years earlier—had been the basis for the plans

Palpatine had finally given him to implement. Well, perhaps it wasn't so surprising, given the vagaries of war and politics. Nothing that went into the Empire's vaults was ever completely lost, although sometimes things were mislaid. And concepts rejected when they came from someone else often looked better when rethought as one's own. Even the Emperor, it seemed, was not immune to that particular hubris.

After a prototype design had been built and refined in the heart of the swarm of black holes known as the Maw cluster, Tarkin and Bevel Lemelisk, the head of design, had had the Death Star project moved several times to avoid possible Rebel sabotage attempts, ultimately relocating it to the Horuz system for added security. Of course, on a project this huge, there was little hope that it could be kept secret forever—but knowing that it existed, even knowing where it was being built, was not the same as being able to do anything about it. Admiral Daala, commanding four *Imperial*-class Star Destroyers and countless smaller attack craft, kept constant vigilance from her station within the Maw; any unauthorized ships that entered the region would not leave to carry tales elsewhere.

Tarkin stared at the incomplete spheroid, floating serenely in the void, eerily backlit by the solar glow reflected from Despayre. It wasn't even a complete skeleton yet. When done, however, the battle station would be 160 kilometers in diameter. There would be twenty-four zones, twelve in each hemisphere. Every zone, called a sprawl, would have its own food replicators, hangar bays, hydroponics, detention blocks, medical centers, armories, command centers, and every other facility needed to provide service for any mission deemed necessary. In an emergency, auxiliary command centers located in each sprawl provided full weapons and maneuverability control, for a redundancy depth of twice a dozen. When fully operational, the battle station would be the most powerful force in the galaxy, by far.

And it was Tarkin's to command.

As the commander of such a vessel, he would, perforce, be the most powerful man in the galaxy. The thought had certainly occurred to him that not even the Emperor could stand before him, did he choose to challenge Palpatine's rule. Then again, Tarkin knew the Emperor. If their positions were reversed, he knew that there was no possible way he would sanction anyone having such power—not without some kind of fail-safe. Was a destruct device already built into the station somewhere, with the red button safely installed in Palpatine's chambers? Was some equivalent of Order 66 known only to certain onboard officers and troops? Or was it something even more devious? Tarkin was certain the Emperor had some kind of insurance against any theoretical rebellion. Not that the Grand Moff intended such a course; he wasn't a foolish or suicidal man.

Aside from the fearsome, world-destroying "superlaser" itself—which was based upon the Hammertong Project and used a power source secretly taken by the 501st Stormtrooper Legion on Mygeeto during the Clone Wars—the station would mount a complement of craft, both space and ground, equal to a large planetside base: four capital ships, a hundred TIE/In starfighters, plus assault shuttles, blastboats, drop ships, support craft, and land vehicles, all ultimately totaling in the tens of thousands. It would have an operational crew numbering more than a quarter million, including nearly sixty thousand gunners alone. The vessel could easily transport more than half a million fully outfitted troops, and the support staff—pilots, crew, and other workers—would be half that number. The logistics of it all were staggering. Oh, it would be a fearsome monster indeed. But a monster tamed and under Tarkin's control; a monster sheathed in quadanium steel plating, invulnerable and impervious.

Well, *almost* invulnerable. Lemelisk had disappointed him in that instance. The greatest challenge in designing the battle station, he had said, was not creating a beam cannon big enough to destroy a planet, nor was it building a moon-sized station that would be driven by a Class Three hyperdrive. The greatest challenge was powering both of them. There must be trade-offs, he had said. In order to mount a weapon of mundicidal means, shielding capabilities would have to be downgraded to a rudimentary level. Power, Bevel had said, was not infinite, even on a station this size, fueled by the largest hypermatter reactor ever built. However, given the surface-to-vacuum defenses, the number of fighters, turbolaser batteries, charged-particle blasters, magnetic railguns, proton torpedo banks, ion cannons, and a host of other protective devices, no naval ship of any size would be even a remote threat. A fleet of *Imperial*-class Star Destroyers—even a fleet of *Super*-class Star Destroyers, should such a thing ever exist—would offer no real danger to the battle station once it was fully operational. Given all that, a shield system that was less than perfect at times wasn't such a high price to pay for the ability to vaporize a planet.

Once the station was fully online, then the Tarkin Doctrine—officially recognized by the Empire and named as such—would hold sway throughout the known worlds. The Tarkin Doctrine was as simple as it was effective: fear would keep the galaxy in line. Once the power of this "Death Star" had been demonstrated, its very existence would be enough to maintain peace. The Rebel Alliance wouldn't dare risk facing it. An insurgent who would gladly accept his own death in the cause would quail at the thought of his entire homeworld being turned to incandescent plasma.

Tarkin turned away from the viewport. Already there had been sabotage and setbacks, and more would occur; it was inevitable on a project this size. Slaves had tried to escape, droids had malfunctioned, and men who should have known better had thought to gain personal power through political machinations. In addition to these annoyances, Darth Vader, the Emperor's pet, was wont to show up unannounced now and again to lay his heavy hand upon the whole process. Vader, unfortunately, was beyond Tarkin's command, even though, as the first of the new Grand Moffs, he was a man whose whim was law in the entire Outer Rim Territories. It was true that Vader's own manner of function was essentially the same philosophy as the Tarkin Doctrine, albeit on a smaller scale; still, it was . . . disquieting . . . to see the man cause an admiral or a general across the room fall over with a mere gesture as if shot. Vader called it the Force, that mystical power that had supposedly been unique to the Jedi and the Sith. Tarkin had seen him knock blaster bolts from the air with his lightsaber—or even, at times, with naught but his black gauntlets—with no more effort than swatting flitterflies. Vader was something of a conundrum: the Jedi were extinct, so it was said, as were the Sith, and yet the man in black possessed one of the signature weapons favored by both groups, along with the skill to use it. Puzzling. Tarkin had heard it said that Vader was more machine than man underneath that armor. He knew that the cyborg droid General Grievous had been able to wield four lightsabers at once, so perhaps it was not so surprising after all that Vader was adept with one. No one could say for sure, of course, since no one, except possibly the Emperor himself, knew the identity of the face behind the black helmet's visor.

Tarkin, however, had his own theory about the Dark Lord's former life, based on information he'd gleaned from privileged files and conversations, as well as from public records. He'd heard about the supposed death of Anakin Skywalker, the Jedi war hero, on Mustafar, and knew that no body had been found. Of course, it might easily have disappeared in one of the white-hot lava rivers . . . but was it really just a coincidence that Darth Vader, encased in a life-support suit and demonstrating a mastery of the Force supposedly only attained by the most powerful of Jedi, had become the Emperor's new favorite immediately after Skywalker left the scene?

Tarkin shrugged. Whoever or whatever Vader was, or had become, he was not without great personal power, and it was well known that he had the Emperor's trust. But that didn't matter. All that mattered to Tarkin was that the construction of the battle station was proceeding apace. Should Vader or anyone else attempt to obstruct this, they would be dealt with, summarily and completely. His ultimate dream *must* be realized. Nothing else was important, compared with that.

Nothing.

IMPERIAL PRISONER TRANSPORT SHIP *GLTB-3181,* IN SUBORBITAL TRAJECTORY FOR PROCESSING STATION NINE, DEATH STAR

Teela Kaarz sat in her assigned seat, staring at the blank hull next to her. The shuttle had no viewports in the passenger area, so there wasn't much to see, save other prisoners. There were maybe three hundred such—males and females of perhaps a dozen different humanoid species, packed into the transport in tight rows. The smell of various body odors was sour and potent. She saw no other Mirialans such as herself. She knew there were some from her homeworld down on the hellacious world of Despayre—at least, there were if they were still alive. The prison planet was rife with danger—wild animals, poison plants, violent storms, and extremes of heat and cold due to an erratic orbit. Not a place to which anybody of her species, or most others, would voluntarily go, unless they had a most serious death wish.

Teela didn't harbor a death wish, but it mattered little now what she wished. Her right to wish, along with just about every other right, had been taken from her. She was no longer a galactic citizen. As of a standard year ago, she was a criminal and a prisoner.

Her "crime" had been simply to back the wrong political candidate in a planetwide election on her world. The Emperor had decided that the man running for office was a traitor, as were his most influential supporters. He had thus ordered a score of well-to-do Mirialans to be rounded up, given a speedy "trial," and convicted of treason. Given the public outrage over this travesty of justice, it had been deemed politically inexpedient to execute them then and there, and so Teela and her compatriots had been shipped off to die on a world many light-years away—a world so dangerous and inhospitable that it almost seemed to have been designed for the sole purpose of being a prison planet.

It had been quite a shock to be among those so chosen. In the span of a single planetary rotation, she had gone from being an influential and well-to-do professional to a criminal, and had existed in the latter state for a standard year. She had been lucky—and astonished—to have survived that long. She had been an architect, specializing in encapsulated arcology design—not a profession that prepared one for survival on a world where every other animal slinking around considered you prey, or every other plant had thorns from which a tiny scratch could cause agonizing pain before its poison killed you.

Before her fall from grace she had been near the top of her game, a much-sought-after professional who had designed the Ralthhok Encapsulization on Corellia and the Blackstar wheelworld in the Sagar system. She had been fêted and lionized, a guest of monarchs and Senators, heads of industry and starfleet admirals. She had thought nothing of taking an atmo-skimmer halfway around Mirial to dine with friends on different continents for each meal.

Now just having a dinner that didn't bite back was a luxury.

She had been lucky, but her survival hadn't been entirely due to luck. Her father had been fond of the outdoors, and as a young girl she had gone camping with him frequently. He had taught her woodcraft, and while the plants and animals on the prison world Despayre were different from those on Mirial—to say the least—the principles of dealing with them were the same. If it had teeth and claws, it was best to avoid it. If it had thorns or serrated edges, it was not a good idea to stray too close. One kept one's awareness firmly in the here and now and did not indulge in the luxury of daydreams and reverie unless one was safely barricaded behind makeshift walls constructed of cast-off battleplate or jury-rigged fields. And it was a good idea not to let one's guard drop even then, because there were predators inside the compounds as well as out; predators with two legs instead of four or six, but nonetheless deadly.

One year. And until this morning, there had been no reason for her to believe she would ever leave Despayre, however much time she might have left to live. But when Imperial Guards landed outside the makeshift shantytown the prisoners had named Dungeontown, the rumor had quickly spread. There was a project in orbit, the word was, and they needed more labor.

"I hear they got twen'y t'ousand Wookiee slaves workin' this t'ing," the man sitting to her right said. He was talking to the prisoner on his right, and not Teela, but as close as he was, she'd have to be deaf to miss the conversation. The prisoner to her right was a Bakuran; coarse, and convicted of multiple crimes, according to the bragging he'd been doing to their mutual seatmate: robbery, gun-running, assault, murder. He smelled like slime mold.

"That right?" The prisoner seated one away from Teela was a Brigian, a tall, purple-skinned humanoid whom Teela had seen in Dungeontown a few times. The only Brigian in their town, she had heard. He was soft-spoken when he answered the Bakuran, but she'd also heard that he had been an assassin good enough with his hands that he seldom needed a weapon. There was a story that he had once killed a virevol—a kind of wolf-sized, saber-toothed rat found only on Despayre—with nothing more than a stick. And then cooked and eaten it.

Thieves and murderers. Pleasant company for a woman who had, until she had been arrested for a poor political stance, never gotten so much as a skytraffic ticket. Not that she had made that knowledge public. The more dangerous criminals in Dungeontown thought you were, the greater the chance they would leave you be. When anybody asked her what her crime had been, Teela always just smiled. That tended to make the questioner think twice about whatever his intentions might be toward her.

"Yar," the Bakuran said. "Half a million droids, plus a load o' construction bots—extruders, shapers, benders, like that, too. Big sucker they be buildin', whatever t' kark it is."

The purple humanoid shrugged. "Die on the planet, die in space. No matter."

The transport slowed, then stopped. After a moment there was a *clank!* that vibrated though the ship.

"Sounds like a ramp just locked on," the Brigian said. "Looks like wherever we're going, we're there."

The Bakuran turned to look at Teela, giving her a long up-and-down leer, then a toothy grin. "Wouldn't mind a bunkmate, if space b' tight," he said. "You'll do."

"Last 'bunkmate' I had accidentally died in his sleep one night," Teela said. She smiled.

The Bakuran blinked. "Yar?"

She didn't say anything further. She just kept smiling.

The Bakuran's grin faded.

A guard appeared. "Everybody up and single-file," he said.

The Brigian was closest to the aisle, the Bakuran behind him, and Teela behind the Bakuran. He kept glancing back at her, quick and nervous looks, as they filed out of the ship and into the sinuous tube of the pressurized ramp.

At the entrance to a huge and cold assembly area, Teela saw there were thousands of other prisoners entering through scores of ramps connected to other transports. She could smell the perspiration and fear from the prisoners, mixed with the stale, metallic tang of recycled air. Guards stationed at scanners monitored each incoming line. As each prisoner passed through a scanner, there sounded a musical tone.

Reading their implants, she guessed. Most of the notes were the same, but now and again a different tone would sound, a full step lower, and the prisoners connected to them would be separated from the others and directed away from the main body toward a stairway to a lower level. Maybe one in fifty, she figured.

Who were they? she wondered. Rejects? Culls? People bound for a one-way trip out the nearest air lock?

When Teela passed the scanner's arch, the tone emitted was the lower one. She felt her heart race faster, her breath catch, as the guard brusquely ordered her to step out of the line.

Whatever that sound meant for those it selected, she was apparently about to find out.

4

THE SOFT HEART CANTINA, SOUTHERN UNDERGROUND, GRID 19, IMPERIAL CITY, CORUSCANT SECTOR, CORE WORLDS

"Should I break their skulls?" Rodo asked.

Memah Roothes said, "No. Just throw 'em out."

"You're sure? I don't mind."

"Much as I admire a man who enjoys his work, I'm asking you to try to curb your enthusiasm."

"You're the boss."

From behind the bar, where she occasionally took a turn mixing drinks, the owner of the Soft Heart Cantina watched as Rodo, the pub's peacekeeper, went to attend to the off-duty and getting-progressively-louder customers. That there were two Imperial stormtroopers soused and gearing themselves up for a fight didn't worry her. Rodo—if he had another name, nobody she knew had ever heard it—was one of the biggest humans she had ever seen. Born and raised on Ragith III, a descendant of human colonists who had been genetically bred and selected for generations to adapt to the one-and-a-half standard-g environment, Rodo, at over two meters and 110 kilos, was not a man you wanted to have mad at you. Somebody once parked a landspeeder in his spot on the street outside the cantina. Rodo had considered this an insult, and he had been direct in dealing with it.

Seeing a vehicle picked up and turned over without help makes an impression—people didn't park in Rodo's spot anymore. He was also extremely fast and very, very good at some weird kind of martial art, which he could use to tie a drunk and belligerent patron into a knot faster than you could call the Imperial cools to come and haul the problem away.

Rodo's presence was why things tended to stay pretty quiet in the cantina, even on a payday like tonight. When somebody got too loud or combative, usually Rodo's arrival at the table was enough to solve the problem.

Usually, but not always . . .

Memah turned to finish a drink order. She saw—out of the corner of her eye—a human male, a spacer by his garments, gazing dreamily at her, chin supported by one hand as he leaned over his drink. She gave no acknowledgment of his admiration. A Rutian Twi'lek from Ryloth, with teal skin that seemed to glow under the fullspec lights, she was used to such looks. Her skin, in both color and tone, was one of her best features, which she tended to showcase by wearing short and sleeveless dresses.

She knew that, to most humanoid races, she was startlingly beautiful; even her lekku, the two large, fleshy tendrils that hung about her shoulders instead of human hair, seemed to have an erotic attraction for humans. And she was fit enough, due to a daily swimming and zero-g workout regimen, although it always seemed to her that she could stand to lose a kilo from her hips.

Memah had managed this place for two years, and owned it for two more, before the galaxy had gone crazy. Of course, war was good for business in a cantina. Beings about to ship off to battle in the middle of nowhere on some backrocket planet knew they wouldn't be relaxing in a place like hers the few times they weren't blasting Rebels or droids. This tended to promote a certain to-vac-with-tomorrow attitude, which translated into considerable profits for her.

The Heart was crowded, and it took Rodo a minute to work his way to the would-be fighters, who were at a two-seat table near the east wall. One of them was on his feet and the other rising when the big bouncer arrived. He was a head taller and nearly as wide as both of them put together. He eclipsed the light, and both men looked up to see what was casting such a gigantic shadow.

Memah grinned again. There was no way she could hear what Rodo was saying to them. The place was noisy with conversation and laughter, the clink of glasses toasting, the scrape of chair legs on the hard floor. She had two more tenders working the bar, both busily mixing drinks and drawing down the taps. It wasn't a quiet environment. But she knew essentially what the big man was telling the two troopers. They had disturbed the spirit of the Heart, and they would have to leave—now.

If they were wise, they'd smile and nod and hustle themselves to the door. If they were stupid, they'd argue with Rodo. If they were *really* stupid, one or both would decide that how they behaved wasn't any of the peacekeeper's business, and they'd be happy to demonstrate their Imperial combat training to him, thank-you-very-milking-much!

Rodo's response was always based on their attitude. Play nice, and they could come back tomorrow and start fresh, with no hard feelings. It went on a sliding scale from there. In this case, the two must have decided that the enforcer wasn't as tough as he looked, and worth at least a few choice words, probably concerning his parents or siblings and his immoral relationships with them.

Before either trooper could do or say anything else, Rodo grabbed each one by the shirtfront, moving incredibly fast for such a big man, and, in an amazing display of raw strength, lifted both clear of the floor and banged their heads together. If they weren't unconscious after that, they were certainly stunned enough to cease hostilities. Holding them thus, Rodo walked toward the door, as if doing so was no more effort than carrying two large steins of ale.

It didn't take him long to achieve the exit—everybody between him and the door moved with great alacrity, clearing a broad and empty path. The room went almost quiet as the door hissed open and Rodo tossed the two into the street.

When the door hissed shut, the noise level returned to normal, and Memah went back to her drink order. Nobody was hurt, and so there was no need to worry about the authorities. And if the troops were foolish enough to come back with others like them, seeking to exploit their Imperial status . . . well, there wasn't an overabundance of support downlevels for such officiousness.

Memah sighed. When she'd first started in this line of work, waitressing in a dive deep in Gnarlytown called Villynay's, most of the Imperial troops had still been clones, and every one of them had been uniformly polite and easygoing. It was true that, after a bit too much ferment, they could get a tad boisterous, but they'd never been a problem, and had also never been at all hesitant in helping to street anyone who was. She'd heard that they'd all been programmed, somehow, to only show hostility toward the enemy. Whatever the reason, the clones had been a pleasure to serve.

Well, that was then and this was now. Maybe she was looking at the past through rose-colored droptacs, but it seemed to her that a lot had changed. Now a night when Rodo didn't have to eject a few obstreperous drunks was a night to remember.

As she put together a Bantha Blaster, stirring in the ingredients, Memah noticed another pair of customers. They weren't causing any ruckus; if anything, they were too quiet. Humans, a male and a female, they were, like much of the crowd this time of the evening. Both were dressed in nondescript black coveralls. They nursed mugs of membrosia and sat facing each other at a two-seat table in the corner, from which they seemed, without being obvious about it, to be watching the room.

And even though she never caught them staring directly her way, Memah got the distinct feeling that they were particularly interested in her.

Rodo arrived back at the bar like a heavy-gravity crawler docking. He scanned the room, looking for more trouble. None seemed to be in the offing at the moment.

Memah finished the Blaster and put it on the bar. "Ell-Nine, order up!"

The new server droid, a trash-can-sized one on wheels whose model she never could remember, rolled to the bar. "Got it, boss," it chirped. It grabbed the tray with extendible arms, anchored it to the magnetic plate atop its "head," and took off to deliver the drinks.

Memah drifted down to the other end of the bar. "Rodo, you see the two in black in the corner?"

Rodo didn't look at the pair, nor directly at her. "Yep."

"Know who they are?"

"Not who. Haven't seen 'em in here before. Got a good idea what, though."

There was a long pause that Memah finally broke. "You want to finish that thought and educate me here?"

He cracked a small smile. Rodo liked her, though he'd never made a move on her, and she knew he never would. "Imperial Intelligence ops."

She frowned, surprised. What would a couple of Eyes be doing in her place? She ran a workingbeing's bar, and there wasn't much likelihood of any high-level skulduggery or spying being done here. This was the Southern Underground, after all; most underdwellers couldn't even spell *espionage,* much less engage in it.

"You sure?"

"Pretty much. They got the look. You want, I can poke around some, check 'em out."

She shook her head. "No. Don't stir up trouble we don't need. Just keep an eye on them."

Rodo settled back. "That's what you pay me for, Boss Lady."

5

OFFICERS' BARRACKS, ISD *STEEL TALON,* HORUZ SYSTEM

Master Chief Petty Officer Tenn Graneet rolled out of his sleep rack and put his bare feet onto the cold metal deck. That woke him up fast enough. *Really ought to get a rug to put down there.* He'd been meaning to do it since he'd been assigned to the ship, eight weeks ago, but other things kept taking priority, and neither S'ran Droot nor Velvalee, the other CPOs who shared the cabin, seemed bothered by it. Of course Droot's feet were more like hooves, and Velvalee was used to temperatures a lot colder—the blasted floor might feel warm to his feet, for all Tenn knew. Those two were on graveyard shift this week, so they'd be heading back to the cabin about the time he got to his post.

Tenn mentally shrugged. Someday he'd get around to it. Maybe cozy up to that Alderaan woman who did knitting when off duty, get her to make him enough of a synthwool carpet to cover the deck—it wouldn't take all that much. He always could sweet-talk a fem into doing all kinds of things for him.

He padded down the hall to the refresher, took a quick sonic shower, splashed depil on his stubble, and wiped it clean. Then, wrapped in a towel, he went back to don the uniform of the day.

Tenn Graneet was past fifty, but he was in very good shape for a man his age. He had a few unrevised scars from various battles when his station had been hit by enemy fire, or from when something had gone wrong and blown up, and a couple from cantina rumbles when he'd been slow to get out of the way of a broken bottle or vibroblade. Still, he was lean and muscular, and he could keep up with grunts half his age, though not as easily as he used to. The days when he could party all night and then work a full shift the next day were past, true, but on the obstacle course even the newbies knew enough to not get in front of him unless they wanted to get run over. It was a point of pride that, even after more than thirty years in the navy, nobody in Tenn Graneet's gunnery crew could outdrink, outfight, or outwomanize him.

He picked out his oldest uniform clothes, the light gray faded to the color of ash, and slipped into them. They were going to get dirty and smelly anyway today, so no point in messing up new ones. Word from uplevels was there was going to be another surprise battle drill around midshift. The Port Heavy Blaster Station CO, Captain Nast Hoberd, was a drinking buddy with Lieutenant Colonel Luah, who was the admiral's assistant, and as a result the PHBS always got the heads-up when a drill or inspection was about to be sprung. The captain wanted his unit to look good, and since they always knew in advance when it counted, they always did look good. White-glove a surface in any of the six turbolaser turrets or two heavy ion cannon turrets, and there wouldn't be a speck of dirt. You could eat off the floor in Fire Control on inspection days. Light the battle alarms, and the port battery was the first to report battle-ready. Every time.

Rumor was that Hoberd was up for major, and his unit's pretty-much-spotless performance during every drill and inspection didn't hurt his chances any. Not that the blaster crew had any slouches on it. You didn't get to shoot the big guns unless you had plenty of practice shooting the little ones, and anybody who couldn't pull his weight, Tenn got rid of fast enough to leave friction burns. He had his own reputation to keep up. CPO Tenn Graneet was the best gunnery chief in this being's navy. If somebody gave them a target and it could possibly be hit, his crew would hit it, sure as there were little green beings living on Crystan V.

Dressed, Tenn looked at himself in the mirror. A face that was every centimeter the grizzled old navy chief looked back at him. He grunted. He'd joined the Imperial Navy before it was the Imperial Navy, and he expected to die at his post. That was fine by him. A lifetime of military service wasn't a bad life at all, as far as he was concerned. He left his quarters and headed into the hall.

The *Steel Talon* was the ninth ship upon which he'd served; on the last four of them his duty had been that of a gunnery chief. An *Imperial*-class Star Destroyer, the *Talon* was the backbone of the fleet. Tenn hoped to be transferred, one day, to one of the four new *Super*-class Star Destroyers that were currently being built. Those were monsters indeed, eight or ten times the size of the *Imperial*-class ships, which were themselves over a kilometer and a half in length. The SSDs looked like nothing so much as pie-shaped wedges sliced out of an asteroid and covered with armament. Perhaps if he called in the right favors at the right time, he might wrangle an assignment on the next one scheduled to roll ponderously out of the Kuat Drive Yards. He still had a few good years left in him, and who better to run the big battery on one of those monster ships than him? He had his request in, and maybe, if Hoberd got his promotion, he'd put in a good word for Tenn before he left. As long as Hoberd was running the battery, though, that wasn't likely to happen. He didn't want to lose the best CPO in the sector, so he said.

Well, thought Tenn, *it's nice to be appreciated.* Still, he knew, deep down, that he wouldn't be satisfied until he could say he'd run the biggest and the best.

Shift change was coming, and officers and crew filled the halls on their way to their duty stations. Even though it would only be a drill, Tenn was looking forward to hearing the generators whine as the capacitors loaded, followed by the heavy vibrations and scorched-air smell as the ion cannons and lasers spoke, spewing hard energy across empty space to destroy the practice targets. To be able to reach out a hundred klicks or more and smash a ship to atomic dust was *real* power. And nobody was better at it than he was.

Tenn got to the array five minutes early, as always. Fifty meters in diameter, the unit was quiet as shift change neared. He saw Chief Droot and nodded at him. "Chief. How're we doin'?"

"Shipshape, Gee." The big Chagrian, one of the few aliens to rise to any kind of rank in the Imperial Navy, glanced around. "You know there's a surprise drill at eleven thirty hours?"

"Yeah."

"We cleared the decks, got the caps charged, ready to blaze."

Tenn grinned. "Thanks, Droot. I owe you one."

"Nah, I'm still two down—you had the station shining like a mirror on that last inspection. I got a smile out of the admiral himself that time."

Tenn nodded. Everybody kept track of who owed who what on a ship, and you didn't let a fellow chief catch flak if you could help out. Even if it wasn't your watch, it was your station, and what made one look bad made them all look bad. And vice versa, of course.

"Station's yours," Droot said. "I'm gonna go get some supper. I hear the mess hall has some berbersian crab on the menu."

"More likely doctored soypro," Tenn said.

Droot shrugged. "Yeah, well, it's the navy, not the Yuhuz Four Star." He left, ducking to make sure his horns cleared the hatch.

The morning shift crew was already in place—CPO Tenn Graneet wanted his people onstation fifteen minutes early, and if you weren't, you'd be sorry. Once, and you got your rump chewed like a starved reek was gnawing on it. Twice, and you were looking for another job.

"Good morning, people," Tenn said.

"Morning, Chief," came the echo from the crew.

"Polish your buttons, boys," the chief said. "I don't want anything sticking just in case we have to shoot something today."

Most of the crew smiled. They all knew about the drill. They were all ready. None of them wanted to be the being who disappointed Master Chief Petty Officer Graneet. No, sir . . .

MEDICAL FRIGATE *MEDSTAR FOUR,* POLAR ORBIT, PLANET DESPAYRE

"Captain Dr. Kornell Divini?"

Uli nodded. "Yeah."

"Medical Technician Class Two Vurly, sir," the man said. Human, as Uli was, or at least close enough that he couldn't tell otherwise, and Uli was something of an expert on humanoid anatomy.

"This way, sir."

The meditech led him down featureless gray corridors, deeper into the ship, to an office complex. Uli marked the route half consciously, knowing he could find his way around pretty quickly if need be. He had a good sense of direction, though it wasn't anything he could claim credit for—he'd been born that way.

Sure enough, it was the Medical Admin section he found himself in. Ships' medical suites all looked alike; the same pale off-white walls, wide corridors, and color-coded luminescent floor stripes that led you to various departments. There were a dozen or so people working: secretaries, mostly, some biologicals, some droids. The hands-on medical stuff would be done elsewhere down the hall, he knew.

"Commander Hotise, Dr. Kornell Divini."

Hotise was a short, rotund man, probably seventy or so, with white hair and a cropped beard. He wore office grays, and the clothes were cut well enough that they had to be tailored. He was checking off a list on a flatscreen. He looked up, nodded at the tech. "Thanks, Vurly."

The tech nodded, said "Sir," and left.

"Welcome to *MedStar Four,* Doctor," Hotise said. "Glad to have you aboard."

Uli nodded. "Thank you, sir," he said. His apparent lack of enthusiasm must have showed. The old man cocked an eyebrow that had more hair than a leafcrawler.

"Not happy with this assignment, son?"

That earned Uli's new commander an incredulous look. "Not happy? I did my first tour in a Rimsoo unit on a swamp world where your lungs could fill with spores in five minutes if you weren't wearing a filter mask. I patched up maybe a thousand clones, and I was supposed to be rotated back to my homeworld and discharged a civilian at the end of it. That was . . . five? six? hitches ago. I lost track."

Hotise nodded. "Imslow," he said.

"That's right." IMSLO stood for "Imperial Military Stop Loss Order." Too many skilled people who'd been drafted had had enough of the military after the Clone Wars, and when their compulsory service ended, wanted nothing more than to go home. With the action against the Rebels heating up, the Empire couldn't allow that. Doctors, in particular, were in short supply; hence, IMSLO. A retroactive order mandating that, no matter when you'd been conscripted, once you were in, you were in for as long as they wanted you—or until you got killed. Either way, it was kiss your planned life good-bye.

Imperial Military Stop Loss Order. An alternative translation, scrawled no doubt on a 'fresher wall somewhere by a clever graffitist, had caught on over the last few years: "I'm Milking Scragged; Life's Over." The memory brought a faint, grim smile to Uli's lips.

"Sorry, son," his CO said. "It's not my policy."

"But you *are* career navy."

The older man nodded. "We each have our chosen path."

"Not exactly true, is it? If I was on *my* chosen path, probably you and I would never have met."

Hotise shrugged. "What can I say? I don't run things back in civilization—I just do what I'm told. We were short a surgeon. I requisitioned a replacement. You're him. You weren't here, you'd be someplace else where the Empire deemed you necessary.

"It ain't Imperial Center General or Big Zoo, but it's quiet here. Not like a Rimsoo tent out in the tall grass. Nobody is shooting at us. Most of what we see is the occasional industrial accident or normal wear and tear. You could do better, Captain, but you could also do a lot worse. War is ugly, but that's how it is."

"Yes, sir."

"You can drop that part. We're pretty informal around here. I'll have a droid show you to your quarters, and you can take the tour and settle in." Hotise looked at Uli's orders. "Says here you're originally from Tatooine, Dr. Divini."

"Uli."

Hotise squinted at him. "Beg pardon, son?"

"People call me Uli. It's a Tusken word—means—"

An alarm blared, cutting him off. Uli didn't need a translation: *Incoming!*

A secretary droid rolled up on a single wheel. Its gyroscope squeaked a little right at the edge of Uli's hearing as the spinning wheel kept the droid upright and stable. It stopped in front of Hotise. "Sir, Ambulance Ship Nine is on the way to Dock B with twelve workers injured by an oxygen tank explosion at the construction site."

Uli noticed that the droid's vocabulator had, for whatever reason, a kind of musical lilt that he found pleasant. It was as though the droid were a character from a light opera, about to burst into song at any moment.

"It should be arriving in six-point-five minutes," the droid continued. "Field medics list primary damage due to compressive injuries, shrapnel wounds, and vacuum ruptures. Four critical, two of those in shock; three moderate; five minor. Species breakdown is six Wookiees, three humans, one Cerean, one Ugnaught, one Gungan."

Uli frowned. That was an interesting mix—*six* Wookiees? Working for the Empire? That didn't seem right.

"So much for quiet," he said. "Which way to Emergency Receiving?"

"You don't have to jump right in yet," Hotise said.

Uli shrugged. "Might as well. It's what I do."

Hotise nodded. "Fourmio will show you." He nodded at the droid. "Leave your gear here; I'll have it taken to your quarters."

The droid said, "This way, Dr. Divini," in a pleasing tenor. Its wheel squeaked as it rolled down the hall. Uli followed.

6

SLASHTOWN PRISON COLONY, GRID 4354, SECTOR 547,
QUADRANT 3, PLANET DESPAYRE

As a Zelosian, Celot Ratua Dil could, if pressed, live on sunlight and water—at least for a while. He didn't know his species' origin, but he did know that his people all had green eyes and green blood. While nobody outside the species had ever been curious enough to do full genetic scans, the theory that there had been some unique melding of animal and plant in the dawn of Zelosian history was accepted as fact on his homeworld. Sunlight and a little water, and he could go a month, two months, without eating a bite, though he'd rather not. He'd rather eat a nice meal of bahmat steak and feelo eggs, and, as long as he was rathering, he'd *much* rather be home on Zelos than on a prison world full of nasty criminals.

Unfortunately, that wasn't how it was.

He looked around the inside of the rude hut in which he lived, a ramshackle collection of local wood and cast-off Imperial packing crates lashed together with vines, wire, and bits of twine. Not much, but it was home. He rolled off the pad he used for a bed, essentially a blanket over some evergreen boughs. Fresh and layered right, it was pretty comfortable. The branches were getting dry, though; it had been a couple of standard weeks since he'd changed them. He'd have to do that soon;

not only were dry branches uncomfortable, but scorpion slugs would quickly infest them, and one sting from a slug's tail could cause members of just about any humanoid species agony for weeks—if they were lucky.

For the thousandth time Ratua mentally railed against the bad luck that had sent him here. Yes, he was a thief, though not much of one. And yes, he'd been a smuggler, though he'd never made any real credits at it. He was a pretty good scrounger, which helped him survive here. And he was not above taking advantage of a poor trader in a spirited transaction now and again. But being scooped up in a Trigalis port pub that just happened to have a pirate gang in it, and being lumped in as one of their crew? That was *wrong*. All he had done was stop in for a mug of ferment. The fact that he had been doing a little haggling with one of the pirates over some meelweekian silk that had "fallen" from a commercial hovervan earlier didn't mean he was a member of the crew.

The judges, unfortunately, had not been convinced. Ratua had offered to undergo a truth-scan, but somebody would have to pay for that, as he didn't have the coin, and the judges weren't willing to spend taxpayers' credits when he was so obviously guilty of something, even if it wasn't this particular crime on this particular world. And so he'd been tossed in with a crowd of hard-bitten types, all of them wedged into a cargo hold not big enough for half their number, and summarily tossed off the planet.

Being on a prison planet with some seriously bad criminals was not a walk in a quiet park. Even without the exiled thieves, murderers, extortionists, and so on, Despayre wouldn't be anyone's first choice to build a winter home. The land was mostly jungle, consisting of one large continent and one considerably larger ocean. The rampant growth was nourished by a gravity level of less than three-quarters a standard g, and by seasonal gales that roared in from the distant ocean, fueled by tidal forces due to the erratic orbit.

The jungle flora and fauna had responded to the environmental challenge of the gales by producing large, close-knit growth that stabbed roots deep into the ground. In some places the entwined rain forest was totally impenetrable. The animal life had adapted as well, by becoming, for the most part, sinuous and serpentine, the better to forage through the tightly interwoven vines and boles. There were poisonous crustaceans, as well as a few flying creatures such as small winged lizards and manta-like things, the latter with an interesting life cycle that began in the ocean and ended in the jungle.

And everything—*everything*—seemed to be the most vicious, savage, and generally unpleasant representative of its species possible. It wasn't so much an interdependent ecological system as it was all-out biological war, with each of Despayre's myriad indigenous species seemingly hardwired to attack and destroy all others. Everything that moved, it seemed, had fangs that dripped venom, and everything rooted to the ground had poisonous thorns, barbs, burrs . . .

And on top of all *that,* there were the prisoners.

The guards, safe in their floating patrol barges, were there to make sure nobody escaped; short of that, the prisoners could do pretty much whatever they wanted to one another, and not a night went by without somebody being thumped, sometimes hard enough that they died. It was the law of the jungle in here, just as it was out there, and the big predators ruled. They took what they wanted, and if you objected, you got squashed. Ratua tried to keep a low profile—if they didn't notice you, they weren't as likely to take you out just for the sport of it. He kept his mouth shut and his head down, and concentrated on survival.

He washed his face, using fairly clean water in a stasis field generator dome, then headed outside. Sergeant Nova Stihl, one of the more easygoing of the guards, taught a self-defense class nearby every morning. Mostly the students were other guards, but there were some prisoners, and Ratua enjoyed watching other people sweat. Plus, it was a gathering in which biz could be conducted. Swap a little of this for a little of that, get by a little better. Ratua had a pretty good biz going bartering goods and services, and that helped buy off the predators who did spot him now and then. Say, fellow being, which would you rather do? Stomp me into green mush, or get a new battery for your music player?

Among criminals, as among most people, greed was pretty dependable.

Ratua arrived shortly at the cleared spot where the self-defense players gathered. There were eighteen or twenty of them, plus about that many prisoners and guards watching. He circulated, hoping to find somebody with a couple of spare sunfruits he could score for breakfast.

Sergeant Stihl was talking about what to do if somebody attacked you with a knife as Ratua worked his way around the gathering.

"Anybody know the first thing you do if somebody comes at you with a blade?" Stihl asked.

"Run like a fleetabeesta," somebody said.

To the general laughter, Stihl replied, "You took this class before?" More laughter. "Monn has it exactly right," the sergeant continued. "You make tracks away, fast as you can. Bare-limbed against a knife, you get cut, no ifs, no buts. And unless you scum of the galaxy have been industrious since last time I looked, you don't have much of a medcenter anywhere around these parts. You could get cut bad, bleed out, or get infected and leave the party by the slow and painful exit, hey?"

There was a murmur of agreement. Everybody knew that. Lose a body part here, it was gone for good if you weren't a natural regenerator. The state of local medicine was rudimentary: a few docs and other healers, but not a lot of equipment or meds. Of course, the closest bacta tank was a mere three hundred or so klicks away; unfortunately, the direction was vertical rather than horizontal, and most of the prisoners had few illusions about their chances of being hoisted up to the orbiting facility if they were in harm's way.

"But if you don't have a weapon and you can't run, then you need another option. And it has to be one that doesn't depend on great skill because it won't work unless you have that, and even then, maybe not." Sergeant Stihl looked around. "Hey, Ratua, lemme borrow you for a minute."

Ratua smiled. He'd done this before.

"Lot of self-defense teachers, they say you have to trap and control the knife arm," Stihl continued. "That, not to put too fine a point on it, is pure mopak. If you aren't faster than the guy with the knife, that gets you gutted, no matter how much you know."

Ratua strolled into the ragged circle made by the watchers. Stihl tossed him the practice knife, a forearm-length dagger made out of softflex. Stiff enough to work like a real knife, but with enough give that if you hit somebody with it, it would bend without doing damage. The point and edges were coated with a harmless red dye that left a temporary mark on whatever they touched.

"I'm twelve years deep in teräs käsi," Stihl said. "I was the First Naval Fleet's Unarmed Middleweight Champion two years, runner-up for two more. Bare hand-to-hand, I expect I can take anybody my size on this planet apart, doesn't matter which species. Blade-to-blade, I can duel to a draw. Bare against a knife? I'll get cut. Show 'em, Ratua."

Ratua smiled and stepped in as if he was in no hurry. He made a lazy thrust with the knife. Stihl went into a crouching move to grab his arm, only—

Ratua did his trick.

As the sergeant reached for his wrist, Ratua pulled his hand back, and while it looked like no big deal to him, he knew the watchers would see his hand *blur.*

It wasn't a Zelosian thing, it was Ratua's own. He didn't know where it had come from, but once he kicked in the booster rocket he was, for a short time, faster than most ordinary beings. *Way* faster. Some medic who'd examined him once and tried to clock his reflex time had said something about mutation, about abnormally fast nastic response in the cellulose fiber that made up a large part of his muscle mass. Whatever the cause, it had come in handy more than once during his exile on Despayre.

As the sergeant continued to move in what seemed like slow motion to Ratua, the latter whipped up the knife and made three quick slashes and a stab. Then he took a step back.

Time resumed normal speed. Several people who had never seen the demonstration gasped or swore.

Sergeant Stihl had two thin red lines across his neck, one on each side, another across his throat, and a little red dot under his rib cage just below his heart.

After the sounds of amazement had died down, Stihl said, "You see?" He turned to Ratua. "How much fight training you have, Ratua?"

"Counting today?" He grinned. "Uh, that would be . . . none."

Stihl pointed at the slashes and stab marks. "Any of these would have been enough to kill me. Green-Eyes here has no training. I'm an expert, but if that knife had been real, I'd be fertilizing the plants—if somebody bothered to bury me. Yeah, he's fast, freaky fast, but that's the point: you never know who or what you're going to be up against, especially here on Despayre. Makes you stop and think, doesn't it? Thanks, Ratua."

Ratua nodded and moved out of the circle. These occasional little demonstrations were another reason he managed to stay alive. Predators preferred helpless victims, and while Ratua wasn't a fighter—the sight of blood, even if it wasn't green, made him ill—there were a lot slower folks to prey upon. Why risk your neck if you didn't have to?

Stihl would go on to talk about position and preemptive strikes and such, but Ratua had heard it all before. He was more interested in finding a sunfruit, and after his moment in the spotlight, that would probably be easier. Everybody loved a star.

Most days, Sergeant Nova Stihl felt as if he was part of the solution and not part of the problem. Being a guard on a prison planet was, at best, not a particularly glamorous duty. In fact, even at its best, you could carbon-freeze it and it would still stink to high orbit. He'd much rather be out in the thick of things, fighting Rebels on a real field of battle, using his hard-earned skills where they'd matter the most. But somebody had to be here, and he was philosophical enough to shrug off the fact that he'd been one of those so assigned. He'd learned a long time ago to make the best of the situation. That was all you could do if you were a trooper in the Imperial Army.

He remembered a quote from the Mrlssi philosopher Jhaveek: "I know myself to be only as I appear to myself." It was a deceptively complex concept, couched in simple words. Nova smiled slightly as he thought of the probable reaction his fellow soldiers would have if they knew that the holos hidden beneath his bunk were not racy images of Twi'lek dancing girls, but rather dissertations on various schools of metaphysical thought detailed by the galaxy's finest philosophers. Not that he had anything against Twi'lek dancing girls. But his studies, over the last few years of his post here, had kept him sane—of that he was convinced.

Most of the prisoners were indeed the dregs of the galaxy—bad beings who had broken major laws and who deserved to be put away for life, if not jettisoned from the back of a Star Destroyer along with the rest of the garbage. A few had been collected and shipped here by bad luck or accident, though he knew that most of those weren't exactly pillars of society, either. Ratua was a good example of this, although Nova owed him big-time for getting him the holos with only an eyebrow raised in reaction. But the vegetable man was an exception. If you checked the data on the majority, you'd probably find that most of them had gotten away with some full-out evil hurt aimed at the rest of whatever world they came from, so you didn't feel too bad about them being here. There weren't too many of the truly innocent who wound up on Despayre, though he knew of a few; political prisoners, most of them.

Backed the wrong candidate, spoke up at the wrong time, didn't toe the party line. Nova felt some sympathy for those, though given how the galaxy was these days, probably more sympathy than they deserved. If you're dumb enough to stand in front of a riot trooper and make an obscene gesture at him, you ought not to be surprised if he shoots you. Troopers were people, they had feelings, and on a bad day dancing in front of one and calling him names could be a very bad idea.

It was the same thing with politics. Anybody with more than vestigial sensory organs could tell which way the Imperial wind was blowing, and there was a war on, even though it hadn't been officially named as such. Free speech sometimes had to be tempered for the good of society, and what would have been a spirited discussion back when the Republic was in full flower was often now considered treason. That bothered him some. Maybe not as much as it should've, but some.

Nova sighed. Despite his fascination with the conundrums posed by some of the galaxy's foremost scholars, he didn't consider himself a particularly deep thinker—he just did what he was told, which mostly consisted of keeping prisoners in line and trying to avoid situations in which he had to shoot them. Teaching self-defense classes he did on his own time; it helped some of the weaker inmates, maybe gave them a chance against the real predators here. At any rate, it made him feel better about himself. He liked a level playing field, and while his "classes" weren't going to accomplish that, they did smooth out a bump in the terrain here and there. Now and again he'd hear a story about how someone from his classes used what he taught to avoid being maimed or killed, and that made him feel good. He was pretty careful screening his would-be prisoner students. Yes, they were all crooked as sand snakes, but he tried to keep out the ones who were aggressive—the ones who'd take what he taught them and use it for something other than self-defense. He had a lot of smaller beings as students, weaker ones, and those convicted of crimes that were about money rather than violence. He absolutely did not want to make a stone killer better at killing. More than enough of that went on in the galaxy already, much of it right here on Despayre.

His comlink chirped on his belt, signaling the morning recall. Time to wrap up the class and get back to the guard station, check in, get his next assignment. Some of the other guards thought he was foolish for mingling with the prisoners—you didn't get to carry a blaster or even a shock baton unless you went out in a quad or a platoon-sized group, for fear that the prisoners would attack you and take your weapon. But Nova wasn't concerned about that. The really bad actors here knew enough not to mess with him bare-handed, and if they pulled a beam or projectile weapon and took him out, they knew the chances were excellent they'd be dead before the next sunrise. Guard troops took care of their own, and if you attacked one, you attacked them all. They were protective of one another, but there were limits observed for the greater good. If you took a guard hostage and tried to use him or her or it for leverage, it got you and the guard and anybody within a hundred meters turned into a smoking crater. No negotiation, no compromise, just a big, sleek thermal bomb arcing out of the compound and onto your position. You couldn't hide, because the bomb zeroed in on the guard's implant, which couldn't be turned off or destroyed unless you knew exactly where it was, and that location was different for every guard on the planet. You'd have to completely skin the guard alive before finding it, and, while that wasn't a deal breaker for a lot of the planetary inmates—more, in fact, like a bonus for some of them—the catch was that even if you killed the guard, the implant kept working and reported its wearer dead. Which meant the bomb was on its way, and not even a fleetabeesta with its tails on fire could get out of range in time.

This was a big planet, but not so big that they couldn't find you. Knowing this tended to keep a lot of the more violent prisoners in line. Because of all this, not to mention his own considerable skills, Sergeant Nova Stihl wasn't worried about going among the scum. Tough beings recognized each other, and nobody looked at him and saw an easy target.

And besides all that, he had Blink.

The comlink chirped again. "Stihl?" came the lieutenant's voice from it.

"Yes, sir."

"You going to play pattycake with those slime beetles all day or are you coming in?"

"On my way, Loot."

7

IMPERIAL-CLASS STAR DESTROYER *DEVASTATOR,* EN ROUTE TO HORUZ SYSTEM

Darth Vader stood on the bridge of his warship, staring out through the forward viewport at the kaleidoscopic chaos of hyperspace. The effect, even moving at the relatively stately speed of a Star Destroyer, was akin to tumbling down an endless tunnel of amorphous, whirling patterns of light—starlight and nebulae smeared into impressionistic blotches by the ship's superluminal speed. He knew that even experienced spacers and navy personnel often hesitated to look out at it. Standard operating procedure was to keep the thick slabs of transparisteel opaqued while traveling through the higher-dimensional universe. There was something profoundly *wrong* about hyperspace, composed as it was of more than the three spatial and one temporal dimensions that most sentient species were used to. Looking too long into hyperspace promised madness, so the stories went. He had never heard of anyone actually succumbing to "hyper-rapture," as it was called. Nevertheless, the legends persisted.

Vader enjoyed staring into it.

He had, of late, become aware of the sound of his breathing, the rhythmic and even pulses of the suit's respirator. The mechanical device that helped keep him alive was most efficient, and he usually tuned it out. Now and again, however, usually during quiet or contemplative moments, it would intrude, reminding him that it was the will of his Master that he had become what he had become. In many ways, so much less than he had been before.

And in other ways, so much more . . .

The creation and construction of the suit had been perforce hasty, since the maimed and burned thing that had been Anakin Skywalker was dying, and would not have survived for long even in a bacta tank. There had been no time to tailor all the life-support systems specifically to his needs. Many of the suit's features were adapted from earlier technology, such as had been designed for the cyborg droid General Grievous over two decades before. It was hardly state-of-the-art. It could, Vader knew, be rebuilt now and made infinitely better, more comfortable, and more powerful. There was only one problem with doing so: to be completely excised, even temporarily, from the suit would kill him. Not even the safety of the hyperbaric chamber—indeed, not even his command of the dark side—could ensure his protection during such a procedure.

Like it or not, the suit and he were one, now and forever.

"Lord Vader," came the voice of the *Devastator*'s captain from behind him. There was only the smallest hint of fear in it, but even that much was obvious to one steeped in the dark side of the Force. Vader felt it as an icy frisson along his nerves, a plangent chord that he alone could hear, a flash of lightning across a darkling plain. Fear was good—in others.

"Yes?"

"We are approaching the drop back into realspace."

Vader turned and regarded the man. "And?"

Captain Pychor swallowed. "N-nothing else, my lord. I just thought to inform you."

"Thank you, Captain. I am already aware of it."

"Yes, my lord." The captain bowed, and backed away.

Inside the helmet, Vader smiled, though it caused him pain to make the expression. But pain was always with him; a little more meant nothing. It wasn't even necessary to call upon the dark side to deal with it. It was purely a matter of will.

The smile faded as he contemplated the immediate future. This trip, he felt, should not be necessary. Governor Wilhuff Tarkin—"Grand Moff Tarkin," as he had been recently designated; a ridiculous rank, in

Vader's opinion—knew his duty. He had been charged by the Emperor to create this behemoth that was supposed to strike fear into the hearts of the Rebels, and certainly he knew what would happen to him if he failed in his duty. Tarkin's philosophy was sound: fear *was* a useful tool. And the battle station would undoubtedly be useful, though the power all its vaunted weaponry and battleships could produce paled against the power of the Force. But the Emperor wished it, and so it would happen.

There had been, however, setbacks—accidents, sabotage, delays—and these were troubling to the Emperor. And so Palpatine had sent Vader to once again convey his displeasure at these setbacks to Tarkin's pet project, and to suggest—strongly—that the Grand Moff find ways to avoid them in the future.

Tarkin was no fool. He would understand the message: *Fail, and suffer the consequences.*

The *Devastator* segued from the hallucinogenic chaos of hyperspace to the more stable vista of realspace. Vader turned away from the view, his cape swirling about him. Now that they were nearly at their destination, he would be able to spend a few hours in his hyperbaric chamber, free at least of his helmet. Time to reflect on his memories, to allow his anger and rage to rise, and for a brief time the dark side would feed on that rage and free him of constant pain. The healing never lasted, however. It was impossible to maintain for long, even within the confines of the chamber. As soon as his anger ebbed and his concentration lapsed, he reverted to what he had become—to what Obi-Wan Kenobi, his erstwhile Jedi Master, had made of him.

Most of the Jedi had been destroyed. Some of the few who mattered the most, however, had not. Some had escaped, among them Yoda. This was disturbing. Old as the green little imp with the querulous voice was, he could still be a threat.

More important, though, was the knowledge that Vader's nemesis still lived. He would have felt it through the Force if the old man had died, of that he was certain. And this was a good thing, a very good thing indeed. Because someday, somehow, Obi-Wan Kenobi would pay for what he had done to Anakin Skywalker, and it would be Darth Vader who collected the toll. He would strike down Kenobi as he had so many of his fellow Jedi, be they Masters, Knights, or Padawans. Eventually the inevitable would become reality, and the Jedi would be no more.

That thought was worth another painful smile behind the ebon mask.

8

GRAND MOFF'S SUITE, LQ FLAGSHIP *HAVELON*

"Sir, there has been . . . an incident."

Seated behind his desk next to the panorama of his viewport, which occupied most of the wall to his right, Tarkin stared at the captain. "An incident?"

"Yes, sir. An explosion in the oxygen supply tanker arriving from the planet. It was just off the northeastern quadrisphere's Main Dock when it happened."

"How much damage?"

"Uncertain, sir. There is still a lot of debris flying about. The tanker was destroyed. Fortunately, most of the crew were only droids. A few navy beings and officers—"

"Don't address trivial matters, Captain. How much damage to the *station*?"

"So far, what we know for sure is that the dock portal and bay took the brunt of the explosion. Our security teams can only guess at—"

"Then do so."

The captain looked uneasy. Officers had been sent to the front for lesser offenses than delivering bad news, and he knew it. No doubt this was why the admiral in charge of security had not come to deliver the report himself.

"Sir, both the portal and dock are demolished. The bay is a mass of twisted girders and ruptured plates. Easier to tear it apart and start from scratch than to repair them."

Tarkin would have spoken aloud the curse that rose from his throat had he been alone. But of course, a mere captain could not be privy to such utterances from a Grand Moff. He simply said, "I see."

"Emergency construction teams have arrived and are doing an assessment," the captain continued. "A full report will be tendered as soon as possible."

Tarkin nodded. Outwardly, he was calm, collected. His voice was cool and even as he said, "I want the cause determined, Captain. Without delay." A millimeter below the surface, however, he was seething with rage. How *dare* anyone damage a single bolt, or rivet, or weld of his station!

"Of course, sir," the officer replied.

"If it was a failure due to someone's error, I want to know. If it was sabotage, I will have the entire life history—or histories—of whoever caused it, and the name of the senior officer who slipped up and allowed it to happen."

"Yes, sir."

"You are dismissed, Captain."

"Sir!" The captain saluted, turned, and departed, a lot quicker on his feet than when he'd arrived.

Tarkin stood and stared through the viewport at the infinite blackness, shot with points of light. So cold and empty out there. Well, before too long it would be fuller, by an infinitesimal degree, with the frozen and contorted body, or bodies, of whoever was responsible for this outrage. Retribution would be swift and certain. That was the only way there would be even a remote possibility of making other would-be saboteurs think twice about imitating such a heinous act.

At times like this, he wished Daala were here. Clever, beautiful, and utterly ruthless when the situation demanded it, she could be most diverting—a great relief for a man such as himself, beset on all sides as he was with weighty problems. But the only female admiral in the Imperial Navy was still stationed at the Maw with her four Destroyers, protecting the hidden base where the battle station's plans and weaponry were in ongoing development.

Abruptly, Tarkin made a decision. He waved his hand over the comm on his desk.

"Sir?" came the immediate query from his aide.

"Is my ship prepared?"

"Of course, sir." The aide's tone was polite, but with just a bit of surprise to indicate what an unnecessary question it was.

"Meet me at the flight deck."

"Yes, sir." Cautiously: "Might one ask where we are going?"

"To inspect the damage to the battle station from the explosion. I want to see it for myself."

"Yes, sir."

Tarkin stood, feeling a glow of fierce satisfaction. He had not always been a desk-bound commander. He had spent plenty of time in the field. Now and again it served the rank and file to know that he was still capable of getting his hands dirty—or bloody, depending on the situation.

GRAND MOFF'S LIGHTER, 0.5 KILOMETERS FROM THE DEATH STAR

"Look to the forward viewport, sir," the pilot said.

Tarkin, who had been poring over a schematic hologram of the station that showed where the damage was, turned and stared through the port at the real thing.

It was indeed a mess. It appeared as if a giant hand had smashed the dock, then petulantly ripped sections of it loose and flung those into space. Debris of all sizes and shapes whirled and tumbled aimlessly, not having had time yet to settle into any sort of orbit.

Tarkin's expression was pinched tight in anger, but his voice was level as he said, "Bring her around and let's have a closer look."

"Sir." A pause. "There's a lot of debris, sir."

"I can see that. I suggest you avoid running into it."

The pilot swallowed drily. "Yes, sir."

As the pilot began to swing the small cruiser into a wide turn, Tarkin's aide approached.

"Yes, Colonel?"

"The forensic investigation team has a preliminary report, sir."

"Really? This soon?"

"You did indicate a desire for alacrity, sir."

"Indeed." Tarkin offered the colonel a small, tight smile. "Hold off on the flyby," he instructed the pilot. "I'll take the report here."

"Sir." The pilot was visibly relieved at this.

A moment later, the holoprojector lit over the command console at which Tarkin stood, displaying a one-third-sized image of a security force major standing at attention.

"Sir," the major said, giving a military bow.

Tarkin made an impatient gesture. "What do we have, Major?"

The major reached off-image to touch a control, and a second holoimage blossomed next to him. It was that of an Imperial gas tanker. As Tarkin watched, the images grew larger and translucent as the point of view zoomed closer. A flashing red dot appeared toward the rear of the ship, and the POV zoomed in closer still to reveal the interior of the vessel.

"From the dispersal pattern of the ship's interior and hull, which we backtracked by computer reconstruction, the source of the explosion was here—" The officer pointed into the hologram, only his hand and pointing finger becoming visible in the blown-up image before Tarkin's eyes. "—in the aft cargo hold. The precise location was plus or minus a meter of the pressure valve complex on the starboard tank array."

"Go on."

"Given the size of the tanks and the pressure—the oxygen is liquefied, of course—and the estimated explosive potential and expansion, we have calculated that a leak and subsequent accidental ignition of expanding gas in an enclosed compartment is highly unlikely to have produced the level of damage recorded."

Tarkin nodded, almost to himself. "Sabotage, then," he said. "A bomb."

"We believe so, sir." The image zoomed back out to encompass the major again. "We have not yet recovered parts of the device itself, but we will."

Tarkin gritted his teeth, feeling his jaw muscles bunch. He made an effort to relax, giving the major another of his tight smiles. "Congratulate your team on their efforts thus far, Major. I am pleased with your efficiency."

"Thank you, sir." The man smiled.

"But don't pat yourselves on the backs too much just yet. I want to know what kind of bomb it was, who made it, who planted it—everything."

The major stiffened again. "Yes, sir. We will report as soon as we have new information."

"You're already late with it," Tarkin said. "Dismissed."

The holo blinked off, and Tarkin stared into the blank space that was left, as if looking for answers. Sabotage was, of course, to be expected. This wasn't the first time it had happened, and it almost certainly would not be the last. A project this size, no matter how tight the security, was impossible to keep entirely hidden. An astute observer could gather a number of disparate facts from far-flung sources—shipping manifests, troop movements, vessel deployments, and the like—and from those, if he had even the cleverness of a sunstroked Gungan, deduce some general ideas. He might not know exactly what, or precisely where, but he could figure out that something big was being constructed. And with sufficient resources, time, and cunning, this being, and others like him, could discover a trail that led back to this system and this station.

There were shrewd beings among the Rebels; Tarkin had no doubt of that. And there were, more than likely, Rebels among the human detritus down on the prison planet. Perhaps even traitors among the Imperial Navy or troops.

A very tight lid was being kept on this project. Communications had been, and continued to be, squeezed tighter than a durasteel fist. But *somebody* had blown up that cargo ship, and had not done so just because they were bored and had nothing better to do.

Such travesties could not be abided. Nor would they be.

9

INTERIOR OFFICE ANNEX, ASSEMBLY HALL, CONSTRUCTION SITE BETA-NINE, DEATH STAR

He had a name—Benits Stinex, and anybody who knew anything about architecture recognized it. Stinex? Oh, sure, the designer. The one who still gets written up regularly in *Beings Holozine*. The one whose price was always more than one could imagine, let alone afford. Among themselves, the staff doing the interiors referred to him as "the Old Man." Old he was, too—Teela guessed his age at three, maybe four times her own, and she was nearing twenty-five standard years. Human, with more wrinkles than hyperspace, the chief architect was; the head of interior design and construction, and still mentally as sharp as a vibroblade.

He waved at the holo, which glimmered blue and white over the projector in front of them, depicting the schematics for the finished assembly hall. "What do you think, Kaarz?"

Standing next to him in the recently pressurized but still-cold office annex, Teela knew she was once again being tested. Every time she was around the Old Man, he did that. She'd heard that it took awhile for him to trust you—but once he did you were golden in his eyes. It seemed that everybody worth the salt in their bodies who worked for him wanted him to feel that way.

And why shouldn't they? A missive of recommendation from Stinex, even just a line or two, was worth just about any conceivable torture one could imagine and endure. It was a ticket for the hyperlane that could lead to wealth, fame, and the most desirable thing of all:

Freedom.

The freedom to design what one wished, to give free rein to one's artistic expression, to create something that might truly outlast the ages, that might—

Teela realized that the Old Man was waiting patiently for an answer to his question. She shrugged. "It's standard Imperial design; works enough to serve."

The Old Man gave her a slow, disappointed look.

"But," she continued, "if you want it to work *well,* then the egress and exit portals need to be relocated." She pulled the finger-sized electronic scribe from her belt, thumbed the eraser stud, and waved it at the drawing. "Here, here, and here," she continued, "and possibly there, as well." The portals vanished as she gestured, replaced by skeletal wall lines. Quickly she sketched in new doors. "Reposition these portals, skew the walkways, like so, the flow-through improves at least twenty-five percent, like the presentation says. Doesn't cost any more."

The Old Man smiled and nodded, pleased. "What about the ventilation?"

"Specs call for a superannuated System Four and what you need is a minimum of a Five. A Six would be better."

"The Empire deems a Four adequate."

"The idiot who drew up the engineering specs was interested in saving money—if he had to sit in this hall with four thousand other beings, each putting out between sixty and a hundred and forty watts of heat and copious amounts of carbon dioxide, not to mention various body odors, while listening to some long-winded admiral blather on for two hours, he'd upgrade the air exchangers as soon as he could get to a requisition form."

The Old Man laughed. "I can see why you were sent to prison. Political delicacy is not one of your strong points, is it?"

She shrugged. "Form follows function."

"The defense of the idealist. I will grant you that the Empire is slow to learn basic architectural concepts." He nodded at the three-dimensional image. "All right. Make the portal changes. I'll allow a Five for the exchangers. What else?"

Teela could not stop her grin. She was a political prisoner of the Empire, but at least she was being allowed to do work she knew how to do. As vast as the project was, they needed all the help they could get, and she was very good at her job. The Old Man knew it, even though he kept verbally poking at her every time they spoke. He himself was a willing tool of the Empire, but he had designed everything from refreshers to superskytowers, skyhooks to sports stadiums, and he had forgotten more than most architects learned in a lifetime of study. She had trained with some of the best, and she knew the hand of a master when she felt it. She didn't enjoy being tested like a third-year arcology student this way, but she also felt a little surge of pride every time the Old Man smiled and nodded at one of her suggestions. It was good to be acknowledged by someone of his ability.

As she pointed out other inefficiencies in the standard design, however, she felt it again: that tiny twinge, that brief moment of discomfort. She was working for the *Empire,* a thing she had sworn she would never do, helping design a vessel that would, in all probability, be the most fearsome weapon the galaxy had ever seen. While it was true that improving the biometrics and seating pattern in an assembly hall was not the same as devising a superlaser that could melt moons, still . . .

Still, one was either a factor in something's success, or a factor in its failure.

Working for the enemy, said the little voice she sometimes heard in her head. She often visualized it as a miniature version of herself, shaking a chastising finger. *How sad is that?*

Not as if I had a choice, *is it?* she replied mentally. *Nobody asked me if I wanted the job, now, did they?*

You could have turned it down, the avatar of her conscience shot back.

And been sent back to that serpent's nest of a planet to rot and die? To what end?

Her inner self fell silent.

"We can't do that," the Old Man said to her suggestion of natural lighting in the complex. "I have limits."

She nodded. She had thought that would be his response, but there was no harm in asking. The Old Man had considerable power when it came to design alterations. Several times Teela had seen specifications upgraded and improved to heights well beyond what she had expected.

This project had support at the highest levels. While the admirals who controlled the credits were always trying to pinch and hold on to as many as they could, nobody was going to stint on anything that would make it function as intended.

Too bad the original designers hadn't had that mandate.

Teela hadn't seen all of the master plans—she didn't think anybody below the Old Man's standing had seen all of them—but there were plenty of design flaws in the subplans she had reviewed. Nothing so major that the place would fail to function or fall apart if somebody bumped into a wall, but enough little bits and pieces here and there said without a doubt that the designers had paid less attention to details than they should have. Another draft or two of the schematics would have corrected most of those; many were being caught and fixed on the fly, such as she had just done—poorly placed entrances and exits, less-than-adequate ventilation systems, thermal vents badly located . . . the usual minutiae that cropped up in big construction projects. There was just more of it, but then there was a lot more vessel for mistakes to happen in, wasn't there? This Death Star was, after all, as big as a Class IV moon, with a *minimum* of over a million beings making up the crew. Nothing this size had ever been built before . . . at least as far as Teela was aware.

What it all came down to was, she would do what she could do. Working for the Empire was bad, no getting around that, but not as bad as living in a makeshift hut on a world that was, for the most part, either jungle or swamp, and whose inhabitants would sooner kill you than look at you. After all, what could *she* do? Architecture wasn't exactly the sort of exciting and dashing thing that people could rally around. She would, in all probability, just get herself killed if she tried to aid the Rebels. But by doing what she knew how to do, she might actually save a few lives, or at least make those lives more comfortable. Yes, those lives would belong to servants of the Empire, but after all, not every single being here was evil.

As rationalizations went, that one wasn't so bad. Her inner self almost bought it.

10

MEDICAL FRIGATE *MEDSTAR FOUR,* POLAR ORBIT, DESPAYRE

The secretary droid C-4ME-O stood gyroscopically balanced on its single wheel in the hallway as Uli exited the surgery theater. The procedure had been routine, an operation to graft in a new liver for a Wookiee slave injured in the recent explosion at the construction site. Some of the enslaved species were considered expendable, as there were always more potential conscripts on the planet below, but Wookiees were too valuable to lose, a colonel had told him. They were worth three of just about any other worker, and Uli had already heard it at least ten times since he'd gotten here: if you want a job done right, get a Wookiee to do it. They were able to better withstand the temperature extremes of vacuum, they had more endurance than the other species, and their work ethic was unimpeachable—they seemed incapable of giving less than 100 percent, even on a project they had been conscripted for. The only drawback was that their vacuum suits had to be specially made to accommodate their huge, hairy forms. Uli had wondered why he'd seen so many of them when he'd arrived. He'd soon realized that like himself, they were not here by choice.

"Dr. Divini," the droid said, in its pleasing tenor. "How are you?"

"As well as can be expected, Fourmio. Is there something you need?"

"I am quite self-sufficient, thank you, Doctor. But Commander Hotise would like to see you when it is convenient."

Inwardly, Uli groaned. He'd been pretty much on the go ever since he'd gotten here, and now that his rotation was finally over, he'd been looking forward to some sleep. "Did he sound urgent?"

"Actually, sir, his precise words were, 'Get Divini's butt up here on the double.'" The droid did a perfect imitation of Hotise's voice.

Uli had to smile at that. Hotise might be a career man, but he was honest and direct in his speech and actions. And he was just another cog in the Empire's giant machine—no point in blaming him for the situation.

Uli was wearing surgical blues, which he did not waste time changing. While standard service protocols ordinarily required more formal dress when attending a commanding officer in a noncombat area on board a ship, the medical units were less stringent. Most medics were draftees and didn't give a Psadan's patoot what the navy thought of them anyhow—they were just hoping to get out and go home. And like him, any doctor worth his laser scalpel knew he, she, or it was far too valuable to be stuck in a brig for failing to observe some piddling uniform code. The Empire was sometimes hidebound and slow, but not altogether foolish.

When Uli entered, Hotise was seated behind his desk, tapping his fingers rapidly on two different input consoles. Holoimages danced and flashed over the consoles as the codes flowed. It was impressive to watch, like seeing someone able to write in two languages at the same time, one with each hand.

"Sit. Be with you in a few seconds."

Uli parked himself in the chair, a flowform device that hummed and adjusted itself to his contours for a perfect support. Sitting down was a mistake, he belatedly realized. If he leaned back, he could fall asleep faster than . . .

Hotise, true to his word, jarred Uli from his doze only a few seconds later. "The construction crew has gotten a couple of equatorial med stations operational—not full-service plexes, but they have two surgery suites, pre-op and recovery rooms, and twenty medical beds each. Not to mention bacta tank wards, nursing stations, supply rooms, offices . . . you know the drill. More than a Rimsoo, less than a medcenter."

"And . . . ?"

"And I want you to go run one."

"I'm not an administrator," Uli said.

"Teach your grandfather how to put his boots on, son. I know you're not an administrator, but we're shy a few dozen of those right now. Construction is running ahead of schedule, at least in our field, and we're slow getting fresh help.

"You're qualified as chief surgeon, and I'll send Fourmio along to handle the secretarial stuff. We need three surgeons and a couple of internal medicine docs, all with broad-species experience, plus nurses, aides, orderlies, and some computer operators. It's no worse than running a clinic. Caseloads'll be mostly workers getting banged up, some infections, age-related illnesses—the usual med-surg stuff on a construction site. Nothing you can't handle. If you get bogged down, you can call for help."

There was no way out of this, Uli realized. Still, he couldn't resist asking: "Why me?"

"Well, frankly, son, I don't have anybody else I can spare."

What did it matter? Uli asked himself. Here, there, or somewhere else—it was all the same, really. This wasn't a combat situation, like so many in the past had been. Nevertheless, he could feel a tiny worm of uneasiness begin to writhe slowly in his gut. "All right," he said.

"Thought you'd say that—not like you have much of a choice. Pack your gear—you leave on the third-shift shuttle."

As Uli headed for his quarters to gather his few belongings, he considered his life yet again. It had been two decades since his first assignment on Drongar. He'd helped staff a few more Rimsoos since then, and when the Clone Wars had ended he'd been more than ready to practice in the private sector. But that wasn't the life he'd been dealt. And now, when he should have been long free of his bondage, he was going to yet another post—this time on the behemoth called the Death Star.

Generally he tried not to think about Drongar—even after all this time, reminiscing led to certain memories that were too painful. But he couldn't help but remember a phrase that the scrappy little Sullustan reporter Den Dhur had often used: *I've got a bad feeling about this.*

Right, Uli thought.

SLASHTOWN PRISON COLONY, DESPAYRE

Ratua first heard the rumor from Balahteez, the Pho Ph'eahian spice smuggler. Balahteez had, over the years, developed numerous contacts, and, perhaps not surprisingly, many of them had ended up here. As a result, he always seemed to have good sources of information. The price you had to pay to hear that information was to listen to his sad story of unjust treatment by the heartless Empire.

Spice smuggling by itself usually wasn't enough to rate a trip to the prison planet for a life sentence, but Balahteez had been involved in an unfortunate accident while being pursued by an Imperial patrol near the Zharan moon Gall. Realizing that his ship would soon be overtaken by the navy gunboat chasing him, Balahteez had jettisoned his illegal cargo. The drug, packed securely in a block of carbonite the size of a luggage trunk, had hurtled down Gall's gravity well and punched a large hole into the outer hull of a barracks housing a large unit of TIE fighter mechanics. The hole was big enough that thirty of the hapless mechanics had been blown through it and into vacuum by the explosive decompression, and a dozen more had run out of air before the emergency and repair droids could reseal the compartment. Not to mention the other fifty or so who had died immediately from the impact; the carbonite block had been traveling at about two kilometers a second and had left a crater thirty meters in diameter.

It had been an accident, pure and simple, and the odds against the block striking one structure in a few thousand square kilometers of utter emptiness were so large that calculating them would have caused a throbbing headache in a Givin. Needless to say, the Empire hadn't seen it like that.

Ratua had heard the story enough times that he knew it almost word for word: the smuggler had been tried, convicted, and put on a ship to Despayre, all in less than a standard week's time. Ratua had heard it said that Pho Ph'eahians were great raconteurs, entertaining enough to keep their audience spellbound. And the Pho's story had been interesting—the first five or six times Ratua had heard it. But he'd lost count of how many times it had been told to him by now. And the Pho couldn't be hurried along: Ratua had to sit and smile and pretend to be interested, offering sympathy in the right places, nodding, clucking his tongue and shaking his head in amazement, or the smuggler would get miffed and wouldn't reveal what he had recently learned. It was rather like performing a well-rehearsed play: if Ratua did his part correctly, he'd be rewarded; flub his lines, and he'd be left joyless.

"Truly, truly, you have been mistreated," he said. "So unfair."

Balahteez nodded. "I have, indeed I have."

"Sad. There is no justice." Ratua judged that they were at the point where he could now ask, "So, any news?"

"As it happens, my leafy friend, yes. I have it on dependable authority that the EngSat Complex and Dybersyne Engineering Systems have begun production on the largest focusing magnet ever built—the gauss equivalent of a small iron moon's field, so they say."

"Well, that's, uh . . . interesting," Ratua said. "Probably the most exciting thing this year at the Interstellar Conference of Dull and Boring Science Twits."

"My apologies for any inadvertent rudeness, my young sprout, but you know naught about which you jest." Balahteez glanced up at the ceiling but was clearly intending that his gaze pierce the roof and extend into space.

"Yon construction, upon which so many of our fellows have been conscripted to menial labor, along with thousands and thousands of slaves, droids, and private contractors, not to mention army, navy, and Imperial engineers, is the destination for this colossal apparatus."

"Yeah—so?"

"Well, let me enlighten you. Beams of coherent particles, such as electrons, positrons, and the like, as well as amplified photon emissions, are often focused with large magnetic rings. Let us postulate that one could, in this fashion, generate a weaponized beam with enough force to blow a large asteroid apart with a single blast."

"Is there such a thing?"

"In theory, yes, though it requires a power source so large as to be impractical to perambulate, even on a Star Destroyer. But," Balahteez continued, raising one phalange in emphasis, "aboard something the size of, say, a moon, one could easily install and house such a mechanism."

"You're saying the battle station they're building up there is going to be that large?"

"Oh, my, yes. Easily. But this is not the point. The magnetic ring being built by Dybersyne is much, much larger than would be needed to focus such a beam, even a beam of such astonishing power."

Ratua frowned. "You've lost me."

The smuggler smiled. "Let us say, for the sake of argument, that the battle station under construction is large enough to hold, oh, six or eight such weapons, as well as a hypermatter reactor that could power a small planet. And that it is possible to focus all of this energy into a single beam—by the largest and most powerful magnetic ring ever made." He looked expectantly at Ratua.

"Milking mopak," Ratua said softly.

"Indeed, indeed. I see you comprehend at last. Not so dull and boring after all, eh?"

Ratua shook his head. That was for sure. If the Empire could make something like that work, there wouldn't be any place a Rebel force could hide—the superweapon could, with a single blast, destroy whole continents. Maybe even whole planets. Just knowing such a thing existed, it seemed, would be enough to keep the peace. You certainly wouldn't want to see it coming into *your* system with malign intent . . .

Ratua was not the political type. He'd never cared much who was in charge, since he lived on the fringes anyhow, and now that he was condemned to spend the rest of his life on this dreadful planet, it mattered even less. If the Rebels somehow won out against the Empire—a thing that seemed beyond possibility, especially given this latest news—they wouldn't be likely to offer him amnesty for his crimes any more than the Empire had. Sure, there were some political prisoners here who might be freed, but thieves and smugglers and murderers wouldn't be going anywhere no matter who won the war. Even those who had truly been unjustly convicted, as he and Balahteez had been, couldn't expect commutation. No, he was doomed, it seemed, to rot here on Despayre for the remainder of his days.

But . . .

If he could somehow manage to secure a spot on that station, he could be reasonably certain of two things: one, it wouldn't be hanging around the Horuz system very long after it was operational, and two, it would be one of the safest places in all the galaxy. All things considered, *there* would be a much better place to be than *here*.

Unfortunately, Ratua had no particular talents that would make an Imperial recruiter want to choose him for station-side duty. Probably the Empire had little need of a scrounger on such a vessel. Still, when you considered it, on a station the size of a planetoid, a single being could easily escape official notice. Once there, he could fade into the shadows and, with a bit of luck, become effectively invisible. There had to be literally millions of places to hide up there.

The problem was, *up there* might as well mean the other side of the galaxy, as long as he was down here. Still, it might not be an insurmountable problem . . .

"Let me get you a mug of tea," Ratua said, "and we can continue our talk."

11

IMPERIAL-CLASS STAR DESTROYER *DEVASTATOR*

Refreshed from his time in the hyperbaric chamber, Darth Vader once more contemplated his unique fate. He had become accustomed to what he was, for the most part. It was hard, after all these years, to even visualize the face of Anakin Skywalker, Jedi Knight. But that was as it should be. Skywalker was dead. He'd been killed on the bank of one of the lava rivers of Mustafar, and the Sith Lord Darth Vader had risen from his ashes.

He became once again aware of his breathing, and the demand-respirator sped up as he let the dark side take him, let it envelop him in anger and hatred. The power of the Force flowed into him, filling him, fueling his rage. It was, as always, his choice: he could absorb the dark energy, keep it pent within him, a no-longer-quite-human capacitor that could discharge it anytime, directing it toward anyone or anything. Or he could let it flow through him now, be not the vessel but the conduit, and thereby find momentary surcease from the fury that was always so much a part of him.

He decided on the latter.

He left his lightsaber clipped to his belt. Ordinarily he would have used it to practice on the dueling droids that had been specially designed and constructed to test his mettle. Programmed with the knowledge and skills of a dozen different martial artists, and armed with deadly cutting or impact weapons, they were formidable opponents indeed, and had been an integral part of Sith training since time immemorial. But not everything was about the lightsaber. There were other attributes, other weapons in his arsenal, that needed exercising as well.

Vader inhaled, holding the dry and slightly bitter air for as long as his scarred lungs could manage it. When he allowed the breath to be drawn from him by the respirator, he thrust his right hand toward a nearby mirror.

The aluminized densecris shattered into a thousand pieces, struck by the dark side as if by a metal fist.

Vader was aware of the "unbreakable" substance splintering and falling, tinkling onto the floor, myriad reflections sparkling in the light as they seemed to move in slow motion. At the same time, the Force alerted him to the presence of someone in the doorway behind him.

"Yes?" he said, without turning to look. He knew who it was by the greasy feel of the man's thoughts. Had he been unable to sense those, the mere fact that the intruder had come here to interrupt his exercises would have been enough to reveal his identity. No one else would dare.

"My lord," said Admiral Motti. "Grand Moff Tarkin requests a word with you."

Vader turned, surprised. Why would Tarkin seek an audience now? Yes, the man knew he was on the way to the construction site, but it was bad protocol to break comm silence.

Whatever the ostensible reason, it was a certainty that a hidden agenda lay behind it. Tarkin's deviousness could flummox a roomful of Neimoidian barristers, Vader reflected. Fortunately, the Force was a most useful tool against such intrigue.

Without a word, Vader swept past the admiral and headed for the privacy of his quarters. Motti's mind was not weak, but the emotions roiling beneath the calm exterior made his thoughts easy enough to sense: could he have struck Vader dead in that moment, he would have. The man's mind was a cauldron of seething anger, of hatred and envy, most of which was directed toward Vader. A pity Motti had no connection to the Force, the Dark Lord mused. He could have proved most useful.

"Lord Vader," the holo of Tarkin said. The greeting and the slight bow with it were stiff and formal. The image was full-sized, if a bit transparent and fuzzy, occupying the holoplate in Vader's anteroom as if the governor were standing before him.

Vader studied the simulacrum. Whatever the issue was that had prompted Tarkin to call, it wasn't a small one. The man's face was even more dour and saturnine than usual.

"Grand Moff Tarkin," Vader said. He made no effort to disguise an edge of contempt for the title. The military did love its pecking order.

Tarkin wasn't a man to dally with pleasantries; he got straight to the point. "There has been an explosion on the battle station—sabotage. Significant damage."

"And . . . ?"

"We have determined several suspects in its cause."

"And . . . ?"

"Our medical teams have not yet received the first supply shipment of mind-probes."

Vader nodded. "I see. You wish me to examine these suspects."

"Yes. If there are any preparations you need to make, speed is of the essence. It is paramount that we determine who caused this incident, and why, and deal with it forcefully."

"I need no preparations. My ship will arrive in a few hours. I shall speak to the prisoners as soon as I board your vessel. Have them ready. I will determine who among them are responsible."

Tarkin gave him another crisp military nod. "We look forward to your visit, Lord Vader."

Vader gestured for the comm unit to disconnect without responding. *Yes,* he thought. *I'm sure you do.*

This was most interesting news. If the Rebel Alliance was responsible—and who else could it be?—this action certainly gave the lie to the official image of the dissidents as disorganized rabble posing no real threat. Vader felt a small ember of satisfaction glow within him. He had known for some time that the malcontents were growing both in organization and in power. They had staged guerrilla raids on space stations and supply depots, had managed to obtain military matériel and warcraft from sympathetic industrial and shipyard designers, and had allied themselves with many alien species, playing upon the latters' resentment at being reduced to inferior status in the eyes of the New Order. They were more than just a motley collection of wild-eyed idealists; they now numbered among their ranks former Imperial strategists, programmers, and technicians, and their network of spies was growing more intricate daily. They were scum, true enough, but enough scum could clog any system, even one as complex and pristine as the Empire.

They had to be dealt with, and they would be. This Death Star of Tarkin's could be effective to a degree, but one need not use a proton torpedo to swat a fire gnat.

Vader turned and left his chambers. The dark side would tell him who the miscreants were—tell him, and deal with them as well.

12

THE SOFT HEART CANTINA, SOUTHERN UNDERGROUND,
GRID 19, IMPERIAL CITY

Memah Roothes frowned at the delivery droid. Local weather systems were acting up, and the air was hot, too moist, and cloying, not to mention smelling of lube and a hint of rotting garbage drifting through from the alley behind her cantina. She had been up late and arisen early, she already felt lousy, and she certainly didn't need this latest piece of bad news.

"Excuse me? I don't think I heard you correctly. Please repeat that."

The droid, a standard loader/unloader utility model, said again, "Your liquor shipment has been delayed. Our dispatcher tenders apologies for the mistake."

"And what are my customers supposed to drink in the meanwhile? Water?"

The droid's basic intelligence was sufficient for making liquor deliveries; it wasn't up to sarcasm. "Water is drinkable by all sentient carbon-based beings."

"Yes, and even here it is *free* from any Imperial tap."

The droid did not respond to that. Memah shook her head in disgust; a human mannerism she'd picked up. It was pointless to argue with a droid; might as well argue with the ferment dispensers under the bar. "All right. When may I expect the shipment?"

"Tomorrow."

"Well, I guess I'll just have to make do somehow, won't I?"

That question was evidently also beyond the droid's comprehension. Sighing, Memah waved it away.

Rodo, who had been in the front repairing a broken hinge caused by the impact of a combative patron, came back to the delivery portal. "Problem?"

"Yes. Today's delivery—there isn't one."

"Hmm . . ."

Memah turned to look at him. "Do I detect some kind of meaning in that monosyllable?"

"It's probably nothing," Rodo replied. "But I saw the food staples airtruck fan past Kenloo's Market this morning without stopping. They get their deliveries same days we do."

The market was two buildings down, on the other side of a vacant shop that had once housed exotic offworld pets. Some kind of exobiotic plague had run through the animal stock seven months back, and half of them had died. The Empire had quarantined the place, had the remaining creatures put down, and that was the end of that. The building had sat empty ever since.

She pulled herself back to Rodo's comment. "What are you getting at?"

The big man shrugged. "Just seems odd that two businesses right next to each other, with service from different delivery companies, would both get bypassed on the same day."

"A coincidence," she said.

"When I was with the Strikebirds, we had a saying: Coincidence can get you killed." Rodo yawned and stretched his arms over his head, displaying muscles that would make a Whiphid look scrawny. "Maybe I'll check around," he said, "see if Chunte's and Ligabow's are also having delivery problems."

"And if they are?"

He shrugged. "Then it means something."

She couldn't help the exasperated tone that crept into her voice. "Like *what*?"

Rodo shrugged again. "Dunno. Could be a lot of things. Maybe just problems with dispatcher programs. Maybe the start of somebody trying to depress real estate values so he can buy up the block. Hard to say. Could be nothing at all."

Memah nodded slowly, not quite sure what to make of Rodo's sudden and studied casualness. "Yeah, well, we're going to have to dust off some of the reserve stock to get through tonight's crowd. And even then, it'll be iffy."

He nodded. "I'll be back before the evening crush," he said. He headed for the mouth of the alley, and she went back inside.

Rodo's worry aside, a missed delivery was probably nothing to be concerned about, Memah told herself. There was, after all, a war on, and little glitches were to be expected, even if the war never actually came close to this planet, save for a few incidences of sabotage. And what Rebel with half a brain was going to come down to the Southern Underground to blow something up—here, where there was a good chance somebody would waylay him and steal everything he had on him, including his bomb? Unless you knew your way around these parts, it was risky being a tourist without a couple of armed guards. Plus, there weren't any targets down here that would make much of a headline in the holocasts—who cared about the slums below the streets anyhow?

She thought then of those Eyes who'd been in the other night. Yeah, okay, that had been unusual, but whatever their reasons, it wasn't as if there was anything covert going on . . .

Was it?

Memah snorted. Probably some computer had burped somewhere and lost a couple of routing files. As long as it was a onetime glitch, she could live with that. After all, where local government was concerned, it wasn't as if she had a lot of choice these days.

NCO CANTINA, ISD *STEEL TALON*

The NCO cantina was half full, the air blowers working hard to get rid of the smoke and body odors, and almost succeeding. MCPO Tenn Graneet sat across the four-person table from Olzal Erne, the second-watch chief from the starboard array. Both humans had their elbows on the table, right hands clasped in arm-wrestling position. Their left hands were linked on the tabletop.

Erne was bigger—twelve, maybe fifteen kilos heavier—ten years younger, and he liked to pump iron, so he had the muscles of a weight lifter. To look at them, it should be no contest—Erne clearly had the advantage.

"You about ready, old man?" Erne said.

"Just a second." Tenn freed his left hand, grabbed his frosted mug, and took a long swallow of ferment. He put the mug down, grinned, and relinked with Erne's left hand. "Good when you are, Olzal."

A dozen members of both gunnery crews and a couple of deck polishers stood around the table, watching as both men settled in, the muscles on their arms beginning to bunch slightly. Other than that, the clasped hands could have been molded in durasteel.

"Five on Chief Erne, thirty seconds max," one of Erne's gunners said.

"I got that," somebody on Tenn's crew said.

"Ten on CPO Graneet," one of the proton railers, also of Tenn's crew, chimed in.

"Time on that?" a woman asked.

"As long as it takes."

"I'll take that bet."

"Hey, Numbers, how much does our side win?" Tenn asked.

Numbers was a Givin, a species of beings who were, on the whole, obsessed with mathematics. Only a few dozen Givins had been conscripted, but their ability to survive for short periods, unsuited, in hard vacuum, even more than their aptitude for juggling integers, had resulted in more favored treatment than most other nonhumanoids got from the Empire.

Numbers had an uncanny ability to do all manner of arithmetic in his head, almost as fast as a droid. Now was no exception. Tenn had no sooner posed the question than the gaunt creature replied, "Eighty-five credits among us. Twenty in your pocket."

"Counting your money, Tenn? You gotta beat me first, don't you?"

"Oh, that." With a quick snap of his wrist and flexion of his chest and shoulders, Tenn slammed Erne's hand to the tabletop. It took maybe an entire second.

He let go of the other man's hand to a smattering of applause and cheers. Erne looked stunned. He rubbed his biceps. "Milking son of a tairn!" he said. "How the kark did you do that?"

Tenn grinned. "Clean living, Chief."

The truth was otherwise, but only he knew it. Back in a dustup during the final days of the Clone Wars, when he'd been an assistant gunner on his first assignment, some idiot of a loader had switched leads on a heavy capacitor and then forgotten to set the safeties. As soon as the discharger opened it, the cap had blown and showered the gun crew with shrapnel, a piece of which had severed the tendon connecting Tenn's right pectoral muscle to his arm.

It had been lucky for the loader that he'd been killed instantly; otherwise, those of the crew who weren't already maimed or dead would have made it a point to see him die slowly.

When the medic had reconnected the tendon in Tenn's upper body, he hadn't liked the old attachment, which had gotten pretty banged up by the piece of hot metal. So he'd done an organic-screw embed and reattached the ligament a little lower. It looked fine, and eventually the screw was reabsorbed, leaving nothing more than a tiny bone nub. The result of this creative endeavor had been about a 25 or 30 percent improvement on the leverage in his right arm. With a little training, Tenn's right pectoral was effectively almost half again as strong as his left. It didn't look it, it wasn't any larger, but the result was nonetheless impressive. It had won him a lot of bar bets on arm-wrestling contests over the years.

Numbers slid a little stack of credits under Tenn's mug. "Your cut, Chief."

"My elderly mother thanks you kindly, son." He looked at Erne. "So, I buy the next round?"

"Works for me," the bigger man said.

"No dishonor in being beaten by the best."

The chief grinned. "Give me a couple of days to heal up, we can have a rematch."

"Always happy to take a fellow navy man's money."

After the watchers had gone back to their own brews, Erne said, "So what's the scut on the new battle station?"

"The Death Star?" Tenn lowered his voice to a conspiratorial level. "I hear that anybody who can hit a resiplex wall from a meter away can have a berth if he wants it. But if you can *really* shoot, they'll let you run the big guns—including one that'll make our biggest weapons look like pocket slugthrowers."

"No kidding?"

"Guys like us, we got no problem," Tenn continued. "All we have to do is ask."

"You gonna go for it?"

"Now *you're* kidding. I'm a lifer; why wouldn't I? When this thing is finished, nothing anybody anywhere can field against it will even scratch the finish. Running a gun that will pop Star Destroyers like soap bubbles, maybe even knock a moon out of orbit—what kind of gunner would pass that up?" He grinned. "Bigger *is* better."

"I hear security will be tight. No leaves once you sign on until after the station becomes operational."

"And this is different from what we're now doing how? Besides, look at the size of it. It's gonna be like living on a moon—or in one. *Thousands* of decks. You can scan it and plug it so that everything a man could want will be somewhere in that sucker. Who needs shore leave when all you have to do is punch up the turbolift?"

Erne allowed as how Tenn's evaluation of the Death Star's prurient possibilities made much sense. Both men drank more of their ales.

"I've already told my exec I'm ready to sign on," Tenn said. "Soon as they get a gun working, enough air to breathe, and enough gravity to tell which way's up, I'm *there.*"

"Speaking of everything a man could want . . . ," Erne said. He nodded at the door.

Tenn turned. Ah. A pair of civilian workers from Supply—young, good-looking fems—stood there, having come, no doubt, to check out a place where real men drank.

"I like the blond," Erne said.

"Fine by me," Tenn said. "Hair's all the same color in the dark."

Erne stood. "Good evening, ladies. Might my father and I buy you both drinks?"

The two young women smiled. Tenn gave them his best grin in return, feeling the contentedness that only liquor and competitive victory could bring. A good job, the respect of people you worked with, and a nice-looking female sitting next to him, in a cantina full of excellent Ortolan blue ferment. How much better could life get?

13

PILOTS' PUB, REC DECK, ISD *STEEL TALON*

Vil Dance had a stack of tenth-credit coins balanced on his upturned elbow, up to a dozen now. Around him, other pilots were making bets on whether he'd make it.

So far, so good . . .

He took another sip of his ale. The game was simple: You pointed your elbow like a gun sight and aimed in front of you, forearm held at a ninety-degree angle and parallel to the floor. With your open palm next to your ear and facing the ceiling, you snapped your hand down and tried to catch the coins balanced on your elbow before they fell. Anybody could do one. Most could do three or even four. Once you got past ten it was harder. Vil's personal best was eighteen, so a dozen wasn't that hard. It was a hand–eye coordination test, and if you were a pilot, you'd better have that in a goodly amount. The trick was to snap your cupped hand down fast enough so that you got to the coins while they were still stacked together. After a few centimeters' free fall in normal gravity, they started to break from the stack, and once that happened you couldn't pull it off. The movement had to be fast, but it also had to be smooth. The slightest off-angle jerk would torque the stack enough to separate the coins. You could manage most of them if that happened, but you'd miss some, guaranteed.

It wasn't as though the honor of the squad or anything was riding on him, but Vil did have a reputation to keep up. His times on the pilot reaction drills were always in the top two or three, and that's what this was, essentially. A test of reflexes. There were other species, like the Falleen, for example, who could catch twenty or more with no problem whatsoever. But few humans could manage even ten, other than acrobats, martial arts masters . . . and pilots.

"C'mon, Dance. You're slower than a ronto in eight g's." That was Benjo.

"Yeah, while we're young," Raal added. "Well, some of us, anyway . . ."

Vil grinned, snapped his hand down, and grabbed the dozen tenths, no problem. "Easy money," he said.

There was a moment of surprised silence among the squad, then:

"Five says he can't do fourteen."

"I'll take that bet."

"Ten says he can."

"Odds?"

"Odds? What, do I look like a Toydarian bookie? Even!"

While the pilots argued, Vil collected two more coins from a stack on the table. Fourteen, eh? Still four less than his top number, though he didn't see any real point in mentioning that right—

The scramble horn blared, a series of short, insistent hoots. The pilots dropped the chatter, along with whatever else they were holding except for their credits, which they stuffed into pockets as they ran toward the exit. Vil set his mug down on the table and followed. There had been only one swallow of ale left; it would haven taken all of two seconds to finish it, but when the horn howled, you stopped whatever you were doing *right that instant* and hauled butt for your station. First, it was the right thing to do; everybody knew that. Second, you never knew when an Imperial holocam might be watching you, and if you got caught dragging your feet during a call to station, instead of being a crack TIE pilot, you might find yourself transferred to a few months of "droid duty" scrubbing out garbage bins and latrine holding tanks.

And third, Vil liked flying even more than he liked drinking.

"Gotta be a drill," somebody said. "Not likely another prison break after that last batch we cooked."

Vil didn't speak to that. Somewhat to his surprise, he'd had a couple of uncomfortable nights after that experience. Yes, they had been criminal scum, and it was his job to stop said scum, and they *had* been shooting at him, but even so it hadn't been a real contest. The *Lambda* hadn't had a chance. He'd blown that ship out of vac and watched the remnants of the crew whirl through the coldness, freezing in clouds of their own bodily fluids. One tended to think about it as shooting blips, like in the holo sims, not people, but seeing the carnage that had resulted from his weapons had . . . *Well, let's be honest here,* Vil told himself, *since it's all just between me.* The truth was . . . he'd had a few dreams.

No, not dreams. Dreams were innocuous fragments of this and that, things like not having studied for a test or flying without a craft or being naked in public. These hadn't been dreams.

These had been *nightmares.*

Thankfully, he'd forgotten the details almost immediately after waking up, save for one night. That had stayed with him. One of the flash-frozen corpses, drifting through the void about ten meters away from the cockpit of his fighter. Its head and body had been ravaged by shrapnel to such an extent that Vil couldn't tell if it had been male or female. He'd watched, fascinated, as the lacerated body rotated slowly, bringing its face into view. He'd noticed that, by some miracle of chance, the eyes had been untouched by the sleetstorm of metal . . .

And then the eyes opened.

Vil suppressed a shudder. That had been the worst. He told himself that it wasn't unusual, that it was part of the job. That he'd get used to it.

It helped. A little.

As Vil approached the hangar, he saw the assistant to the command officer on deck waving the pilots in.

"Move like you've got a purpose, people! A pregnant Pa'lowick could run faster! Let's *go*!"

"ADO," Vil said as he approached. "What's flyin'?"

"You and your squad, among nine others," the ADO said. He kept waving at the still-approaching pilots, down now to only a handful. "VIP escort for the *Imperial*-class Destroyer *Devastator.*"

Vil blinked. "We got a rainbow-jacket admiral? A Moff?"

"Not exactly. The guy running this ship is more of a monotone," said the ADO. Noting Vil's blank look, he added, "All black."

Vil got it then. "Darth Vader."

"Friend of yours?"

Vil laughed. They were side by side on the stairs, almost to the flight deck. Vil said, "Never met the man—or whatever he is. Saw him fly once. TIE school, out of Imperial City Naval Base. Against Barvel."

There was no need to specify that he was talking about Colonel Vindoo "The Shooter" Barvel, one of the most decorated TIE pilots ever. During the Clone Wars, Barvel had taken out more than thirty confirmed enemy craft in ship-to-ship combat, twice that many more probables, and nobody knew how many he hadn't even bothered to report. Vil knew he himself was a good pilot, a hot-hand even in training, but Barvel, who had been cycled out of combat by jittery brass to make sure the Empire had a live hero to parade around as a recruiter, was the best. Even though he was only a captain at the time, he'd been put in charge of the pilot school at ICNB. Barvel could power-dive the wings off any other craft and hit a target the size of a pleeky on the way down at top speed, port or starboard cannon, you pick which gun. In training missions he'd flown with the man, Vil had felt like a small child who could barely walk trying to keep up with a champion distance runner.

During maneuvers for the about-to-graduate pilots, Darth Vader had shown up. He didn't have any military rank per se, but he was the Emperor's wrist-hawk and everybody knew it. If it came from Vader's augmented voxbox, it might as well have come from Palpatine's lips, and you argued with it at your peril, no matter how high your rank.

Vader had watched for a time, then asked for a TIE fighter. He had climbed in, taken off, and joined the mock battle. Within seconds, his electronic guns had painted half a dozen ships, and it had come down to Vader versus Barvel. Vil, whose ship had been hit in a three-on-one early in the pretend fight, had been in a holding pattern waiting for the engagement to finish, and he'd watched it all.

Vader hadn't exactly flown circles around Barvel, but every time The Shooter jigged or jinked, Vader was half a second ahead of him. Barvel was doing things Vil didn't think were possible in a TIE, and Vader not only matched him, move for move, he just plain outflew him. It was—no other word for it—astounding. Vil quickly realized that Vader could have taken the flight school commander out at any time—he was only playing with him.

That had been as spooky in its own way as Vil's nightmare. He'd never seen a human pilot move like that. Damned few alien ones either, for that matter.

After a few passes, and with what had seemed a slow, offhand, lazy series of rolls and loops, Vader came around, nailed Barvel with his training beams, and it was "Game over." All the pilots hanging there in space had to reach up and shut their mouths manually.

The ADO looked down the hallway, but no more pilots were inbound. He turned and pointed. "Better get to your ship, Dance." A short pause, then: "Vader's good, huh?"

"Better than good. If it was him against me, I'd just overload my engine and blow myself up—that way I'd get to pick my own moment to die."

What Vil hadn't mentioned, mostly because he still didn't believe it himself, was that the mechanic who'd serviced Vader's borrowed TIE fighter afterward had come out of the bay shaking his head. The nav and targeting comps had been turned off, he'd said. Cockpit recorder showed that Vader had done that *before* he'd left the dock. So if the mechanic was to be believed, not only had Vader beaten the best pilot in the navy as easily as if Barvel had been a crop duster on some backrocket world, he had done so on *manual.*

Which was simply *impossible.*

"Go," the ADO said. "Hit vac—you don't want to be late to the party."

"No, sir." *Not that Vader needs the escort,* Vil thought. *Nobody here could get in his way.*

Vil hurried onto the deck, his mechanic waving him to his TIE. "Been takin' a nap, rocketjock? Get in!"

As Vil clamped down his helmet and checked his readings, he had a moment to ponder the purpose of the escort. *Darth Vader, commanding a big Destroyer. Wonder what he's doing here?*

Had to be something big. You could have a headful of hard vac and still suss that out.

The air lock doors opened. Vil lit his engines and was gone.

14

RECEIVING DECK SEVEN, *HAVELON*

Tarkin frowned as he waited on the receiving deck for Vader to arrive. It was certainly true that the Emperor could send whomever he liked, whenever he liked, to check on the station's progress. Tarkin had no reason to be anything but grateful to the Emperor—how many Grand Moffs were there, after all? Who had elevated him to that puissant position and given him command of the most important military project in galactic history?

All that was true. And he *was* grateful—to Palpatine. But one feels differently toward the one holding the leash than toward the one on the leash.

There was something about Vader that set his teeth on edge. It wasn't just the prosthetic suit with its mask and breather, nor the fact that he couldn't see the eyes behind those polarized lenses. Vader had power, both personal and as the Emperor's tool, and Tarkin's sense of him was that he cared about as much for a human life standing next to him as he did about a mistfly in the far-off swamps of Neimoidia. Standing next to Vader was like standing next to a giant thermal grenade—it might just go off at any moment.

And the man in black had a temper, no doubt about that. Thus far, he had not unleashed it in Tarkin's direction, but Tarkin had seen it loosed on others, and those who thought to give Vader grief quickly realized that it was a fatal mistake. No matter how much people decried the Force as being a superstition that hadn't saved the Jedi from annihilation, it was real enough to enable Vader to stop a man's heart or keep the breath from his lungs simply by willing it. Not to mention knocking blaster bolts from the air with that lightsaber of his. True, nothing would be able to withstand the force of this battle station's armament, once it was operational. But it wouldn't be fully operational for another few months, and anybody who was both strong enough and foolish enough to slay Vader would have to deal with the Emperor's wrath—and *he* made Vader seem like an Iridonian hugglepup.

The shuttle hatch opened. With most military VIPs, there would be an honor guard of elite stormtroopers or even Imperial Red Guards emerging first. Not so with Vader. He strode through the hatch and down the ramp alone, his cape billowing behind him in the wind of his own passage, fearless, not the least bit worried about any possible danger. He was arrogant, but then he had reason to be.

Tarkin waited, his admirals shifting nervously behind him. Some of them couldn't stand the very idea of a man like Vader, who existed outside the chain of command and was able to come and go as he pleased, not truly subject to military orders. Well, it was what it was, and there was no help for it.

Vader approached to stand before Tarkin. He always seemed larger and taller than Tarkin remembered, a dark presence, a force, as it were, of nature. "Grand Moff Tarkin," he said, offering not even the slightest nod of a military bow. Vader bent the knee to no one, save the Emperor, Tarkin knew.

"Lord Vader." There was no point in offering small talk or pleasantries; Vader had no use for them. "Shall we begin the tour?" Tarkin asked, extending one hand in a gesture that encompassed the entirety of the station.

"Proceed."

"This way. We'll take my lighter."

Vader could sense the hostility of some of the men behind Tarkin, but that was of no importance. Hostile words or actions he could and would deal with, but thoughts of the weak-minded were no threat. Tarkin, oily and smooth as always, was a man who knew where his best interests lay, and as long as his own plans matched those of the Emperor, he was a useful tool. Which was good, because Vader would not hesitate to use that tool.

The Rebels were turning out to be more troublesome than many had expected. The Emperor had known it would be thus, of course; the resistance had not been a surprise to him. The Emperor was completely in concert with the dark side of the Force. He was the most powerful Sith who had ever existed.

As would Vader be, someday.

But that was in the future. Now he had more mundane duties. There were problems with the construction of this station. When Vader left, those problems would be corrected. He would return as necessary to correct more troubles as they appeared, and he would also return at times when things were proceeding smoothly, just to remind Tarkin and his senior officers that the Emperor's eye was always watching them.

Always.

15

LOWER LEVEL TROOP BARRACKS, SECTOR N-ONE, DEATH STAR

The N-One sector, a huge area equal to one twenty-fourth of a hemisphere, had been partly pressurized and heated, so at least Teela didn't have to wear a vac suit to work anymore. Thank the stars for that; she was sick to death of ending each day fatigued by the effort of manipulating the stiff joints and servos, the limited vision, and the inability to scratch—to name only a few problems. She'd worn vac suits before on jobs, and those experiences hadn't been pleasant, but this was by far the worst, because the Empire, no doubt in a cost-saving effort, had mandated the use of outmoded constant-volume suits instead of the newer, elastic one-piece designs.

The suits had been necessary for a time, however. On a project this size there was no way to complete the entire hull, pressurize it all, and then start building the interior—the amount of air necessary would be tremendous. Once the vessel was functional, then the multitude of converters installed in every sector could easily handle the task, but until those were online, air would have to be sucked from a planetary atmosphere and hauled up out of the gravity well by cargo ship—either that, or build a huge conversion plant in space and truck water to that, which would be even harder. A tanker full of water was more unwieldy than one full of air bottles, and without proper heat it just turned into blocks of ice when you unloaded it, which in turn resulted in problems with increased volume. The sheer magnitude of the project wouldn't allow a full exterior hull construction first.

Thus it had been reasoned early on that, while the hull was being laid, individual sectors would be built and sealed. This allowed plenty of storage space, at least at first, for supplies, as well as habitats for workers to stay close to the task. Hundreds of thousands of laborers needed someplace convenient to live—shuttling them back and forth for any distance after every shift was neither cost- nor time-effective.

The hull-plate extruders were only a few hundred kilometers away, hung at a fixed orbital point where the gravitational forces of the prison planet and the raw-material asteroids being towed to the gigantic masticators all balanced. The process was simple enough. An asteroid sufficiently high in nickel-iron content was hauled from the outlying belt to the masticators and fed into a maw; the whirling durasteel teeth chewed the asteroid to tiny bits and mixed them with alloy ores mined and brought up from Despayre, including quadanium. The resulting gravel had water added and was put under high pressure to form a slurry, then fed into pipelines that led to the smelters. These were essentially huge melting pots that refined the mix, burning off impurities. The resulting scarified ore was conveyed to extruders that pressed out the hull plate, rather like food paste from a squeezed tube. There was still a lot of slag left over, but this was just gathered together, pointed at the local star, and given a hard push. Months later, these slag-rafts would fall into the sun and be burned up.

Teela had been on projects before that used deep-space masticators and extruders, of course, such as skyhooks and wheelworlds. She'd never seen as large or as many as there were here, however. The amount of plate being produced was beyond any amount ever used in one place before.

Sector N-One was shaped like a large crescent slice of juicemelon, cut in half midway. It was thirty-one kilometers wide at the base, which would be the equator when the station was finished, narrowing almost to a point only a few dozen meters wide at the other end, and just over ninety-four klicks long. Most of the sectors would be identical in this hemisphere, save for a select few and including, of course, those through which the superlaser would be constructed.

It was hard to visualize the scope of the whole orb. *Big* didn't begin to do it justice. The habitable crust alone was two kilometers thick, and included in it the surface city sprawls, armory, hangar bays, command center, technical areas, and living quarters. Below that would be the hyperdrive, reactor core, and secondary power sources—none of which, fortunately, concerned her.

What concerned her at the moment was an old and somewhat cranky Wookiee who was giving her a hard time.

Teela's command of the Wookiee language was rudimentary. The problem with speaking Shyriiwook wasn't so much the vocabulary as the pronunciation; a human's vocal apparatus just couldn't handle the grunts, groans, and howls necessary to be understood. Like most people who'd ever been around serious construction projects, Teela was used to dealing with the tall and furry bipeds—they seemed to gravitate to such sites, even when they weren't being enslaved and forced to labor on them. Fortunately, on the big projects most Wookiees understood Basic, even if they couldn't wrap their tongues around it any more than humans could deal with Wookiee-speak. Given all that, Teela usually managed to communicate well enough with them.

Usually.

The chief on this shift in this subsector was a grizzled old Wook named Hahrynyar, who probably would have joined up voluntarily if he hadn't been grabbed and enslaved. His coat was gray from muzzle to ankle, he was stubborn and intractable, and he had the annoying habit of forgetting how to understand Basic whenever Teela made an indisputable point. Which was what was happening now.

"Haaarrn," the Wookiee said. *"Aarn whynn roowarrn."*

"I understand that it's on the plans. What I'm saying is I don't want you to build it. It doesn't make any sense to put a heat exhaust port there. The main exhaust port is already done, and if there is a need for additional ones—which I don't believe there is, at all—there are better places to put them than right next to the main one. We don't need it in this sector, and certainly not *there.*" She pointed at the holo schematic of the polar trench.

"Harnkk whoom?"

"On *my* authority, that's whose."

"Arrk-arn ksh sawrron."

Teela chuckled. She'd understood that well enough. "Yes, yes, I'll put it in writing."

These old metal benders and rivet pounders always thought they knew better than the architect when it came down to the actual construction. Sometimes they did, which was fine. But no matter what, they'd stick to the approved plan like a preprogrammed droid with permabond on its wheels to make sure they didn't get scalded by the sector work boss.

She couldn't blame the Wook for wanting it in writing. Early in her career Teela had taken verbal orders from a designer. No big deal, just some interior frame spec on a resiplex he thought was silly, so he'd told her to use a different grade of durasteel and, when she'd seemed uncertain, had assured her it was plenty strong enough to handle the job and a lot cheaper, so what was the problem? She'd shrugged and done what he'd asked. When the inspectors came around and refused to approve the building, the designer had been very quick to point out that his assistant must have made that decision all on her own, because the plans—and he—had *specifically* called for 9095-T8511 grade on that scaffold frame, and if his assistant had used 9093-T7511? Well, it didn't matter that the alloy and heat-treat could easily take the load if the plans called for the higher grade, now, did it?

He had hung her out to twist in the breeze. Later, when Teela had stormed into the designer's office to give him a piece of her mind, he had laughed at her. She needed to learn how to play in the real galaxy, he'd told her. If you got caught, you passed the blame along. What she should have done, he'd said, was laid it onto the obviously blind and stupid construction crew chief who had selected the wrong alloy. He could read a plan, couldn't he?

Teela couldn't prove anything and she wasn't stupid. After that, she made certain to get any deviations from the plans appended to the work order in writing. So she knew exactly what the old Wookiee was thinking.

"Don't worry about it now," she said. "You have to get the heat exchangers into the barracks before you'd start on piddly stuff like ports, anyhow."

"Arrrrnn rowwlnnn." Well, yes, Hahrynyar allowed, that was the way a smart builder would do things.

"Go, then. Somebody has mislaid my shipment of triaxial fiber-optic cable and I've got to run it down. Get the exchangers unpacked and a crew started installing them, and we'll get back to the philosophy of exhaust ports later, okay?"

The old Wookiee nodded and headed off. Teela watched him lumber away for a second, then turned her attention to the next problem. Never a dull moment, the day was never long enough, and they sure didn't pay her enough . . .

She had to smile at that. The pay might not be much, but it was better than living in a pesthole down on a planet full of murdering scum. Even cantankerous old Hahrynyar couldn't argue with that.

GUNNERY COMMAND, ISD *STEEL TALON*

Tenn Graneet stuck his head into the CO's office. "You wanted to see me, Cap?"

His commanding officer looked up from his flimsiwork. "Come in, Tenn."

Tenn ducked slightly to pass through the hatch. Captain Hoberd's office looked, as usual, like the local A-grav had somehow suffered a massive flux in just this room; datachips were piled haphazardly on the floor, the two holopics on opposite walls—one was an image of Hoberd's graduating class, the other of his wife, Linesee, and their two kids; Tenn could never remember their names. The holos hung constantly askew, and Hoberd's Silver Valor medal was dangling from the upper hinge of a wall cabinet. Every time Tenn entered the CO's office, the medal was dangling from a different location—on one or the other of the family pics, from the small alumabronze sculpture on his desk, even swinging slightly in the breeze directly beneath the air vent . . . he couldn't recall ever seeing it in the same place twice. Droot and some of the others reported the same experience. No one ever saw him move it, and no one knew why he did. It was just a quirk of the captain's. Those unfamiliar with his war record might think he had a disrespectful attitude, but nothing could be further from the truth—at least, not in Tenn's opinion.

"What's up?" He couldn't read anything from the man's face, which wasn't unusual; Hoberd, it was said, could outstare a Weequay. Normally this didn't bother Tenn, but today, for some reason, he began to feel a little uneasy. The energy in the room was subtly different. He didn't go in for woo-woo concepts like that, but sometimes he couldn't deny it.

"Sit down, Tenn." Hoberd's expression didn't change. Tenn looked at the chairs, both of which were filled with various objects, and perched on the edge of the less cluttered one. "I've got some bad news, I'm afraid."

Uh-oh, Tenn thought. Had to have been that last inspection; he couldn't think of any other possibility. What had gone wrong? An improper calibration? Not up to spit-'n'-polish standards? What was it?

The CO let him sweat for a moment, then grinned. "Bad news for me, anyway—I'm losing my best noncom."

"Sir?"

"Pack your bags, Chief. You're for the Death Star. They're giving you the big gun."

At first the words didn't make sense to Tenn. Then the meaning broke through, like a sun through clouds, and he grinned.

"No poodoo, Cap?"

Hoberd held up a small datachip. "Orders just came down." He tossed the chip, and Tenn caught it in midair. He was aware that he was grinning like a kid. "Thanks, Cap!"

Hoberd frowned slightly. "You sure you want to do this?"

"You're kidding, right?"

The CO shook his head regretfully. "How am I going to replace you?"

Tenn blinked. "What, you aren't coming?"

"Not me. My tour is over soon, and I'm mustering out. One of my in-laws runs a good-sized industrial operation—I have a job waiting."

"Oh, *that* sounds exciting. Making widgets? Moving sewage? C'mon, Cap. You and me, pulling trigger on the biggest—"

"Job pays three times as well and the only thing dangerous about it might be having the wife find out where I'm hiding the girlfriend."

They both laughed. Then Hoberd continued, "No guns're operational yet. There are only a few sectors even pressurized, but you're the best shooter in the fleet and they're lucky to have you. They want you over there as soon as possible to begin orientation."

Tenn felt like his head would split in half if his grin got any bigger. The CO was right: who better to pull the firing lever on the superlaser? This was the biggest, most powerful weapon ever built. *Ever.* This was as good as it got. He could bask in the warm glow of that for quite a while.

"Well, what're you waiting for? Go on! Next time I see you your ugly mug had better be hidden behind one of those snazzy black visors they wear over there."

CPO Tenn Graneet walked out of Captain Hoberd's office feeling as though something had gone wrong with the corridor's gravity, because he was definitely walking on air. Just wait until Droot and Velvalee heard the news. The best shot in the galaxy paired with the biggest gun . . . Tenn slapped his hands together, rubbing them with enthusiasm. He couldn't wait to get his hands on those controls.

16

THE SOFT HEART CANTINA, SOUTHERN UNDERGROUND, GRID 19, IMPERIAL CITY

Memah stood on the walk in front of what had been her cantina, stunned beyond words. The Soft Heart was no more than ashes and cinders, still warm, soot and smoke twirling up toward the exhaust fans in a dirty breeze.

And it wasn't just her place. The whole block had burned. The fire-suppression sprayers had unaccountably malfunctioned, according to the unofficial reports, at least, and the droid fire crews had been sent to the wrong location, so that by the time they arrived and began their efforts to control the blaze, it had been too late by far. They were lucky to have kept it from spreading to the whole sector, they said.

Memah still couldn't get her mind around it. This wasn't just a building reduced to ashes. This was her *life*.

Rodo came to stand next to her, his face grim. "Varlo Brim was discovered dead in his cube this morning."

She frowned. "Who?"

"An arsonist, a professional. I know someone who works for the medical examiner. 'Heart failure' was entered on Varlo's certificate—*before* his body ever arrived at the morgue. Word from above was that there was to be no detailed examination of the corpse."

She turned away from what had been her reason to get up every day and blinked at him. The ash-laden air made her eyes watery. It seemed important that she understand what Rodo was trying to tell her, but, though he was speaking in Basic, the words didn't seem to make sense. "Which means . . . what?"

"Think about it. A block of the underground goes up in flames. The suppressors, which passed inspection less than two months ago, suddenly don't work. The fire crews get here late, and the next morning a man who sets fires for a living is found dead of 'natural causes' in his cube. Plus all those deliveries that didn't get made? It doesn't take a construction engineer to put it together."

Memah stared at him. "Kark," she said.

"Yeah. Somebody is collecting a fat insurance voucher. What d'you want to bet that construction's gonna crank up on a new row of shiny new businesses that are gonna be owned by some uplevel bosses who just happen to be bureaucrats responsible for the firefighters and automatic suppressors?"

"And we can't do anything about it," she said.

"Not if the fix was in. You had it covered?" He nodded at the ashes. "Insured?"

"No. I never saw the need, what with the suppressors and all."

Rodo nodded. She was grateful for the lack of rebuke in his face and voice. "What are you gonna do?"

Memah shook her head. "No idea."

There were others wandering through the ruins, humans and aliens, looking at what had been their shops, the repositories of their hopes and dreams. And gawkers, fire-control droids still checking hot spots, local police . . . the strangely silent crowd, moving in and out of the smoky mist like revenants, made it all seem quite surreal.

A man in black coveralls approached them. His gaze took in the pile of smoldering cinders, and he shook his head. "Sorry for your loss, Memah Roothes."

Again, she understood the words, but they meant nothing. "Do I know you?"

"No. I'm Neet Alamant, a recruiter for Civilian Adjunct to the Imperial Navy."

"Yeah—so?"

"I have an offer you might find interesting."

Memah gave a bark of bitter laughter. "Unless you're looking for plant fertilizer"—she gestured at the ruins—"I don't have a lot for sale right about now."

"I understand. Perhaps we might speak of this later? Here is my contact information. Please comm me when you have a free moment."

He handed her an info button, flashed a patently false smile, and walked across the street toward several people standing in front of what had been a bakery.

Memah stared at the button on her palm. A free moment? Sure, no problem. She'd have plenty of those upcoming. She'd be sitting in her room on the dole with nothing to do, remembering the good old days when she ran a pub.

She looked at Rodo. He shrugged.

Memah looked back at the ruin of her cantina. What was she going to do now?

MEDCENTER, SECTOR N-ONE, DEATH STAR

Uli passed his hands under the UV sterilizer, then wiped them on a clean towel. The orderly droid floated the patient out and toward post-op. They were caught up, no more patients scheduled for surgery or follow-ups until rounds that evening. A break at long last.

"You should come see this, Doc," Zam Stenza, one of the orderlies, said.

Curious, Uli followed the orderly through the staging area and down a half-finished passage that was more catwalk than corridor. His boots thumped upon the cheap expanded metal grate that was the temporary floor of the corridor, and the sound echoed hollowly along the hallway. This section was supposed to be finished, but it looked only half done; less, in places. There was enough air, but there were construction droids crawling like metal spiders on the inside of the hull, welding studs and connectors and adding insulation. Uli saw unsealed gaps in the interior walls. *Sure hope they don't pop a seam somewhere,* he thought nervously. He was fairly certain that carrying on shirtsleeve activity in such a precarious environment was contravening several safety regs, and he was equally sure that it would do no good whatsoever to point this out.

Stenza stopped to look through the window at a lower walkway. Uli moved closer to see what was so interesting.

A group of pedestrians was moving along the wide passage. It consisted of guards, high-ranked officers, and one man in black who towered over them all.

"Who's that?" Uli asked, feeling like he should know.

"Darth Vader," Zam said. "He's here on an inspection tour."

Uli stared at the tall, black-cloaked figure. He knew about Vader, of course. He'd seen vids of the man—if that was what he really still was under the suit, which looked like it contained some kind of cyclic respiratory system, and probably bionic prosthetics as well, judging by his gait. The stiffness was subtle, but there if you knew where to look.

"Inspection tour?"

"Yes," said C-4ME-O, who had come up behind them. "This project is of prime concern to the Emperor."

"And just how do you know this, Fourmio? Tight with the Emperor, are you?"

"No, but I was put into service on Coruscant before it became Imperial Center. I've never had a mindwipe, so I have my memories of that time. Droids do sometimes talk to one another, you know. Word gets around."

Uli nodded. Yes, that was true enough. There was a lot of truth in the old saw that said, *If you want to know what goes on, ask the droids.* They see, they hear, and they don't forget. He had known some droids who were every bit as clever and talkative as any natural-borns or clones he'd been around. There'd been that protocol droid back at Rimsoo Seven on Drongar—what had it been called?—who'd been self-aware enough to play sabacc and gloat over the winnings. It had had a sarcastic circuit a klick wide.

Uli watched the procession pass. "Walked right past us, didn't they?"

"The word is that Lord Vader is not fond of medics," C-4ME-O said. "Apparently he has had some unpleasant experiences in that area."

Uli nodded. He could see why. The only reason he could imagine that someone would be stuffed into a lung-suit with a respirator breathing for him would be because his own breathing passages had been terribly damaged and, for some reason, new lobes and trachea could not be cloned and implanted. That would be a strange malady in this day and age, but not impossible. Some kind of autoimmune problem, perhaps.

There were those rare people, one in a billion, who would reject their own matched genetic tissue implants—even skin grafts. Had to be something like that, Uli mused—nobody would voluntarily walk around looking like Vader otherwise.

"Supposedly he can kill a man just by looking at him," Stenza said. He dropped his voice to a whisper. "I heard a rumor that he was once a Jedi."

Uli nodded. The mysterious Force was fairly amazing when manifested by an expert in its use. Uli had seen it demonstrated by a woman who had been part of the team on Drongar. She had been a Mirialan, a Jedi healer named Barriss Offee. Only a Padawan when he'd met her; later she had become a Jedi Knight. He'd learned a lot from conversations with her, both about the ways of the Jedi and, in broader terms, about life. She'd been strong in the Force, he'd been told. Not that it had been enough to save her. Barriss had died on Felucia, so he had heard, when the clones had turned on their Jedi masters.

The news had hit him far worse than he'd expected. He'd told himself many times, in the nearly two decades since his first posting on that fetid swamp world, that what he'd felt for Barriss had been nothing more than youthful infatuation. It might be true, but he could still see her face in his mind, hear her voice, feel the power that had lived inside her. Even after all these years.

Maybe he hadn't loved her. Maybe he'd been too young to know what love was, back then. But when he had heard of her death . . .

So many people he had cared deeply for were dead because of that karking war. Probably some of the Jedi had escaped death, but the official posture was that they had all been enemies of the people and executed accordingly. And all research into the psionic abilities of the former peacekeepers of the galaxy had been summarily halted. To venture into that area was worth the death penalty these days. Lot of that going around, too. Step wrong and it was prison if you were lucky, and death if you trod too hard on the wrong toes. Given all this, it was amazing that Vader would tolerate even the rumor of him being a Jedi.

He sighed. Well, it wasn't his business. He was a surgeon. Genetics, esoteric mind-over-matter control, connections with the infinite . . . those weren't his concerns. He just went where he was told, cut where he was ordered to cut, and hoped that his forced servitude would end someday, preferably with him still in one piece. Initially he'd thought that the only good thing about being assigned to a battle station the size and power of this one was not having to worry about being blown up. That was before the first influx of wounded workers from the bombed section had come under his knife. Nothing was safe, not even this monstrous Death Star.

Uli turned away. There should be time to grab a bite at the commissary, and a few hours' sleep, before his next shift. Unless there was more sabotage, of course.

He wished he could remember the name of that droid back on Drongar. He knew it was going to bug him all day.

17

CONSTRUCTION SITE BETA-NINE, DEATH STAR

The man dressed in black with the respirator helmet felt to Teela like something out of a long-forgotten nightmare. She could almost sense evil radiating from him in pulsing waves; just being near him made her queasy, set her stomach roiling.

And for all that, she was not even his focus, merely one of the retinue of architects and builders standing in the background as Grand Moff Tarkin arrived with the tour to show off this part of the station. She had not spoken to Vader, nor he to her, but still she felt the way she imagined an insect under a magnifying lens might feel if it looked up and saw a giant eye staring down at it. Vader had his back to her, and yet she could *feel* his attention as a kind of dark pressure, as if a cold hand had been laid on her shoulder.

It made her want to walk away. No, it made her want to *run* away, to get as far from here as she could, as quickly as she could. She'd never felt such a heavy sense of foreboding. The opposite side of the battle station wouldn't be far enough to run. But to attempt such a thing would be a bad career move for anybody, and more so for a criminal paroled as a trustee.

Tarkin was droning on about something to do with firepower, pointing at turbolaser emplacements, and Vader seemed to be listening. But Teela *knew,* somehow, that his focus was not on the Moff's speech. He was probing the minds of those around them, examining them, and finding them . . . lacking something.

Abruptly she became aware that his full attention had arrived at her. Of a moment, she felt as if she had been stripped naked, both her mind and body, and that Vader, like the imagined scientist examining the insect pinned under his lens, beheld her in all her being—the good, the bad, the flaws, the strengths . . . everything that made her who she was.

Instinctively, she threw up a mental wall, a shield to prevent the intrusion, as though slamming a blast door shut. She did it by envisioning just that: a heavy durasteel portal closing, the shaft locks sliding into their collars, the perimeter flange sealing. She'd always had a vivid imagination—a big reason why she was successful in her chosen field—and she could see, in her mind's eye, every seam and seal, every weld and rivet on the hatch, could hear the solid, echoing *boom!* it made as it shut, could even feel the vibration. Just before it closed, she thought she felt a small hint of something from Vader's thoughts: surprise.

And . . . curiosity.

But—that was *impossible.* How could she feel someone else's thoughts?

It had to have been her imagination, Teela thought. But a moment later the tall figure turned and looked directly at her. The lenses in the black helmet hid his eyes, but there was no doubt—he had marked her.

It wasn't just her imagination.

Teela held her gaze as steady as she could, and kept her mental wall in place.

A moment passed. It seemed like a long time, but it couldn't have been more than a few heartbeats. Vader seemed to nod slightly, then turned back to look at whatever it was that Tarkin was prattling on about.

The removal of his attention was like a glass shell shattering about her. Teela nearly collapsed. She gasped, loud enough to cause several of her colleagues to glance at her. She felt shaken to her core.

What had just happened?

SLASHTOWN PRISON COLONY, DESPAYRE

Ratua considered his options, or at least what he thought they might be, and found them less satisfactory every time he recounted them. Only one held any appeal at all, and that one not so much.

As he saw things, he could either spend the rest of his life on this tropical pesthole of a world, until one day somebody or something killed him . . .

Or he could leave.

That is, he could try. The stats were as simple as they were depressing: nobody lived to a ripe old age on the prison planet and shuffled off peacefully in their sleep. Nobody. Either some horrible local disease took them, or somebody wanted their boots, or something with fangs and poison-tipped claws looking for a meal got too close, and that was just how it was. Despayre was a hard place, and sooner or later you were grub food, even if you were as fast as Ratua was.

He was in his shack, alone and brooding. The pitiful interior was illuminated by a glow stick, which gave barely enough light to show the backless chair, the large cable spool that served as his table, with his cracked plate and two mismatched and chipped mugs, and the crab spider as big as his hand nestled in one of the upper corners near the roof. Night had fallen, and the predators that liked the dark were out hunting. Some were prisoners, some animals, and none of them was apt to wish you well. And yet for the path Ratua needed to be upon, he would have to venture out in the night. Moreover, he was going to have to do it real soon, because the only chance he had of getting off this rock was the tiniest of loopholes that could close at any moment. The effort would cost him everything he owned—which wasn't much, and that was part of the problem—and if he failed, yet still somehow survived, he would be starting over again from point zero, with nothing save the clothes he was wearing.

Ratua sighed, staring at the makeshift wall of his hut. Was the life here worse than the risk of trying to leave it? Nothing ventured, nothing gained, but also nothing lost . . .

A tap on the door interrupted his meditation. He grabbed his capacitor, walked two steps to the entrance, and peered out through the peephole. The capacitor, salvaged from a broken gel-cam's battery pack, wasn't much of a weapon. It required contact with an attacker, which was closer than Ratua wanted to be against somebody with a knife, say, but it was better than nothing. The device, once triggered, built up an electrical charge within a couple of seconds. The amperage was low, but there was still enough voltage to knock a full-sized human onto his backside—assuming you could touch bare skin with the contact points. His quickness made it a somewhat better weapon than it might be in the hands of someone with normal reactions, but it was good for only a single zap before it had to be recharged, which would be far too slow in a fight if you couldn't stall the attack long enough to let the juice build back up.

As good a scrounger as he was, he had never been able to score a blaster. Not that he'd tried all that much. Carrying a firearm wasn't the best way to keep under the radar. Still, there were times, like now, when he regretted not having scrounged harder.

He glanced through the tiny fish-eye lens in the door, salvaged from the same cam as the capacitor, and relaxed. It was Brun, the cargo crew boss on the night shift. The one he'd been expecting.

Ratua opened the door, checked to make sure nobody was behind Brun, and quickly shut and barred the door behind the man.

Brun was human, kind of; he looked like nothing so much as a normal-sized male who'd been sat upon by something large and heavy. His trunk was shaped like a canister, and his head was almost wider than it was tall. He was from some planet that Ratua had never heard of before they'd met. Brun had been on the prison world for years, and had worked his way up to a position of some trust in that he was allowed inside the compound to help in the loading and unloading of cargo supplies for the dirtside guard posts.

The only way off the world was by ship, and the guard supply craft were the most likely conveyances. There had been organized breaks in which whole ships had been commandeered, but that was, in Ratua's considered opinion, stupid past the point of suicidal. The Empire had all kinds of firepower up there, and they weren't shy about using it if they knew a transport had gone rogue. That had happened six months or so ago, and there hadn't been any survivors of that attempted escape.

If you couldn't sneak past, you weren't going to get very far. And in a stand-up with Imperial warships, you were going to lose.

Brun was not a man for pleasantries. "Krovvy me th' bitska, floob. M'hitch revs inna cyke."

Whatever world Brun was from was either too far out on the Rim for a decent education program, or its indigent population really didn't care about being understood all that much. After months of conversation, Ratua had picked up enough of Brun's patois to understand the gist of his statement, which was something along the lines of *Tell me your idea, friend. My shift starts in an hour.* The term *floob* was considerably less benign than "friend," but Ratua was willing to overlook that. He pointed at one of the two chairs. As Brun sat, the wood creaking under his weight, Ratua went to his stashbox and came out with a bottle of wine. It wasn't a great wine, but it was from offworld and not a local vintage, so it was better by far than what was available to most prisoners. Ratua had been saving it for a special occasion, and this was about as special as it was going to get.

He unsealed the cap and poured some in the two mugs, handing one to his guest.

"Starry," Brun said, tasting it. *Not bad.*

"Keep the bottle."

Brun nodded. "'Shuwan?" *What do you want?*

Ratua took a deep breath, composing himself as best he could. *Nothing ventured, nothing . . .* "I want you to get me onto the supply ship before it leaves in the morning."

A long heartbeat of silence; then Brun laughed, shook his bread-loaf-shaped head, had another sip of the wine, and replied, to Ratua's surprise, in perfectly understandable Basic, "I can do that, but what's the point? It's not going anywhere except back to the freighter parked up in geosync. Any ship leaving the system'll be scanned down to the rivets, and you've probably heard that none has been leaving lately. You can't *go* anywhere, Ratua. Life in a warehouse won't be any better than here. You do know that every now and then, they open the doors to vac and let it get real cold in the noncritical storage units? Just to get rid of, uh, vermin?"

Ratua shrugged. "Yeah, I know." He wasn't going to stay in the stores area, but he saw no point in telling Brun his plans. The less the squat humanoid knew, the better. "Let me worry about that. Do we have a—"

Brun waved the cup. "Hold up, hold up. Haven't said I'd do it. If they catch you alive and you give me up, I'm back in the pack, with no perks. Why would I risk that?"

Ratua had expected him to make just that point. He went back to his stashbox and dug out a small electronic device, which he showed to Brun. "Know what this is?"

Brun was in for a raft of crimes, one of which was piracy, specializing in stripping and then reselling the electronics from captured ships. He nodded. "Looks like an embedder."

"Exactly right. Onetime spy-killer. Check it out." He handed it to Brun to examine.

"Where'd you get this?"

"You know me; here, there, I get around."

Brun nodded again. That was Ratua's talent, everybody knew that. He could scrounge just about anything. Brun touched some controls on the hand-sized device and nodded at the readout. "Charge is up. Looks good. How much you want for it?"

"Not for sale. It's your guarantee," Ratua said. "I'll let you embed me and set the implant to your name."

Brun looked thoughtful. With a spy-killer installed, Brun didn't need to worry much about Ratua ratting him out if he was caught. The embed unit, about the size of a baby's fingernail, would sit harmlessly in Ratua's skull for the rest of his life. But it would be tuned to a certain word, and if that word was spoken by Ratua, and only Ratua, the device would explode. Not much of an explosion—just enough to fry his brain up nice and crispy.

"So what do I get out of it?"

Ratua waved at the interior of the shack. "I've got some prime stuff here—food, drink, electronics, death sticks. And I'll give you a list of my dealers. I'm gone, they'll talk to you; there's nobody else. It's worth a lot."

"All that'll happen is you'll freeze to death up there."

"That's my worry. Do we have a deal?"

Brun sat there, his short, thick legs barely reaching the floor, wine cup in one hand and embedder in the other. Ratua knew he was weighing the risks. There were some, yes—but if Ratua was dead, he wouldn't be pointing fingers. Greed fought with worry, and Ratua watched the battle play out on Brun's face.

Greed won.

"All right. South Gate, midnight, and keep out of sight until you see me. You see anybody else with me, stay away."

Ratua let out the breath he'd been holding. "Done."

"Don't pack a big bag," Brun added. "Now turn around."

Ratua took the last drink of his wine and did as he was told. Brun put the embedder's muzzle against the back of Ratua's head; he could feel the cold pressure, and then a moment of mild pain as Brun injected the unit into his skull.

"So," Brun said, pocketing the embedder, "how do you know I won't just kill you anyway?"

"Because you're not a killer," Ratua replied. "One reasonably civilized being can usually recognize another."

Brun grunted. "Lem' scan th' fiddymon," he said. *Let me see the goods.* He didn't reply to Ratua's evaluation of him, but Ratua knew it was the truth. He didn't have to worry about the device going off and painting whatever room he was in with his brains. Even if Brun was a killer, it still wasn't a worry, because the device wasn't properly armed. That little bit of reprogramming, and the part needed so that the embedder showed that the chip was armed when it wasn't, had cost him a small fortune in trade goods, and would have been cheap at twice the price. He could jump up and down and yell "Brun!" until his lips fell off and nothing would happen—at least not as far as that bogus implant was concerned. No way was he going to walk around the rest of his life with a bomb in his head, waiting for a slip of the tongue. Brun wasn't a killer, true enough. He also wasn't the brightest star in the cluster, not by several orders of magnitude.

If they captured Ratua, he'd give Brun up in a Jawa's heartbeat. As much as the little humanoid was going to make on this deal, he could stand a little risk for it.

As long as he didn't know about it.

18

J BLOCK BARRACKS, GUARD POST 19, GRID 4349, SECTOR 547,
QUADRANT 3, DESPAYRE

Sergeant Nova Stihl had slept badly. A dream had troubled him; he could not recall the full substance of it, only that he had been in danger, his weapons empty and his fighting art useless. That was all it took to qualify as a nightmare for a soldier.

Likely it was the heat. Even this late, near midnight, the air outside was near body temperature, and the barracks' air exchangers were malfunctioning yet again. There was something wrong with the transformer, apparently; the techs had not been able to keep the coils harmonized properly. When they fluctuated, the coolers couldn't keep up, and it quickly grew hot inside the windowless rooms. Probably hotter in here now than outside.

For a moment, he considered his holos—he was halfway through a discourse on eclectic deontology by Gar Gratius—but he knew that wouldn't put him back to sleep. He arose and pulled on a pair of shorts. Maybe there was a breeze outside; at the least, even though it was warm, the air probably wouldn't be so stuffy in the yard.

He left the barracks building and walked into the yard, which had a grassy, genetically engineered short lawn that felt cool under his bare feet. The charged fence surrounding the compound gave off a pale glow, punctuated now and then by a spark as Despayre's equivalent of an unlucky insect blundered into the field.

The night was cloudy, the overcast sky keeping it dark where there was no artificial light and also acting like a blanket to keep the day's heat in. In the distance a thunderstorm rumbled, following heat lightning that flashed dimly at this remove. A little rain would be welcome—it would cool things off.

Nova timed the flashes to the thunder, to gauge the distance. He made it fifteen to sixteen kilometers, moving closer. *It'll probably rain itself out before it gets this far,* he thought. *Too bad.*

There was a bright pool of light at the dock, where the supply ship was still being off-loaded. They used prisoners for that, droids being in short supply and prone to breaking down in the tropical heat and humidity quicker than they could be replaced. The prisoners were guarded, of course, to make sure none of them decided to hitch a ride offworld when the transport left—not that they had anywhere to go, since the transport was a short-hop vessel incapable of making the jump to lightspeed.

Nova did some stretching, sinking down into a split on the cool grass, rolling over onto his back and then into a shoulder stand, then letting his legs drop until his knees rested by his ears. He held the pose for a few minutes, then rolled to his feet without using his hands.

He felt a little better after that. His shift started early, so he turned to head back to bed. Maybe the coolers were working again.

He caught a glimpse of movement to his left. He glanced that way, toward the South Gate.

Nothing. Nova stood still for a moment, waiting, looking . . .

He didn't see anything out of the ordinary.

Had he imagined it?

Probably a flit, one of the flying poisonous reptiles that sometimes got past the fence and into the compound—no one knew how. If it was a flit, then he'd best take himself inside; the critters were almost impossible to dodge in the dark, and one prick of their poisonous dorsal barbs could put down even a man his size.

Nova headed back for bed.

SECTOR N-THREE, DEATH STAR

"Where are the prisoners?"

Tarkin looked back at Vader. "Don't you want to finish the tour?"

Vader dismissed this question with a wave of his hand. "I trust you can manage the assembly without my help. The prisoners?"

Vader could see the muscles in the governor's lean jaw tighten. "This way," Tarkin said. He was irritated, but did not allow it to show overmuch on his face. And while his mind was perhaps not as flexible as it should be, it was hardly weak. Amazing, Vader reflected, how many highly ranked naval officers did have weak minds. They were good at following orders, but he could read them easily, even without the Force. The language of their bodies spoke volumes about their inner thoughts.

Not everyone here was weak-minded, however. Quite the contrary, in fact. One of the architects, the Mirialan woman, had surprised him. She had put up a powerful shield to cover her thoughts, even though she was untrained at it. He couldn't feel the Force flowing in her—she was no Jedi—but her mind was strong. Stronger than that of any woman he'd encountered in a long time; ever since . . .

Vader quashed the memory that threatened to rise. He did not allow such thoughts any longer. He had made an ally of pain over the past two decades; had let the physical and emotional trials he'd been subjected to make him stronger, instead of destroying him. But stoic though he was, even he had limits to what he could stand.

He looked about him at the huge, curved wedge of the section, which was slowly being filled with girders and columns and vast plates of duralumin. The observation catwalk, and the small area around it, had been fielded off and supplied with gravity, as had a number of other decks and platforms. Vader could see one directly across the wedge from them, with several people garbed in the traditional white smocks and gray jumpsuits of scientists and engineers discussing something. Their local A-grav field made it appear that they were standing upside down relative to his party.

The vast majority of the wedge, however, was still in zero-g and vacuum. Vader watched construction workers—Wookiees, mostly, judging from the size of their vac suits—floating from one level to another, or welding struts and bracework. Droids of various makes and models also moved about on various errands. It was an image of well-organized industry, one calculated to reassure him that work was proceeding smoothly and on schedule. No doubt it had all been carefully orchestrated by Tarkin, but no matter. Vader knew that it took workers who were at least competent to give the illusion of exemplary work.

He would return with a favorable report for his Master. Tarkin and his construction teams would be able to continue building the station. Sabotage could not be allowed. He would examine those suspected of having a hand in the recent explosion. If their mental defenses were feeble, he would pry every thought in their heads loose and act on what he found. Anyone connected to the disruption would be made to pay the ultimate price. One, ten, a thousand—it didn't matter how many. All would regret it.

All would pay.

19

BRIG INTERROGATION CHAMBER, DETENTION BLOCK AA, DECK 5, DEATH STAR

"For whom are you working?"

Vader stood in front of the lieutenant who had been in charge of the night watch at the Despayre air production facility. Tarkin watched as the Sith Lord interrogated the prisoner about the evening when the ship that had blown up had been loaded.

"Th-th-the Imperial Navy," the man managed, in response to Vader's question.

"I think not." Vader's deep and distorted voice carried such an overtone of menace, it made Tarkin want to take a step back. Some of the officers behind him actually did so.

The lieutenant, old for his rank, turned to look at Tarkin. The fear in his eyes was obvious—as was his desperation. He had to be desperate if he thought there would be any help for him from Tarkin. Tarkin held his own gaze cool and steady. The man belonged to Vader now.

"Look at me," Vader said. The lieutenant turned back to stare at him. "This is your last chance." He raised his right hand, fingers spread wide.

"My lord, *please*! I know nothing!"

Vader closed his hand into a fist.

The lieutenant's voice faded to a choked whisper, his throat muscles straining visibly against the unseen vise that had suddenly gripped them. "*Ugghh . . .*" His face purpled, his eyes and tongue bulged, and after a moment, he staggered and fell to the durasteel plate floor. One didn't need to be a medic to see that he wasn't going to be telling anybody anything, ever again.

Tarkin said nothing. He had seen Vader do this before, and, as before, he had no idea how it was accomplished. Whether the Force was some form of telekinetic power or psycho-physiological hypnosis or something else altogether, it was certainly impressive.

Vader turned to Tarkin. "He had nothing to do with the sabotage."

Tarkin frowned. "You know this?"

"His mind was weak. Easily read."

"Then why kill him?"

"He will be an object lesson for those who follow."

Tarkin raised an eyebrow. "A bit harsh."

"The incident happened on his watch. He is responsible. He should have known about it."

There was a line of causality that didn't bear too close an examination, Tarkin reflected. By that logic, anybody who had been on duty at the time, at any point in the construction process, could be found guilty. Taken to extremes, even Tarkin himself might be. And somehow, though Vader's mask was as impassive as ever, Tarkin knew that the Sith Lord was thinking just that.

"I will wait for a time before I examine the remaining prisoners," Vader continued. "Give them a chance to learn of this man's fate. See that they hear of it 'accidentally.'"

Tarkin nodded. It was ruthless, but certainly he could see the value of it. After all, was not this battle station the grandest example of the doctrine that fear itself was the most potent of weapons?

"I will return to my ship now," Vader informed him.

"We have quarters for you here, Lord Vader—"

"I prefer my own." With a swirl of his cape, Vader turned and departed.

Tarkin quelled the annoyance he felt at Vader's dismissive attitude; he'd expected no less. He glanced at the dead man, and then looked at the coterie of guards and officers crowded into the small chamber, several of whom were obviously still stunned by what they had seen. "Take the body to the recycler level and dispose of it. And see to it that the guards allow the prisoners to overhear conversations about what happened here—in florid detail."

For a moment, no one moved. Tarkin looked about the room. "Am I talking simply to hear my own voice?"

That got results. Quickly, a pair of guards bent to gather up the corpse.

Tarkin left the brig, striding down the narrow corridor, flanked by his adjutants. Vader was about as controllable as a rogue reek, but he did get results. Tarkin would be surprised if the other personnel being held in connection with the sabotage were not quick to give up what they knew after hearing of this.

If they knew anything at all . . .

Still, if it cost a handful of prisoners to help keep this from happening again, that was a small price to pay. There were plenty of others to replace them.

TERMINUS FOURTEEN ACCESS CORRIDOR, DEATH STAR

Master Chief Petty Officer Tenn Graneet was in the corridor leading away from the shuttle that had brought him to the battle station when he saw a lone figure striding toward him, all in black, with a cape rippling behind. He recognized the man immediately, from innumerable news holos he'd seen.

It was Darth Vader, the Emperor's enforcer.

Son of a bantha, Tenn thought. He'd known the man was here on an inspection tour, but he certainly didn't expect to encounter him walking down a corridor all by himself, with no protective entourage. Although, given everything he'd heard about Vader's highly touted skill with that Jedi akk-sticker hooked to his belt, why shouldn't he be?

Tenn kept walking. So did Vader. The corridor, one of the peripheral passageways that led from the shuttle terminus, wasn't exactly narrow, but it wasn't terribly wide, either. Tenn realized that Vader's course was such that the mysterious cloaked figure would run smack into him unless one of them shifted to the side.

For a moment, Tenn considered holding to his path, just to see what Vader would do. It was a common game among navy personnel, a test of will and dominance, to see who would veer away first, and CPO Tenn Graneet seldom had to give space to anybody—save, of course, superior officers. Vader, however, wasn't in the navy, so technically he didn't outrank Tenn.

It was tempting, but only momentarily. Vader's pace was fast, and Tenn didn't think the man in black had any intention of altering his course even a hair. Tenn Graneet thought himself as tough as a vacuum seal, but he wasn't stupid or suicidal. He allowed himself to drift to the right, just enough so that when they passed, their shoulders were within a hand span—actually, Vader's shoulder passed within a hand span of the top of Tenn's head. Close enough so that the edge of the flowing black cape slid over Tenn's arm and threatened to catch, for just an instant, on the chief's chrono. The material had a smooth, silky texture, and was cooler than he would have thought.

In fact, the very air seemed cold in the wake of Vader's passage.

Tenn slowed his pace slightly, feeling as if he had just brushed up against a primal force of nature; the edge of a hurricane, perhaps, or an icy comet that simply could not be stopped. Had he challenged Vader by staying in his path, he had no doubt that he would have regretted it for as long as he lived. Which quite probably wouldn't have been all that long.

The chief resisted an urge to glance back. If Vader had even noticed his passing, there had been no sign. "Whoo," he said softly to himself as the sound of the other's boots diminished. That had been an experience he'd remember for a while. He'd almost been the man who'd tugged on Darth Vader's cape.

20

FLUTTERBIRD DINER, SOUTHERN UNDERGROUND,
GRID 17, IMPERIAL CITY

Neet Alamant was a polished fellow, his voice as smooth as drive lube; never an awkward pause or loss for words. Seated in the retro-style dining booth across from him, Memah felt very little in the way of trust or warmth for the human. Rodo was at the counter, overwhelming a stool and not trying very hard to look inconspicuous as he nursed a cup of caf. Memah wasn't afraid of this officious little man, but it did feel comforting to have Rodo nearby, and to have that be obvious, just in case.

"So let me see if I have the gist of your offer," she said. "You want me to run a cantina at a military installation, for which I will be paid a fat signing bonus and a very generous salary, plus a percentage of the profits. This will entail a two-year contract, during which time I will be required to stay at this base full-time. Is that a fair summation?"

"Yes. Recreational facilities will be available. I am given to understand that the installation in question will be on a par, at least, with this area of the Underground, insofar as supplies, traffic, and general working conditions are concerned."

Memah looked thoughtful. That last statement didn't mean much, but she had lived in worse places than the Underground. She didn't need luxury; in the last couple of years she hadn't had occasion to visit the surface but a few times, and she could have skipped those without any real sense of loss. Her life pretty much revolved around her work at this point.

All in all, it seemed a straightforward proposition. Alamant was not forthcoming as to where and what the military installation was, but she could understand that. There was, after all, a war on, and the Empire was, not surprisingly, protective of its secrets. What little clues she could sieve from his words, it was probably a naval base on some far-flung planet. If it was big enough to justify having a civilian-run cantina, it probably wasn't in the middle of a hot war zone. And if it had the comforts of the Southern Underground, without the concomitant dangers, it couldn't be too bad.

Of course, this guy was a recruiter, and he just might be inclined to shade the truth a bit if it served him to do so. He probably got paid for every qualified warm body he delivered. Then again, an Imperial Work Contract had to spell out the reality to be valid, even these days. If you were in the army or navy, you didn't have many rights, but as a civilian you usually got a better deal.

And it wasn't as if she was besieged with offers of work. Cantina operators had certain skills, of course, but there wasn't a formal course of study in the craft that she knew about, and others of her ilk weren't in particularly short supply.

"I can bring my own security chief?"

"As long as he, she, or it doesn't have a felony criminal record and there are no outstanding Imperial warrants for major crimes. An appropriate salary will be provided for such work, and quarters will be provided for you and any security assistant you might wish to bring, as part of the package. Yours includes a single-occupancy room, standard officer's suite," Alamant said. Then he pointedly turned to look at Rodo before looking back at her. "Your security guy gets his own private quarters, too."

She nodded, still thinking.

"Not to pressure you for an answer, but the next civilian crew vessel for this venture leaves from Mainport in three days. If you're not interested, I will seek another for the position." He slid out of the booth and stood up. "I'll need to know your decision tomorrow."

Memah held up a hand. "Wait here a moment, please." She slid out of the booth as well and walked over to where Rodo sat.

"Bad caf," he said, looking at the cup. "Tastes like dishwater." He shook his head.

"And how would you know that? Drink a lot of dishwater?"

He shrugged and flicked his gaze at Alamant. "What does he want?"

"He's offering me a job running a military cantina . . . won't say where. I need to sign on for two years, no leave. Pay is good, plus a piece of the profit, some benefits—housing, medical, like that."

Rodo nodded. "You gonna do it?"

Memah made a show of looking around the diner. "Amid all these other offers to put a roof over my head and food on the table? I don't know; it's so hard to winnow them down." She sat down beside him. "I know someone like you can always get a job—but if I take this, I want you as my security man."

Rodo nodded once. "Okay, I'm in."

"Just like that?"

He grinned. "A chance to thump active military guys who get rowdy? Why not? The guys in the field usually have better skills than the benchwarmers. More interesting that way. Besides, I'd miss you."

She had to smile at that. "You're a Branded Aesthete, Rodo. You don't engage in intimate relations with women."

He nodded again. "Keep 'em on a pedestal where they belong, that's our motto. But everybody's got to be somewhere. Beauty is where you find it."

Memah felt a wave of relief. "Ship leaves in three days."

"No problem. I can pack in five minutes."

She nodded. Yeah. It would take her about that long, too.

"So I'll tell the man we'll take the job."

"Might as well. Caf can't be any worse." He lifted his mug in a salute to the recruiter at the other table.

21

MEDCENTER SURGICAL COMPLEX, SECTION N-ONE, DEATH STAR

When the only tool you have is a knife, the old joke went, *every problem looks like a steak.* Thus Uli, being a surgeon, was primarily concerned with procedures surgical—after all, if your speeder breaks down, you don't call a plumber. But there was more to it than just the operation under the sterilizing lamps. Until the patient was back on his or her or its feet, he or she or it was the surgeon's responsibility, and there was another old saw that spoke to this: *You cut it, you take care of it.*

That was precisely why a surgeon had to know a certain amount of general medicine before he was allowed to pick up a laser scalpel. Because if your wonderful cardio-thoracic procedure to repair a ballooned aorta before it could burst in a deadly aneurism was perfect, but the patient died two days later in recovery, that brought up the third hoary old saying: *The operation was a success, but the patient died.*

There were surgeons who could separate the two and still sleep at night, but Uli was not one of them. And so he found himself standing near the bed of a grizzled old Wookiee construction chief who had been involved in a nasty decompression accident that had required a heart-lung transplant three days past. Despite the best sterile procedures, sometimes patients developed secondary infections, and something like that had apparently happened here. The usual antivirals, antiprions, and antibiotics had been ineffective thus far, and no pathogenic agents had been collected. Nevertheless, the old Wook had a fever, he was coughing, and his blood work showed a strange shift that wasn't bacterial, prional, or viral. The patient had an elevated eosinophil count, hyper to the level of Second-Stage HES. Naturally, Uli had called in more expert help, but the medical specialist had ruled out the usual trans-species suspects—it wasn't kozema, leukemia, asthma, autoimmune disease, or drugs. The only remaining possibilities were some kind of parasitic or protozoal infestation. But the QRI scans were clean, there were no telltale nanocam images, and nothing cultured out. Save for the elevated white cells, there weren't any other real indicators. If this wasn't some previously unknown form of nosocomial infection, the only other possibility seemed to be black magic.

The Wookiee, named Hahrynyar, wasn't critical, but he didn't seem to be getting any better. He was sick enough that he needed to stay in bed. Uli glanced at the array of telemetry gear on the wall and stands, and shook his head in weary bafflement. No change.

His understanding of the Wookiee language was rudimentary on a good day. He could understand "Yes" or "No," and a few other medical responses to questions like "On a scale of one to ten, how much does it hurt?" but he wasn't going to be having any deep philosophical discussions with the big furry biped. Fortunately, he didn't have to. He gestured to C-4ME-O, who was filling a nearby bacta tank with fluid. The droid wheeled over, ready to translate.

"Good day," Uli said to the Wookiee. "How are you?"

"*Wyaaaaaa. Ruh ruh?*" The droid's dulcet tones made the snarls and moans of Wookiee-speak oddly pleasing to the ear.

The patient moaned a response, which 4ME-O translated as, "For you, maybe."

The old Wook had kept his sense of humor, even though he was obviously still feeling pretty bad. Uli was glad to see that: a willingness to fight was the single most important aspect of the healing process, no matter the species.

"We're going to try something new," he continued. "We think maybe you have some kind of parasite. Probably been dormant in your system for years, and the immunosuppressives somehow triggered it. The internal medicine team has a broad-spectrum medication, Nicosamide-Mebendazole Complex, that seems to work on a variety of occult mammalian parasites. If you have what we think you do, this should cure it."

"*Whuahh yun yorra ellihenn?*"

"Well, the side effects are generally mild. There are a couple that might cause some discomfort."

"*Arrn whoon urr.*" This was, according to C-4ME-O, an idiosyncratic phrase structure indicating an affirmation couched in weary cynicism. The droid translated it roughly as "Of *course* there are." Hahrynyar motioned for Uli to continue.

"Um, sometimes there's an associated diarrhea. And very rarely, it affects a patient's finger- and toenails."

"*Yaag?*"

"Well, the nails sort of . . . fall out."

"*Whuahh?*"

"Oh, they grow back in a few months, good as new. And, as I say, it is quite rare."

The next comment was one 4ME-O seemed reluctant at first to translate; when it did, Uli had to hide a smile. He hadn't been aware that members of this species were so imaginative.

"I understand this is distressing, but you can't leave the unit until you're better, and you can't go back to work until we are sure what you have isn't contagious."

The Wookiee scowled.

"Hey, I don't make the rules, I just work here. You have a complaint, take it up with the Emperor."

Hahrynyar snarled an offensive remark concerning Palpatine's personal hygiene that Uli was ready to swear brought a blush to 4ME-O's durasteel skin. Then the big Wook reluctantly conceded to the treatment.

After finishing his rounds, Uli went back to his office and looked at his calendar. Barring an emergency, he had nothing on his surgical schedule until tomorrow, and that was a routine triple bypass on a naval officer who was too fond of fats in his diet. The man was just a hair short of clinically obese; a kilo more, and he'd have to be put on medical waivers to continue serving. Given the nature of the war, that wouldn't surprise Uli—the Empire's need for warm bodies in some arenas was critical, as he well knew. Short, tall, thin, fat, it didn't matter; they always needed more blaster fodder.

He shrugged. Every time he thought about it, it made him angry, but his anger didn't matter. The war kept going. There were times when he thought he'd never get home again, that the war would never end, and that he'd die an old man on some pity-forsaken rock in the middle of nowhere, patching up the endless lines of wounded.

If only there was something he could do to change it.

COMMAND CENTER, OVERBRIDGE, DEATH STAR

Tarkin was pleased. As much as he distrusted Vader and his motives, the coming of the man in black had visibly improved functions wherever one looked. Nobody wanted to face the Sith Lord's wrath, and the best way to avoid that was to do one's job with the utmost efficiency. Vader was a catalyst; he caused reactions that went well beyond his personal sphere of influence, great as that was. The fear he inspired in others was far more than merely the sum of his various and sinister parts. Even Tarkin, a Grand Moff, had sensed it occasionally, like a whiff of ozone presaging an ion storm. It was odd, Tarkin reflected. His rational mind knew that Vader was only a maimed remnant of a man, sealed for the rest of his life in biosupport armor. A figure more to be pitied than anything else. But in person, the last thing he inspired was pity. Vader had *power,* and he knew how to use it, no matter if he was overseeing the scouring of a continent from the bridge of his Star Destroyer or striking a man dead from across the room.

Tarkin shook his head slightly. That which stays hidden and mysterious is always more intriguing than that which can be seen. He certainly couldn't complete with Vader on a physical level, nor did he wish to. But when this dream of his became cold durasteel reality, Vader's vaunted flagship would be yesterday's holos. Why waste time finding and incinerating Rebel bases on various and sundry asteroids and moons when, with a single command, he could see an entire planet decimated?

And he would have that power, very soon now. Repairs on the recent damage were well under way, and the crew chiefs, directing three shifts, reported that over the course of the next few months the original work schedule should be reclaimed. Tarkin had every hope that the fifth-column activity had been scotched. Certainly, anyone who came under Vader's steely gaze who had anything to do with it would be removed forthwith from the playing board—permanently.

This battle station would be built—and when it was done, it would be the ultimate power in the galaxy.

Tarkin could be patient until then.

22

MACHINE TOOL STORAGE UNIT ALPHA-FOUR, POLAR ORBIT AROUND DESPAYRE

Ratua had no specific plan as to how he would get from the orbiting warehouse to the battle station called the Death Star. But he wasn't stupid. The section in which he found himself was apparently dedicated mostly to replacement supplies for assorted kinds of mechanical devices. No kitchen stores and no weapons were apparent on his initial examination of the premises. Things didn't look particularly bright for his immediate future.

Perhaps, though, Fem Fortune had decided at last that Celot Ratua Dil had suffered enough by being in the wrong place at the wrong time, for three very good things happened to him within hours of slipping from the transport ship and into the warehouse.

First, he practically tripped over a huge store of gas tanks, and among these were copious amounts of both oxygen and hydrogen. With two parts of the latter and one of the former and a spark—no problem, given all the gear available—he could produce pure water, which, in a pinch, could keep him alive without any food for weeks.

Second, he found a locker full of vacuum suits, one of which fit him tolerably well, so that in the event the rumors were true and the warehouses were periodically opened to the airlessness of space to get rid of pests that had somehow managed to find their way within, he wouldn't freeze or suffocate to death.

And third, he found a case of dehydrated Vulderanian grain flakes that had obviously been mislaid—it was stacked in a rack of machine tool parts. Add water and, while it would probably not be the tastiest meal he had ever enjoyed, and would certainly grow quite monotonous over time, it would offer sustenance.

So he had food and water, and he could breathe. Things could be a lot worse.

After another day of cautious exploration, Ratua came across a crate containing a general-service droid, and he marveled at his continuing good fortune. Long ago and far away, he had spent some quality time hiding out in a droid repair shop while avoiding the local authorities, due to an unfortunate misunderstanding. After a few days with nothing better to occupy his time, Ratua had taught himself the basics of droid programming. Nothing fancy, but enough that he could upload simple instructions. And general-service droids were often pressed into service as loaders.

Now he had a plan. All he needed was an opportunity, which came a few days later—just after he had finished his preparations for it. How lucky was that?

A troop of droids arrived on an unloaded cargo vessel. Seeing this from his hidden vantage point in a maintenance conduit, Ratua quickly activated his programmed droid and hurriedly donned his vac suit. Then he concealed himself in a packing crate, sealed the crate shut from inside, and waited.

Now it was up to the droid.

He'd programmed it to observe the loaders, see what stores they had come to acquire, and quickly mark the crate containing Ratua so that it appeared to contain the same items. Once this was done, the droid "borrowed" a null-g platform and moved the crate onto the supply vessel. Nobody stopped it—there was no reason to do so. Even if there had been a living security agent on the cargo ship, a mechanical loading a crate of machine parts would be what he expected to see, and that's what he would see.

And since nobody started yelling and trying to open the crate, Ratua felt fairly confident that his ruse had gone undiscovered.

The hold was airless and unheated, but Ratua was protected in his suit, and he couldn't imagine the trip to the station would take more than a short time. If he'd guessed wrong, he would eventually run out of oxygen, but few things in life were without risk. And so he settled down to wait, willing himself into a quasi-dormant state so as to conserve air.

After a few minutes, he felt the cargo ship stir to life and move, presumably, away from the warehouse.

Wherever he was going, he was on his way.

CIVILIAN TRANSPORT VESSEL *PORTMINIAN,* EN ROUTE TO THE HORUZ SYSTEM

The viewports were opaqued, there being nothing to see but a kind of impressionistic fuzzy *strangeness*. Memah had tried looking out into the higher-dimensional realm early in the voyage, and had quickly realized that the resulting headache and nausea were not to her liking. Rodo, who had undertaken more than a few FTL voyages, had warned her, but she'd had to check it out for herself. Memah Roothes had never been one to take another's word for something when she could investigate herself; a trait, she reminded herself wryly, that had led to more than one headache over the years.

The vessel, while not a first-class starliner, was comfortable enough. Small but decent cabins, four passengers to a unit. Aside from Rodo, there were two other humans from Imperial Center in their cabin, both civilians contracted for troop services—one was a Corellian who specialized in recreational gaming, the other a woman who was somewhat less forthcoming as to her origins and exactly what her duties were to be.

Nobody had told them about how long the trip would take or where it would wind up, but they had been cruising at superluminal for several days, at least, so it had to be no small distance. Unless, of course, they were going around in circles or other random patterns to make it seem that way. Memah didn't seriously believe that, though. The Empire might be willing to expend drive fuel and pilot pay to confuse high-ranking officials or important civilian clients, but a tavern keeper, a bouncer, a gamer, and a "dancer"? She doubted it.

And when all was said and done, it didn't really matter, did it? She was going somewhere, and when she got there, she'd be running a new place and getting paid pretty well for it. Things could be worse. Things could be—and had been—a lot worse. At least no one was likely to burn down a tavern run by the Empire.

23

SSD *DEVASTATOR*, POLAR ORBIT, DESPAYRE

Darth Vader emerged from his hyperbaric chamber, refreshed insofar as the word had meaning for him. He had been thinking about the incidents that had impeded construction of the battle station, and they seemed to him to be ill formed and poorly operated. This surprised him somewhat, as he considered the Alliance more of a threat than even the Emperor did. That said, he knew that the Rebel network, like any large group, mostly comprised those who were at best adequate to the jobs with which they had been tasked. There were always a few who were adept, even brilliant, of course, and Vader was sure there were those among the Rebels who qualified for that description. Those were the ones to be concerned about, for they would fight to the last breath. Some of the Jedi had gone down very hard; the Emperor's visage itself was testament to that.

Before Vader had himself been transformed, he'd watched Mace Windu inflict ghastly injury upon his Master. Had that been a test, as Vader suspected, to see if Anakin Skywalker would commit himself to the Sith Lord's cause? Had Darth Sidious been in control the entire time, only pretending to be losing, and willing to absorb such malevolent energies purely to make a point? If so, it had been a heavy price for his Master to pay to learn what he'd needed to learn.

But be all that as it might, there was no Yoda, no Mace Windu leading this insurgency . . . no one who shone so brightly in the Force that Vader could not miss him. Whatever few Jedi might be left in the galaxy had nothing to do with this latest attack.

He would tell Tarkin as much. The cadaverous administrator had little imagination, but he was doggedly methodical, give him that. He could keep things on track. The project was not slowed so much that it needed Vader's personal attention toward its completion. He had come to see what he needed to see, had corrected the problem he had found, and now it was time to move on to other, weightier matters. There was a war being waged, after all.

In the hallway outside his suite, Vader found a captain. "Find the admiral and tell him we are leaving within the hour."

The captain saluted. "Yes, my lord." He hurried away.

Vader entered the suite. It was well appointed but scarcely luxurious; it had been many years since he had taken notice of such things. He moved to the comm station to contact Tarkin and tell him he was done here. With any luck at all, Vader told himself, he would not have to return until the battle station was finished.

GUARD POST, SLASHTOWN PRISON COLONY, DESPAYRE

"Say again?" Sergeant Nova Stihl asked.

"Pack, Sergeant," the loot said. "You are being transferred."

"To where?" Not that he cared overmuch—after all, one place on this pestilent world was as good, or bad, as another. But to his surprise, the lieutenant pointed at the ceiling. "To that pile of I-beams and durasteel plate in the sky."

Nova blinked. "To the Death Star? Why?"

The lieutenant sighed. "These insignia look like a Moff's rankings to you?" He gestured at his uniform. "Not yours to reason why, Stihl, yours is only to do and die. There's a shuttle leaving at midday; your orders are to be on it and so shall you be. Kiss your favorite prisoners good-bye and stuff your duffel."

Nova shook his head in disbelief. "This makes no kind of sense. I'm doing good work here; since I started the lessons, murders and general population violence have been down by twelve percent."

"Yeah, and we're all gonna miss watching you, Sarge, but the military wants you there and not here, so there you will go."

Nova shrugged. No way to argue against that. Orders were orders.

In his room, he was able to pack his gear in half an hour; it wasn't like he'd been able to put down deep roots or anything. He'd supposed he would be moving on at some point, but he hadn't ever really considered it all that much. And now here it was, and, when he got right down to it, what difference did it make? Watching convicts here or working a brig on a station—same difference. He'd miss the open air and sunshine, and the very few folks, either prisoners or guards, whom he thought of as friends. But he could work out anywhere he had a space big enough to lie down in, and he'd always been able to make new friends.

Nova looked around. It was just a place. He'd spent some time here; now he was leaving. Such was life. If he'd learned nothing else from his studies, it was that one went with the flow.

He wondered what kind of duty he'd be assigned on the station. Perhaps he'd contact a few people who owed him, try to find out.

Forewarned was forearmed, after all.

24

MACHINE TOOL STORAGE UNIT ALPHA-FOUR, CARGO TRANSPORT KJB-87, APPROACHING THE DEATH STAR

The smart thing for Ratua to do would be to stay in his crate until it was off-loaded and safely in a storage area somewhere. But after a couple of hours, he couldn't stand the cramped monotony anymore, and so he undogged the hatch and cautiously emerged.

Save for the droids, which were all powered down for the flight, he was alone. The ship was on programmed remote control, so it was no risk at all for him to peep through a viewport to see what was out there.

He'd heard about the battle station, of course, even observed it once or twice through a dioptric scope he'd managed to scrounge from a guard. But he wasn't prepared for this. Though only about half finished, the Death Star still loomed like a skeletal monster. He had no idea how far away it was; the lack of an atmosphere to blur distant objects rendered it stark and vivid, seemingly close enough to touch. The scale was unbelievable, and he wouldn't have been able to tell how large it truly was save for the Star Destroyers and massive cargo ships that hung about the construction site, looking like so many children's toys compared with the station itself.

Amazing.

Ratua thought, *Should be no trouble at all finding places to get lost in on something that size.*

He went back to his crate, latched himself back in, and began masticating some grain flakes.

CIVILIAN TRANSPORT VESSEL *PORTMINIAN,* APPROACHING THE DEATH STAR

Rodo whistled. "Check it out," he said.

Memah moved to stand next to the much taller human. "Whoa!"

"*Big* sodder," Rodo agreed. He pointed. "That's a Star Destroyer moving off over there, see?"

"What is it? Some kind of troop transport?"

Rodo shook his head. "Battle station's my guess. Too big for a troop carrier; you could probably stuff a couple million stormtroopers into that thing with room left over for a fleet of battleships, once they get it done—more than you'd need for any one Rebel outpost."

"But why is it so *big*?"

He shrugged. "Dunno. I'd guess it packs a load of firepower."

"You think *that's* where we're going?"

"Bet big credits to boiled chork it is."

Memah stared at the huge, unfinished spheroid, already bristling with armament. Once completed, it would probably be able to blow ships, asteroids, maybe even entire moons, into cosmic gravel. She felt her lekku bristle in nervous anticipation.

Well, she'd hoped for a locale in which to ply her trade that would be safe, hadn't she?

"Be careful what you wish for," she murmured. Rodo glanced at her, but said nothing.

The station, already huge, kept growing larger as the transport approached.

MILITARY SHUTTLE NGC-1710, APPROACHING THE DEATH STAR

Nova had seen the holorecordings, but they didn't even begin to give you the real scope of the construction site. The blasted thing was *huge,* big as a moon! He'd heard the scut, naturally, the military comm-vine was hot with it: the Death Star was going to carry an armada of ships, it would have more guns than an Imperial fleet, there were super-secret weapons that could pop Star Destroyers like soap bubbles, burn a continent down to the bedrock, trigger solar flares, and so forth. But he'd figured most of that for jaw-wag that wasn't worth the air it took to repeat it. Now, however, seeing the place as the shuttle drew nearer, he revised his opinion. No way the Empire would spend this kind of effort and money if this thing didn't have a big trick it could pull off.

One thing for sure: it promised to be far more exciting than herding prisoners around on a tropical pesthole like Despayre.

It looked like interesting times lay ahead.

25

CIVILIAN TRANSPORT VESSEL *NORDIEUS,* APPROACHING HANGAR BAY 1271, DEATH STAR

Commander Atour Riten—a rank that meant less than nothing to him—leaned back in his seat and looked at the viewer inset into the bulkhead next to him. *My,* he thought. *It certainly is . . . big . . .*

Of course, he had known that. Despite all the secrecy concerning the project, and even though he had not been cleared to top levels by the Empire, he had known that. One did not spend forty years working for the Library Galactica without figuring how to read between the lines.

So yes, this battle station was huge. He had known it, intellectually, but the reality of being able to see it with references that gave one an idea of its size was something else entirely. There were only a dozen or so sections of it finished enough for normal habitation, but even those portions were exceedingly large.

Atour mentally shrugged. It didn't matter how big the thing was, only that the library inside it was worthwhile. And this one certainly was, if what he had been told was true. It wasn't as large and encompassing as, say, Imperial Center Main, but it was much more complete than many planetary libraries—or at least it would be when he got done with it.

"Big suckah, idn't it?" The man sitting next to him was some kind of construction worker, a contractor who specialized in magnetic containment vessels, a subject that had come perilously close, during the course of the flight up, to breaking Atour's belief that nothing was boring, provided the person speaking of it understood it properly. Flux, gauss, m-particle and graviton shifts? Even with his not-inconsiderable general knowledge, those technical details were but mildly interesting, at best.

Still, Atour Riten believed firmly that there was no excuse for discourtesy, and so he nodded. "Indeed." Unfortunately, this was taken as encouragement by his seatmate to launch into an enthusiastic description of the power requirements, in megajoules, that it took to run such a huge station.

Atour let him babble on while he waited for the docking procedure to begin and considered the vagaries of fate that had led him here, so late in life. That the library was a potentially good one had been an unexpected bonus, because he had not been posted here as any sort of reward. He'd been shunted off into this world-forsaken assignment as a way of getting rid of him, at least in a manner of speaking.

It had been, in a sense, his own fault: Atour Riten was, admittedly, not always circumspect when it came to controversial subjects—politics, government, personal relationships—and there were a fair number of people who hated to suffer his opinions as a result. Fortunately for him, those with enough power to have him killed with a snap of their fingers seldom had pristine pasts. Archivists, as a rule, knew how to dig into data banks and find just about anything, including bodies thought safely long buried. And old and smart archivists knew how to rig dead-man switches so that if they themselves suddenly died, no matter how natural it might seem, the locations of those bodies—many, many bodies—would come to light. Sometimes they literally were bodies; mostly they were bits of damaging, often illegal, information that would cause much consternation in high levels of government should they pop up on the daily holonews.

There were a whole lot of people who did not want that to happen, and some of them were passing smart, smart enough to at least realize that promoting Atour Riten to commander and shuffling him off into the middle of nowhere to run a military library and archive was a lot safer than deleting him. And so it had come to pass.

Truth to tell, he wasn't that unhappy about the solution they'd found. His glory days of revamping and innovation were behind him.

Weeks where he could stay awake and alert for three or four sleep cycles and burn in a work-fever were long past. He could still put together a top-rack system as well as anyone—false modesty aside, better than most—but these years it took longer than once it had. He was much nearer the end of his road than the beginning. And all in all, he had few regrets.

He sighed softly. Long had he been a thorn in the foot of whoever was in power. This latest shift didn't really matter all that much: Republic, Empire, it was six to one, half a dozen to the other. It meant little to the average person struggling to make a life. Either form of government could make the mag-levs run on time, and both stepped on individual rights far more than they should. As far as Atour was concerned, the best government was that which governed least. Something a step or two above anarchy would be ideal.

Now there was a power-hungry Emperor running things. Both history and personal experience had taught Atour that in as little as a few years, or as much as a few centuries, there would come evolution—or revolution—and this, too, would pass. The new rulers would start out full of promise and hope and good intentions, and gradually settle into mediocrity. A benevolent but inept king was as bad as a despot.

The warning bell chimed, and the pilot's voxcast said, "Attention all passengers, docking will be complete in five minutes. Please check and make sure you have all your belongings before debarkation."

Atour Riten chuckled softly. There was a word you didn't hear that often. *Debark,* from Old Low Frusoise, meaning "to leave a small sailing ship's secondary boat." Who on board knew that, save for himself and perhaps the pilot?

Probably no one. And probably no one cared in the least. When you got to be Atour's age, you had to take your amusements where you could. Especially with a seatmate nattering on and on about hypermatter reactions.

MIDLEVEL CANTINA, DECK 69, SECTOR N-ONE, DEATH STAR

The *size* of the station was mind-boggling. Memah still couldn't get her head around it. Her tiny part of it, which was to become a working cantina, was half again as large as the place that had burned to the pavement back in the Underground, and she had been given more or less a free hand to furnish and run it. At least, so far. She'd been assured that, as long as she didn't go crazy and try to outfit the place with platinum draw taps or the like, the Empire would cover the cost.

If she kept getting news like that, she might just have to revise her opinion of the new regime.

Rodo drifted past the desk where she sat working up an order form for refreshments and intoxicants. If there was a fermented, brewed, or distilled spirit that wasn't in stock, she had yet to learn of it. There were beers, ales, wines, liquors, malts, brandies . . . both generic and brand-named. The legally allowed chemicals that could be eaten, inhaled, dermed, or otherwise taken were likewise available across the board. All she had to do was tick it off on the complex Imperial order form and then wait for delivery. It was apparent that whoever had set this station up had planned ahead for such things.

She looked up from her chore at Rodo. "What?"

"Contractor's on his way to install the tables and chairs. He says it's a two-day job, tops."

"Yeah, right. And the Emperor's packin' a lightsaber."

"Apparently there was a recent visit from the Emperor's favorite envoy." He cupped his hands over his mouth and did a creditable impression of Darth Vader's respirator sound. "Since he left, things have run *very* smoothly. I believe the contractor is sincere."

The comm on the computer blipped. Memah answered it. "Yes?"

"Memah Roothes, please."

"Speaking."

"This is the scheduling droid for Sector Medical. When might it be convenient for you to meet with one of our doctors to complete your physical examination for preadmission to the station?"

"I hate to point this out, but I arrived here some days past. Besides, they gave me the standard once-over before I dusted Despayre."

The droid politely acknowledged the error, citing shorthandness and overscheduling problems; nevertheless, a physical was required SOP. Memah could see that she wasn't going to get out of it; the droid was firm and nonyielding as only a machine could be. She acquiesced to the following day at eleven hundred hours.

"You are scheduled to see Captain Dr. Divini. Please bring any medical records you have with you. Do you need a reminder call on the morning shift?"

"No, I can remember that far in advance, thank you."

She shut off the comm and looked at Rodo. He gave her another shrug. "I went yesterday. Apparently I am not a carrier of any transmittable diseases and thus am deemed fit for habitation."

"Well, if I were Sangi Fever Sal, this would be a day late and a dozen credits short," Memah said. "I could have infected hundreds of people by now. There'd be bodies dropping like brindlebugs in the hot sun."

"The Empire grinds slow but fine," Rodo said. "And they did check everybody before we got on the transport dirtside, like you said, so why do it again? There's no chance of catching something on the way up."

"That's the government—everything and everyone gets shunted through the Department of Redundancy Department." Memah looked back at the requisition form. "So tomorrow I'll go get thumped and probed by the medics. See if you can't get the guy doing the exhaust fans and baffles in here while I'm gone, too, okay?"

Rodo nodded, but somewhat absently; his mind was obviously otherwise occupied. Memah thought about asking him what he was chewing over but decided not to—when he was ready, he'd mention it. In the meantime, she had a choice to make: Corellian ale or Zabrak ferment?

26

DECK 92, SECTOR N-ONE, DEATH STAR

Ratua didn't have any connection to religion—he didn't subscribe to any of the doctrines or dogmas, more than a few of which he had been exposed to in his life. However, if there was one that promised a thieves' paradise, it might not be too different from this battle station.

He'd been afraid at first that he'd have to skulk about the outlying corridors and hallways, staying in the shadows, taking service tubes and stairs to avoid being stopped by station security. But he had walked past guards scores of times, hesitantly at first, then with less worry, and finally with nothing but confidence. As far as he could tell, nobody had even lifted an eyebrow in his direction. Nobody stopped him and asked him what business he was on; nobody asked for identification, as long as he stayed away from corridors and chambers plainly marked off-limits to unauthorized personnel; in short, nobody seemed to notice him at all. The prevailing attitude seemed to be that if you were on the station, then you must belong here, and as long as you weren't doing something that looked suspicious, you were free to come and go as you liked.

Ratua wasn't quite to the point where he swaggered about as if he owned the place, but he did move now with a certain confidence that belied his true status, and which, no doubt, made him even more invisible to the cools. He strolled into the public cafeterias, selected food and drink, and ate unmolested. No ID was necessary for that; food was free. He'd even slipped into a supply depot and, using his speedy mode, had "borrowed" fresh clothes—a basic freight handler's coveralls.

The first few days he had been on the station, he'd found a few empty trash chutes that didn't seem to be used, where a clever being could rig a couple of crosspiece supports and camp out of sight. Of course, you had to be careful that somebody didn't open the chute and dump trash onto your impromptu bivouac, but that had only happened once. Still, it had been sufficiently discomfiting to send him looking for more congenial hiding places—that, and the suspicion gleaned from sounds and smells that there were things living on the garbage levels. Big things.

After that, he found all manner of storage spaces that were empty or nearly so, and for a being with his skills, slipping into these when nobody was around was child's play. He could sleep there without much worry at all.

Food, shelter, clothes—he had all the basics. And after he had gotten the lay of the place, some artful scavenging had provided basic items for barter.

"Ho, trooper. You know anybody who might have use for a D-nine battery pack in pretty good condition? As it happens, I have one and find myself a little short of coin until payday. Worth ten c's, easy, but I can let you have it for seven . . ."

Within a week he had a pretty good stash of trade goods hidden in a recycling station storage bin, enough credits to buy small items he couldn't get for free or "borrow," and a line to a couple of quartermasters who were making a little extra in the gray and black markets.

No matter where you went, people were the same. There were honest ones, dishonest ones, generous, greedy, all across the spectrum, and if you were paying attention you could tell which were which and use them to your benefit. If he had learned nothing else living on a prison planet, he had learned to pay attention.

By creating a false identi-tab he became Teh Roxxor, an inspector employed by a civilian contractor who built storage bins for recycling stations, which gave him a reason to be in such places. Not that it seemed necessary; the one time a guard had seen him going boldly into one of his storage spaces, Ratua had just smiled and nodded at him, and the guy had waved back and gone on about his business.

Unbelievable. Give him a year like this, he'd be running this battle station . . .

27

REC ROOM 17-A, LEVEL 36, DEATH STAR

Lieutenant Vil Dance looked around the interior of the rec room. It was of basic design—tall ceiling, mirrors along one wall, an expanse of padded floor—and otherwise empty save for seven or eight people, all of them humans but one, a tall Rodian with a vibroblade scar across his face. Didn't see a lot of them in the military—didn't see many aliens at all, given how generally xenophobic the Empire was—but Vil had heard that some of them were pretty good bounty hunters. Given that, he could understand why the Rodian might be here. It helped explain the face scar as well.

Vil checked his chrono. Class was supposed to start in five minutes.

Most of the others looked to be in pretty good shape, which wasn't unexpected. Not a lot of do-little types would bother to stir their backsides to come and try something that required any physical effort. He knew plenty of pilots who, outside of the required calisthenics, got most of their exercise from walking to the cooler to get another bottle of ale. Vil kept in pretty fair shape on his own; he wasn't here so much for the workout, or even the knowledge, as he was for the possibility that he might gain a tiny edge as a pilot. At the Academy, somebody had done some research and found that people who studied this kind of thing had slightly better scores in the flight simulators due to decreased reaction time. He'd never really had a chance to try it before. He was, he knew, already an excellent pilot, but every little bit he could add to that was worth checking into.

The door slid open. A man in gray workout skins walked into the room. He had a rolling, muscular gait and a big smile, and appeared to be in his early thirties. He wasn't particularly big or impressively muscled, but something about the way he moved, the economy of his motion, said to Vil that this guy knew his stuff.

"I'm Sergeant Nova Stihl," he said, "and I'd guess that almost everybody here outranks me. But let's get this straight from the start—I don't care if you're a gasser or an admiral, this is *my* class. What we are talking about is teräs käsi, a martial art designed for close work. Hands, feet, elbows, knives, sticks. I expect I know more about this stuff than any of you, so what I say goes. You can't live with that, walk now. Unless, of course, somebody can demonstrate they are better than I am, in which case, I'll take lessons from you." He paused. "So do we have any fighters here?"

Vil felt he could handle himself reasonably well when the furniture started flying, but there was no way he was going to step up to that kind of comment. It wasn't the sort of invitation anyone in his right mind would extend unless he was reasonably confident of what the end result would be.

He looked around. A couple of the men looked to be ground-pounders, thick with enough muscle to be dangerous. There was one guy, a little smaller than most, who had a feral gleam in his eyes. Vil's impression was that he wouldn't want to have the guy behind him in a dark corridor. And there was the Rodian, but he didn't know enough about Rodians to judge that one.

One of the men he'd pegged as ground-pounders said, "I c'n handle m'self okay."

Stihl gave him a welcoming grin. The ground-pounder was taller, heavier, and he did look like a man you wouldn't want mad at you. Vil had the feeling, however, that that wasn't going to make a whole lot of difference to Sergeant Stihl.

"Okay," the instructor said. "Come and show me something. Knock me down and I'll buy your drinks for the next month."

The ground-pounder grinned at that. "Comin' right up, Sarge!"

Vil thought, *This'll be interest*—and before his mind could finish the thought, it was over. The big ground-pounder stepped in, swung a punch that would have dented quadanium plate, and a second later was lying flat on his face.

Vil didn't have a clue what the sergeant had done to cause it. He'd just made some kind of fast sidestep and what looked like a wave of his hands, and *bam!* the attacker hit the floor hard enough that Vil could feel it vibrate.

Ouch . . .

There was a surprised murmur from the others that indicated they didn't know what Stihl had done, either. *Bet the next class is a* lot *bigger once this gets around,* Vil thought.

"Anybody else want to give it a shot?"

Much shuffling of feet, inspection of fingernails, and sudden interest in the ceiling. Nobody did, apparently.

"Good." Stihl reached one hand down and helped the ground-pounder to his feet. "Then let's get started."

MEDCENTER, DEATH STAR

Because there weren't enough medical doctors or droids to go around, Uli found himself, somewhat to his annoyance, doing routine physical exams on new arrivals to the station. Using a surgeon for such work was rather like using a protocol droid to run a water converter—the task would be accomplished, speedily and efficiently, but it would definitely not be the most effective use of the droid's time and skill.

He gave the diagnoster printout of the just-finished scan a look-over while his latest patient got dressed. The man was human, originally from Corellia, but he'd been eking out a grim existence on Despayre for the last four months. Nowhere on his dossier did it list the reason he'd been banished to that pesthole. Why should it? No point in wasting pixels on a man who, for all intents and purposes, was dead.

The stats were unsurprising: elevated urinary nitrogen, compromised immune system, vitamin and mineral deficiencies, incipient scurvy . . . borderline malnutrition, in short. The man was lean as a Givin, with no excess fat at all to soften sinew and musculature. He'd been able to survive, but, if he hadn't been scooped up in one of the regular sweeps for more workers, he wouldn't have lasted much longer. Now his problems were over, for the short run at least. No more subsisting on boiled knob-blypears and roasted ratbats; the mass-produced rations that were the workers' diet might not be particularly tasty, but they would be nutritious enough to keep him alive and laboring for the Empire.

Until he was, most likely, worked to death.

After the Corellian had been led out by a med droid, Uli rubbed his eyes and asked, "Who's up next?"

C-4ME-O said, "Memah Roothes, female, Rutian Twi'lek, Ryloth, arrived onstation nine days past from Imperial Center."

"Coruscant," Uli corrected the droid. "I always hated that name change." He glanced at the wall chrono. Nearly eleven forty-five hours; he'd been on his feet since twenty-three hundred.

"Memah Roothes is a civilian contractor whose designation is RSW-Six, subgrade two, Miscellaneous Entertainment and Services."

"Which means what?"

"She was hired to run a cantina in this sector."

Uli couldn't help but feel slightly peeved at the droid. "Why didn't you just say that in the first place?"

"I did, Captain Dr. Divini. If you had studied your *Imperial Designation Manual,* you could hardly have reached any other conclusion."

"I don't need a droid telling me to read the manual, thank you very much."

C-4ME-O made a snorting sound.

"What was that?"

"Condensation on my vocabulator. It needed to be cleared."

Uli grinned and shook his head. "Give me the chart."

In the exam room, the Twi'lek female sat on the table in a disposable wrap, dangling her bare feet over the edge. Her skin tone was teal, and at first glance, she certainly looked healthy enough. "Memah Roothes, I'm Dr. Divini."

"Doctor." A cool and noncommittal acknowledgment.

He looked at the flatscreen. "Says here that you're originally from Ryloth, by way of Coruscant."

"By way of a lot of places."

"No major illnesses or injury on the record."

"Nope. I had cavern fever as a child—I'm from the Darkside—but that was common enough. Most of the younglings caught that sooner or later. Other than that, nothing to speak of."

Uli nodded. It had been a long time since his medical rotations and he'd never seen that many Twi'leks even then, though he had cut open a few since. Her chart indicated pretty standard stuff. He'd test her reflexes, listen to her heart, and then let the diagnoster check the rest, including a broadscan for any possible pan-species communicable diseases; not that it mattered much, since she'd already been here for a week and a half. Everything by the numbers; any third-year medical student could do it. He turned to the instrument table and fitted an auscultator to his ears, then turned back to her, saying, "Well, let's have a listen to your heart. Would you mind—"

He stopped as she slid off the table, shucked her wrap, and tossed it onto the table, all in a single, smooth motion. Then she faced him.

Uli wore his professional expression. "I was going to say, Would you mind taking a deep breath?"

She shrugged. "You would have gotten around to asking eventually."

Uli wasn't sure in what context her remark was meant, and not in a big hurry to find out. Roothes was definitely an attractive female, no two ways about it; still, he was a doctor. He'd seen more than a few beings of various sexes naked before. It was all part of the job.

He poked and listened and examined, didn't find anything remarkable, and noted such on the flatscreen chart. She was a well-nourished, well-developed sthenic Twi'lek female who looked a bit younger than her stated age and was within normal limits for a being of her species, at least according to the old-fashioned physical exam.

"Step in front of the diagnoster, please."

She did so. The machine hummed as it sensed her presence on the exam pad. A bright light flashed, and in an instant she was weighed and measured, her various bodily systems—digestive, respiratory, nervous, circulatory, and musculoskeletal—scanned. The machine ran a battery of more than a hundred tests in a heartbeat, both generic and species-specific, and sent the results to his flatscreen. They testified that Memah Roothes was normal, healthy, and disease-free. No surprises.

"You can get dressed," he told her.

She looked at him. "So I pass?"

"Yes. Everything checks out fine."

"Two hours of my life I'll never get back," she muttered as she began to re-dress.

Uli left the room, suppressing a smile. He knew just how she felt.

28

CENTRAL COMMAND DECK, OVERBRIDGE, DEATH STAR

Tarkin found himself wishing once again that Daala were here. It surprised him how much he missed her company. She had military responsibilities at the Maw Installation, of course, but the truth was that the nature of that area of space, in which a congeries of black holes orbited one another in an elegant, complicated dance, made casual passersby unlikely in the extreme. And if that weren't enough, the four Star Destroyers on duty there were more than capable of discouraging any errant ships, Rebel or otherwise.

And now that the station was being constructed here in the Horuz system, the importance of the work at the Maw was somewhat less than it had been. It was true that Qwi Xux's other projects—the Sun Crusher, the World Devastators, and other potent superweapons—were still in development there, as well as the installation being full of valuable scientists and technicians, but if Daala were to leave for a week or two, there would be no problem whatsoever with her captains maintaining security in her absence.

Of course, Daala had officially been given express orders to maintain her post until relieved, since there had to be a ranking admiral in charge. But there were orders and then there were orders, and since both sets came from Tarkin, he could alter them as he deemed necessary. As the galaxy's only Grand Moff, he had extensive leeway in how he ran his portion of the navy. Nobody could question him, save the Emperor—and as long as he got the job done, the Emperor wouldn't care what he did to accomplish it.

Tarkin stared out the viewport at the partly assembled battle station, and thought about it.

The standing protocols at the Maw Installation were not open to interpretation. If a non-Imperial ship happened by and managed to avoid being swallowed by one of the many singularities surrounding it, the ship was to be captured and the crew interrogated as to how and why they were there. Failing the ability to capture it, there was but one other option—the vessel was to be blown to atoms. There were no exceptions, and any deck monkey with a rudimentary brain could follow those protocols. There was no need for Daala to be standing over the gunners repeating what they all already knew.

Abruptly, Tarkin made his decision. He went to his quarters and engaged his personal communications holo-unit, then sat back and waited for the connection. It was not long in coming.

"Wilhuff! How good to see you!"

The image of Daala over the holoplate was life-sized, and the resolution very sharp—it wasn't the same as her being here, but the holo did capture her facial expressions, as well as her cold and haughty beauty, well enough. Like him, she sat in a command chair.

She was happy to see him, he could tell, and that pleased him.

"And you, Daala. How are things at the Installation?"

She made a dismissive gesture. "Less than exciting. You have news?"

Due to the secret nature of the experiments being done at the Maw, outside communications were, for the most part, forbidden. With the exception of this circuit, Daala and her crew were cut off from the rest of the galaxy save for the Emperor himself, and perhaps Darth Vader. Tarkin could justify this contact for reasons of security—and, if you couldn't trust a Grand Moff, then who was trustworthy?

"Nothing that concerns your command," he said. "We are winning the war."

"Of course," she said with a knowing smile.

He smiled in return. "We have had some small problems here. But they've been rectified, fortunately, with the help of a certain Imperial representative of whom you are no doubt aware."

Daala nodded. She certainly knew to whom he was referring, though she would not speak Vader's name aloud, either. This was supposed to be a secure circuit, the signal encoded and encrypted on both ends, but neither Tarkin nor Daala trusted that. Vader had ears everywhere, and what one technician could hide, another could uncover.

"However," Tarkin continued, "I need to give you a . . . personal briefing, and to that end, I would have you pay us a visit."

"Really? When?"

"Whenever your duties make it convenient."

Both of them smiled at that one. They both knew that, at this point, her "duties" were about as exciting as a dish of curdled droat milk. The crews could do disaster and battle station drills in their sleep.

"Well," she said, "I expect I can get away starting . . . what time is it now?"

He chuckled. Daala was the only person in the galaxy who could make him laugh. Aside from her beauty, ambition, and brains, it was one of her most endearing characteristics.

"Let me know when you depart. I look forward to seeing you, Admiral Daala."

"And I you, Grand Moff Tarkin."

After he disconnected, Tarkin felt something surge in his breast. Happiness? To be sure. But something more as well, something he could not quite put a finger on. Daala was an exciting woman in many ways, not the least of which was her physical attractiveness. But her ruthlessness also called to him. She was the highest-ranking female in the Imperial Navy—due in large part to his machinations, of course, but Tarkin did not doubt that she would have eventually risen on her own. When people did not know she was female and judged her on performance scores alone, she could contend with almost any male officer in the service—and had done so.

Perhaps she would not have gone so far, so quickly, without his aid, but without any doubt a woman of her skill and talent would not be held back. He would not have been attracted to any woman less capable. If a man could not have an equal as a mate, at least it was good to find one who could run with him.

He looked around his quarters. Was it a bit dusty in here? He'd have the cleaning droids come in and put it in sparkling order straightaway. Daala was coming, after all. Things must be perfect or he would know the reason why.

He smiled. They called him old behind his back, but he had fire left in him. He was sure his subordinates would be surprised if they knew just how hot that fire burned.

29

CIVILIAN LIVING QUARTERS, DELTA SECTOR
CONSTRUCTION SITE, DEATH STAR

Teela had come to the conclusion that her boss liked throwing problems at her, just to see her initial reaction. This one was easier than some, harder than others, and overall another chore she could have as well done without.

Stinex looked at her expectantly. "What do you think?"

"I think you must get some kind of perverse pleasure out of bedeviling me."

He laughed. "The older one gets, the harder it is to find fun things to do. Your solution?"

"Tee-my. Either that, or you-buh."

Stinex laughed again, louder. *Tee-my* came from TMAI, which was the acronym for Throw Money At It; *you-buh* was from UABH—Use A Bigger Hammer. Both were terms that builders and mechanics liked to toss around. A whole lot of problems could be solved if one but had enough credits to buy whatever was needed to fix them. And brute force had its place, too. Neither was workable here and she knew it, but she did like making the Old Man laugh.

"Seriously," he said.

Teela stood and walked to the holo of the sleep-space proposal.

Closed, it looked like nothing so much as a coffin, and she knew that she wasn't the only one on whom it would leave such an impression. She gestured, and a line of glowing stats and dimensions appeared.

"Come on, boss," she said. "You know the stats as well as I do. If we try to stuff five hundred civilians who haven't had the training or the acclimation to phobespace dimensions into things like this, the minders will have them coming out their ears. We overload the med section, the civilians don't do the work . . . there is no upside."

He nodded. "Yet we have to figure out a way, and since I am in charge, I'm making it your task."

Teela muttered a particularly vile curse word.

The difficulty was that they had X amount of space within which to house Y numbers of living beings. It was well known by builders throughout galactic space that many species would, without sufficient living space, become claustrophobic, often violently so. Humans were particularly susceptible to this, which was a problem, as something like 95 percent of the Death Star's projected crew were human or genetically very similar. There were ways of training human troops—combinations of hypnosis, drugs, and periods of acclimation—to offset this so that the problem would not be epidemic among the military contingent, but the civilians generally had no such training. Put folks into a sleep space the size of a coffin, and a great number of them would quickly develop psychological problems. Some nonhuman species, such as Gamorreans and Trandoshans, could not be made to enter such places voluntarily no matter what.

You didn't want someone welding a critical joint at a crucial juncture of an air-supply line to be half crazed from sleep deprivation because her fear of tight places had kept her awake for several cycles.

You'd think that on a station this large, the last problem they'd have would be living space. And yet some idiot who'd created the initial plans years before had thought that a chamber measuring a meter by a meter by two was sufficient room for somebody human-sized if all she or he was going to be doing in it was sleeping. Which is all one could possibly do in it; there wasn't room to do anything else. You had to crawl into the slot and, once inside, you couldn't sit up or even turn around. If you went in feetfirst, you came out headfirst, and vice versa.

So the question here was: How to give the tenants more room? At the very least, one needed a two-meter-square box, so that most of the occupants could stand erect without smacking their heads into the ceiling, or stretch out their arms without hitting the walls—and even that was marginal. You needed four times the room currently allotted. The problem was, where was it to come from? The available space in the civilian sectors had already been designated for other uses.

Stinex knew this as well as she did. And he most likely had an answer in mind. But it was always a test with him. It wasn't as if he wanted her to fail; she didn't think that at all. But she knew he took delight when she came up with solutions, and the more novel, the better.

This one, however, wasn't going to roll off the top of her head anytime soon. She'd have to think about it.

She said as much. He nodded. He was of the measure-twice-cut-once philosophy, and knew that it was better she considered the problem with due gravitas rather than just blurting out whatever came to mind.

"You have until tomorrow," he said. "Zero eight hundred."

G-12 BARRACKS, SECTOR N-SEVEN, CONSTRUCTION SITE, DEATH STAR

Nova ducked a wild swing, caught the attacking guard's arm, and spun him into the trooper behind him. Both men fell, but he had no time to rejoice—there were others coming for him, lots of others. He waded into a pair of guards and hit both at the same instant with a double punch, smashing their noses, then dropped and swept, upending another one, and before that one hit the deck he was up again firing a side kick into the belly of yet another—

He was aware that someone was fighting at his side, a human like himself, but huge, and just as good a fighter as he was. His nameless ally grabbed a guard by his front, lifted him off his feet and head-butted the man, knocking his helmet off, then dropped him, whirled, and took out two more with a spin kick.

"We're having fun now, aren't we?" the big man said. He laughed.

Nova had no idea where he was or why he was here, fighting an entire phalanx of stormtroopers. He didn't know who his mysterious ally was, either. He only knew that they were going to lose. They'd taken out a goodly number of guards, but there were still seven or eight of them standing, and the only reason Nova and the big man hadn't been roasted yet was because the fighting had been too close for the guards to use their blasters. That was about to change, however. The guards were backing away, going for their weapons. The game was about to be over.

Nova felt fear welling inside him. Not for himself; he knew he was a dead man fighting. Two against fifteen, the latter armed with blasters? A win was never in those cards. But it was vitally important that he prolong the fight as long as he could, to give the others—

To give them what? To give *who* what?

He didn't know. All he knew was that this would be his last dance, and he wanted it to be the best he could manage. Going up against impossible odds, going down swinging, using what he knew.

There were a lot worse ways to check out.

He saw the trooper draw down on him, saw the blaster's muzzle aimed at his head, knew he could never reach it in time—

Nova awoke, sitting up soaked in sweat, his heart hammering.

Blast!

The glow of the life-support monitors bathed the small room in dim blue and green lights, enough to see that Mantologo, the other NCO who was also off-shift, was sleeping like the dead, snoring lightly. It was just the two of them; the other two sergeants who shared the room were working.

Nova sat up on the edge of his rack, then slid off onto the cold floor plates. He padded into the refresher, a small unit that held a sink, a toilet, and a tight sonic shower pad. He splashed tepid water onto his face, toweled it off, looked at himself in the small mirror over the sink.

The same dream.

This was the fourth time he'd had it since he'd transferred onto the battle station. There were slight variations in it—sometimes he was fighting alone; sometimes there were more guards, sometimes fewer. The last time he'd had it he'd been crisped by the laser's energy beam and "died." That had been bad.

Maybe I should have the medics check me out, he thought.

Yeah. Right. And wouldn't *that* look good on his record? Bad dreams? *What kind of tough-guy martial arts expert are you, Stihl, going to see the doctor because of a dream?*

He shook his head. No. He wouldn't be doing that anytime soon.

Besides, it didn't happen that often. He was usually able to go back to sleep, and he never had a repeat of the dream on the same night. Nova shrugged. Most likely it was something that the filters would eventually strain out of the air. Nothing to get all in a lather about. He'd start practicing one of the mind-clearing meditations he knew before he went to bed. That might help.

If not, well, he could learn to live with it. But that sure wasn't his first choice.

30

CANTINA, DECK 69, DEATH STAR

"Come up with a name yet?" Rodo asked as they looked around the inside of the finished cantina.

"I think so." Officially it was going to be given a deck, area, and room number, but unofficially people liked descriptive names. Her Southern Underground establishment that had burned had been "the Soft Heart." This new one, while she didn't own it, was hers to run, and given where it was and the patrons who'd frequent it, Memah thought a variation on the old name would fit.

"I'm calling it the Hard Heart."

Rodo nodded. "Works for me."

The construction droids and a couple of Wookiee supervisors had worked quickly, but as far as she could tell they'd done a good job. Rodo had inspected bits and pieces and seemed satisfied. The basic layout was the standard military pub/cantina model she'd seen in dozens of places throughout what was now Imperial Space. The main room was more or less square, with the bar running nearly the length of the east wall. In the northeast corner was a small stage, just in case they were lucky enough to get live talent for skits or music, or in case some of the drunker patrons felt moved to render heartfelt versions of their favorite songs. Unisex/

unispecies refreshers were sited off the northwest wall, and a manager's office next to those. There were three entrances—one each on the south and north walls, plus an emergency exit on the west wall behind the bar.

Twenty tables filled the room, bolted to slides inset into the deck, each with half a dozen low-backed stools adjustable for height. If a large party came in, as many as five tables in any row could be scooted together into a larger module. The stools could be also moved, but normally were held in place with electric locks controlled by the tender from behind the bar. People could adjust seating as necessary for their size or number, but once all was in place the tender could flip a switch and lock the stools. That way, if the crowd got rowdy, they wouldn't be using the furniture on one another. Not that such a scenario was likely with Rodo on the job, but better safe than trashed.

The consumables were all behind the bar, on shelves running up the wall or underneath the counter—liquor, puffs, eats. Food was generally pull-tab heated modmeals; you could live on them, but that was about all. A cantina was not the place for fine dining.

The ceiling and tabletops had blowers and vacuums built in, and the table's units could be controlled either at the table or by tenders or servers at the bar. If the boys at table six were smoking pickled rankweed and producing billowing clouds of fragrant, intoxicating blue smoke, they could adjust the vacuums so it didn't drift like fog over the girls at table seven, who were licking up spirals of kik-dust, or the drinkers at table five chugging down steins of Andoan ale. The air scrubbers weren't 100 percent, of course, but effective enough.

The serving droid, SU-B713, aka Essyou, rolled up, looking very much like a large domed ale can. Essyou had been programmed with a feminine vocabulator: "Stocks are topped off, boss. We are ready to soak and smoke."

Memah smiled. Whoever had programmed SU-B713 must have had fun doing it. "Good. Run a final check on the credit interface, make sure all the readers are online."

A multicolored light array sparkled on the droid's computer screen. "Copy, money readers are green and mean. I'm going to go run internal systems checks and then defrag, keep my drive alive."

After the droid rolled away, Rodo said, "Professional comedians starving on the HNE circuit and we get a head server droid who does stand-up."

"Hey, if it keeps the troops happy."

"Yeah, but how am I going to get my workouts if the patrons all behave themselves?"

She grinned. "Come on, you can help me adjust the scrubber in the oversized 'fresher stall. We get a couple of Hutts or a Drack in there, we don't want the air circ to be overwhelmed."

With the last few tasks completed, they were probably as ready as they were going to get, Memah decided. Everything she could think of had been seen to as best as could be managed, but she was still a little nervous. A new cantina opening was a fluttery-gut thing at best. True, it was just a cantina, nothing huge in the cosmic scheme of the Galactic Empire, but when it was *your* cantina, you wanted it to go well. A station like this would be around for decades, and a good reputation out of the box never hurt business. She was, after all, getting at least a small piece of the action, and the better things went, the more she would make.

ISD *STEEL TALON*

"Systems reports are all normal, Admiral."

Motti nodded. This tiresome business on the ship had to be done, of course, but he wanted to get it done quickly and return to the station. He felt an almost superstitious concern when he was off-site for very long. Yes, Tarkin was the Moff, and he was in charge, but the real running of the station fell to Motti—as well it should. No man in the Imperial Navy had more of an interest and investment in the "Death Star" than Admiral Conan Antonio Motti.

The captain reporting saluted and departed, and Motti glanced up at the chrono inset into the bridge wall. In another hour he could leave, shuttle back to the station, and get back to important functions. Because, superstition aside, there were also practical, real-world reasons for Motti to be wary of long enforced absences from the station. The biggest being that he didn't trust General Bast or General Tagge.

Both were officers from the Imperial Army contingent, and technically both outranked Admiral Motti, despite the fact that the station was a navy venture. Tarkin, of course, being Grand Moff, was above the petty distinctions of service branches. He outranked everyone.

Motti feared Tagge the most. The House of Tagge was an old and wealthy family, well respected in the corridors of power back on Imperial Center. Tagge held sway with the Emperor, and he knew how to use it. He'd used it to land his current position as adviser to Tarkin.

Bast, Tagge's subordinate, was also a focus of worry. Although possessed of no personal aspirations beyond serving the Empire, he was loyal to both Tagge and Tarkin, and might become an obstacle at some future point.

Motti had tried to enlist Tarkin, subtly, in the idea that the man who controlled the battle station, once it was fully operational, would effectively be the most powerful person in the galaxy. It was true that the Emperor and Vader supposedly had that mystical connection with the Force, and Motti well remembered, as a young man, witnessing firsthand some of the astonishing accomplishments of the Jedi during the Clone Wars. But not even superhuman abilities could stand against a weapon that could blow a planet to pieces.

In any event Tarkin had either not picked up on the hints or, more likely, he had, but had chosen to keep his options open—and to himself. No matter. If Tarkin wanted to pretend loyalty to the withered old man who sat at the head of the Empire, that was fine—for now. Motti knew the ins and outs of the station better than anyone. And he had developed a certain loyalty among the senior officers. Eventually, the time would come. If Tarkin wasn't with him, then it was the Grand Moff's misfortune. The risks were high, but so were the stakes. To be the ultimate power in the galaxy—maybe the universe? Who could walk away from that, given the chance to have it?

31

HALF A LIGHT-SECOND FROM DOCK ONE-A,
EQUATORIAL TRENCH, DEATH STAR

"Pull up, Kendo!" Vil Dance said. He waited for the acknowledgment, but none seemed to be forthcoming. "Lieutenant Kendo, have you gone deaf?"

Vil's own TIE vibrated as he leaned into the sharp turn, port and "up," accelerating hard to avoid the robotic target drones grouped in a tight formation only six hundred klicks ahead of him.

"Pulling up, sir," Kendo finally said. Through the commset, the man's voice sounded—what? Laconic?

No, more like . . . *bored.*

Vil watched Kendo's ship peel away from the course that would have smashed him into the drones in another two heartbeats. *A sliver is as good as a parsec,* the old pilots' saying went, and while that might be true, following orders was more important.

A fact that new recruit Lieutenant Nond Kendo badly needed to learn.

The rest of the squad hung back a few hundred klicks, watching the newbie Kendo and the veteran Dance as they made their first warm-up run at the targets. They kept the chatter down, because it didn't take a petahertz processor to see that their squadron leader was ready to bite somebody's head off and spit it halfway to the Core, given this newbie's performance.

They all thought they were the hottest pilots to ever lay hands on a stick when they first arrived, every one of them. Vil had felt the same way. But he had learned pretty quickly that when the squad leader told you to do something there were reasons, and if you decided you knew more about flying than he did, it could cost you. Severely.

There was no way he was going to have anything less than perfect performances on his first few weeks at his new assignment. He'd shipped over from the *Steel Talon* to the Death Star only a couple of weeks before, and he wanted to make sure that the brass had no reason to rethink their decision.

This was a simple training exercise; each of the squad members got solo runs at the target drones, with Lieutenant Commander Dance behind them, looking over their shoulders. The first pass was to check range and distance. On the second, it was targeting lasers only—you painted the target, got the kill electronically, and the squad leader rated your run. Only on the third pass did you get to shoot for real. The drones—old freighters refitted for naval exercises—were heavily armored, and it would take a lot more than a blast from a single TIE to seriously damage them, so a dozen squads could hit them before they had to be repaired; the Imperial Navy thus saved a few credits. Where you put your shot was important, and you learned how to do it by full-speed runs and full-power guns—but only in steps and by the numbers.

Vil had seen Kendo's targeting lasers sparkle on the lead drone, and the practice shot had been pretty good to his eyes. He checked his ship recorder on the second run's completion, and it confirmed his opinion as they curved around for the third and final run.

Okay, fine, the kid could shoot. Which got him no slice at all in Vil's eyes—he was still a potential supercritical reaction.

"Listen up, Kendo, and pay close attention. You fire five seconds out, target the aft sensor array, and break off *immediately,* you copy?"

There was a two-second pause, then: "Ah, copy, Squad Leader. Request permission to target the aft pilot port. I can hit either gun—you call it."

"I am sure you can, Lieutenant, but that's not the *assignment* I just gave you, is it?"

Another pause. "No, *sir.*"

"Good. You're teachable, at least. Now bring it around and let's run it by the book."

"Copy."

That last word had an unmistakable ring of contempt. It was as if all the arrogance of a young, full-of-himself, simulator-trained pilot was compressed into it. *Hey,* it said, *I can do this! I don't need some gutless old squad commander I can fly circles around holding my hand!*

He couldn't help but grin. He had only three years on Kendo; nevertheless, sometimes he felt more like thirty years older than the newbies. He made no reply, just hung zero and watched Kendo make a sharp and well-executed half roll as he lined up for his run. The kid could fly. But could he do what he was told?

Ahead, the six drones sailed serenely through the blackness. They were programmed to activate defensive weapons—low-powered beams that were enough to rattle your teeth if one hit your fighter, but not strong enough to cause any real damage. Anybody paying attention could avoid these, but it took practice. In the real world, even a freighter could get lucky and blow you out of the void, and that's what training was for, to teach you how to avoid such mishaps. TIEs were fast, but they had neither life support nor shielding; a solid hit from any real weapon could crisp you like a mulch fritter.

Kendo accelerated—a hair faster than called for, but Vil held off calling him on it. *Let's see what you can do with it, kid . . .*

The newbie zipped toward the target. Vil checked his Doppler-ping. Seven seconds. Six . . . five . . .

"Shoot," Vil said.

No response.

"Kendo, shoot and pull up!"

But Kendo kept boring in, drawing closer to the lead drone.

The stupid mopak! He's going for the pilot port!

"Pull up, Lieutenant! That's an order! Pull up, *now*!"

The drone fired its port guns. The attenuated strobe hit Kendo's fighter. It wasn't enough to hurt him, but it must have been enough to startle him. He fired, flared to port—

Too late.

A quarter second sooner on the turn and he'd have missed, but as it was the TIE's starboard solar array hit the drone's nose. The impact tore the array from the fighter, the energy collection coils unraveling spasmodically, like a beheaded snake; the power lines sparked in cold vacuum as they were torn apart. The housing snapped and the impact spun the craft into a wild tumble.

Vil shoved the stick, feeling g-force slap him hard, knowing it was far too late to do anything but watch. "Kill the power! Kill the—!"

The fuel tank separated from the hull. The seal held, but the fuel line stretched, stretched . . . Vil could see it happen, slowly, as if time had stalled out . . .

The line snapped, spewing the radioactive gas in a sudden cloud toward the tumbling craft. Something—a shattered circuit board, perhaps—sparked. There was a soundless, eye-burning *flash*—

"Blast!" Vil shouted. "Blast, blast, *blast*!"

32

THE HARD HEART CANTINA, DECK 69, DEATH STAR

Ratua's identification wasn't bombproof, but short of a destructive analysis it would pass any casual scan by anybody—not, he marveled yet again, that anybody seemed to give a braz's behind enough to bother to ask to see it. From the look of this station, it would, when finished, be impregnable from outside attack; nobody was going to be able to throw much of anything at it that was going cause it any real problems. And yet here he was, walking around like it was his personal ship, ostensibly a contractor. Had he been a Rebel saboteur, he could have been busy causing a world of problems absolutely unchecked for weeks. How ironic was that?

Of course he wasn't a Rebel of any kind. He didn't have much use for politics, never had, couldn't see that he ever would. For a man in his, ah, profession, whoever was in charge—Empire, Alliance, his dear old uncle Tunia—didn't really matter. Unless Black Sun managed to take over, whoever ran the show would want to see Ratua stashed in a cell somewhere.

But he wasn't in a cell now; in fact, he had it pretty cushy. Plenty of credits stashed here and there, a fake identity that nobody questioned, even a legitimate, semi-private room, courtesy of a bribe to a poor clerk with a slight gambling problem. Everything a man might want.

Okay, almost everything. He could use a little female companionship, and he was working on that. A new cantina had just opened a few levels from where he roomed. He'd heard people talking about the place, and it sounded like fun, so he was on his way to check it out. He wasn't big on chems, but he didn't mind having an ale now and then to brighten up a dull evening.

The cantina, which had a small glowing sign that read THE HARD HEART above the double portal, seemed fairly busy. He stepped in through the air and caught the smells of a working pub—fragrant smoke, warm beverages, some body odors from patrons who should have showered before they came in. Mostly navy guys, some contractors, more males than females, which was hardly surprising. Most of the customers were human, or humanoid stock close enough that it was hard to tell the difference. Lighting was low enough to afford a kind of privacy, but not so dim it didn't offer a useful spectrum. His species could see a little deeper into the ultraviolet than some, but not as far into the infrared as others. Still, he wouldn't be bumping into the walls here.

The tables were mostly full, but there were a few empty spaces at the bar, which ran most of the right-hand wall from where he'd entered. Ratua moved through the crowded tables, being careful, with an ease born of long practice, not to bump anybody or loom into anyone's space unexpectedly. Surprise some folks and they'd shoot without a second thought, and military types were faster on the trigger than a lot of civilians.

But it looked like that wouldn't be a problem here. He noticed a sigil over the mirror behind the bar: U. Stood for "unarmed." That was a good idea. Navy guys seemed to enjoy wearing a sidearm everywhere they went; get them soused and angry, and stray blaster bolts could be a problem. Bad enough if you annoyed somebody to the point where he was ready to pull his weapon and cook you; even worse if you were minding your own business and you caught a bolt aimed at somebody else.

Ratua achieved the bar. There were a couple of droid servers working the floor, one behind the bar, and a most attractive Twi'lek woman with lovely teal-colored skin that showed wherever her short-sleeved coverall left her bare—places that added up to a satisfyingly large number.

"How may I serve you?" one of the droids said.

"House ale," he said.

"Two credits. Your debit number?"

"Cash." Ratua dropped two coins into the droid's cash drawer, which extruded from its torso to receive them. After a moment, the droid tendered a mug of amber-colored ale with a centimeter of frothy foam for a head.

"Thanks," Ratua said. The ale was cold, crisp, with a hint of something tart under the hops. Nice.

He turned slightly, mug in hand, and observed the room.

Next to the far wall, just to the right of the second entrance, stood a large human. He was watching the patrons without looking at anyone in particular. Ratua felt the man's gaze touch him and move on. This would be in-house security and, from the looks of him, not a fellow with whom you'd want to argue. Ratua had seen many violent men on many planets, many of whom were just naturally mean, and some who had a certain competent look about them that bespoke training and ability. This guy was one of those. Step crooked here and you'd find yourself unceremoniously displaced to the outside corridor. Start a real fuss and you would, clearly, soon wish you hadn't.

"That's Rodo," a female voice said from behind the bar. "He doesn't bite. He doesn't have to."

Ratua looked. The Twi'lek woman stood there, smiling at him. He nodded, saluted her with his ale. "And I would guess that a sensible person would not care to become the object of Rodo's irritation."

"In that, you would be correct. I'm Memah Roothes. I run the place."

Ratua nodded again. He considered giving her his fake identity, but for some reason he could not begin to understand, he went with his real name instead. "Celot Ratua Dil," he said. "I liked the joint when I walked in, and I like it even better now that we've met."

"Oh, a ladies' man." Her voice was amused, but there was also a hint of interest. At least, he hoped so.

"Not me, Memah Roothes," he replied. "Just one who appreciates good ale and beautiful females."

"Welcome to the Hard Heart, Celot Ratua Dil. You're a contractor?"

"Actually, I recently escaped from the prison planet. I'm just conning my way along."

She raised an appreciative eyebrow. "A sense of humor is worth a lot around here."

He looked around, noting the bright colors and decorations that softened but didn't completely disguise the hard angles and general severity of the architecture. Impressive as the Empire's new weapon was, it wasn't going to win any design awards. "I can see that. I guess there's more than one reason for calling it the Death Star. And," he added, "call me Ratua, please." He smiled and raised his mug again. "May I buy you a drink?"

"Too early to start this shift," Memah Roothes said. "But if you're still here in an hour or so, maybe I'll take you up on that."

Ratua grinned. "A herd of wild banthas couldn't drag me away."

She turned aside to serve a new customer, and he watched her, admiring the lithe way she moved. Oh, yes, he was definitely going to be spending some quality time in here.

33

OPERATING THEATER, MEDCENTER, DEATH STAR

The surgery was not going as well as it should have. Uli was getting frustrated.

"Get a pressor on that bleeder, stat," he said.

The surgical assistant, an MD-S3 droid, was a stationary unit built into the suite. It used a thin and flexible arm to clamp a field reader onto the cut vein; the flow of blood stopped. The droid adroitly sponged up the blood in the cavity, said, "Sponge four," aloud, removed the sponge from the endoscopic incision, and dropped the soaked pledge into the waste bin.

"Wipe," Uli said.

The droid used another of its multiple arms to run a sterile cloth over Uli's forehead, blotting away the perspiration that threatened to run into his eyes. There were anti-sweat films that could be sprayed on to temporarily keep perspiration at bay, but Uli didn't like them; most of them made him itch.

Carving humans and humanoids was generally no problem for him—he could do clone surgery in his sleep, might actually have done so a couple of times back when he was in the field, working long shifts and patching up scores of wounded every day. But natural genetics sometimes threw a sport at you, a body that wasn't built exactly the same way most of that particular species were normally constructed. The navy major here on the surgical table was one of those sports, and if Uli didn't figure out what he needed to know, and fast, the major could become an interesting statistic.

Three hours earlier, a forty-year-old human male from the planet Bakura had presented to the screening medic complaining of nausea, loss of appetite, low-grade fever, and pain in his abdomen. Symptoms were classically consistent with an inflamed appendix. The medical examiner made the diagnosis and sent the patient along for surgery.

Normally a surgical droid would have handled an operation like this, quickly and efficiently. But the battle station was still understaffed and underequipped. So Uli had shrugged and scrubbed. It should have been a routine appendectomy, the kind of ho-hum surgery any first-year resident could do one-handed. Except when Uli shoved an endoscope into the major to find the inflamed appendix, he encountered a slight problem:

It wasn't there.

At least, it wasn't where it was supposed to be. This was impossible, but Uli didn't waste time questioning the image on the screen. "Do a tomographic axial scan and find that appendix," he told the MD droid.

"Yes, Doctor," the droid replied. Its imaging scanners hummed. A thin green line appeared and moved from the patient's groin to his chest, mapping the length and width of the scan. "TA scan complete."

"Show me."

A hologrammic projection, life-sized, appeared over the patient, floating in the pale bluish glow of the OT's UV sterility lamps.

Uli looked. "I still don't—oh, there it is. What the frip is it doing there?"

It was a rhetorical question, but the droid answered it anyhow. "Cross-checking against my datafiles indicates an anatomical abnormality, Doctor."

"Brilliant." Uli shook his head. Fates save him from literal-minded droids. But there was no time to be annoyed at the MD-S3. The appendix was swollen to what looked like four times normal size, though its unusual location made it hard to see even though he now knew where it was. His mind ran through various choices. He'd have to open the man up a bit more, or get an endoscopic arm in to snip and glue . . . yeah, that would be the best way. Least invasive.

"Extrude a number six endoscope with an SS clamp and seal off that appendix."

"Yes, Doctor."

Another thin appendage snaked from the droid's housing. This one bore a two-tined fork. The upper one was a self-cleaning cam lens, while the lower tine, five centimeters longer, held an open surgical-steel clamp. The droid deftly inserted the arm into the patient. The holo appeared over the man, showing the fork's progress.

Unerringly, the droid positioned the clamp at the base of the inflamed appendix and then snapped it shut. A second arm, an endosnipper, slid in and, with an actinic flash of laser light, removed the appendix. A vacuum attachment sucked out any possible contaminants. The droid removed the surgical arms and tissue.

Uli breathed easier. "Do a scan of the appendix for any pathogens and order antigen motes effective for anything you find."

"Yes, Doctor."

"Send me a copy of the lab work and prescriptions."

"Yes, Doctor."

"Okay. Close him up and have an orderly take him to the ward."

"Yes, Doctor."

Uli turned away from the patient. Before such things as axial scans and precision surgical droids, they might have lost this patient, digging around looking for a lost appendix that was about to pop. But the major would survive, and likely go on to slaughter hundreds or maybe thousands more people before the war ended.

The irony of it all wasn't hard to see.

SUPERLASER FIRE CONTROL, THETA SECTOR, DEATH STAR

"So whaddya think, Chief?" Mekkar Doan slapped the main control console.

Tenn Graneet grinned at his fellow petty officer. "Oh, it's a first-class craft, right enough."

The two men were standing in a small nexus chamber overlooking the eight radiating particle accelerator tubes designed to feed the superlaser beam. The walls were covered with readout meters, fluctuating bar graph monitors, banks of controls, and other equipment. Much of it was beyond CPO Tenn Graneet's knowledge, but that was all right. He didn't need to know everything about *how* it worked. He just had to be able to work it.

Chief Doan laughed. "You think you can shoot it, once everything's hooked up?"

Tenn gave him a fake astonished look. "*You* shot it, didn't you? When I can't hit anything you can, I'll retire."

"You read the specs?"

Tenn nodded. "Yeah. It could be a planet cracker, if it works like it's supposed to."

"Engineers say it will."

"Engineers." Tenn put a considerable amount of sarcasm in the word.

"Yeah, I hear that. But they're pulling out all the stops on this baby." He rubbed his hand on the control console. "Any problem they had, they threw enough money at it to bury it to the rails. We'll have the power, no worries there."

"And if somebody didn't forget to dog a bolt tight, maybe it won't blow us all to the other side of the Rim."

"Hey, I'm telling you, word is the worst piece of gear on it is still triple redundant."

"I had a nephew who was a deck monkey on the *Battle Lance,*" Tenn said.

Doan's smile faded. "Yeah. I knew a couple of guys shipped on her. It was a freak accident."

"Maybe. A backfire could overload the HM reactor and turn this station into radioactive dust, too."

Doan shook his head. "Never happen. They got the Emperor himself looking over their shoulders on this one. They won't frip it up."

Tenn shrugged. There was little point in worrying about equipment failure. If the thing worked, it would prove the Death Star to be, as Tarkin had put it in one of his many inspirational addresses to the station's population, "The ultimate power in the galaxy." If it didn't work—well, the hypermatter reactor was capable of generating an energy burst equivalent to the total weekly output of several main-sequence stars; if anything went wonky, it wasn't likely he'd be around long enough to notice. Nor would anyone else.

"Yeah, well," he replied, "if they can build it so it holds together, I'll shoot it."

"Let me show you how it works. You and your team will be practicing on the simulator until the real thing here's online."

As Doan explained the intricacies of the sequencing relays, Tenn found it somewhat difficult to concentrate on what the other man was saying. He wasn't sure why. After all, he'd dreamed of this moment for months: the day he'd finally stand in the control chamber of the superlaser and be officially given command of it. Even though construction wasn't finished yet, you couldn't tell it from in here. He listened to the susurration of the klystron tubes and thermistor couplers, smelled the astringent scent of insulation lube, felt the breath of conditioned air adjusted to a constant twenty degrees, and wondered why he was not content.

There was only one reason that seemed remotely feasible.

The *Battle Lance.*

His nephew, Hora Graneet, had been a navy spacer on the *Imperial*-class Star Destroyer Mark II class vessel, which had been selected for a shakedown cruise testing one of the improved prototype hypermatter reactors. Tenn didn't know the specifics of what had happened, and didn't have anything close to the math needed to understand it anyway. He knew that hypermatter existed only in hyperspace, that it was composed of tachyonic particles, and that charged tachyons, when constrained by the lower dimensions of realspace, produced near-limitless energy. How this "null-point energy" had become unstable he didn't know. He only knew it had been powerful enough to turn an ISD-II and its crew of thirty-seven thousand people into floating wisps of ionized gas in a microsecond.

So? Don't tell me you're scared, *Graneet. You knew the risks. This is a war, declared or not. Wars have casualties.*

No. It wasn't that. It wasn't even so much that Hora had been a favorite nephew, or that the younger Graneet had admired his uncle so much that he'd enlisted, which made Tenn feel a considerable amount of responsibility for his death. It was the thought of that much power, and the possibility of it becoming uncontrollable. Again Tenn surprised himself. He'd never been overly concerned about fallible technology before. His was not to reason why; he was the trigger man. And he was being handed the biggest gun in the galaxy—with the safety off.

But was he capable of wielding such power wisely?

Was anyone?

34

DOCKING BAY 6, ALPHA SECTOR, DEATH STAR

Daala came down the ramp looking every centimeter the Imperial admiral. She didn't just walk, she *swept,* and it was a joy to watch her stride. Strong, smart, ambitious, dedicated, funny, *and* beautiful—what more could a man possibly want in a partner?

Well, a bit more proximity would be good. But they were both creatures of duty, and Tarkin knew that wasn't apt to change anytime soon; certainly not until the battle station was finished and unlimbered. Perhaps not even then. He knew that Daala looked upon him with much favor, but the relationship had always been secondary to her career. He understood that. More; he admired it. He wouldn't want a woman who thought any less of herself. That was the ultimate paradox, of course.

"Grand Moff Tarkin. So good to see you again, sir."

Tarkin held his smile in check. One had to be proper about such things out in plain sight. "Admiral Daala. The pleasure is mine. I trust your trip was uneventful?"

"Yes, sir. Nothing untoward whatsoever."

"Excellent. Allow me to show to your quarters. Your suite, as it happens, is right next to mine."

He saw a flicker of anticipation cross her face—hardly enough to notice unless one was standing right in front of her. In a very quiet voice, without moving her lips, she said, "How convenient, Wilhuff."

He couldn't keep from smiling, despite his best efforts. "This way, Admiral." He extended one hand to show her the direction.

She gave him a military nod, and they moved off past the honor guard. As they walked, she stared about the hangar, impressed. "I knew it would be huge, but the reality of it hadn't quite come home."

"Save your awe for when it's finished and operational. Which will be quite soon now."

"The Rebel Alliance won't know what hit them."

"Oh, they'll know, my dear. Everyone will know. That's the point."

She had cut her hair shorter than when last they had been together. It was flattering on her, but then, he'd never seen her with a hairstyle that wasn't flattering. There weren't really any regulations about how female admirals should dress or groom themselves—Daala was the only one, after all, and who would dare to tell her?

She had risen on merit alone, but certainly her ascent to the command ranks had caused some speculation about her relationship with Tarkin and how that might have smoothed the way. Nobody speculated about it in earshot of him, of course. Not anymore, because those foolish few who'd done so had had their ashes scattered to the four solar winds. Tarkin had not reached the unique rank he held by allowing his enemies any quarter whatsoever. Yes, Daala had been his protégée, and yes, he had opened doors for her a bit sooner than she might have managed on her own, but she had made flag command without his help. There were plenty of male admirals unfit to polish her boots.

They soon reached the door to her quarters. "Shall we go inside and discuss this further?" he murmured to her.

"By all means, Grand Moff Tarkin."

Before the door had slid completely shut behind them, she was in his arms.

LIBRARY AND ARCHIVES, DECK 106, SECTOR N-ONE, DEATH STAR

The library aboard the battle station wasn't the biggest Atour had ever seen by any means. He had done his apprenticeship in the Baobab Archives on Manda, although these days he didn't deem it exactly prudent to highlight that fact on his résumé. And from there he had gone on to be the archivist of such repositories as the Dorismus Athenaeum on Corellia and the Holorepository on the wheelworld Arkam 13. The latter was known for having the largest collection of lore on the Old Republic outside the Temple.

It wasn't the most exciting of lives, that of an archivist, but it was one that suited him well. He had not, as many supposed, always been introspective and scholarly; as a young man he'd fought for the Janissariad in the Balduran Civil War. The experience had left a foul taste in his mouth for any and all forms of centralized government. Disgusted with politics, Atour Riten had retreated, in soul if not body, into the misty past. It was a decision he'd never regretted.

The Death Star Library—as his mind insisted on naming it—was supposed to eschew the use of holobooks, tapes, and 'crons and rely instead on phononic lattice storage. This would allow storage of a huge amount of information in a very small space. Part of Atour's brief in this new job was to supervise the droids scanning information from other media into lattice form. Even on something the size of the Death Star, space was at a premium—at least for such things as data storage.

Though he'd seen bigger and better, the amount of data accrued was impressive nonetheless. The files were extensive, the retrieval systems were thick with memory to speed up downloads, and the broadcast-to-reader circuitry was top-notch. It was a pity that most people didn't actually go to libraries anymore, not when they could sit in the comfort of their own quarters and access files electronically. Want to read the new hot interstellar caper novel, or the latest issue of *Beings* holozine? Input the name, touch a control, and *zip*—it's in your datapad. Need to study the history of winged intelligent species? No more difficult than inputting search parameters, then scanning the bibliographic references and choosing a place to begin.

There were, of course, old-fashioned beings who would still actually trundle down to where the files were. On some worlds the most ancient libraries kept books—actual bound volumes of printed matter—lined up neatly on shelves, and readers would walk the aisles, take a volume down, sniff the musty-dusty odor of it, and then carry it to a table to leisurely peruse.

There weren't many of those readers left, and they were growing rarer all the time—this Atour knew from experience. But there were some who still knew how to actually turn a page—and for those who were willing to do so, the rewards could be great indeed.

Of course, Atour was no Luddite antiquarian who grumbled and inveighed against the modern world. On the contrary, he'd been praised by experts as a slicer of excellent quality. And it had served him well more than once to have knowledge he wasn't supposed to. One didn't normally think of the data storage and information retrieval business as being particularly cutthroat, but it must be remembered that, in Palpatine's Empire, every business was cutthroat. And if one was the head librarian and archivist, such files were accessible, even without high-level clearance. He hadn't spent a lifetime among the stacks without learning a trick or two.

Thus it was that Riten found himself looking at a set of plans for this battle station, aka the Death Star. He was no engineer to understand all the schematics, and the documents were fat with technical jargon, but anyone with even a smattering of a general education could see the wonder of the place. It was a monster in size, and in intent, as well as in killing ability—or it would be once they assembled all of the weaponry and got it operational.

Fascinating material . . .

For more than a few years Atour Riten had, when he discovered such interesting and potentially useful files, copied them and logged them into a personal folder that was virtually impossible to slice. In addition to the best military wards and pyrowalls, the folder was also protected by a random number generated by a quantum computer, said number being forty-seven digits long. Moreover, the program would shift each digit one value lower or higher every six standard hours, and only somebody with the code to access the program running it could keep track of this shift—one had to know the date and hour the program generated the number in order to follow the sequence. It was a slow and unwieldy process, hardly suitable for files that needed to be accessed with any frequency, but workable for him.

Once the files were copied, he needed a safe place to keep them. For some time, ever since he had run the military base's library there, he had sent the files to Danuta, a planet of no great import or value save for its mildly strategic location. It was easy enough to piggyback the coded information onto an Imperial message comm or even a holocomm—another trick he had learned in his years of accessing military secrets.

Someday, if he lived long enough, Atour intended to write a history of the times that had begun with the Clone Wars and run through the current conflict between the Empire and the Rebel Alliance. Of course he had to wait and see who won before he could get to that part, but he was always on the lookout for research material. The plans for this battle station, upon which the war-in-progress might well hinge, certainly seemed worthy of a place in that research. He'd have to write the account under a pseudonym, of course. No matter which side won, they would want to have words with the author of such a tome, which would hold both sides up to a bright light that would flatter neither. Likely the information would be suppressed, but that didn't matter. There would always be copies of it floating around, and beings who wished to know its contents. Knowledge was like that—once it was ushered into the light, putting it back into the shadows was difficult, if not impossible.

Atour leaned back in his formchair, which offered a silent adjustment to his contours. Had to give the Empire its due—when they wanted to, they could provide first-class environments. His office was testimony to that.

He gestured at the computer's cam, moving his fingers in a pattern that said *Wipe all records of this access.* The holo blinked once, and it was done. Now he needed to find a comsig leaving the station, and link and route his stolen files to it. Communications were restricted at this base, of course, but if you went high enough up the chain of command, there was always someone who was allowed to talk to someone else. And since any officer foolish enough to risk his career by stealing a ride on a superior officer's communications probably wouldn't have been assigned here in the first place, the techs most likely didn't bother to look too closely at the messages they were generating. And even if they did, they wouldn't see Atour's addition if they didn't know exactly where and how to look.

The chink in the armor of powerful beings was that they believed power made them smarter, as well as blaster-proof. It had been Atour Riten's experience that neither of these things was true.

He wove a complicated two-handed pattern at the computer cam, which began scanning comm frequencies, looking for a ride. Eventually, it would find one. There was no hurry.

Meanwhile, it was time for lunch.

35

EXERCISE SUITE, EXECUTIVE LEVEL, DEATH STAR

Motti prided himself on keeping fit. Stripped to a speed-strap and drenched in his own sweat, he was working out in the executive officers' heavy-gravity room, which he'd set at a three-g pull. Just standing in such a field was an effort. Every movement required three times the energy it normally did. Even jumping was risky—land at a bad angle and you could break an ankle. Trip and fall and the impact could fatally crack your skull.

Motti picked up a trio of denseplast workout balls, each the size of his fist. Anywhere else on the station they would weigh about a kilo each; in the HG room they were three apiece. Juggling them caused his muscles to quickly burn. His shoulders, arms, hands, back—all were protesting the effort as he tossed and caught the balls. He could manage the three most basic patterns: the cascade, which was the easiest; the reverse-cascade, a bit harder; and the shower, in which the balls all circled in the same direction. If he dropped one it was usually during the shower pattern, and the first thing he had learned when juggling in the HG room was to move his feet out of the way quickly if he dropped a ball. Three kilos moving three times faster than normal could easily break bones or crush toes.

Today, despite the burning in his muscles, he was a machine, moving perfectly, and the balls stayed aloft, moving in sync without any flaw. He was aware that a couple of other senior officers were watching him from one corner of the room, and he smiled to himself. Being fit was important. If you were physically stronger than the men around you, it made them look upon you with the most basic level of respect: *Cross me, and I can break you in half.* He was not, nor would he ever be, some fat and out-of-shape formchair officer who'd wheeze and run out of breath if he had to climb a flight of steps.

He began to juggle the three heavy balls faster, shortening the arcs, bringing his elbows in closer to his body, tightening the pattern. The balls, which had been flying over his head, settled lower, and persistence of vision made them almost look as if they were a wheel rotating on an axle in front of him. Soon he would be able to add another one to the circle and juggle four. It might seem a trivial thing, but it wasn't. It was a metaphor for how to live one's life. A man could do almost anything he wished, if he wanted it enough.

THE HARD HEART CANTINA, DEATH STAR

Sergeant Stihl didn't spend much time in pubs or cantinas. Now and again he'd go, mostly to show he was a regular trooper who didn't mind having a couple of brews with the other men, but not all that often. An evening spent in a cantina would be one in which he could have been working on his fighting art or reading some epistemological treatise. Also, mind-altering substances did bad things for your motor skills, and it was hard to overcome the inertia of a few ales or some brain-fogging chem once you were done. Much easier then to sit on a soft chair and watch the entertainment holos than to go work out, which was definitely not the road to mastery.

One of the troopers in his unit had gotten engaged, however, and the shift had an excuse to celebrate, so Nova had gone along, since the man was also a student of his.

It was a nice enough joint. Clean, well ventilated, the crowd noisy but not over the top. Obviously the place to be off-hours in this sector, as it was standing room only. And the ale was cold.

He noticed a security guy watching things, and after a few minutes of surreptitiously watching him watch the crowd, Nova had marked him as a player. He stood head and shoulders over most of the crowd, but he wasn't dependent just on his heft—that was obvious. The man was a fighter. Nova didn't know which art he favored or what kind of combat moves he had, but there was definitely something there. After so many years of dancing the dance, you could tell, just by the way a man stood or leaned against a wall. It was subtle—there was an attention to balance and stances, a way of shifting weight that, if you knew what to look for, was easy to see. This guy could take care of himself and anybody else in here who might want to give him trouble as well.

Except for Sergeant Stihl, of course.

He smiled into his ale. It was only his second in two hours, and there was still three-quarters of the purple liquid left. He'd already burned up the alcohol from the first mug, and he had no intention of continuing to drink enough to dull his wits. His days of getting hammered in public were long past—what was the point in having skills in a martial art if you were too fuzz-headed to use them when the need arose? He'd once seen a Bunduki player, a guy who had won top-level matches, get soused at a cantina in a dirtside dive. The player had gotten into a tiff with a local, and because he was drunk had gotten his butt thumped pretty good—despite his skill. Nova wasn't going to find himself in that position, not if he could help it. And he didn't go to cantinas to fight—that was just plain stupid. You never knew who had a vibroblade tucked away in a back pocket, or a couple of friends who would jump in unexpectedly to help out when you squared off.

Nova was to wonder, later, if there really was anything to the metaphysical theory that thinking such thoughts gave them a higher probability of actually occurring. Maybe if he'd been thinking about doing his laundry or herding workers into the mess hall, the guy walking past wouldn't have stumbled at that moment. Maybe. Or maybe it had something to do with Blink.

Blink was his private name for a knack he had for anticipating things, particularly movements of opponents. Many times, during a fight, he would know somehow, *before* the movement began, that the other guy was going to throw an elbow or a kick. Of course, being able to anticipate your rival's next move was the essence of good fighting, but Blink went beyond that. Not even years of practice could tell you, for example, if an antagonist was about to activate a hidden portable confounder, a sensory scrambling device that could momentarily throw you off-balance. Or if another fighter was coming around the corner as backup to the first. But these things, and others, had happened to Nova. And he'd known. Somehow.

Whatever the reason, he saw the man, who was carrying a platter of mugs filled with ale he had collected at the bar, catch his boot on a stool leg, and because the stool was locked down, the leg didn't move. The guy started to fall, directly toward Nova who, without thinking, stood, reached out with his left hand, and tapped the falling man on the shoulder, deflecting him to the side so that instead of dropping the platter of mugs into Nova's lap, the man fell past him half a meter to the right.

The mugs flew, showering fizzy ale in gouts every which way. The platter hit the floor well ahead of their former owner, who managed to break his fall with his hands. Then, big, drunk, and really irritated, he shoved away from the floor, came up, and spun to face Nova.

"You okay, friend?" Nova asked.

"No, I'm *not* milking okay! What did you trip me for?"

Nova shook his head. "I didn't. You caught your foot on the stool right there."

"You calling me a liar?"

"Just telling you what I saw."

"You tripped me, then you *shoved* me!"

"Nope. I just kept you from landing on top of me. Sorry. It was a reflex."

The man balled his hands into fists. His face, already red, got more so. Nova sighed. He knew the signs. Any second now . . .

The man stepped in and threw a hard, straight, right-lead punch at Nova's face. Nova turned his head, brought his left hand up to deflect the fist a bit, and with the open palm of his right hand smacked the attacker on the left temple, staggering him. Before the guy could do more than blink, Nova switched hand positions and thumped the heel of his left hand into the man's right temple. The man fell again, not unconscious, but not far from it.

"You about done, Sergeant?" came a soft voice from behind him.

Nova had felt, rather than seen, the big security man come up from his right side.

"I think so." Nova turned to find the bouncer looming before him.

"Teräs käsi," the bouncer said. It was not a question.

"Yep."

The big man nodded. "Highline, mirror-tools. Nice. I'm Rodo."

"Nova Stihl."

A couple of heartbeats passed.

"You were a little slow getting here," Nova said.

"Not really. I saw you come in. I didn't think you'd need any help." Rodo looked down at the dazed man.

"And you wanted to see."

Rodo shrugged. "Sure. Wouldn't you?"

Nova grinned. "Oh, yeah."

Rodo's grin matched his own. "Next ale is on me."

"I think I'm done drinking."

"Yeah, that's why I offered." He paused, then added, "There's a guy teaches teräs käsi classes downlevels."

"That would be me."

"Maybe I might drop by?"

"I'd like that. You're welcome anytime."

Rodo bent and, with what looked like almost no effort, lifted the still-confused man to his feet. "What say we call it a night and head home, hey, friend?"

The man nodded. "Yeah. I'm very tired. What happened?"

"You tripped."

"Oh, wow."

Nova Stihl waited until Rodo had the drunk firmly in hand before he sat again. He noticed that the other troopers at the tables were looking at him with a certain amount of . . . something . . . in their faces. Wonder? Amazement? Respect? Fear?

All of the above, probably.

"Next round is on me," Nova said. "To celebrate the union of Sergeant Dillwit here and his poor unlucky betrothed."

The men laughed, and that was the end of that.

Memah Roothes was preparing a drink made up of ten different-colored layers of liquid, and it required some precision to keep the fluids from bleeding into one another. She had the first seven poured into a cylindrical crystal as long and as big around as Rodo's forearm. The last three layers were the hardest, but as long as she kept a steady hand, she'd manage. It was a pain in the glutes manipulating the various densities, but the concoction, which would serve four, went for fifty credits, so it was worth the five minutes it took. When it was finished, Memah sat back and looked at it. Perfect.

Rodo appeared at the end of the bar as the server droid collected the drink, called, for some reason Roothes had never understood, "A Walk in the Phelopean Forest," and wheeled away with it. "Nice work," he said.

"Thanks. You, too. I noticed you didn't kick the sergeant out?"

"Nah. Pure self-defense. I'd have done the same."

"Went down pretty fast."

"Yeah. Guy is really good—system-class fighter, easy. Didn't expect to find somebody like that out here in the middle of nowhere."

"Why not? It's a warship, right?"

"Yes, but the really good ones are either out in the killing fields *using* the stuff or back in civilization teaching it to recruits. First one is okay, second is a waste. Here, it's just unusual."

Memah shook her head. "Males. Always with the violence. You want to go a couple of rounds with this guy, don't you?"

Rodo grinned. "I wouldn't mind. You want to stay sharp, you got to hone yourself against the best you can find. Just friendly competition. Nobody gets hurt—well, not hurt too bad."

Memah shook her head again.

Rodo drifted away.

Even though she was busy, she caught a glimpse of Green-Eyes sitting over in the corner, sipping an ale. Now, there was an interesting male. A Zelosian, he'd said; not a species she'd ever run into before. She'd warped the HoloNet a little looking for general data on his kind, and found surprisingly little. They seemed to be a strange genetic mixture of plant and animal, unable to crossbreed with any other humanoids—not that she was overly concerned about that, as she saw no urgent need for younglings in her future.

She found him oddly compelling. Yes, he had an easy smile and a relaxed manner, plus he wasn't hard to look at, but it was more than that. There was a kind of . . . resonance, if that was the right word. As though they had known each other for a long time, even though they had only met recently.

He pretended to be a moderately successful contractor, but whatever he was, that wasn't it. She'd had Rodo do a little checking on him as well, and as far as this station was concerned, no such person as Celot Ratua Dil existed. Which meant he was a rogue of some kind, working the angles, and her heart had sunk when she'd learned that.

She shook her head as she filled half a dozen mugs with black Mon Calamari seaweed mash and she pondered, not for the first time, the question: Why couldn't she find a decent, hardworking, ordinary kind of male who wanted to grow old together? Why was she always attracted to the bad boys, the ones without two honest credits to rub together, the ones with no real prospects?

Memah sighed as she prepared another drink. Ah, well . . . if it wasn't for kissing bad boys, she'd never get any kissing done at all. Not that she'd gotten a lot of even that lately.

She put the drinks up. "Order up!" she said.

The server droid rolled up to collect the tray.

Well, she was going to be stuck here for another year-and-some before her contract ran out. Maybe Green-Eyes could help the time go easier.

36

SUPERLASER SIMULATOR, THETA SECTOR, DEATH STAR

CPO Tenn Graneet had been assured that the mock-up of the battery control room for the superlaser was an exact replica of the as-yet-unfinished one, down to the last rivet. Every function that was to be found in the soon-to-be-working ultimate weapon was replicated in the simulator. The gunnery team would spend long hours training at the mock-up's consoles, programming the complicated firing procedure into their brains, so that when the actual control room became operational, switching to the real thing would be as easy as falling off a bantha.

Which was a good thing, because the superlaser battery wasn't a simple installation. It was, in fact, far more complex than any gun control in any ship in the Imperial Navy that Tenn had ever encountered. There were banks of lighted switches color-coded for each of the eight tributary sub-beams; monitors double-stacked around the wall that showed every function of the hypermatter reactor and generator; sensor readings from the heart of the reactor to the field amplifiers, the inducer, the beam shaft . . . taken all together, it made a heavy destroyer's biggest gun look like a child's toy. Each component had to be precisely tuned and focused. If the primary beam focusing magnet was off a nanometer, the tributary beams would not coalesce, and there was a good chance of imbalance explosions in the beam shaft if the tributaries weren't pulsed in at *exactly* the proper time and in the proper sequence. The techs and engineers tended to wave that possibility off as too small to worry about. One chance in a hundred million, they said. Tenn wasn't swallowing that. When it came to something this potentially deadly, no odds were long enough. It was true that there were automatic fail-safes, but Tenn—and any chief worth his salt—trusted them just about as far as he could stroll in hard vac. Some of those engineers lived in skyhooks so far up past the clouds that they'd forgotten what the ground looked like. If a gun's designer wasn't willing to stand next to it when it was being tested, well, Tenn saw no reason to be there, either.

Triggering a monster like this wasn't like pressing the firing stud on a blaster. At optimum it would take fifteen or twenty seconds from the given command to fire until the main beam was ready to be unleashed, and they hadn't gotten close to that yet. Half the time during firing simulations they couldn't balance the phase harmonics enough to shoot the primary beam at all. And even if the magnetic ring was precisely stabilized, all it would take was one of the tributaries warbling so much as a microhertz out of phase, and the others would desynchronize as well. The result would be a feedback explosion along the beam shaft and back to the main reactor that would turn the battle station into an incandescent plasma cloud in less than a single heartbeat, and the Empire thanks your family very much for your sacrifice.

That wasn't going to happen on his watch, Tenn vowed. By the time the actual battery was operational, Tenn expected his crew to be running the program smooth as lube on polished densecris plate. But they weren't there yet. Not even within a parsec of close.

Fortunately, they had plenty of time to practice. The crew, half of whom Tenn had swiped from his old unit with help from his new commander, were sharp enough, but it took twelve people working the battery to properly light the big gun and make it go bang, and every one of them had to nail his or her part dead-on. There was no margin for error. So far, in the first dozen run-throughs, they had been able to fire the primary beam five times within a minute of the order. Once they'd taken two minutes, and four times they hadn't been able to focus the tributaries properly at all, resulting in complete failures to fire. One time the computer had registered a late minor beam-warble that would have resulted in an automatic shutdown of the primary power feed to avoid damage, which meant it would have taken an hour to get back up for ignition sequencing. And wouldn't *that* be a delightful job, recalibrating everything with the land batteries of a Rebel base spewing hard energy at you?

In addition to the real problems, there had been a simulated major run malfunction with multiple beam-warbles and disharmonic phasing. The computer, in theory, could have shut that one down in time, but Tenn thought that report was optimistic. In a real situation, with a fully powered weapon, that one would more than likely have turned a whole lot of beings, equipment, and everything else into sizzling ions racing toward the edges of the galaxy.

"All right, boys, let's see if we can get it right this time. I want everything by the numbers and clean. Throw the wrong switch, you are on kitchen patrol for a week. Too slow on the phase-balance, better get some nose plugs, because you *will* be scrubbing the trash compactors until they sparkle. Drop a reading on the inducers, and you'll find yourself shoveling out the animal pens until you smell like the south end of a northbound reek. Are we clear?"

"Yes, Chief!" came the chorus of replies.

"Say again, I didn't hear you!"

"Yes, Chief!"

He smiled under the blast helmet, then grimaced as a rivulet of sweat ran into one eye. The milking headgear would be less than useless if the gun backfired, but it would make a dandy torture device for interrogating real spies. True, it was navy policy that gunners wear them, but whoever'd designed these black buckets hadn't had to leave one on for a whole shift. They just made the job harder by restricting peripheral vision and essentially guaranteeing that you spent most of your shift clonking your head on pipes, struts, bulkheads, and the like. They were also hot and stuffy. Tenn was pretty sure some boot-head had designed them for looks and not function. When nobody was around, he let the men take the helmets off and breathe a bit, but given the nature of this sim battery, some by-the-book officer was always dropping by to gawk.

"We have an order to commence primary ignition," he said. "Commence . . . *now*!"

He tapped the timer control and watched the seconds flick past as the chorus of reports began:

"Hypermatter reactor level one hundred percent. Feeds on tributaries one through eight are clean . . ."

"Primary power amplifier is online . . ."

"Firing field amplifier is green . . ."

"We are go on induction hyperphase generator feed . . ."

"Tributary beam shaft fields in alignment . . ."

"Targeting field generator is lit . . ."

"Primary beam focusing magnet at full gauss . . ."

Tenn watched the timer. So far, so good. But then:

"We have a hold on tributary five. Repeat, we have *orange* on T-five! Disharmonic in the subrouter."

"Fix it, mister!" Tenn said. He looked back at the timer. Twenty-four seconds . . . "Get it straight right milking *now*!"

The sweating T-5 tech tapped buttons, moved sliders, pivoted shift levers. "Reharmonizing . . . the warble is flattening out—in five, four, three, two . . . T-five is clean, we are *go* on T-five!"

Tenn scanned his board. The last orange light blinked off, and they were green straight across. He thumbed the safety button on the shifter above his head and pulled it down.

"Successful primary ignition achieved," the computer said.

There was a cheer from the crew, and Tenn smiled. "Thirty-eight seconds. That's a new record, even with the glitch, but we can do better." He took off his helmet. "Restart it. If we break thirty seconds before swing or third shift does, I'm buying the beer."

They cheered, and fell to work with a will. Once again, he smiled. Nothing seemed to motivate a crew like the lure of free beer.

37

SIM SEVEN, DELTA SECTOR, DEATH STAR

Vil Dance was flying like a man possessed by an unfettered spirit, as well as he had ever piloted a TIE fighter, really sharp, he knew it—and it still wasn't good enough. No matter how he jinked or stalled or dipped, the attacker was right there behind him! He couldn't shake him—the other ship was like some impossible shadow, mimicking his every move.

Vil did a power stall, but the bogey stayed right behind him as if he were welded to Vil's TIE. He rolled, went vertical—and the tail was still there. He hadn't fired a shot—yet.

"All right," he muttered through clenched teeth. "Let's burn some g's, my friend." He shoved the TIE into an almost ninety-degree break to starboard, nearly blacking out from the overpowering tug of gravity as he pulled at least four g's. And the mysterious black fighter not only matched him, but made it look easy. Vil could almost hear his nemesis behind him yawning. If he could shake him loose long enough to turn, at least he might manage a last-ditch maneuver that pilots called a WBD: We Both Die. He'd take the son of a raitch with him.

But it was too late for that. Abruptly his pursuer's ion cannons flared. White light filled the cockpit, and as it blinded Vil, he heard:

"Your ship has been destroyed." The flight simulator's voice wasn't supposed to have any inflection, but Vil was sure he heard a smug *gotcha!* tone to it.

"Sim off," Vil said. He was disgusted with himself. The holoprojection winked out, and he leaned back in the control formchair and sighed.

He'd thought—hoped—that the martial arts stuff he'd been studying would make a difference. After a couple of months' worth of classes, he'd felt as if he had been honed just a little sharper. And it was true, he'd realized when looking at the readouts; the timers had verified his reaction time. He *was* faster.

But not fast enough to ace the simulator.

Ever since the newbie Kendo had died, over a month ago, Vil felt he'd been off his game. It wasn't anything dramatic—he could still outfly anyone else on the battle station, hands down. But he still felt less than optimum.

It hadn't been *his* fault. The kid had been reckless. He'd wound up chewing vacuum for it, and there was nothing Vil could have done.

But he'd been one of Alpha Squadron, and as such, Vil felt responsible. He'd never had a death in his squad before. He felt that he should do something more than the obligatory memorial service, the expressions of grief to the family via holo. But he had no idea what.

It would have been one thing if Nond Kendo had died in the heat of battle. But to go out on so foolish a thing as a training exercise . . . it was so *pointless.*

There were times, in fact, when the whole thing seemed pretty pointless to Vil. And these thoughts, these feelings, disturbed him—almost as much as the kid's death did.

He'd signed up to be a fighter pilot for the Empire; had pictured himself rocketing through the cosmos, gunning down evildoers in the name of everything right in the galaxy. But so far, the only deaths he'd seen were those of a group of motley escaped convicts who'd stolen a shuttle, and a kid too cocky to live.

It wasn't exactly how he'd visualized it.

"Time of fight?" he asked.

The computer said, "Two minutes, fourteen seconds."

Vil's eyebrows went up at that. It hadn't seemed that long during the fight. That was a personal best against the sim of Colonel Vindoo Barvel, the only man who'd held his own for even a few breaths against Darth Vader. Vil wondered how he would fare against a sim of Vader.

Not that he'd ever find out; he'd like to meet the fool crazy enough to ask the man in black to be scanned and holoed while he pretended to pilot a TIE. Like as not, Vader would take the man's head off with that fancy laser sword of his.

Anyway, he'd held his own two seconds longer than he'd ever managed before. Maybe this hand-to-hand stuff Stihl was teaching had some merit, after all. He felt a little better.

"Where do I rank overall?"

"Of current-duty Imperial pilots, you are currently ranked nineteenth in this simulation."

Hmm. "Out of how many?"

"Two hundred and thirty-four thousand, six hundred and twelve."

Okay, so that wasn't *too* bad. Only eighteen pilots ahead of him, out of nearly a quarter million? Certainly nothing to be ashamed of . . .

Vil sighed. He leaned back in the formfit. "Set it up again," he said.

"Beginning simulation in ten seconds. Nine . . . eight . . . seven . . . six . . ."

Vil took a deep breath, and gripped the controls.

LIBRARY AND ARCHIVES, DECK 106, DEATH STAR

Atour had been laboring over a data retrieval problem for nearly an hour when he realized that somebody was standing behind his chair. He frowned and turned, ready to chastise whoever it was for intruding into his office sanctuary.

But the words died unspoken. Standing behind him, close enough to touch, was a droid, one of the new librarian models. He hadn't had a chance to see one before now, other than in holocatalogs and sales material. It looked something like a standard bipedal protocol droid, save its color was a metallic blue instead of gold, complete with a bluish glow to its photoreceptors. The head was a bit larger also, reflecting its increased memory capacity. "Yes?"

"Good midday, sir. I have been ordered to report to you for assignment."

What was that accent? High Coruscanti, it sounded like. Very posh and clipped. He'd never heard a droid affect an accent before, and the upper-crust sensibility it conveyed made Atour hide a smile.

"In what capacity?"

"Sir, I am a librarian. I am here to assist you in whichever way you deem felicitous."

Felicitous. Not a word that one usually heard from the vocabulator of a droid. Or anybody else, for that matter. Sometimes Atour thought he was the last classically educated man in the galaxy.

"Sent by whom?"

"Sector Admiral Poteet, sir."

"I see. And your name?"

"I am model P-RC-three."

"No, no, not your model number. Your name."

"I have no name, sir." The polished tone sounded somehow disapproving. "I am a droid."

"Who programmed you?"

"My primary programming was installed by Lord Alferon Choots Bemming, the owner and chief operating officer of Bibliotron Systems."

Ah. "On Imperial Center."

"Yes, sir." Again the subtle subtext, which managed this time to imply, *Where else?*

Atour had, of course, heard of Lord Alferon, the amateur inventor and heir to the Bemming Shipping fortune. The family owned one of the largest private libraries of hard-copy books in the galaxy, more than seven million volumes, some ranging back to the Golden Age. Lord Alferon was supposedly so rich that he could buy a planet, cover it knee-deep in precious jewels and metals, and then use the rumored doomsday weapon on this battle station to blow it all to atoms without putting a noticeable dent in his exchequer. He was also something of a tinkerer, and owned a droid-design company where he spent much of his personal time. Atour thought wistfully of the rich man's library. There were people who would kill to work there, and he was foremost among them. Seven million books. He sighed. It made one's heart ache.

"All right, then. Henceforth, you will answer to the name 'Persee.' Unless you have some objection?"

"No objection, sir." Was the droid's tone slightly icier? Well, if so, that was just too bad.

"Good," Atour said. "Now come here and make yourself useful. There is a bottleneck in this access system, here—" He pointed at the holoscreen. "—and I want it eliminated. Find a way."

"Very good, sir. Will that be all for now?"

"That's enough, I imagine. How long do you estimate it will take?"

The droid stepped forward and touched several controls on the holo-console, then watched as a crawl of words and numbers scrolled up so fast that no human could possibly read them. After a few seconds it touched a second control. The alphanumerics stopped, and the droid stood there silently.

Atour counted slowly to five. "You were going to give me an estimate of the time necessary to clear the bottleneck."

"Unnecessary, sir. The problem has been cleared."

Atour blinked. "Really?"

"Of course, sir. Will there be anything else?"

Atour smiled. A competent assistant! How wonderful! Better a single droid that knew what it was doing than any number of fumbling organic beings. "No, I think that will do for now. Thank you, Persee. I appreciate it."

"It is my function, sir. Would you care for some tea while you determine my next chore? I have checked the kitchen stores, and can offer you a choice of Manellan Jasper, Kosh, Bluefruit Kintle . . ."

Now Atour Riten laughed aloud. Perhaps this post wouldn't be so onerous after all.

38

DOCKING BAY 35, *IMPERIAL*-CLASS STAR DESTROYER *UNDAUNTABLE*

Admiral Motti was pleased that Admiral Helaw had done such a good job with the *Undauntable*. She was an old ship, on the line for a decade before any other in this quadrant, and despite that, she gleamed like a shiny new credit coin. All systems were in order, and Helaw, who was going to retire as soon as this project was finished, was old school, a man who had earned his flag rank on the front lines of a dozen major battles. When the guns started working, you wanted a man like him watching your back—he'd take the beam in his own chest before he allowed it to hit you from behind.

As the two men walked down the corridor to the docking bay where Motti's lighter waited, their talk was easy and informal. They went way back—Helaw had been a captain on the *Ion Storm* when Motti had gotten his promotion to first lieutenant. That Motti had eventually done a desk tour on Imperial Center and made contacts that allowed him to rise past his old commander spoke to his ambition and intelligence in such matters. Helaw had never enjoyed politics, even though Motti had tried to interest him. The older man just didn't care—all he wanted to do was take his ship out and smoke the enemy, and he was as good at it as any man in the navy. Assigning him a desk would have been a waste, Motti knew, even though he would have been a formidable Moff, had he wanted to go down that road. Better by far than Tarkin, whose political skills were superior to Motti's own, but whose grasp of working strategy and tactics was much inferior to Helaw's.

"So you think this big tank of a station Wilhuff is building is coming along all right?"

"It is. And now that I'm aboard, it will do so even faster."

Helaw laughed. "Never a lack of self-confidence in you. Zi."

Motti smiled in return. "You know what they say: Sometimes wrong, but never in doubt."

"I still think it's putting too many spawns in one bin."

"Come on, Jaim, you've seen the specs, even though you weren't supposed to. The station is a fortress. It has more guns than a fleet, and a weapon that will crack open worlds like they were ripe wuli nuts. Nothing the Rebels can throw at it will slow it down by as much as a meter. Nothing *we* have will give it pause. Whatever else he might be, Wilhuff's ideas about this are solid. The Rebels won't be able to run fast enough, and if we can blow a planet out from under them, where can they hide?"

"Maybe."

They were almost to the deck. Motti turned to look at his old commander. "'Maybe?'"

"Did I ever tell you 'bout Lieutenant Pojo?"

"I don't think so."

"Thirty-five, forty years back, Kan Pojo was the range officer and small-arms instructor on the training ship *Overt*. He was fleet champion with any arms you could carry—carbine, sniper rifle, sidearm. He could use a blast pistol to pick flies off a wall at ten paces. I never saw a man who could shoot as well as he did. It was uncanny."

"Uh-huh." Motti resisted the urge to yawn. He admired and respected Jaim Helaw as he did few men, but the old trooper did take his time spinning a yarn.

"We ran into a bit of trouble in the Vergesso—pirates had taken over a moon. We were sent down to teach them the error of their ways."

Motti nodded. "And?"

"Pojo wanted to get into the fray. It was a lot of close-quarters stuff: the only city on the moon was domed—we're talking a maze of alleys and narrow streets. Nobody could use big guns, because anything larger than a blaster rifle might rupture the dome. So the CO thought, Why not?

"I was doing a tour as a naval adjunct, a second loot, and Pojo was assigned to our squad. So we drop, access the dome, and start hunting pirates. They were a ratty bunch, maybe a hundred, hundred and twenty of 'em, but spread out.

"Our squad came across a group of 'em, about twenty-five men, and we all commenced to have a shootout. Pojo was knocking them down, left, right, and center, like targets on the range. Only thing I've ever seen to compare it to is that old holo of Phow Ji taking out the mercenaries. Ever seen it?"

Motti nodded. What soldier hadn't?

"So Pojo takes out half the group before any of us can even crank up our guns, using nothing but his sidearm—a blaster modified with a heavy-duty capacitor to fire more charges than your standard model.

"The survivors broke and ran, and we started chasing them. Pojo and I took off after a group of four—three men and a Rodian, I think. Pojo's grinning like an overfed sand cat; this was what he was born to do.

"The pirates couldn't shoot for sour whool poop, so they split up. I took off after the first two, and they shot their guns dry, at which time I plinked 'em. Then I circled back to Pojo. He had the last two cornered, they had drained their blasters, and he had holstered his."

"He holstered his blaster?"

"Yeah, to give them a chance. They were six, eight meters away. So Pojo says, 'Okay, boys, here's the deal: Take off, and if I miss, you're free.'"

Motti shook his head. Un-fripping-believable.

"So the two, figuring they're dead men anyway, charge him. Pojo pulls that customized blaster faster than you can believe—his hand, the gun, they were just a blur—those guys hadn't taken two steps. He cooks off a round and shoots the sodder on the left right between the eyes, *zap!* Then he aims at the second pirate, who's still running at him, and squeezes off another bolt."

"Let me guess: he missed?"

"Nope. Blaster shorted out. *Hiss, pop, crackle.* The capacitor must have overloaded, and the gun flared. Pojo drops it, goes for his backup—no gunnery loot would carry just the one gun, but by that time, the pirate was in his face. Sodder had a shiv. Just a low-tech blade, not even a vibro, one step above a flint knife.

"By the time I lined up and shot the pirate, he'd buried that knife in Pojo's throat. The medics couldn't get there in time."

Motti smiled. "A multibillion-credit battle station is not exactly a pijer-rigged blaster, Admiral."

"The more complex a weapon, the more likely it is to have flaws," Helaw said. "Kan Pojo was the best pistoleer I ever saw, then or since, but he was waxed by what was essentially a whittled rock when his state-of-the-art weapon failed."

"I'm not too worried about pirates with knives, Jaim."

"You should be, son," the grizzled old admiral said. "You should be worried about *everything*."

ADMIRAL MOTTI'S LIGHTER, TWO HUNDRED KILOMETERS OFF *UNDAUNTABLE*'S PORT STERN

Did the old man have a valid point? Motti wondered. It was hard to see how. The Death Star was a true Dreadnaught, a giant among midgets. Of course, just about every fable about giants tended to end with the midgets triumphing somehow. Perhaps it wouldn't be a bad idea, once he was back on board, to order a detailed inspection of the superstructure and the plans. Maintenance would howl, but that didn't matter. After all, Motti hadn't gotten to his rank by assuming everything was as it should be. Like as not the old man was just being paranoid. But in situations like these, with the fate of the galaxy literally riding on the outcome, it was hard to be too paranoid . . .

Motti was still musing about Helaw's story when the Star Destroyer *Undauntable* suddenly ceased to be the oldest ship of the line in the quadrant behind him.

In a brilliant, silent white-hot blast the *Undauntable* blew apart.

39

COMMAND DECK, OVERBRIDGE, DEATH STAR

"You were there," Tarkin said.

"I didn't blow it up," Motti replied.

Tarkin silently counted to ten. Behind him, at a discreet distance, Daala stood, pretending not to hear their conversation.

"What could have happened?"

"It could have been an accident," Motti said.

"You don't really think that."

"No more than you do, sir. Admiral Helaw was as good as any commander in the Imperial Navy and better than most. I cannot imagine an accident of this magnitude would happen on a ship he ran."

"The *Undauntable* was an old ship."

"Even so."

Tarkin nodded. "I'm afraid I agree." He paused. "It would be better if it *had* been an accident."

Motti said nothing, but Tarkin knew the man was no fool. He understood.

"Darth Vader's recent visit was supposed to have eliminated the threat of sabotage," Tarkin continued.

"So I understand. Apparently it did not."

"If that is the case, we could, I expect, depend on another visit from Vader in short order. Not the worst thing that could happen to us, but certainly another burden we don't need, with sprawl construction nearly complete."

"One would expect such a visit, yes."

"Whereas if there was an accident, on an old ship—a leaky hypermatter containment valve, perhaps . . . that would be unfortunate, but understandable, and there would be no need for the Emperor's representative to come all the way out here again."

Motti frowned deeper. "It would be a shame, however, for such an 'accident' to be laid at the feet of Jaim Helaw, whose memory would forever bear that blot on his otherwise perfect record."

"It *would* be a shame. However, with Jaim dead, that won't really bother him, will it? And he had no family."

Motti said, "The navy was his family."

"Just so. And Jaim was loyal to the bone. He would not wish his 'family' to suffer, would he?"

Motti didn't like it, that was plain, but Motti was also a loyalist. There was no need for Tarkin to remind him of his duty. The admiral nodded, a crisp, military motion. "So, then: an unfortunate accident, and a single black mark on an otherwise brilliant career."

"Unfortunate, indeed," Tarkin replied. "And we all move on."

After Motti was gone, Daala moved over to stand next to Tarkin. "Isn't this a bit risky?"

"Not really. Motti is ambitious, and he knows this station is his transport to greatness. He'll be promoted to Moff as soon as the Rebels are vanquished, and it would be foolish for him to raise a fuss about this. He liked the old man—I was rather fond of him myself—but nothing we can say or do will bring him back, and better that his death serves us rather than gets in our way. So, it was a terrible accident. These things happen."

She nodded. "But that doesn't solve the problem entirely, does it?"

He sighed. "You are quite right, Admiral. We still have among us a traitor who somehow managed to vaporize a Star Destroyer. We need to find the ones responsible, before the Rebels can claim credit for this heinous action. And by *we*, I mean—"

"Me," she finished. "Do you think that wise? I should be getting back to my duties at the Maw."

"They will keep. I need you here more than they do there."

Daala nodded. "Well. I suppose that if it is my duty, what else is to be done?"

She smiled. He returned it.

"I'll start immediately," she said.

Tarkin cleared his throat. "Perhaps not immediately. I seem to recall there were some other matters we intended to discuss."

"In the privacy of your quarters?"

He smiled again. "Just so."

THE HARD HEART CANTINA, DECK 69, DEATH STAR

Teela Kaarz wasn't much of a drinker. Sure, she'd have a little wine with dinner, a social drink now and then, but she was too happy a drunk, too willing to go along with whatever anybody wanted just for the fun of it, and that had gotten her in trouble more than a couple of times. Better to stay sober than to have to deal with the regrets later—she had enough of those as it was.

But here she was, in this cantina, listening to a young woman on the small stage playing a stringed instrument, something classical and quiet, barely audible over the sounds of people drinking, laughing, and talking. She was here because she had won a bet—one of the other architects had doubted her ability to redesign a dining hall to a specification change suddenly required because somebody had mistranslated a measurement system. Whereas the specs said the room's floor was to be nine hundred square meters, whoever had written the blueprint had somehow used the Trogan meter instead of the Imperial standard meter, and the difference could not be made to fit in the available space, since there was a 25 percent variation in the measures.

Back when she had been in school, such an error would have been unthinkable, but the relationship of academe to real construction was that of night to day. It happened all the time. Just last week an automated supply ship had plowed into a warehouse on Despayre, destroying the ship entirely and half the building it hit, because somebody had set the autopilot's deceleration speed to *centimeters* per second instead of *meters*. If you impact at a hundred times the velocity you're supposed to, it makes something of a difference.

Vishnare, the architect who had proposed the bet, lifted his cup in salute, as did the other five people from her workgroup, and she raised her own cup in acknowledgment.

A noisy group entered the cantina just then, drowning out whatever toast Vishnare had to offer, along with the music. Teela looked at the new arrivals: half a dozen human males all dressed in pilots' informals.

She sipped a tiny bit of her drink and put the cup down. The pilots were loud, full of themselves, oozing overconfidence and arrogance. She had dated a former military pilot once who'd left the service and taken a job flying commercial transports on her homeworld, but he hadn't left the attitude behind. *Look at me,* it said, *I'm so much better than everybody else. I can fly!*

That relationship hadn't lasted long. Being secure in what you did was a good thing, but being obnoxious about it? Not so much.

The pilots took a table, and a droid went over to take their orders.

Teela surreptitiously glanced at her chrono. She had to stay for a while more just to be polite, but since she wasn't much for small talk, mostly she'd just sit there and smile and nurse her drink until she could make an excuse and take off. She had some journals she wanted to read, and crowded, noisy rooms had never been her favorite spaces. She needed to go to the refresher, though, and while she preferred to do that in her own cube, when you had to go, you had to go.

She smiled, stood, and worked her way toward the 'fresher.

She was on her way back to her table when a large fellow wearing storage workers' greens decided he would give her an opportunity to enjoy his company. The man lurched to his feet and blocked her path. "Hey, sweetlook, wha's y'hurry? Lemme buy you a drink!" He was at least half soused, from the smell of his breath and his unsteady motion.

"Thank you, but I already have a drink. I need to get back to my friends there." Teela nodded at her table, four meters past where the storageman wavered on unsteady feet.

"Naw, naw, y'll'v *much* more fun here't *my* table, 'strue." He belched, and a rum-tainted miasma drifted past her nostrils.

Teela was aware that she was not altogether unattractive, and over the years since puberty had resculpted her body, she had learned how to deal with unwanted attention well enough. Sometimes you could smile them away, sometimes you put a little steel in your voice, and most times you just flat out told them you weren't interested. Drunks didn't always get the subtle hints, so she went for direct: "Sorry. Not interested."

She moved to go around him. He slid over and kept her route blocked. "Y'don' know what y're missin', sweetlook. I'm *prime*!"

"Good for you. Tell somebody who cares." She turned, intending to go back the way she'd come and loop around—

He grabbed her wrist as she started away. "Y'sayin' no t'*me*?" His tone was definitely less friendly now.

Teela twisted her wrist, trying to pull free, knowing in advance that it would only serve to make the storageman hang on tighter. She was right.

Conversation at the tables immediately surrounding them lagged as the patrons, mostly male and mostly as drunk as or drunker than her aspiring boyfriend, watched in bleary interest. The storageman was as large as he was drunk, which made him quite formidable. Teela stopped struggling, because at this stage that was what her assailant wanted. She had heard that the cantina's bouncer was fast and reliable. She hoped so, because she knew from past experience how quickly a situation like this could get really ugly . . .

"Oh, look," a man's voice said.

Teela turned. It was one of the pilots. He looked about twenty-five, and he also looked like, if he worked out hard and ate his Flakies every morning, he might someday have a chest as big as the storageman's neck.

Great, she thought. *A hero. Where's the fripping bouncer?*

"Your shin hurts," the flyboy continued, smiling at the big drunk as guilelessly as a freshly decanted clone.

The storageman frowned. "My *what*?"

The pilot kicked, a short, low move, and the inside edge of his boot sole impacted the bigger man's lower leg, just below the knee. He scraped his foot down the bigger man's leg and stomped on the storage-man's instep.

"Ow—*feke*—!"

The pilot put his right hand on the big drunk's chest and shoved. Since the other was hopping on one foot, clutching his insulted leg and yelling, it took very little effort to move him backward, where he sat down heavily into his seat.

Before he could do more than blink in bleary surprise, a *very* large man appeared as if by magic directly behind the storageman and laid a hand the size of a wampa's forepaw on the seated man's shoulder. "Is there a problem here?" he asked in a quiet voice. It was a pleasant voice, with no anger in it, but it nevertheless made Teela think of a sheath covering a razor's edge.

"Nope," the pilot said. "Our friend here is a little over his limit, and felt unsteady on his feet. The lady and I were just helping him regain his seat safely."

The bouncer standing behind the storageman smiled. "Ah. Well, then, enjoy the rest of your evening." He looked down at the befuddled storageman. "And you were just leaving, weren't you?"

"Whuh?"

"Nicely put. Let me help you to the exit."

When they were gone, Teela said to the pilot, "I don't want to seem ungracious, but that wasn't necessary."

"When a man lays unwanted hands on a woman, I believe it is. It's discourteous at best; brutality, at worst." He smiled. "I'm Lieutenant Vil Dance, by the way."

She had to admit that his smile was attractive. *Down, girl,* she cautioned herself, but despite that she couldn't deny the tingling that had started in her stomach.

"Teela Kaarz," she replied. "And I appreciate the sentiment, Lieutenant, even if I don't necessarily agree with it."

"Appreciation, even without agreement, is certainly better than a poke in the eye. Would you allow me to buy you a drink?"

"Thanks, but no. I'm not much of a drinker."

"Me, neither, really. I'd rather be in my cube studying technical journals."

"Really?"

He grinned again. "Actually, no. But I'm hoping that if you believe I'm the serious sort, maybe you'll think better of me."

His smile was infectious. Teela couldn't help smiling in return. "Does that work for you often?"

"Pretending to be studious?"

"No, pretending to give away your pickup line that way."

Now he laughed. "Oh, I like a smart and funny fem." He dimmed the smile a little. "Let me buy you a caf or sucosa. Water, even. Sit and visit with me for a little while."

"I don't know . . ." Which was a lie; she knew very well what she wanted to do. In her mind's eye, the small mental projection of her conscience and common sense gaped in disbelief. *I can't believe you're seriously contemplating this,* it scolded.

"Come on. It's war, I'm a pilot, my number could be up any moment. Wouldn't you feel better knowing I went out to meet my end smiling at the memory of you?"

You just barely escaped a dangerous situation with one man, her conscience avatar said, *and here you are letting yourself be sugar-talked by another.*

Teela laughed at Dance's line. "You pilots and your platinum tongues. All right. I suppose it won't hurt anything."

Her conscience threw up its hands in resignation and stalked off into the gray corridors of her brain.

As they approached the table, she saw the other pilots look at them. More than a few looked twice, or closer, and all were blatantly impressed. They stood. "Hey, Vil," one of them said. "We have to shove off. See you back at the barracks."

Dance eyed him. "You're sure about that?"

"Oh, right. Um . . ." The flier was obviously uncomfortable, and the concealed smiles of the others, not to mention the glare he was getting from Dance, weren't making things any easier for him. "Right. We have to, uh . . . go over our technical specs. Down in the hangar."

The five pilots left. Teela gave Dance a measured look. "You had a bet going with your friends," she said. It was not a question.

He shrugged. "Of course. First man back with a woman wins the table. They'll go see if the odds in the pub on Level Six are better. One doesn't need a bunch of comrades cramping his run if one gets lucky."

"You aren't going to get *that* lucky, Lieutenant. Not tonight, anyway."

He flashed that high-wattage smile at her again. "You're too sharp for me, Teela Kaarz. I really like a woman who makes me have to stretch."

She sighed. No way was she getting into anything remotely serious with a navy pilot. No way.

But a cup of caf couldn't hurt . . .

40

THE HARD HEART CANTINA, DECK 69, DEATH STAR

Memah Roothes was aware that she was—well, not to put too fine a point on it—primping. That was a bad sign, she knew, when she started to care what a new male thought of her appearance. The actions themselves didn't look like much: a slight adjustment of her posture, a little brush over the brow to smooth out a bit of makeup, a quick glance at her reflection when she passed a mirror to check her lekku positions. Nothing major. But she knew. She wanted to look good, and she wanted Ratua to notice that she did.

She wasn't too old, ugly, or fat, and she wasn't stupid. He already did like her—you didn't run cantinas for as long as she had without being able to feel the heat come off a male when he looked at you. Still, the fluttery sensation she felt, the quickening of her heartbeat and breath—those were all bad signs. She didn't need a new complication in her life right now.

And Green-Eyes was definitely that. For one thing, he didn't exist, according to what Rodo had found—or hadn't found—in his HoloNet search, and that meant he was a bad boy of some kind. Could be a legal bad boy—a sub-rosa agent for the Empire, say. Or he could be a Rebel spy. Or some kind of criminal . . .

But he made her laugh, he was quick and clever, and those eyes . . . she'd never seen any quite that color before. They were like liquid emerald, bright and alert.

Hence, the primping.

At the end of the bar, a pair of CPOs were talking about a rumored prison break in the detention area. Memah overheard one of them say, "Way I heard it, nine guys broke out, one of them a Jedi."

The other petty officer laughed. "Hate to point it out, but Jedi are real scarce these days."

"Just telling the story, Tenn."

"Yeah, I heard it, too. Only I heard it was fifty guys, all captured Rebels, led by five Jedi. And they took over the superlaser and started blasting Star Destroyers. 'Course, the big gun isn't even operational yet. Anyone knows that, it's me. But hey, why let facts get in the way of a good story?"

The first chief laughed and sipped at his ale. "Sounds almost like a sim run, don't it? A really wacky sim run."

The second CPO said, "Time this war's over, want to bet that story'll have a Rebel army nearly destroying the station? Every action I ever been in, stories like that pop up. One floob spits on the slidewalk, by the end of the cycle it's turned into a crack unit of Rebels knocking over a fortress."

The first one laughed again. "Yeah. Next they'll be saying it took the Five Hundred and First to put 'em down."

Both men laughed.

Memah smiled. She had heard some of those stories, too. Why people felt the need to embellish the truth, or even fabricate something completely different, when reality was all too often quite fantastic enough, was light-years beyond her.

She happened to be looking at the door when Ratua came ambling in as if he owned the place. He caught her glance, smiled, and headed for the bar. Once there, he looked her up and down in frank appreciation.

"You," he said to her, "look like the reason the riot started."

She realized to her astonishment that she was blushing. "Well," she replied, "*you* look like you could use a drink. What'll it be?"

He laughed. "I'll have the unusual."

"Which means what, exactly?"

"Surprise me. Something exotic. Expensive enough to justify me sitting here and occupying your bar and attention."

"I don't think we have anything worth that much."

"You wound me. Right here." He put a hand over his heart, or at least where a human's heart would be. "Here I am, seeking sanctuary, trying to stay out of trouble—"

Memah said, "I think you *are* trouble, Ratua. It would probably be much better for me if I stayed as far away from you as I could."

"Probably," he agreed, in a more serious tone. "But where's the fun in that?"

She built him a drink, a simple one, with a lot of alcohol and some sweeteners and colors. It was potent stuff. So far she'd never seen him drunk—at least, not so she could tell. *Must have a hyperdrive metabolism,* she thought.

She put down his glass, then planted both hands on the pleekwood bar and leaned toward him. "Fun starts with the truth. Who are you?"

He sighed, and didn't say anything for a couple of seconds. "I've always found truth to be highly overrated."

"Nevertheless . . ."

"Okay." He took a fortifying swig of his drink, then said, "I'm Celot Ratua Dil, second son of the First Counselor Nagat Keris Ratua and his Tertiary Wife, Feelah Derin. Of late, I resided on the planet Despayre, where I was incarcerated for a crime I actually did not commit—though in balance, I can't claim to be an upstanding citizen."

"So you weren't kidding before?"

"Nope."

"What was the crime?"

"Guilt by association. Wrong place, wrong time."

"And how did you come to be here?"

"I escaped."

"Really. Just like that?"

"Well, I won't bore you with the details—"

"Oh, please—bore me. I so seldom find myself bored these days."

"It doesn't bother you that I'm an escapee?"

Memah stood back and folded her arms. "You were pretty sure it wouldn't, weren't you? Or you wouldn't have told me."

"I was hoping. And you did demand the truth."

"So I did. And I'm wondering when I'm going to get it."

Ratua studied the drink for a moment, then looked up at her, and she had to physically tense up to resist the earnestness in those remarkable eyes. "Now, if you want it."

"What have you done for which you might have deserved to be imprisoned?"

"I was a smuggler. Among other things. Nothing violent."

"That's good." She refilled his drink. He smiled into it, then at her.

Smile and use those eyes as much as you want, she thought. *If I have to turn you in, I will.* "Think hard before you say anything more, Celot Ratua Dil. If you're guilty of any crimes against the Empire, then I could be endangering my cantina just by talking to you. You might want to turn around and walk out of here right now, because if your presence is a danger to me and my livelihood, you'll find out where this place got its name."

He stared at her. "I believe you're the kind of person who'd do it."

Memah nodded. "That I am."

"Good," said Ratua. "If you weren't, I wouldn't be talking to you."

41

REC ROOM 17-A, DEATH STAR

Sergeant Nova Stihl was tired. The fighting classes he taught weren't part of his regular duties, and now that word had gotten around he had four full sessions, with about twenty-five students per class. Each of these ran an hour and a half, and he had two sessions every evening after his shift ended. He didn't eat until after the second class, after which he would go back to his cube, shower, and hit the sleep pad.

Such a schedule made for busy light and dark cycles.

He kept himself in shape, but he hadn't been sleeping well. The bad dreams he'd sometimes had back on the prison planet had grown more frequent on the battle station, and some of them were extremely realistic and violent. More than a few times he'd come out of a sleep to find his heart pounding rapidly and his coverlets drenched in sweat.

He didn't understand why it was happening. He had considered having medical run a check, to make sure there wasn't something amiss going on in his brain, but he kept hoping the sleep sorties would ease off. He'd give it a little more time, and then he would go see the medics, he told himself. Maybe there was something in the air, some trace element the filters weren't straining out.

Besides, when did he have time to go see a doctor?

Most of the students were rank beginners; even though some of them could fight well enough, they had to learn the system of teräs käsi to overlay what they already knew. There were reasoned patterns of movement, principles, laws, and these were more important than any particular technique. It didn't matter if you had a punch that would knock down a wall if you couldn't deliver it, and to do that, you needed a system that would allow it frequently.

Even though his students were newbies, Nova always felt as if he learned as much from them as he taught. If you had to explain something to a being who knew nothing about it, you had to understand it pretty well. Sometimes words would come out of his mouth that he didn't expect—words that suddenly rang in a way that the essential truth just . . . blossomed suddenly, like a desert flower after a sudden rain. Now and again he himself couldn't believe some of the things he'd said. Where had that come from? He hadn't known it was there until he'd heard himself say it.

He realized that someone was standing before where he sat, cross-legged, on the matted floor. "Divo, you had a question?"

The student, a squat power lifter who looked strong enough to pick himself up with one hand, nodded. "Yeah, Sarge. That distance thing. I'm a little confused."

Usually there was one student who asked most of the questions, and while the others would sometimes cut their gazes to the ceiling and look bored, the questioner was usually speaking for more than just him- or herself. That was why Nova always answered questions as completely as time allowed.

"Bare hand-to-hand, there are four ranges," he said. He counted them off on his fingers. "Kicking, punching, elbowing, grappling. You can't grapple effectively at elbow range, you can't elbow at punching range, and you can't punch at kicking range.

"Add impact weapons and you alter the distances. A cane extends your punch to kicking range. A knife extends your elbow to punching range. Sodder has a knife in his hand, you don't want him closer than a step and a half unless you're doing something active to him—inside that, he's too close. He'll get you with that blade more often than not, and it only takes one time to ruin your day.

"So—let me show you the step-in to steal that crucial distance again . . ."

The drills went on. The students practiced the moves with Nova walking around, making corrections, offering direction, telling them when they had it wrong and when they had it right. He liked to think he was an encouraging teacher. He always seemed to develop a core of regulars, even though turnover among newbies was usually pretty good—a lot of folks wanted to be able to kill someone with their bare hands, but they didn't want to do the months or years of work necessary to develop the skills.

The air in the rec room seemed to change, suddenly and subtly. Nova could feel it without having to look around.

Danger had entered the room.

Without making it obvious as he helped a student find the proper hand position for a punch, he turned slightly.

Standing just inside the door was Rodo, the bouncer from the Hard Heart.

Nova grinned slightly, and caught the other's grin in return. The class would be over in five minutes, and he knew Rodo's timing wasn't an accident. His smile became wider, as well as slightly rueful. He was tired, he was hungry, and he hadn't been expecting it—but that's how it always went, wasn't it? Those were the conditions one trained for.

He'd gotten his First Level Adept after a grueling two-hour class that had involved a lot of groundwork, athletic rolling around and grappling. That kind of stuff wore you out pretty quickly. His master had waited until the class was over and the students headed for the sonic showers when he'd pulled Nova aside. "I think it's time you took the test," he'd said.

The sudden adrenaline rush had gripped Nova, briefly washing away his fatigue. "Really? When?"

"Right now."

Nova smiled at the memory. The test had taken almost four hours. The old man had turned him upside down and inside out; he'd taken him apart like a malfunctioning droid. And he'd been right to do so. After all, a footpad on the street wasn't going to wait until you felt your best. You had to be ready at any moment to fight to the death, if necessary. Otherwise the teachings weren't worth knowing.

At the end of the session, Nova dismissed his students, many of whom were obviously wondering what the Hard Heart's bouncer was doing here. Nova moved over to where Rodo was holding up the wall. *He's big enough to hold it up,* he thought.

Might as well get to it; he wasn't getting any less tired.

He said, "So, you want to go a couple of rounds?"

Rodo shrugged, his shoulders shifting like tectonic plates. "I wouldn't mind. 'Course, if dancing with your charity cases has tired you out—"

"Thanks for your concern. Light spar?"

Rodo nodded. "Fine by me."

Back when Nova had been a beginner, there had been two kinds of sparring matches generally allowed. Heavy sparring required the donning of bulky, padded biogel suits. Even though the gel was relatively lightweight, it added five kilos to you at minimum, not to mention slowing reaction time and reducing range of movement considerably. A suited-up attacker charging you could shrug off a strike that would deck an unprotected fighter and keep coming.

Early on in his training Nova learned to answer the question *Light or heavy sparring?* with the former. Of course, the only difference in the two was the suit—you hit just as hard in "light sparring," but since you knew you could get seriously damaged if you made a mistake, you were more careful.

Nova closed the door and latched it. "You need to warm up?"

Rodo shook his head. "Nah. You need a nap?"

Nova shook his head and grinned. He walked to the center of the padded room and turned to face Rodo.

Teräs käsi had half a dozen basic stances, and Nova was comfortable with them all, having practiced them thousands of times. But as Rodo ambled toward him, he didn't shift his feet into one of the TK defensive plants. He stayed in a neutral pose, shoulders relaxed, feet about shoulder width apart, his left foot a hair ahead of his right. No point in giving his opponent any clues as to his style until the fight began.

Nova knew he was starting at a disadvantage. Even beyond his being tired, there was the simple fact that Rodo outmassed him by a good twenty kilos and stood almost a head taller. Everything else being equal—and so far, Nova'd seen nothing to indicate that Rodo's fighting skills were better than his own—the advantage always lay with the bigger man.

But Rodo didn't know about Nova's Blink. That probably made them even.

Probably . . .

Rodo stopped just outside his own step and a half, slightly longer than Nova's range. A two-step position was too far to attack; the defender would have plenty of time to get set. A single step was too close.

Nova held his ground.

Rodo circled to his left.

Nova turned, shifting slightly, his weight on the balls of his feet and pivoting on both incrementally. He bent his knees a bit, sinking a little lower.

Rodo moved his hands, circling to a high–low, left-over-right position, pulled them in closer to his body, leaned away a hair, and stole half a step closer.

It was a good fake. That upper-body motion would make you think Rodo had moved back when in fact he had moved in.

Nova stepped off neutral to a side stance and used the angle to steal back the half step, maintaining their distance. Rodo nodded. "Nice," he said.

Nova did a back crossover step, right foot behind the left, giving Rodo what looked like an unbalanced and awkward target. The bigger man shook his head. "Maybe not."

Nova circled to his left, stopped, and pivoted, putting his left side forward at about forty-five degrees.

Rodo mirrored the move and dropped his center of gravity a couple of centimeters. Since he was taller, if Nova got to his attack range, Rodo would already be there. The bouncer was a big man, and that no doubt tended to favor him in distance fighting. But he also worked in a cantina, where encounters would be close.

Rodo begin to sway ever so slightly, turning his hips. Nova repressed a smile. Did the other man think he could be lulled like a rikitik facing a naga? He couldn't be fooled that easily. He knew that if he grappled with a guy that much bigger and stronger than him, he'd have to have angle, leverage, and a base, or he'd lose. That wasn't a matter of skill so much as it was simple physics—

Rodo charged, and Nova barely got out of the way in time. He cursed himself for a fool even as he dropped and did a fast leg sweep. He'd lost focus for just an instant, and that's all it had taken to almost lose the match. If it weren't for his ability to sense another's moves, Rodo would have had him. The big man was *fast.*

Their shins connected, smacking together like boards, but Rodo was more flexible than he appeared. He jumped, foiling the sweep, but having to step far enough out in doing so that he couldn't punch in passing. Nova did a stutter step, broke it short, and got within range. He went in with a triple punch, high, low, high. There was no way to block all three, but Rodo didn't back up; instead he stepped in and threw a horizontal elbow strike. Nova sensed that one coming before Rodo started it, blocked with an open hand, and tried a lock. Rodo countered with one of his own, stepped out, and turned—

And they were back where they started.

Rodo chuckled, and in a moment it turned into a laugh, and Nova joined him. Both men straightened from their fighting crouches and relaxed. The actual fighting time Nova estimated as thirty seconds or less.

"We done?" Rodo said.

"I think so," Nova said. No point, really, in continuing; they were too evenly matched. There was no alpha male here.

"You have some outstanding moves, friend," he told the bouncer.

"You'd know," the bigger man said. He extended his hand, as did Nova.

"Where'd you get that hip fake?" Nova asked.

"Changa bushfighting. What about that sweep? That's not classical teräs käsi."

"Sera Plinck, Jalinese knife."

Rodo nodded. They had given each other new moves. A valuable exchange.

Nova realized that his tiredness was gone. He hadn't had a chance to play with a fighter this good in years. It was rare, these days, to run into someone skilled enough to learn from.

"You ever see any Velanarian boxing?" he asked.

"Yeah, the crosscut version. Used to know a guy had some of that. Hard to get the moves down when you've only got two arms, but . . ." He shrugged. "Gotta get back to work. C'mon along—drinks are on me."

This, Nova told himself, could be the start of a great friendship.

42

ARCHITECTURAL OFFICE SUITE, EXECUTIVE LEVEL, DEATH STAR

Teela Kaarz blinked at the man in front of her. "Where's the Wookiee chief? Hahrynyar?"

"He took sick," the man said. "Had to go to the clinic, isn't well enough to come back to work yet. I'm pushrodding this shift."

"And it was your idea to build this exhaust port?" She gestured at the expanded holo of the station's plans. The much-debated port, near the "north pole" of the meridian trench, was clearly visible.

"No, it wasn't my idea. It's on the plans."

"I talked to the Wookiee about that."

The man, a graybeard who was a hand span shorter and fifty kilos heavier than she was, shrugged. "Yeah? Well, sorry, but what you told him didn't get passed on. The plans called for an exhaust port and that's what they pay me to do, follow the plans. Unless you, uh, maybe got an exception and wrote it down?"

Disgusted with herself, Teela shook her head. "I didn't have a chance to get to it."

He shrugged again. "Not my fault."

She nodded. That was true, it wasn't his fault. "Okay," she said. "Done is done. What about the heat exchangers on the barracks levels?"

"Ninety-eight percent complete, down to routers and capacitors, and we'll have those online in a couple more shifts, no problem."

That much was good, anyway.

"The walkway escalators from Six to Seven?"

"Done. We can crank them anytime."

"And the pocket park on Nine is where?"

"Laid out, greensward all seeded, the big trees and foliage planted, pumps and pipes installed, and the channels and ponds cast and hard-set. All we need is for Hydrology to deliver the water and power to light it up."

Teela looked at her datalog. Everything was coming along on time, and some things, like the tiny patch of greenery up on Nine, were actually ahead of schedule. Hahrynyar's substitute was certainly keeping the Wookiee's rep spotless. Okay, so they'd put in a heat exhaust port that wasn't really needed. It hadn't slowed down anything else, and it certainly wouldn't hurt anything by being there. In fact, given the size of the reactor, and the heat it would generate at full power, it was probably better to have too many vents than too few.

It was always a good idea to err on the side of safety.

"All right," she said. "Just keep me in the circuit."

"Of course."

After he left her office, Teela looked over the schedule again. Her portion of the construction was on time and on budget, true enough, but she wasn't the only architect on the project, and as it sometimes happened, the good suffered for the faults of the bad. She expected a call from her boss anytime now, telling her she was going to have to cut costs or speed up—or both. It wasn't fair or right, but if you could carry your load, then you were often asked to help somebody else carry theirs.

"Teela Kaarz?"

Teela looked up. Her receptionist droid stood in the doorway of her office.

"Yes?"

"Senior Project Manager Stinex sends his regards and asks that you come by his office at your convenience."

Teela nodded. Well, there it was, just like she expected. "Inform the senior PM I'll be by in an hour, if that's okay with him." There was no help for it. That was how things worked.

She noticed the droid was still there. "What?"

"You have a call incoming from a Lieutenant Villian Dance."

Teela grinned. "Put that through. And close the door on your way out."

Despite her resolve, the dashing TIE pilot had charmed her. He was funny, clever, and not bad-looking. Given her job and trustee status, it wasn't as though she had much time for recreation, and a man who made her laugh was worth something.

Her viewscreen blossomed with the image of Vil Dance. He tossed her a jaunty salute, two fingers off his brow. "Good shift, Lady Teela?"

She smiled. "Not too bad so far, Lieutenant. I hope your own is going well."

"It just improved a thousand percent."

Smooth, she thought. As smooth as the surface of a neutron star. "To what do I owe the honor of this call?"

"Ah, well, as it happens, I know somebody who knows somebody who is a friend of the cook in the new Melahnese restaurant that just opened on the Rec Deck food court. You fancy fodu in green fire sauce?"

"One of my favorites."

"I thought maybe you'd like spicy food. I can get us a table, swing shift. My treat."

"How can a lieutenant afford such exotic cuisine? I hear it's very expensive to eat there."

He gave her a disarming shrug. "Not a lot to burn credits on out here," he said. "And since at any moment I might be leaving on a mission from which I won't return, I figure might as well spend the money on something—someone—worthwhile."

She laughed. "How long are you going to milk that particular routine?"

"I can see I'll have to try something else, since you are a coldhearted fem unaffected by the prospect of my possible demise. So—dinner?"

She could see her conscience in her mind's eye, shaking its head. *You'll be sorry . . .*

Space it, she told her inner self. "Well, I do have to eat," she said aloud. "What time?"

He flashed her that gigawatt smile. "Nineteen hundred?"

"I'll meet you there."

"Just made my day, Teela."

"We do what we can to keep the troops happy."

After they disconnected, she leaned back in her chair, feeling somewhat bemused with herself.

Nothing would come of any liaison between them, not in the long term. He was a pilot and—despite his ironic bravado—likely to get blown out of the vacuum sooner or later. And she was a prisoner who might get some consideration after the station was built, but there were no guarantees there, either.

Still, there was a war going on, and you had to take your joys where you could find them. When built, this battle station would be weaponproof, and she might be allowed to stay on assignment after the basic design was finished—perhaps even after this thing was ready to roll out and over any resistance in its way. There would still be changes, both in design and construction, taking place. The fact that she was working for the enemy still troubled her occasionally, but she'd rationalized it away, for the most part. And anyway, a job and a place to sleep weren't the only considerations in a woman's life. It was better, in the present circumstances, to take it one day at a time and enjoy each as best she could.

And Lieutenant Vil Dance sounded like he knew how to make life enjoyable.

MAIN CORRIDOR OUTSIDE THE HARD HEART CANTINA,
DECK 69, DEATH STAR

This new deal he had in mind, if he pulled it off, would leave Ratua sitting very pretty indeed. It was technically illegal—which was moot because, given his situation, everything he did was technically illegal—but in this case, nobody would come to any harm. The Empire was pouring credits into this project like water onto a forest fire; a few buckets here and there wouldn't be missed, and what was beneath their notice would fix things so he wouldn't have to work for a while.

He was feeling pretty good, all in all, as he walked confidently down the gently curving corridor toward the recreation area. He mulled over his plans on his way to see Memah Roothes, the most beautiful and interesting female he had run across in, well . . . forever. The cantina was just ahead, up the corridor a hundred meters or so, when the bouncer, Rodo, emerged. Ratua started to call out and wave, but then, half a step behind Rodo, a second man exited the cantina. It took him a second to place the second fellow, the context and surroundings being utterly different from where Ratua had last encountered him. When he did, a chill washed over him like a splash of liquid nitrogen.

It was Sergeant Nova Stihl, the same man for whom he'd sometimes participated in martial arts demonstrations back in Slashtown.

Without missing a step Ratua turned into the next doorway, a shop featuring femwear, resisting the urge to kick in the afterburner. He pretended to peruse the racks of selections and gaze at the holomannequins. As he did, he could feel fear roiling in his belly like one of the dianoga rumored to infest downlevels. Stihl was a decent man, but there was no doubt where his loyalties lay, and it wasn't with escaped prisoners.

A droid rolled up, gyroscopically balanced on a single wheel. "How may I assist you, sir?"

Calm down! "I need, uh, something, ah, festive for a female friend."

"Species?"

"Twi'lek."

"Skin tone?"

"Um, teal."

"How festive, sir?"

"Oh, you know. Very."

"Right this way. We have a selection of Twi'lek wear in the correct color coordinates. Something in hisp-silk, perhaps? Sleep gowns? Microgarments?"

Ratua followed the droid to the back of the shop. There were no other customers or staff about that he could see. There was a window at the shop's front, and all he wanted was to be sure his back was to it. He paid scant attention to the droid as it held something filmy and nearly transparent up for his inspection. "Yes, yes, that's nice. What else do you have?"

His mind whirled. He hadn't expected to see anybody he knew here. None of his fellow prisoners were likely to be wandering the station on their own, and what were the chances one of the few guards he had known personally on the prison world would be transferred here?

Apparently much greater than he had expected.

When you thought about it, it made sense. They'd need guards on the station, because a place as big as this was becoming would definitely have crime popping up, even if it was no more than deckhands getting drunk and disorderly. And that wouldn't be the only problem. Put a million people into an enclosed space, even one as huge as the Death Star, and there were going to be a fair number of bad eggs. Military discipline wasn't the easiest thing to live under, plus there were all those civilian contractors. Yeah, they'd definitely need detention centers and guards, and who better than guys who had hands-on experience on a planet full of real criminals?

Okay, so it was reasonable. But that wasn't the problem, was it? If Stihl saw him, he was cooked, no two ways about it. And that was definitely going to put a bend in his ability to court Memah. He couldn't risk going into the cantina if, as he suspected, Rodo and Stihl had become pals. It certainly wasn't surprising—given their joint love of hand-to-hand violence, it was inevitable that they'd either be bosom buddies or mortal enemies. Regardless, his potential romance was over before—

Hold on, hold on, wait a second. He had told Memah who he was. For maybe the second time in his life, he had offered the truth. She knew he was an escapee, and—so far, at least—had done nothing. He could just tell her about this. They could work out something . . .

"How about this item?"

He looked at the droid. It held up a piece of crimson silk that he could easily hide in his hand, with two fingers left over. The mental image of Memah wearing nothing but this filled his thoughts, momentarily banishing that of Sergeant Stihl. Oh, *my.*

"I'll take that. And that other thing, too."

"Very good, sir. Debit code?"

"How about hard currency?"

"That will be fine, sir. Shall I gift-wrap these for you?"

"Uh, yes. That would be good."

Ratua walked out of the store carrying the packages, in a considerably more sober mood than he'd been in a few minutes before. He had a few nice gifts for Memah, though they might be a bit premature, given the nature of their relationship. He would hold on to them for a while and hope to see her in one, someday soon.

And when he thought about it, maybe Stihl wasn't so much a threat after all. The man was in the military, so his work schedule had to be somewhere in the ship's computer. Those files could be accessed by somebody with sufficient expertise—and with enough credits, such expertise could be purchased by a careful person. If you knew when and where someone was going to be a large portion of the time, you could avoid accidentally running into him.

He felt himself relax a little. Things weren't so bad. Once again, luck had been on his side. He was almost coming to believe that he led a charmed life.

43

LIBRARY AND ARCHIVES, DECK 106, SECTOR N-ONE, DEATH STAR

"Hold still, Persee."

"I am motionless, sir," the droid said.

Atour Riten frowned. If that was true, then his hands must be shaking a bit. Was he really that old?

"Almost done here," he said. "A bit more patience . . ."

"I have infinite patience, sir, being a droid. However, I am constrained to point out that your current actions would seem to be in violation of the Imperial Legal Code, Section Fourteen, Subsection Nine, Part C-dash-one, which forbids tampering with autonomous droid function without official permission."

"So it would seem. But I have permission." He inserted the photonic cable and turned it until it locked into place.

"I show no record of such permission, sir."

"Hand-delivered this morning," Atour said. "My-eyes-only, very hush-hush."

"Really, sir? This is most unusual. I feel I must verify—"

The droid's last comment was interrupted when Atour touched the transfer button on his datastick, and the program contained therein began to download into Persee's memory. The droid sagged slightly, and its photoreceptors dimmed.

The personality substrate would remain the same; Atour did not want to disturb the droid's abilities, good help being so hard to come by. There were only two items that would be substantially changed. First, Persee's spyware, which required it to monitor its work environment and to report on any activities that might be remotely illegal according to Imperial statutes, would shortly be disabled. Second, its basic loyalty module, set up to put the good of the Empire at the top of its function pyramid as defined by its Imperial programmer, was being altered to shift this loyalty to Atour personally.

Persee was, in a few more seconds, going to become Atour Riten's servant first and foremost, and anything it saw or heard its master do from now on, it would keep to itself. Any tampering with its memory chip in an attempt to bypass the new programming would result in a total memory wipe, right down to the primary nodes. What would be left wouldn't be able to walk, talk, or do much of anything else. After all, an assistant who might consciously or unconsciously betray him to Imperial agencies, either covert or overt, wasn't of much use.

Atour had been able to access some wonderful material over his years of filing and cataloging. This droid-altering program had been one of his best finds. Hook it up, pop it in, and *zip!* Just like that, you had a new best friend who would do anything to keep you from harm. Anyone who queried Persee would get reasonable assurances that Commander Atour Riten was a prince of a fellow, as honest as the galaxy was wide, and this would hold true no matter how insistent the questioner. If it went past a certain point, Persee would suffer a firmware breakdown and, whatever anyone might suspect, there would be nothing to find indicating sedition.

The memory of the transfer itself would also be erased from Persee's mind. The droid wouldn't have a clue that any tampering had been done, or that it was any different when it walked out of the office than when it had walked in.

There was a *ping!* as the download ended. Atour unlocked and then removed the cable; the entire process had taken only a couple of seconds. He counted to ten.

Right on schedule the droid's photoreceptors lit. "Will there be anything else, sir?" Persee asked.

"No, I think that will do it for now. Systems check."

The droid replied, with no discernible delay, "My circuits, modules, and mechanics are all operating at optimum, sir."

"Well, good," Atour said. He made an airy gesture of dismissal. "Toodle off, then."

After the droid left, Atour felt better. There was no way he could do many of the things he was accustomed to doing with a blabbermouth droid looking over his shoulder and transmitting it all to the local security computer. The chances of anybody ever grilling Persee until it blew a circuit were very slim, but still, chance favored the better-prepared life-form.

He had a group of new junior librarians coming in for orientation later in the day, and tons of things to do before they showed up. His personal files were proof against any of them stumbling across anything secret by accident or intent. He assumed as a matter of course that one or more of them had to be some kind of Imperial spy. That was usually the case in any organization, and even if it weren't, it was better to make that assumption and be wrong than to not make it and be thrown into prison for underestimating the powers-that-were. A man didn't get to be his age and status by being completely foolhardy, even though he had certainly stepped over the line a time or ten. In his lifelong war against authority, he had won more battles than he had lost, even if they didn't know it.

Much to do, he reminded himself, and little time in which to do it. Best get moving.

44

GRAND MOFF TARKIN'S QUARTERS, EXECUTIVE LEVEL, DEATH STAR

Daala stepped from the shower, a waft of hot water vapor following her out. Tarkin smiled as she dried herself with a fluffy black towel made of virgin cotton from the Suliana fields and slipped into a matching robe. She stood under the air jets and dried her short hair, then came into the bedchamber and sat on the foot of the bed.

"Feel better?" Tarkin asked.

"Much. So much nicer to have hot water than the sonics."

"Yes. Rank has its privileges. You have news for me?"

"I do. You won't like it."

He sat up and looked at her.

She went to the desk, opened a drawer, and removed an info disk. She dialed his computer terminal to life.

"You have my access codes?" Now he slid out of the bed, the silk of his sleepwear causing static electricity as it moved across the sheets. His gown crackled and clung to his body, but he ignored it as he walked to where she stood.

She smiled at him. "Of course."

"Did I give them to you?"

"You don't remember? Well, if you didn't, I know you meant to."

Tarkin wasn't sure if he should be angered or aroused by this evidence of Daala's boldness. Before he could decide, a hologram blinked on. It showed rows of sealed cargo containers, the white everplast boxes stacked three-deep, with corridors between them to allow access. They looked like standard two-point-five-meter units, but it was hard to say just by looking.

"Security cam," she said. "Aft cargo hold on the *Undauntable*."

"A security cam that was not destroyed in the explosion?"

"Oh, it was blown up with the rest of the ship. But it was rigged to feed a signal to a receiver. I obtained the recording."

"How?"

"A moment. Watch."

There was a date/time stamp in the lower right-hand corner of the image, the seconds flashing by . . .

A figure moved into view. Tarkin frowned. It was still hard to judge size without some kind of scale.

As if reading his thoughts, Daala moved her hand over a sensor, and a grid overlaid the image. The figure was slightly less than two meters tall. That still didn't tell him much. With the cloak and hood concealing it, it could have been any of a hundred species.

The mysterious being walked along the row of containers. It reached one in the middle of the cam's field and tapped the keypad on the door with one gloved finger.

"Why didn't we have bioscanners going as well?" Tarkin asked, annoyed. "We'd have data on species, sex, age—"

"Shh," she said. "We were lucky to have gotten this much. Now watch."

The door rolled up and the figure entered the container.

Thirty seconds passed. The figure emerged, closed the door behind him—or her—and moved out of cam view.

Daala waved the recording off. She looked at him, waiting.

Tarkin was nobody's fool. "The explosive device was in the cargo container and ready to go. All the agent had to do was trigger it."

"Yes. He didn't bring anything with him, so it had to be in place already."

"And?"

She turned to the console's controls. Another image appeared, this one a routing manifest.

"The rigged container's ID number is not visible in the recording, but the number of the one eight down is, so it was a simple matter to figure out the one we want."

True, Tarkin thought. Loading droids were not known for creativity. They stacked cargo containers by the numbers.

"You can see that this container came from the cargo vessel *Omega Gaila,* itself from the ammunition stores at the Regional Naval Supply Area near Gall. The container carried high explosives, so that's what a scan would show—if anybody bothered to do one."

She waited again.

Tarkin thought about it. "The RNSA at Gall is a high-security facility. Extremely tight. Nobody on or off the base without top clearance, even the cargo handlers."

"Yes."

He frowned. Shook his head. "Not possible."

"Yet somebody got into a container and rigged it with a bomb powerful enough to blast a Star Destroyer apart. And they weren't shooting in the dark, hoping to hit something, because it took somebody on the other end to arm the device."

"So they knew where it was bound," he finished for her. "No way to have agents at every possible destination. Once it got to our storage facility, it could have gone to any of several ships."

"Or to this station," she said. "It was the luck of the draw that *Undauntable* needed ammo before we did."

"So it's being run by somebody higher than a cargo handler. At the very least, there had to be somebody from Routing involved, and enough of a conspiracy to be able to place or contact an agent already here. We are talking about a Rebel spy in the Imperial Navy with more than a little reach."

"Just so."

"We can probably determine who loaded the container, and who routed it."

"Which is good, but also doesn't stop something similar from happening again if the next shipment comes from a different source."

"Correct. We need to find whoever is running the agents here," he said.

"I concur."

He looked at her. "How do you plan to do this?"

"I'm assuming that the agent did not choose suicide. We have the day and time the device was activated. He or she would have had to arrive before that time, and depart before the explosion. *Undauntable*'s operational logs were backed up on the station's computer, the last entry coming just before the ship's destruction. It might take some time, but we can access those and narrow down the possibilities."

"Good," Tarkin said. "Do so immediately."

She smiled and adjusted the lapels of her robe. "Immediately?"

He did not return her smile. "Yes. There are times for dalliance, and times for action. I want a report by zero five hundred hours."

Daala nodded and began to dress, quickly.

45

MEDCENTER, SECTION N-ONE, DEATH STAR

Uli looked at his commander incredulously. Since Hotise had arrived and set up shop on the station, they hadn't seen each other that much, and Uli wasn't happy to be seeing him now.

"What?" Hotise said. "You seem to think that I personally run this war, Doctor. Believe me, if I did, it'd be run a sight better. As it is, there are things that are simply in short supply. Medical doctors, not to mention psychiatrists, are hard to come by, even here with the big green light. It won't kill you to step into the breach now and then. You did rotations in both disciplines during your residency."

"Of course I did. I'm not complaining about the work. But I'm a surgeon, not an internal meds doctor. My skills are rusty outside my specialty."

"Well, you have state-of-the-art robotics backing you up, as well as the top-of-the-line diagnosters in the galaxy. A first-year medical student or a competent droid could run those and hit the mark ninety-five percent of the time."

"You're making my point for me, Doctor." Uli held his hands up. "These are for cutting, not tapping knees and treating headaches. It's not the best use of my talents."

Hotise shrugged. "Making best use of talent has never been the military's mission, son. They change about as fast as a space slug molts. If they want to have a doctor digging trenches in the field of battle, they will have him do just that—because they can.

"If routine physicals get in the way of your surgery, then let them slide. But as long as you aren't slicing and gluing, we don't have enough help for you to sit around waiting for another body to open up." He leaned forward, putting his hands on Uli's cluttered desk. He looked, Uli thought, about twenty years older than he had months before, when he'd assigned Uli his duties. Uli could also smell a faint whiff of alcohol on his breath.

"Eventually," Hotise continued, "we'll be fully staffed, but until then, we have to spread ourselves around."

"And if the spread is too thin for the good of the patients?"

Hotise straightened. "Suck it up, Dr. Divini. There is a war on, after all."

Uli sighed and nodded. He hadn't really expected anything else. And tired or not, drunk or not, the man was right. A surgeon lying on a couch could just as easily be treating routine lumps and bumps.

Didn't mean he had to like it, though.

"You have patients to see," Hotise said. "So I'll get out of your hair. Have a nice shift."

The older man exited the office, and Uli glared at Hotise's back as he left.

"I'm unfamiliar with all the nuances of human behavior," C-4ME-O said, "but I think it's safe to say that you didn't come out the best in that exchange."

"You're the second wise-mouth droid I've met. If I never meet another one, my life would not suffer a bit."

"Here's the next patient's chart, Doctor."

"Go find something useful to do before I decide you need to be reprogrammed as a latrine cleaner. We can do that in the military, you know. Take a medical droid and put him to that use."

"Idle threats do not become you, Dr. Divini."

Uli smiled despite himself and looked at the chart. It described the complaint of one Sergeant Nova Stihl, a guard, who was having . . .

Bad dreams?

Great. Wonderful. He knew less about psychological maladies than he did Rodian influenza.

In the exam room, the patient sat on the table wearing a disposable flimsi gown. Offhand, he looked fit and muscular; on the face of it he didn't appear to be beset with any major psychosis. His affect was calm.

"Sergeant Stihl. I'm Dr. Divini. What seems to be the problem?"

The man gave him a little shrug and looked embarrassed. "Trouble sleeping."

"I see. Says here you've been having nightmares?"

"Yeah. I hate to waste your time on piddly stuff, Doc, but I'm starting to doze off at work. Maybe you can give me a pill or something?"

"No problem there, we have all kinds of sleeping meds. But we should probably try to figure out the cause before we try curing it."

Stihl shrugged again. "You're the doctor."

"How long has it been going on?"

"Hard to say. I used to have a bad night once in a while at my last posting, but they've gotten worse since I was transferred up here. More frequent."

"Uh-huh. Any stress at your job?"

Stihl laughed. "I'm a guard. I deal with sodders locked in detention who don't want to be there, most of whom did something illegal to get there. Stress goes with the territory."

"Been doing it awhile?"

"Since I joined up. Eleven standard years."

"Okay. So the stress level now is what? More, less, the same?"

"A little less, actually. I was posted dirtside before. Some real touchy types on Despayre, most of 'em crazier than a rabid Shistavanen. Guys detained here on the station are generally military or civilian contractors who got too frisky or greedy. Not many career criminals. Easier to deal with, 'cause they got more to lose."

"Okay. Recreation?"

"I do martial arts."

"Getting hit in the head more than usual?"

Stihl laughed. "Other way around. I'm the teacher—I don't get tagged, much."

"Anything new or different so far as diet? Alcohol? Quarters? Relationships?"

"Not that you'd notice. I get along with my unit, eat the same stuff I usually eat, don't spend my time drinking. Basic barracks are the same all over the galaxy; I share a cube with a few other NCOs; they aren't any trouble. I tend to serial monogamy and don't have anybody I'm seeing right now."

Subjective analysis seemed normal. "Could be an allergy. Lot of construction chaff and microscopic dust floating around before the filters catch it. Let's do a physical, make sure all your systems are online, run some analyses of blood and urine and stuff like that, do a mag-scan. If we find something we can fix, we'll fix it. If everything checks out, I've got meds that will knock you out like you were hit with a mallet, and guarantee a dreamless sleep for six hours."

"Sounds good."

Uli did a physical exam, which was unremarkable. The man was as fit as he had first thought, at least to the trained eye. He had C-4ME-O take the patient to the diagnoster array and run the standard battery of tests, covering all the major systems. The machines were fast; the first results started coming in before the second batch of tests began.

Things looked unremarkable. Stihl was in great shape for a man his age, better than most humans twenty years younger. Myoconduction, brain scan, EEG, MEG, dendrite function were within limits. Afferent/efferent speeds were slightly better than normal; heart, lungs, kidneys, liver, spleen, pancreas, repro, bowels . . .

Uli looked at the blood composition readout. Platelets fine, WBC normal spread, hematocrit, hemoglobin, all normal.

Except—

His midi-chlorian count was over five thousand per cell.

Uli blinked. That was unusual. Normal human range was less than half that. He didn't know a lot about midi-chlorians; nobody did anymore—most of the research on the subject had been done at the Jedi academy by their own healers, and their records were not available for study. A shame. The Jedi were all gone . . .

Like Barriss . . .

He shook his head. He didn't want to rocket down that particular space lane, thank you. When he'd met Barriss, he'd been up for his first tour in the field, young and idealistic. Now Barriss was gone—and so was his idealism.

This blasted war . . .

He pulled himself back to the task at hand. Could the high midi-chlorian count be somehow responsible for the sergeant's dreams? If the Jedi were correct, these were the vital living components that connected everything to the Force. And he'd heard that the Force could sometimes cause strange, even prescient dreams. It seemed to make sense, especially given that it was the only anomaly on the tests.

"So what's the drill, Doc?"

Uli explained the stats to him. The sergeant looked blank. "Mini whats?"

"Midi. Chlorians."

"And you think that might be the problem?"

"Frankly, I don't know. Not my specialty. I'll check into it and get back to you, but in any case it shouldn't be dangerous at your levels. You aren't going to die from it."

Stihl looked relieved. "That's something, anyhow."

"I'll give you some tablets that should allow you to rest."

"Thanks, Doc. I appreciate it."

"Just doing my job," Uli said.

After the sergeant was gone, Uli accessed the station's medical library. Not surprisingly, there was no more to be had on midi-chlorians than he already knew.

Maybe there was a doctor with specialized knowledge of cell biology on the station, or assigned to one of the warships in the area. He started to post a query on the MedNet, but then stopped. *Was this a good idea?* he asked himself. The Emperor had ordered a complete ban on any and all data having to do with Jedi and the Force. So thorough had been the revisionism that now, barely two decades after the Jedi heroism of the Clone Wars, nearly every reference in every data bank in the galaxy had been purged of matters and information relating to the order. Most beings born since then knew little, if anything, about those larger-than-life characters whose names had once been on everyone's lips, and their elders were smart enough not to talk about the subject. The ban, as far as Uli knew, was still in effect. Did he really want to put up a query on a public forum concerning such a highly sensitive topic? After all, Sergeant Stihl seemed to be in no danger, immediate or long-term. He'd never heard of midi-chlorians being associated with any pathology. Did his oath to heal extend so far as to put himself in harm's way by asking for information on a forbidden topic, especially when the patient seemed to be in no danger?

Yes, he reluctantly decided. If there was the slightest chance that the midi-chlorians were causing, or had the potential to cause, ill health for Nova Stihl, It was Uli's duty as a healer to pursue all courses of inquiry.

C-4ME-O entered. "Your next patient is ready, Doctor."

As he interviewed the next patient, Uli realized that, while he'd resented Hotise's laying additional work on him initially, now he was glad of it. It took his mind off what a moral quagmire the galaxy had become.

46

ISD *DEVASTATOR*, ARKONIS SECTOR, OUTER RIM

"Lord Vader?"

"What is it, Lieutenant?"

The lieutenant practically stank of fear. Normally that was to be expected and not a problem, for fear was a useful tool. But occasionally it could be time consuming.

"You aren't afraid," Vader said, drawing his fingers together to concentrate the Force.

"I'm not afraid," the lieutenant echoed. The tightness in his face and body relaxed, somewhat.

"You have something for me?"

"Yes, sir." The lieutenant held up a printout flimsi sheet. "One of your warning flags has been tripped. A surgeon on board the battle station has requested from the local MedNet information on midi-chlorians."

"Very well. Leave it here. You may go."

"Sir." The man left. Weak-minded idiot he still was, but at least he wasn't shaking in his boots.

Vader read the new dispatch with interest. He considered the knowledge therein. Why would someone on the battle station be looking for information on midi-chlorians?

Vader knew all about midi-chlorians, of course—he personally had the highest count per cell ever recorded, more than twenty thousand. More than Yoda, and, he knew, more than his erstwhile Master, Kenobi. Which meant that, potentially, he could have a stronger connection to the Force than anyone. Since most, if not all, of the Jedi were no more, that was all the sweeter, though Vader was convinced that Obi-Wan had remained hidden all these years, as had Yoda, assuming the latter had not finally shuffled off into death. Yoda had been very old, after all, and the defeat and deaths of the Jedi could not have helped him age any easier. He could be dead. But it was unwise to make such assumptions about such a powerful Jedi Master.

Back to the subject at hand. It might be wise to have a word with this medic and see what he was up to. Midi-chlorians did not normally figure into the medical treatment of most beings. This was unusual.

Not unusual enough to leave his current mission and go investigate, however. Soon enough he would have reason to return to the battle station. He would deal with this doctor and his strange request when he went.

For now, it was time to go again to his hyperbaric chamber, to rest and recharge. There was much that needed to be done in the service of his Master, and never enough time to do it all.

ARCHITECTURAL OFFICES, EXECUTIVE LEVEL, DEATH STAR

Teela saw the flowers on her desk when she arrived for her shift, a spray of everlilies, rojos, blueblossoms, and purple passions, artfully arranged by somebody who knew how to mix and match them for the most visual appeal. She could smell the spicy, peppery scent of the rojos wafting in the office air currents as she drew nearer.

The card with the arrangement said, SO WHERE DO WE GO FROM HERE?

That, she thought, *is a good question.*

There wasn't any real future for them. He was an Imperial TIE fighter pilot on war duty, and she was a convicted criminal working as a trustee on the biggest battle station ever designed and built. Their backgrounds were too different, their loyalties too far apart. While it was true that they would both go where the Empire told them to go, and do what they were ordered to do, Teela did so because there was no real choice, whereas Vil gloried in his work.

Construction on the station kept getting faster as the crews learned from the first sections built and were able to build new ones with less wasted effort. Some parts of the process had been so streamlined that the work went nearly twice as fast as it had before. The army of construction droids worked tirelessly, day in and day out; an interior structure that would ordinarily take months to finish with organic labor would often be completed in only a few days. It was amazing and, to an architect, most gratifying to see such constructions appear as if by magic. The only ones who came close to matching the droids' speed were the Wookiees. Teela remembered an old saying: Give a Wookiee a knife and send him into a forest in the morning, and by evening he would have carved you a table to eat dinner on—and a house to put it in.

They were on schedule in many areas, ahead in many more, and behind in only a few. Teela felt mixed emotions at this. After the station was completed, it would go off to engage the Rebels and help destroy the insurrection, and Vil would be in the thick of all that. And where would she be? Probably back on the prison planet for the rest of her life.

Then again, life was always uncertain. You could get hit by a hovertruck crossing a street. There were myriad diseases that would kill you in short order. Somebody could forget to weld a seal and a decompressive blowout could spit you into cold vacuum, where you'd be dead and frozen solid before anybody came to collect you, if they even bothered. You didn't get up every morning expecting such things to happen—that way lay depression as deep as space itself—but you had to know that life was short and there were no guarantees.

So at the moment she had a spray of beautiful flowers on her desk that probably cost a couple of days' pay, and the attention of a not-unattractive man who wanted to spend his time and energy with her. Today, tomorrow, a month, a year . . . nobody knew how long they had, so why not seize the moment and enjoy it as much as possible?

Her inner self allowed as how that made sense. *Go for it, girl.*

She moved her hand over her desk's console and lit the comm. After a moment, the holo came up. Vil smiled at her.

"Hey," he said.

"Hey, yourself. The flowers are lovely. Thank you."

"We still on for dinner tonight?" he asked.

"Yes. But I'm betting I can do a better fogu than any restaurant on board. Why don't you come to my cube and let me cook for you?"

PART TWO

Shakedown

47

CORRIDORS ADJACENT TO DETENTION BLOCK AA,
LEVEL FIVE, DEATH STAR

"Sergeant Stihl, we have intruders! There's a breakout on Level Five, Detention Block AA-Twenty-three. Take a squad and get over there!"

Nova stared at the lieutenant in disbelief. Intruders? A breakout? How was that possible?

"Sergeant!"

No time to wonder about it now. "Copy, sir, on our way! Bretton, Zack, Dash, Alix, Kai, with me! Mahl, Cy, Dex, Nate, on point! Move out, people!"

The squad hustled out of the barracks and into the hall, the sound of their armor rattling as they moved. The corridors were strangely deserted, which Nova chalked up to luck. Fewer people meant fewer civilian casualties.

"Who are we after, Sarge?" That from Dash.

Nova didn't know. Who were they after?

Well, kark it, he'd know them if he saw them.

"Just shoot who I tell you to," he told the trooper. Then he raised his voice to include the rest of the squad: "Double-time it, people!"

They ran through the gray-and-black halls, following the four guards on point, their sidearms held up, fingers outside the trigger guards, as per regulations. The ceilings and floors were covered with blaster-proof absorbital, so if somebody accidentally cooked off a round it wouldn't do any damage. If you carried your weapon pointed at the floor, however, there was a good chance in a crowd that you'd shoot somebody's foot off, and the walls and vent grates weren't all that sturdy, either.

The corridor branched ahead. As they approached, Nova was desperately trying to remember which one led to D-Unit when a blaster bolt sizzled through a cross corridor ahead. The four guards on point skidded to a stop, then moved ahead slowly toward the intersection to peer around it.

Nova suddenly realized this was all familiar. It was as if he had been here before, seen the events that were now unfolding. He knew, without knowing how, that in the next few seconds a squad of stormtroopers was going to—

"*Aaahhhh!*" Somebody beyond the bend in the corridor screamed, and a moment later half a dozen troopers barreled around the corner of the hallway intersection, heading toward Nova and his men.

They were being chased by a single man with a blaster, yelling like a berserker as he ran. The man—Nova saw that he was dressed like a down-on-his-luck spacer—stopped, realizing that there were suddenly overwhelming odds in front of him. Then he turned and ran back the other way, putting on a burst of speed as he disappeared around the corner.

"After him! Go!" Nova led the pursuit, followed by his squad and the others. Once around the bend, he saw that the fleeing spacer had been joined by a Wookiee, and both of them were now shooting back at their pursuers as they fled. A blaster bolt took the man next to Nova. He tried to line up on the runners, but was jostled by somebody from behind; his bolt scorched the plating just behind the two escapees. The human zapped another round at them.

Time slowed down. The bolt crawled toward them, impossibly slow. But as slowly as it was moving, Nova found he was moving even slower . . . the deadly energy burst was going to hit him, and there was nothing he could do to stop it.

The blaster bolt slammed into him, penetrating the chest plate easily. It pierced his chest, burned out his heart, and he fell, dying—

Nova jerked up in bed, his pulse racing, as one of his cubemates hollered, "Hey, Stihl! Wake the frip up, you're yelling in your sleep again! Some of us are trying to get some milking rest here!"

"Sorry," Nova gasped. He slowed his breathing, using calming techniques he'd learned over the years. He felt his pulse rate drop, felt himself grow calmer.

But not calm enough. Nova laid back down, staring at the ceiling. So much for the sleeping meds helping things.

COMMAND CENTER, OVERBRIDGE, DEATH STAR

Tarkin looked at the data running up the screen, pleased. The station was nearly operational—at least enough so that they could begin basic maneuvers. The superlaser was only partially functional, true, but it was hot enough to test, and he had some ideas about how to do that.

All in all, things were going very well indeed.

There had been a few glitches. Daala had not been able to find those responsible for the destruction of the *Undauntable*. She had returned to the Maw, but would be back again, soon. Tarkin looked forward to her next visit.

An intelligence report had just come to his attention. There had been some kind of break-in and theft at an out-of-the-way military base on Danuta. While normally this would have been of little interest to Tarkin, the investigating agents had heard some intel—no more than rumor, really—that one of the files stolen was a set of plans for this battle station. Tarkin frowned. On the face of it, that seemed unlikely—how would the plans have gotten to that backrocket planet in the first place?

Then again, military secrets were notoriously hard to keep, and a file could be transmitted across the entire galaxy, given enough power in the generating signal. Some low-level functionary might have, at some point, come across the plans and decided to copy a set. There could be many reasons for doing so—knowledge was power. How much would the plans be worth to the Rebel Alliance? A fortune, certainly; well worth the small risk of being found out.

And if there was even a remote chance that such a thing had come to pass, if those plans had fallen into the clutches of the Rebels, that could be bad. The station, when fully operational, would be invulnerable from without, of course, but a saboteur who knew exactly where to do the most damage from within could be a real threat.

This needed to be addressed, and Tarkin knew who was best suited for the task. It was galling to have to ask the man for help, but the station's safety was paramount.

He moved to the holoplate and activated it. It was a priority-one communication, and the connection was made almost immediately.

The shimmering image of Darth Vader appeared before Tarkin, lifesized, as if he were standing in the same room.

"Grand Moff Tarkin. Why have you called?"

"I understand there is a remote possibility that a set of plans for this battle station may have been stolen by Alliance agents."

"Yes."

Tarkin clamped his teeth tight enough to make his jaw mucles ache. "You knew this?"

"I have my own agents."

The black helmet had no way to change expression, of course, but Tarkin could hear the amusement in the Dark Lord's voice. "I see," he said, his tone carefully neutral. Now was not the time to be at odds with the Emperor's lackey.

"I will find out if it is true, and if so, I will deal with it." The black helmet inclined questioningly. "That is why you called me, isn't it?"

Tarkin nodded. Vader might be many things, but fainthearted he was not. Once he began a task, he seldom swerved from finishing it. Odds were that the story was no more than a baseless rumor, but if not, no one was better equipped to determine the facts and eliminate the problem than Darth Vader. A useful, if dangerous, tool—no matter how Tarkin might feel about him personally.

"Keep me advised," he said.

"Of course." The image of Vader vanished.

ISD *DEVASTATOR,* NEAR TOPRAWA, KALAMITH SECTOR, NORTH QUADRANT

Vader broke the comm connection with Tarkin. How had the man found out about the stolen plans so quickly? There must be a leak somewhere. There were always leaks. The only way to prevent them was to keep everything to yourself, and that was not always possible.

Vader, of course, knew much more about the situation than he had told Tarkin. It was true: a set of plans had been stolen from a military base, and those plans were, indeed, now in Rebel hands. They had been smuggled to Darkknell, and then to Toprawa. There a band of Rebels had seized an Imperial communications tower and transmitted the plans to a blockade-runner orbiting the planet.

The blockade-runner, he had learned, was the *Tantive IV.*

Princess Leia Organa's vessel.

Bail Organa and his daughter had been among those in the reconstituted Imperial Senate who had cast their lot with the Rebels. The proof was not there yet, but Vader knew. He did not even need the Force to assure him of this. He knew it.

Doubtless her ship was on its way to deliver those plans to some secret Rebel base. Vader had to find and capture the craft before it arrived at its destination. Even though he would have preferred to follow the vessel to its destination and destroy the base, the destruction of another nest of Rebels was not as important as safeguarding his Master's prized battle station.

Thus the *Devastator* was bound for Tatooine, where his agents had predicted the *Tantive IV* was headed. A secret base there made little sense, as the planet was mostly desert and of little military or commercial value. The world was far enough out of the main lanes so that the Rebels might have had a base there once, but that possibility had already been checked thoroughly by Imperial operatives, who had reported that no such place now existed.

It made little sense. The planet was all sand and dunes, sparsely populated by colonists, both humans and other species, and the indigenous Tuskens. Vader knew just how inhospitable the place was. After all, he had spent his early years there—

No. Anakin Skywalker had been raised in the hot, dry wasteland, but who he was now had been forged on a world that made Tatooine look like Hoth. He had been annealed in the molten rivers of Mustafar. Mustafar was his birthworld, not Tatooine.

In any event, why the Princess was going there was unimportant. Perhaps she was just taking a roundabout route to throw off possible pursuit. What was important was that she had the plans for the Death Star, and that in itself was sufficient reason to detain her. The Empire would recover the plans and in so doing rid itself of her meddlesome actions at the same time.

His Master would be pleased with both events.

48

SUPERLASER FIRE CONTROL, THETA SECTOR, DEATH STAR

They hadn't lied. The differences between the simulator and the real thing were negligible. There were more worn spots and scratches in the simulator, put there over months of drills, but the equipment was identical.

Despite all the training, Tenn was still a little nervous. This was the real thing; from here, they could generate a pulse of pure destruction that was stronger than anything ever fired before. Amazing, and not a little intimidating. Not that he expected to ever fire the weapon at full power, certainly not to destroy an entire planet. The whole idea, as he understood it, was that the threat would be more than enough. They'd probably disintegrate an uninhabited moon or two, just to prove they meant business, but the actual targets would be military—Rebel bases, fleets, and the like. For such as those, the superlaser would be a ridiculous amount of overkill, akin to frying a green flea with a turbolaser.

"You've been hands-on in the simulator, you've seen the reads, so I'm not breaking any big news here," his CO said, breaking Tenn's reverie. "This is a monster gun, but it's not a repeater. You miss the first shot, you won't get another one on your shift."

Tenn nodded. He'd asked about power storage first day on the simulator, and the engineers had fallen all over themselves backing away from that one. But once he'd seen the numbers—they had to keep those honest, even in sims—he'd figured it out pretty quick. The capacitors could hold enough juice to light up a planet, true enough, but once they discharged, they weren't going to be filling back up real quick. Once you shot the thing, you might as well turn off the lights and go take a long nap, because it wasn't going to be back up to full power for the better part of a day. True, you could still pump out some pretty nasty low-power beams—and the definition of *low* here was still bigger than what a Star Destroyer could manage, even letting all the hardware spit at once—but it would be a duster instead of a buster. You could scorch a city or two, boil away a large lake or perhaps even a small sea, but that was about it.

And if you were the guy pulling the trigger and you missed, well, you'd be looking for a new job starting ten seconds after you said, *Oops . . .*

Tenn said, "My crew doesn't miss, Cap. You find a target and if we can see it, we will hit it, my personal guarantee."

The CO laughed. "You shooters are all alike."

"Check the records, Cap, check the records. They don't pay me to miss."

The CO's face went serious. "I know that, Chief. But we don't get to pick the targets. It might get ugly."

Tenn shrugged. "I'm not a politician or a Moff, sir. I do my job, let them do theirs."

The CO slapped him on the shoulder. "Good man!" He sounded relieved.

"So, we going to get operational here?"

"Pretty quick, son. Let your crew get familiar with the knobs. It's all supposed to be the same, but we won't be shooting blanks. I don't want anybody to get the jeeblies when it comes time to crank it up for real."

"I hear that, Cap. My crew won't let you down."

"I know they won't, Chief. That's why they get the first shot. You retire and have the great-grandkids at your feet, you can tell them that—how you shot the first round from the biggest cannon ever made."

"Something to look forward to," Tenn said. "That is, soon as I get a wife and get started on the kids who'll get that great-grandkid ball rolling."

Both men laughed.

THE HARD HEART CANTINA, DECK 69, DEATH STAR

"I still find that a pretty bizarre coincidence," Memah said. "That out of all the cantinas in all the galaxy, the one guard who would know you on sight happens to walk into mine."

"Stranger things have happened," Ratua said. "I knew a farmer on a legume co-op on Duro, one of fifty workers there. He was drafted into the navy. So he went through a year of basic training, shipped out, wound up being sent halfway across the galaxy to patrol in the middle of nowhere. He got liberty on a planet called Pzob. He walked into a Gamorrean pub, sat down, ordered an ale. Guy came out of the 'fresher and sat on the stool next to him, turned out to be a shiftmate back on the farm. Nine zillion klicks away from home, they both just happened to be in the same pub at the same time—what are the odds on that?"

She shrugged. "Got me. Math was never my strength."

"You don't seem to have much of a problem counting your credits."

She smiled. Okay, so he was a bad boy, but he did make her laugh. That was worth a lot, these days.

"Speaking of the worthy sergeant," he said, looking at his chrono, "I'd better take off. Stihl's duty shift is over in a few minutes and if he drops 'round to have a brew with Rodo, I want to be elsewhere."

"Good idea."

"Dinner, when you get off? My place?"

"As long as you promise not to cook."

"You wound me, woman."

"Better than poisoning you, like you nearly did me."

"How was I to know your kind can't eat sweetweed?"

"You could have looked it up. You plan to date outside your species, it's on you to know what's poison and what's not."

"You're never going to let me forget it, are you?"

"Not a chance, Green-Eyes. I'll pick up something on the way. Seafood, shellfish, like that."

They smiled at each other. He put out his hand, she took it in her own, and they exchanged gentle squeezes. She could have done worse, Memah knew. She had done worse, more than once.

After he was gone, she sighed and stretched, feeling tense muscles loosen. There were only a handful of customers in the place—it was just before shift change, and people were either on their way to work or about to get off, so it would be another hour or so before the cantina started to fill up. Time to take a break. Business had generally been very good, better than she'd expected. As the station grew, new sections being added and pressurized, there had been new cantinas added regularly as well. There were at least half a dozen of them in this sector alone, and scores of watering holes throughout the other completed portions, but she hadn't noticed that the competition had hurt her any. True, she was getting only a small percentage of the profits, but even so, at the current rate, when her hitch was up she'd have enough saved to start a new place of her own.

She wasn't sure she wanted to do that, however. Chances were good they'd offer her an extension on her contract, and she needed to think seriously about that when it happened. True, it was the military, so there were some rules a little stiffer than on a civilian planet, but even so it was clean, the patrons were generally well behaved, and she was making money like a jewel thief on a luxury spaceliner. She didn't miss the great outdoors—she'd never been much of a nature girl dirtside, and she'd only ventured out of the Southern Underground a few times. Not that there was much "outside" there, all of Imperial Center being essentially one large urban area, save for a few parks here and there.

A cantina on an impregnable battle station, or one next to the spacedocks in the slums of Imperial Center? Put that way, it didn't seem too hard a choice. Certainly this one was a lot safer than any she'd ever run before. Nobody was going to set it on fire by "accident," and from what she'd heard no Rebel ship could scratch the paint, much less really damage it.

Staying on was definitely something to consider. She was having a pretty good time, all things considered, and Green-Eyes being around didn't hurt much, either.

Memah smiled and hummed a tune as she began to mix more drinks.

49

TWO HUNDRED KILOMETERS OFF SECTOR N-FOUR,
EQUATOR, DEATH STAR

Vil slewed into a drifting turn to port, engine and pressors working hard to compensate for the "slide," and his pursuer, one of the newbies in Beta Two, wasn't quick enough to stay on his tail.

He jinked again, this time to starboard, and again the newbie was a hair slow to react. Understandable; this wasn't a move they taught in basic flight school, it was one you learned from somebody with a lot more cockpit time than the instructors had to waste on trainees.

The newbie said something excited that Vil didn't quite catch, but prayer or curse, it didn't help him: Vil had reversed their positions, finishing the loop lined up on the newbie's rear.

Gotcha, kid . . .

Vil thumbed the firing control and painted the newbie's backside with the scoring lasers. If his guns had been at full power, the kid would be dodging debris now, and both of them knew it.

"No big, kid," he said over the comm. "We all got to slide down the learning curve—"

"Attention, all squadrons, attention! Break off your drill immediately, I say again, break off all maneuvers immediately! Arm your laser cannons to combat mode, defensive pattern Prime, and stand by!"

What the kark?

The order was completely out of the black, but Vil was too well trained to question it. He swerved away and toggled his op-chan to his squad's frequency.

"Alpha One, on me, pyramid formation, green and blue, one, one, two!"

He punched the control button, and the signal diodes on his fighter began flashing in the sequence he'd given them, so that his squad would know his fighter and get to their positions. Green, one count. Green, one count. Blue, two counts, then repeated. Dit-dit-dah . . . dit-dit-dah . . .

"What's up, Loot?" That was Anyell, of course.

"How should I know? Stow the chatter and listen!"

The other pilots quickly assembled and moved into the pattern. It was the most basic of fighter maneuvers, practiced hundreds of times, and it didn't take more than a few seconds for all twelve to line up properly.

Vil switched to the main operations report-in channel: "Alpha One is ready."

Other squads logged on. There were 10 of them out there, 120 fighters in all.

After a moment, Command Channel took over:

"All units, this is Grand Moff Tarkin. We have detected an enemy carrier shifting into realspace from lightspeed in Sector Seven, at two thousand, two hundred kilometers' distance from the station, repeat, enemy carrier in Sector Seven. The vessel is identified as the *Fortressa,* a *Lucrehulk*-class carrier. Star Destroyers are moving to engage, but we expect the enemy to launch fighters. They pose a risk to the station. Stop them."

The local op-chan sig flashed, then overrode the main:

"All fighters, all squadrons, this is Flight Commander Drolan, Dee Ess One One. We are deploying in Zone Defense Delta, I say again, Zee-Dee-Delta. We are about to get our feet wet, boys, and I'm buying for the pilot who shoots the most of the fatherless scum out of the vac."

Vil's mind was awhirl. *Lucrehulk*-class vessels were originally Trade Federation ships, mostly modified commercial freighters. They were huge, circular craft, the biggest three thousand meters in length. After the Clone Wars, some of them had fallen under Rebel control. Unless the Alliance had done some major refitting, they weren't heavily armed, nor were they well shielded compared with a Star Destroyer, but they could carry a lot of fighters. Originally they'd spaced vulture droids, but the Rebels would have no doubt switched to X-wings. There might be a thousand of them in that ship, maybe more.

Vil swallowed, his throat suddenly dry. This was it—the real thing, a full-scale engagement, and his squad was going to be among the first ones to arrive at the party.

It was both exciting and terrifying. This was what all the training had been for: not some police action on a backrocket planet but an actual battle with Rebel pilots, some of whom were vets who had flown TIE ships before they defected. This wouldn't be like shooting targets on a range or painting newbies with low-powered beams; this was do or die.

This was why Vil Dance had signed on.

Now it was time to see who had the right stuff and who didn't.

COMMAND CENTER, OVERBRIDGE, DEATH STAR

"Our first wave of TIE fighters will arrive on zone station momentarily, sir. We have scrambled an additional thousand craft from the station." Admiral Motti didn't seem disturbed, but then he didn't have the primary responsibility. Tarkin did, and he was most aware of that as he looked at the hologram shimmering over the operations theater projection. He wasn't really surprised, however. He had halfway expected something like this for weeks, ever since they had lost the *Undauntable* to sabotage. The Rebels—some faction of them, at least—knew they were here, else they would not have been able to blow the ship up. Strategically, it made sense to attack the station now, before it was fully finished and operational. Tactically, a carrier was the smartest way. It would cost much, if not most, of the entire Rebel fleet to get past the Star Destroyers posted here in order to engage the battle station directly. But out of a thousand fighters or more, some might get by the TIE squads and inflict damage, even if the mother ship was taken out. Maybe not enough to destroy it, but if they could slow construction, that would be a victory of sorts.

The lieutenant running the sensor array said, "Sir, the first wave of enemy fighters has left the carrier. Two hundred and fifty X-wings."

As Tarkin nodded, the comm tech said, "Sir, I have a coded message incoming on your personal channel."

Tarkin blinked. Who could that be? "Put it on my personal screen."

Their TIE fighters were holding at a thousand klicks out, and it would take a few minutes for the X-wings to get that close to the station. The Star Destroyers were en route. There was nothing more to be done at the moment. Tarkin activated the message.

Daala's face appeared on his screen.

He tried not to let his surprise show. "Admiral?"

"Grand Moff Tarkin. We're en route to the station, and it seems there is some interesting activity out there."

"Nothing we can't handle," he said. "Though you might want to circle around and avoid it."

"By *it,* you mean that enemy carrier and all those X-wings pouring out of it?"

"Yes. That area is about to become inhospitable."

"You're sending in Star Destroyers?"

"I was, but as of this moment, I have a better idea."

"Ah."

"Precisely."

"Well, I'll move away from—blast!"

"Daala?"

"We have company. Disconnect."

She broke the connection, and Tarkin frowned. Daala was an excellent commander, and her ship was fast and well armed; she could deal with a few X-wings. Still . . .

"Sir, the enemy has disgorged a second wave. That makes five hundred fighters," the sensor technician said.

"We'll put a stop to that." To Motti, he said, "Admiral, have the Star Destroyers stand down. Break off their intercept."

"Sir?" Motti looked at him as if he had just turned into a purple-dyed Wookiee. Tarkin smiled. He moved his hand over his comm.

"Superlaser Control," came the response.

Motti's expression changed. Now he smiled, too.

"Commander," Tarkin said to the comm. "I have a target for you."

SUPERLASER FIRE CONTROL, THETA SECTOR, DEATH STAR

The CO said, "You heard the man, Chief. Can you do it?"

"Sir, no problem."

"Two thousand, two hundred and nine kilometers. Not an easy target."

"If we have the power to reach that far, I will hit it, sir," Tenn replied.

The CO checked a readout. "We have four percent in the discharge capacitors."

"More than we need," Tenn said.

The CO looked relieved. "Go, Chief."

Tenn nodded, turned to the console, and opened the speakers.

"We have an order to commence primary ignition," he said to the crew. "All right, boys, let's pull the hammer back and cock this sodder! Report!"

The various sections reported each operation's status, quickly and enthusiastically:

"Hypermatter reactor level one twenty-fifth of maximum."

"Capacitors, four percent available."

"Tributaries one through eight, green for feed."

"Primary power amplifier, green."

"Firing field amp is . . . green."

"We are go on induction hyperphase generator feed."

"Tributary beam shaft fields aligned."

"Tributary beam shafts one through eight clear."

"Targeting field generator, ready."

"We have primary beam focusing magnet at ten-sixteenths gauss . . . now fourteen-sixteenths . . . now at full."

Tenn scanned his board. All green. Twenty-eight seconds. Not their fastest time, but not bad. "We're good to go," he told the CO.

The CO nodded and said to the comm, "Grand Moff, superlaser is primed."

The Grand Moff's voice over the comm was calm but crisp: "Then fire."

The CO nodded at Tenn.

As he had hundreds of times in simulated practice, Tenn thumbed the safety button on the shifter above his head and pulled the lever down. He counted silently:

Four . . . three . . . two . . . one—

"We have successful primary ignition," the computer's voice said.

Tenn waited. The target was two thousand klicks away, so the time would be only—

"A hit!" the targeting tech said. There was a pause as he scanned his scopes.

"Well?" Tenn asked tensely.

"It—it's . . . *gone,* Chief. Nothing left."

Tenn blinked at the report. He looked at the CO, who looked just as dumbfounded.

They had vaporized a carrier three kilometers across—with four percent power on the beam. Just like that.

A cheer went up from the men in the room. The CO thumped Tenn's back. Tenn grinned in response, but inside, he was still having trouble believing it.

Four percent. The total destructive potential was nothing short of astronomical. The power of a star, at his command.

50

COMMAND CENTER, OVERBRIDGE, DEATH STAR

"Well," Motti said, "it appears that the superlaser works."

Tarkin smiled. "So it does. But there are still five hundred enemy fighters out there and they have no place to go, so they have nothing to lose."

"And we already have them outnumbered more than two to one, with TIE pilots itching to shoot them down, and plenty more where they came from," Motti said. "It's a cleanup operation now, Governor. They can't run, and they can't hide."

Tarkin nodded. "Give the order," he said. "Tell our fighters to hit them hard and fast, while they're still reeling from what they just saw."

"Sir? Your private channel again."

Tarkin nodded and took the call.

The man who appeared before him seemed upset. After a moment, Tarkin recognized the man as Daala's ship runner.

"Yes, Captain Kameda?"

"We were attacked by a squadron of X-wing fighters, sir. We destroyed them, but we took damaging fire."

"Why isn't Admiral Daala telling me this herself?"

"Sir, we lost shielding on the bridge. There was an explosion. Admiral Daala was injured."

Tarkin felt his belly clutch tightly. "How bad?"

"Not life threatening, sir. The medics have stabilized her."

Tarkin let out the breath he was holding.

"But she sustained a head wound and is . . . disoriented. There is a piece of shrapnel in her skull. We need a surgeon."

Tarkin nodded. "Get her to the station immediately."

"We're on our way, sir, should be arriving in a few minutes."

Tarkin broke the call, then activated the station intercom.

Captain Hotise answered. "N-One MedCenter."

"Admiral Daala has been injured in the attack and is on the way in with a head wound. Have your best team of surgeons standing by."

"Yes, sir."

Tarkin sundered the connection. This was not good news. It mitigated his triumph at the success of the superlaser's first firing. He did not want to lose Daala—that would sour the taste of victory.

And of course, he did care for her . . .

A THOUSAND KILOMETERS OFF THE DEATH STAR

The first wave of X-wings outnumbered the line of TIE fighters two to one, but they were flying nonevasive—hoping, Vil guessed, to blow right past the defenders.

That wasn't going to happen. Vil targeted the first X-wing to get within range, fired, and blew it apart, just like that. The enemy pilot never got a pulse off.

With zone defense, you moved around, but you held a certain position within specified limits. The X-wings were trying to get past, not engage. They shot if a TIE was right in front of them to clear a path, but they didn't deviate from their trajectories. They were intent on the Death Star. That made them easy targets.

What kind of lunatic strategy was that?

Vil quickly took out a second ship, then a third.

Behind him, the battle station had scrambled more TIE ships, and behind the X-wings the Star Destroyers were sending out even more. Very soon the odds would be even, if not in the Empire's favor.

The flight commander's voice crackled in his ears: "Alpha One, Beta One, Gamma One, Delta One—break zone and pursue, targets of opportunity!"

Drolan intended for his units to collect as many of the kills as possible, Vil knew. The next wave would stop any who got past, but folks late to the game weren't going to have anything to shoot at when they got here.

Vil shrugged. If the Rebels were intent on suicide, then his men would be glad to oblige them. He blipped his squad: "Alpha One, you heard the man. Fan out and take 'em apart! Ten-klick global pattern; don't get too far away."

He heard the chorus of "Copy, Lieutenant!" as he pulled his TIE around and started chasing the X-wings.

It wasn't a battle; it was a massacre. The X-wings were so intent on hitting the station that they didn't fight back. The eighty or so that Vil's wave couldn't collect were cut to pieces by the next wave of TIEs coming from the Death Star. The second wave of X-wings didn't get a single fighter past the Star Destroyers' TIE squadrons.

When it was done, Vil had ten kills, duly recorded by his nose cam and logged into his file.

Five kills made you an ace. Just like that, Lieutenant Dance had become a double ace, as had more than a few others. The total number of TIE fighters lost was fewer than a hundred.

It had been his first real battle against the Rebels, but Vil took no pride in it. It had been easy.

Far too easy.

51

COMMAND CENTER, OVERBRIDGE, DEATH STAR

"Sir?" Motti said.

"You heard me, Admiral. We are moving the station. The Rebels knew where to find us, and I won't allow that to happen again."

Tarkin had that look on his face that brooked no argument. It was a look that Motti knew well. Nevertheless, it was his duty to point out impediments. "Sir, we aren't really ready for full lightspeed maneuvers yet."

The Grand Moff looked impatient. "I know, Admiral. We don't need to go far; the other side of Despayre will do for now. The Rebels will know that their attempt failed, so they won't try the same tactic again. No one but the commanders of the Star Destroyers and their chief navigators are to be given the new coordinates—and aside from you and our chief navigator and myself, no one else on this station is to be given that information, either. There are spies among us, Admiral, and while we will eventually hunt them down and remove them, I will not risk this station in the meantime. Understand?"

"Yes, sir, I do."

"Within the hour, Motti. Leave two Star Destroyers here."

"By your command, sir."

Tarkin turned away. "I'm going to Medical. Admiral Daala's surgery is in progress."

After Tarkin was gone, Motti considered his task. It made sense to move, there was no questioning that. If a Rebel armada showed up and there was nobody there . . . well, it was a big galaxy. They wouldn't know where to start looking, and it likely wouldn't occur to any of them that their enemies had gone to all the trouble of powering up just to lumber around to the other side of the planet. Every additional hour it took for them to locate the Death Star would be one more hour closer to it becoming fully operational.

And once that happened, the entire Rebel fleet would be powerless to stop it.

That the Grand Moff's paramour was injured was too bad, but hardly any of Motti's concern. He held little respect for her as an officer. Without Tarkin's patronage, she would never have risen to her rank. As far as he was concerned, women didn't have what it took to command. If she died on the operating table, Motti would shed no real tears, though he would, of course, pretend sadness to keep Tarkin mollified. The old man was a bit touchy about her, and it wasn't a good idea to get on his bad side. Daala was a distraction; Tarkin cared for her too much. That was another chink in the Grand Moff's armor, a chink that someday Motti might want to exploit.

SURGICAL SUITE 1, MEDCENTER, DEATH CENTER

Uli was not a neurosurgeon by specialty, but he had learned a great deal about the subject by necessity in operating theaters all over the war-torn galaxy. He'd lost count of the number of hands-on neurosurgical procedures he had done, and he couldn't even begin to estimate the number of species he had operated upon. If you were the only surgeon available, you cut what needed to be cut.

He was not the primary on this case, only one of the three-person team of surgeons digging into the admiral's head. The stakes, as they were keenly aware, were very high. She was the only woman admiral in the Imperial Navy, and she was, according to the scut, Grand Moff Tarkin's very personal friend. It was not beyond possibility that if she didn't make it through the procedure, the Grand Moff might have them all shoved through the nearest lock into unforgiving space.

There were seven more surgical assistants in the room—three nurses and four droids. So far the operation was going well. All vital signs were good.

"Okay, we are removing the artifact now." That was from Abu Banu, the station's only real neurosurgeon. He was a Cerean, one of the few nonhuman species in any position of authority aboard the Death Star—no doubt because he was one of the best brain surgeons in the galaxy.

"Stand by the pressor field in case we get a bleeder," Banu said.

Uli, who was running the field, nodded, but he didn't need to be reminded. They all knew their jobs; Banu was talking for the recorder that was taking it all down. On a high-profile procedure like this, if something happened, somebody would get blamed, and the recording would help pin it down. Sometimes patients died who should have lived, but you didn't want to be the man held responsible for allowing the Grand Moff's lover to expire.

No pressure . . .

A small blood vessel began to ooze, and Uli dialed the pressor field up a hair—enough to stop the seepage, but not enough to put too much pressure on the naked brain upon which they were working.

"Sponge," Banu said.

One of the droids extended a rock-steady arm and blotted the tiny bit of blood that the pressor hadn't stopped.

"Roa, dab a little glue on that arteriole."

Dr. Roa reached in with the applicator's ultrafine tip and touched the torn vessel. A tiny bead of orthostat solution welled, flowed into the cut, and sealed it.

"Got it," Roa said.

Banu straightened, and Uli heard his spine crack. No surprise there; Cereans were notorious for back trouble. It was the price paid for those huge craniums they carried around.

"Okay, crew, what do we think here?" Banu asked. "Uli?"

"The shrapnel went into the hippocampus and adjacent cortex, mostly dentate gyrus. Not much in the Cornu Ammonis fields, or the subiculum, but even so, I'd guess she's going to have some memory problems. Old ones, maybe making new ones."

"Dr. Roa?"

"I'm with Divini. Stick a piece of jagged, hot metal into CA-one, CA-two, and CA-three, wiggle it around, and you've got definite declarative memory loss. Can't tell how much or how bad."

Banu nodded. "I concur. Given the injury, I don't see any problems with general cognitive function, but expressive and factual material will likely be compromised.

"Anybody see anything else we need to fix?"

Nobody did.

"All right. Let's close her up."

Uli was degowning in the post-op changing room with the other two surgeons and the assistants when Grand Moff Tarkin strode in. Uli's first thought was, *He's not supposed to be here.* But—who was going to tell him that?

"Doctors. What is Admiral Daala's condition?"

Uli and Roa looked at Banu. He was the head of the team, so it fell to him to explain it.

"Sir," the Cerean said, "Admiral Daala sustained a neurological injury that chiefly impacted her right medial temporal lobe. She's in good condition and stable."

"What long-term damage will there be to her?"

"We can't be sure yet. That portion of the brain is called the hippocampus—humans have two hippocampi, one on each side. This area is, in large measure, responsible for functions of memory."

Tarkin looked impatient. "Yes. And?"

Banu looked at Uli and Roa, then back at Tarkin. "It's all conjecture at this point, sir. She is in a medically induced coma, so that we may treat her properly to prevent swelling of her injured brain. When she wakes up and recovers, the chances are good that there will be no loss of function, either neurologically or physically; however, there will likely be some memory loss."

"Some? How much is *some*?"

Banu shook his head. "We are not fortune-tellers, Governor. We won't know until the admiral recovers consciousness and can be tested."

Tarkin's face clouded, and Banu apparently saw it. The Cerean hurriedly added, "If I had to guess, I'd say she won't remember the traumatic event, and that she'll likely lose at least some of the past year."

"I see. Well. Keep me informed. Admiral Daala is a valuable officer."

"Of course."

Tarkin turned and left.

"A valuable officer," Roa said. He chuckled. "I heard that she can—"

"Ease up on that," Uli said. "Don't know who's listening."

That sobered all three of them, and with good reason, Uli knew. You didn't want to be making jokes about the Grand Moff's girlfriend and have it get back to him. Not if you didn't want to wind up with your organs harvested.

CORRIDOR, OVERBRIDGE, DEATH STAR

As he headed back to the Command Center, Tarkin was both relieved and worried. He felt great affection for Daala, to be sure, and he was most pleased that she would survive. That she might not recall her most recent visits here and their enjoyable time together was regrettable, but considering the possibility that her injury could well have killed her, not so bad.

It was not so good, though, that whatever she had learned during her investigation of the spies in their midst would also likely be gone. Since she had never been here, officially, there would not be any files tucked away where that data might be found. She was too smart for that.

And it was not the least bit good that she was here and injured, since she was supposed to be at the Maw. That would have to be addressed.

As he walked, Tarkin considered his options. He needed to manage this in a way that would not come back to haunt him. He had not gotten to where he was by pretending politics did not exist. He had enemies, and they would glory in anything that might present him in a bad light to the Emperor.

Daala would recover swiftly; she was young and strong. As soon as she was sufficiently well to travel, he would have her transferred back to the Maw. A story would be put in place—an accident there had caused her some injury. She would go along with that, since her coming to see him would look as bad for her as it did for him. Travel logs could be adjusted, and there wouldn't be any official record that she had ever been here, much less wounded in an action against the Rebels.

And if she didn't remember it, well, not to be hard-hearted, but perhaps that was for the best. Even a truth-scan couldn't find a contradiction if the person undergoing it didn't know it had happened. Regrettable, yes, but one had to make the best of bad situations and, by so doing, keep them from getting worse. He could fill her in later, once the war was over and things had settled down. For now he did not need anybody looking at him askance—not this close to having the station completed and about to begin its mission. That simply would not do.

His decision made, he felt better. Daala would not blame him in the least—she would do as much, were she in his place. Tarkin was sure of that.

52

ISD *DEVASTATOR,* OFF PLANET TATOOINE, ARKANIS SECTOR, WILD SPACE

"Lord Vader, the blockade-runner is in range. Should we open fire?"

"Yes—but do not destroy her. Target the drives and control systems—I want the passengers and crew alive. Once we have disabled them, we will capture and board the ship."

"Yes, my lord."

The captain returned to his business, and Vader moved to stand in front of the forward viewports to watch the fleeing vessel. It was critical that he prevent the plans for the battle station from falling into the Rebels' clutches—and while he was at it, he would find out where they were being taken. Princess Leia Organa was at the core of this operation, and she would divulge what he needed to know—of that he had no doubt. Her mind might be resistant to persuasion by the Force, but there were other ways.

The Rebel ship was no match for Vader's Destroyer, either in speed or firepower. In a matter of moments the drives and control had been crippled by laser strikes of surgical accuracy, their main reactor shut down, and a tractor beam from the *Devastator* generated to envelop the fleeing blockade-runner.

The *Tantive IV* was drawn inexorably into the Destroyer's main cargo hold, gripped tightly in a pressor field that would jam any attempts by the Rebel crew to blow up the captured ship. Vader doubted they were that desperate, but he wasn't going to take the chance.

An assault commander arrived. "Lord Vader, we have entry teams breaching the ship locks."

"Good." Vader turned away from the viewport. "Come with me," he told the commander.

The *Tantive IV* rested in the middle of the huge hold, looking small and defenseless, her white exterior marred by the scorched and blackened areas on the engines. Vader, followed by several stormtroopers, strode up the ramp to the air lock. The lock's hatch had been shattered moments before; clouds of vaporized sealant, paint, and metal still hung in the air. He stepped through the smoke into the corridor and surveyed the damage. The bodies of both Rebel defenders and stormtroopers littered the deck of the blockade-runner. Vader paused to look at one of the Rebels crumpled at his feet, then at a second. They had been brave. Foolish, since there was no escape and no chance of victory, but brave.

Little good it would do them.

The sounds of blasterfire still echoed throughout the small ship; now and then a stray bolt was deflected from a bulkhead and across a cross corridor, the flash of red reflecting fleetingly off the white walls. Vader was not worried about stray fire—he could concentrate the Force enough to stop a blaster's beam with the upraised palm of his gloved hand, if it came to that.

The conclusion was foregone—the Rebels could not possibly win against such overwhelming odds, and they had to know that. Why fight on?

There was some purpose to their continued resistance, of that he was sure. What was it?

Vader and his escort moved through the ship's corridors, continuing his inspection. Some of the Rebel fighters had been captured, although most had gone down firing.

Enough of this. Vader stopped and, with a gesture to the commander, indicated that they bring him a Rebel officer who had just been captured. In another moment the man stood before him, still under guard. Without preamble, Vader reached out and grabbed the officer by the throat, easily lifting him clear off the floor. He gasped and struggled, but in vain, of course. None could escape the grip of the Force.

Before Vader could speak, a stormtrooper approached. He said, "The Death Star plans are not in the main computer."

"Where are those transmissions you intercepted?" Vader asked him. "What have you done with those plans?"

The officer struggled. "We intercepted no transmissions!" he croaked.

Vader tightened his grip on the man's throat, lifting him higher. The officer's half-strangled words could barely be understood: "Aaah! This is . . . uhh . . . a consular ship. We're on a diplomatic . . . agh! mission!"

Vader was not impressed by this pathetic attempt at deception. "If this is a consular ship, where is the ambassador?"

It was a rhetorical question. The man was not going to be helpful, so no more time needed to be wasted on him. Vader crushed his throat and tossed him across the corridor. The body bounced off the bulkhead and sprawled on the deck.

He could sense the reactions of the other nearby prisoners without having to look. Another object lesson: thwart Lord Vader and such would be your reward as well.

He turned to the assault leader. "Commander, tear this ship apart until you've found those plans. And bring me the passengers—I want them alive!"

Vader smiled under his helmet as a file of stormtroopers arrived with Leia Organa in tow. It was reported that she had shot a trooper before they stunned her. It was hard to think of her showing such bravery—she was so young, so beautiful, dressed in that simple white gown. She reminded him very much of . . .

No. He would not allow that thought.

She glared at him, managing to look disdainful even though her hands were cuffed. "Darth Vader," she said, making no effort to hide her contempt. "Only you could be so bold. The Imperial Senate will not sit still for this—when they hear you've attacked a diplomatic—"

He cut her off: "Don't act so surprised, Your Highness. You weren't on any mercy mission this time. Several transmissions were beamed to this ship by Rebel spies. I want to know what happened to the plans they sent you."

She kept to her role: "I don't know what you're talking about. I'm a member of the Imperial Senate on a diplomatic mission to Alderaan—"

Vader's patience was abruptly at an end. "You are part of the Rebel Alliance and a traitor!" He gestured furiously at the guards. "Take her away!"

After she was hustled off, Vader stood motionless, quelling his rage. Anger could be useful, but only when it was anger you brought forth on your own, shaped to your ends. Not when it was provoked by someone else.

He was somewhat surprised by the intensity of his response. There was something about her he could not quite put a finger on, something unusual. It troubled him. Organa's mind was not weak; this he could tell even after a cursory attempt to probe it. And there was something oddly familiar about her, something just outside his grasp . . .

He mentally shrugged it off. It was not important. She would be dead soon in any event; Tarkin had signed the order already. It was only a matter of how much useful information they could pry from her before that came to pass. She was part of the past. He had the future with which he must deal.

He began to walk as he considered his next move.

Next to him the commander said, "Holding her is dangerous. If word gets out, it could generate sympathy for the Rebellion in the Senate."

Vader wasn't moved by such fears. "I have traced the Rebel spies to her. Now she is my only link to finding their secret base."

"She'll die before she'll tell you anything."

"Leave that to me. Send a distress signal, then inform the Senate that all aboard were killed."

Another Imperial officer approached them. "Lord Vader, the battle station plans are not aboard this ship. And no transmissions were made."

Vader stared at the officer. His anger started to burn again.

The officer seemed to sense this. Hurriedly, he added, "An escape pod was jettisoned during the fighting—but no life-forms were aboard."

Ah. So that was why they had continued to resist—to give their precious Princess time to physically remove the plans. Of course. He turned to the commander. "She must have hidden the plans in the escape pod. Send a detachment down to retrieve them. See to it personally, Commander. There'll be no one to stop us this time."

"Yes, sir."

Vader strode through the lock and back into his ship's cargo bay. At the least, they had prevented the Princess from delivering the Death Star plans to the Rebels. Imperial troopers would recover them—and even if they did not, there was little damage they could do on the worthless desert world of Tatooine. There was nothing of value on that world. Nothing at all.

53

THE HARD HEART CANTINA, DECK 69, DEATH STAR

Behind the bar, the liquor bottles rattled on their shelves, and Memah felt a gentle but insistent thrum under her feet.

"What—" she began.

"We're moving," Rodo said.

Next to him, Nova nodded. "Sublight engines, so we aren't going far."

The customers—about a quarter capacity this time of cycle—paused for a few seconds, then went back to what they were doing. Nobody seemed too perturbed by the event.

"Why are we moving? Construction isn't finished yet," she said. "Is it?"

"Apparently enough so that the ship can be relocated," Rodo said.

After a moment, the vibration evened out. The bottles stopped jittering. The hum quieted and became very faint, barely felt.

Memah turned to Nova. "What does this mean, Sarge?"

He laughed. "Oh, right, me being so critical to the running of the station, the Moff called me up and gave me a personal briefing just a minute ago on my comlink. Didn't you notice?"

Rodo said, "I don't believe I'm giving away any military secrets when I say it probably has to do with the battle we just fought."

She looked at him. "What battle?"

Rodo shrugged. "Don't know for sure, but a couple of things just happened that kind of hint at one. Several wings of TIE fighters suddenly decided to leave the station, more than a thousand ships, and shortly thereafter you might recall that the lights dimmed for a couple of seconds? My guess is the power capacitors that fill up a big chunk of this big metal ball got diverted to that big honkin' gun."

"How come you know stuff like this?" Nova said.

"How come you don't?"

"I didn't say I didn't know it."

Memah said, "So is Rodo right?"

Now it was Nova's turn to shrug. "He's not wrong. Word I got was that a Rebel carrier ship popped out of hyper a couple of thousand klicks away and kicked out a load of X-wings, presumably to come and shoot at us. According to my source, they turned the superlaser at the carrier and blew it all the way back to Imperial Center."

She blinked in astonishment. "It's that powerful?"

Nova said, "Oh, yeah. A ship is nothing. The power to the beam was only in the single digits—cranked up full, anything within half a million klicks isn't safe, including asteroids, moons, even planets."

"No!"

"Yes. Why else would they spend all that time and money on this"—he swung one arm to encompass the entirety of their surroundings—"if it couldn't produce some major damage? Why else would they call it 'the Death Star'?"

"It's hard to imagine," she said.

"For you. For me, even. Not for the Imperial high-level mucks who get paid to come up with such things. What I heard, this thing's been in development, in one form or another, for years. And once it starts rampaging through the galaxy, the Rebellion's crisp. If Tarkin even thinks there's a Rebel base on a planet or a moon—" Nova moved both hands in a motion simulating the flowering of an explosion. "Boom. End of base, end of problem. Two or three worlds go up in a flash like that, and the war's over. Who would risk losing billions or even trillions of people to hide a few insurrectionists? It'll be all finished except for the bands and the medals."

"You think?" Rodo asked.

"No question. Maybe when my tour is done, I'll open up a school somewhere quiet, maybe out in one of the arms, settle down, even have a few kids, because war as we know it won't happen with things like this"—he patted the bar top gently a couple of times—"flying around. Build a few more of 'em, you won't need armies or navies or planet-bound military bases. You get a hot spot, some systems get cranky, you send a Death Star, and it'll be game over."

Memah thought about it. The sarge was right. Even with just one Death Star operational, the Rebellion wouldn't stand a chance. Build a whole fleet of them, and the Empire would have the galaxy gripped in a durasteel hand forever.

She saw Nova wince. "You okay, Sarge?" she asked.

"Got a headache that won't quit. Maybe I can kill it with this embalming fluid you sell here. Next round's on me," he said. "We can toast the end of the war."

"It's not over yet," Rodo said.

"Only a matter of time," Nova said.

COMMAND CENTER, OVERBRIDGE, DEATH STAR

"You're confident of this?"

Motti nodded. "Yes, sir. The interior is not finished, but the hull is patent and the hyperdrives will be ready shortly. Enough for a partial shakedown."

"Good. Since the Rebels know our location, we cannot risk staying in the same system until we are at full readiness."

"Prudent."

"And the superlaser?"

"Engineering tells me that we can manage thirty percent power and, after a fast capacitor recharge for an hour or two, that much again."

"How strong will that beam be?"

Motti shrugged. "Theoretical. Nobody knows for sure."

"Well, then we need to test it before we embark."

"That would be wise. Do you have a target in mind?"

Tarkin smiled. "Yes. I do."

Motti wanted to ask how Daala was faring, to show concern, but it didn't seem appropriate to bring it up just now. Besides, he already knew. She had suffered some kind of memory damage and was already on a fast ship back to the Maw. Tarkin might be besotted with her, but he wasn't a total fool. He knew it would unwise to risk Vader or the Emperor finding out she had been here against orders.

Well, no matter. Even though the ship wasn't quite ready for full-scale battle maneuvers, Motti would have it running well enough in a matter of days.

What target did the old man have in mind, though? There weren't any to choose from here; they'd pretty much scoured the system clean. There were two *Bespin*-class gas giants, one in an outer orbit, the other a sun skimmer, but they were too big to be practical. They needed a solar body at least big enough for its own gravity to crush it into spherical shape. Something that size would be the only way to calculate how powerful the beam would be at a third of its projected strength.

CUBE 24556, RESIPLEX 19, SPRAWL 20, DEATH STAR

Vil leaned back on the couch next to Teela, feeling distracted. "So how was your shift?" he asked.

"Pretty good. The crews finished two sets of officers' quarters, another five-hundred-person barracks, and a rec center. It's amazing to stand on an overlook and see these things just sort of appear in a matter of days."

"Sounds like you're pleased."

"Oh, I am. It's not the job I would have chosen, working on a battle station, but it's what I've been handed. And there is a sense of accomplishment in taking a standard design and tweaking it so it costs less and works more efficiently."

"That's great. Congratulations."

"What's wrong?"

He looked at her. How could she know? He hadn't been in all that many relationships, and the ones he'd been in had usually been short and shallow. Teela noticed things that none of the others had seemed to catch.

"Nothing."

She grinned at him. "You might be able to fly, Vil, but that won't. What's up?"

He shifted uncomfortably. "I can't really talk about it."

"You mean the battle yesterday?"

"How do you know about that?"

"It's a big station, but people do talk to each other. Word gets around."

He signed. "Yeah, I guess. Well, I was part of it."

"And?"

"I made double ace. You know what that means?"

"No."

"I shot down ten enemy fighters."

She sighed. "I'm not a fan of war, but that's your job, isn't it? Wouldn't congratulations be in order?"

"Yeah."

"But?"

Vil looked at her. Could he really talk about this with her? Yes, he decided. He could. There really was something different about her, something that said she would understand, even if she didn't necessarily approve.

"It wasn't as much fun as I always thought it would be."

She looked at him with an unreadable expression. "I wouldn't think that killing people would be."

"You can't think of them as people, just as the enemy. It's not that. It was . . . too easy."

She leaned back and blinked at him. "Too easy?"

"It was like shooting at targets. They were so intent on getting to the station, they didn't offer much of a fight. We cut them to pieces."

"I don't get it. You *wanted* them to shoot at you?"

"No, no. Well—yes. I mean, I wanted to survive, of course. I wanted to win, but I wanted it to be . . . I know it sounds stupid, but I wanted to have to work harder."

Teela sighed. "I understand."

He looked at her in surprise. "You do?"

"Sure. Nobody wants to skate along the easy path all the time. You wanted a challenge, so you could feel like you'd accomplished something."

"Yeah. Sometimes long odds are the only ones worth playing."

"Well, I can't say I'm sorry it wasn't more dangerous. Besides, I assume there'll be more battles—"

Vil shook his head. "Maybe not. Knowing that Tarkin could just pull up and blow the whole world right out of the sky? I think wars are going to be a thing of the past pretty quick."

Teela looked puzzled. “And that’s bad because . . . ?”

“Well, it’s not—not for civilization, of course not. Big picture and all that. But for fighter pilots? We’re going to be put out to pasture.”

“You could get a job flying commercial spacecraft.”

“I had it in mind that if I survived, someday I would do that. But . . . not yet.”

She put her arms around him and pulled him closer to her. “You don’t always get your first choice in life. Things happen, you have to adjust. Nobody knows that better than I do.”

He nodded.

“But if you wanted to be an ace, now you are one. That’s something. Congratulations.”

“Well, a double ace, if you want get technical about it.”

“Oh, yeah, let’s you and me get technical, hey?”

Vil laughed. There was definitely something different about this one.

54

THE HARD HEART CANTINA, DECK 69, DEATH STAR

Ratua had trouble jamming his way into the cantina. It was packed, and he understood why. A lot of celebrating was going on. The encounter with the Rebel carrier was all over the station, and if the TIE pilots involved had been cocky before, they would be strutting a lot prouder after that victory.

He wasn't political, and who won the war didn't matter much to him, except that being here meant they'd be moving away from the prison world, and eventually back to civilization. And it would be the safest of safe rides. So all this was to the good.

He saw Memah working frenetically behind the bar. Even with all the droids and servers on duty, he knew he wouldn't get much of a chance to visit with her this shift.

Ah, well. He certainly didn't begrudge her the work. The crowd would thin, eventually.

Meanwhile, his latest scam was getting ripe. A few more days and he'd be rolling in credits. Well, maybe not. But certainly he'd have enough to cover the walls of his cube, with plenty left over to outfit the ceiling and deck.

ISD *DEVASTATOR,* OFF PLANET TATOOINE, ARKANIS SECTOR, WILD SPACE

"What is thy bidding, my Master?"

Vader kneeled in front of the holo projector, offering obeisance to the larger-than-life-sized image of the Dark Lord of the Sith.

As always, his Master's voice was as brittle as crystalline hydrogen. "You have recovered the plans for the Death Star?"

"Not yet, Master. I know where they are and I'll have them soon."

"I have every faith in you, Lord Vader."

Vader inclined his head in a military bow. He felt a sense of pride. Praise from his Master was infrequent, and therefore to be relished.

"I have dissolved the Imperial Senate," Sidious continued. "You will return to the battle station and convey this to Tarkin." He paused. "I want Tarkin to know how important I think this is, that I would send you in person."

"Yes, my Master."

"The station is nearly operational, and I would have it made completely so as soon as possible."

"I will see to it."

"And once you have gotten whatever information you can from Senator Organa, you will terminate her?"

"Yes."

"Good, good. There are strange currents in the Force, Lord Vader, swirling about so that even I cannot see the future, save through a hazy pall. We must move with great care until things become clearer."

"Yes, Master."

The holo blinked off, and Vader stood. His Master's expression of confidence notwithstanding, the conversation had been disquieting. The Emperor was the most powerful Sith in a thousand years, and he was always confident, always in control, able to manipulate complex situations as he saw fit with a celerity that was, to any uninitiated into the dark side of the Force, nothing less than astonishing. There were wheels within wheels, cogs great and small, and Emperor Palpatine was the master machinist who ran all of them.

And yet he had sounded concerned . . . What could possibly concern so powerful a personage?

Vader's agents would recover the jettisoned escape pod from Tatooine. Meanwhile he had been ordered to go to the Death Star, and that was where he would go.

SUPERLASER FIRE CONTROL, THETA SECTOR, DEATH STAR

The CO looked grim, and Tenn understood why. He was feeling pretty grim himself. He would do his job, that wasn't even in question—he was too much the career navy man to do anything else. But he had to say something.

"You're serious?"

"Not really something I'd joke about, is it?"

Tenn felt like he'd just fallen down a pooka hole into some bizarre fantasy world. "For *practice*? Just to see how well it'll work?"

"Engineering hasn't gotten itself together, from what they tell me. They say thirty-three percent power is all they can currently store in the capacitors for discharge. We need to see if that's true."

"What'll it do?"

"Nobody really knows. Nothing has been run up even close to that hot before." There was an awkward pause. Then the CO said, "You okay with this, Chief? Because I can get Beller or Reshias up here—"

Tenn raised his hand. "I'm good, Cap. Not my job to decide where or when, it's to put the spike where they want it. Still . . ."

Still, it's one thing to vaporize an enemy troop carrier or Rebel base, and quite another to destroy an entire world.

"I hear you, Chief. But that's how it is."

"Yeah." Tenn straightened and squared his shoulders. "When?"

"Test is set up for eleven hundred hours."

Tenn looked at the timer on the control wall. Two hours. "No problem," he said.

COMMAND CENTER, OVERBRIDGE, DEATH STAR

Motti wasn't really surprised when Tarkin told him of his decision, but he immediately saw the potential for problems. He voiced his concerns—circumspectly, of course.

"I understand your apprehension," Tarkin said. "But I believe the political fallout will be minimal."

"Still, why risk even that?"

"Because, as you well know, we cannot go into battle without knowing what our biggest weapon will do when we need to use it."

Motti nodded. Tarkin was right. One always tested one's weapons. *How* and *where,* however, were different questions.

It's not your decision, Motti told himself. A fact for which he was profoundly grateful. Aloud, he said, "You're the Grand Moff."

"Indeed I am."

55

THE HARD HEART CANTINA, DECK 69, DEATH STAR

The cantina was closed; the air-purifying system was being cleaned and the ionizers balanced. It was noisy, but with the door closed to her office, the sound of the droid cleaners was muted enough so that Memah and Ratua could have a conversation.

Ratua had the smug smile that she'd come to know over the last few months. "What have you done now, Green-Eyes? You look entirely too pleased with yourself."

"Merely supplied a basic human need," he said.

"Right. C'mon, tell Aunt Memah."

"Nobody got hurt," he said, a bit too quickly. "Nobody will even miss a meal, trust me here. Everybody is happy. The quartermaster merely diverted a shipment of electronics and holoprojectors that would likely have sat in a storage bin for ten years doing nothing, because everything on this station is backed up at least twice already. The chances of them ever needing any of that gear are close to zero."

"Uh-huh." She wondered why she was even bothering to listen to him justifying himself. Theft was theft, no matter the circumstances. But she knew why she listened. As long as he kept talking she could gaze into those green eyes.

"No, look, it's true. It's not doing anybody any good, and there is this market out there for entertainment—people are bored out of their heads in some sectors."

"And what are you going to show on these entertainment systems you, ah, liberated? Skin holos?"

"No, no, nothing like that!" He sounded honestly affronted by the thought. "We're talking sports, crashball, low-g gymnastics, Podracing. Good, clean, family programs."

"And why can't people see those on the station's regular entertainment communications gear?"

"Well, they can—but those terminals are set up where the designers want them. Think about the poor guy who's working in some dark warehouse out on the Rim and gone away from any holo-unit. Sodder's stacking boxes with a grav-loader all day—boring, mind-numbing work. No entertainment terminals there. What's wrong with him having a little viewer on his loader, so that he can sneak a peek at his favorite team when he has a break?"

"Or ram his loader into a wall because he's watching the 'proj instead of paying attention to where he's going?"

He smiled at her. "Well, that's not my problem. I sell them a knife, they can use it to slice their vege-steaks or they can stab themselves in the leg. None of my biz."

She laughed. She couldn't help it. Celot Ratua Dil was a bad boy, true enough, but he was so disarmingly honest about his dishonesty.

"Check it out," he said, obviously relieved at her laughter. He produced a device the size of his fist and set in on her desk, then activated it. The three-dimensional hologram of the station's entertainment net appeared over the 'projector.

"Aside from the regular channels, this particular unit can tap into the external cam feeds. Watch."

He touched the device, dialed up the magnification, and the image of a planet shimmered into view, about the size of a crashball.

"My old stomping grounds," he said. "Despayre. A terrible place to visit, and in fact you couldn't anyway, 'cause once you're there, you're there. But it looks nice from this far away." He cocked his head in consideration of the green-and-blue image. "No, actually, it still looks awful."

Memah glanced at the chron inset into the 'proj. Almost eleven hundred. The maintenance droids should be finishing the filters pretty soon, which was good, because she wanted to be open again by mid-shift, and it would take at least another hour to—

A flash of pale green glimmered briefly from the holo.

The room shook, vibrating enough to rattle the chairs. She felt her viscera become momentarily buoyant, and realized that the ship's gravity field had flickered.

"What is that?" Memah stood, fighting sudden, inexplicable panic. After all, what could possibly pose a danger to—

Ratua held up a hand to quiet her. Those green eyes watched the 'proj. "Wait a second," he said. "Something's wrong."

The image of the planet Despayre seemed to shiver as a thin beam of emerald green—*nearly the same color as Ratua's eyes,* she thought—from off the edge of the 'proj lanced into the center of the single huge continent.

They both watched disbelievingly as an orange spot blossomed on the image of the planet. It seemed no bigger than Memah's thumbnail at first, but it grew rapidly, spreading in an expanding circle. The center of the orange turned black.

"Kark," Ratua said. He sounded stunned.

"What? What is it?"

"They—they're firing at the planet. With the superlaser."

The orange and black spread in irregular waves now, continuing outward from the center. The blue of the ocean didn't even slow it down.

"The atmosphere's on fire," Ratua said. Calmly, as if he were discussing the weather. *Going to be a warm day today, temperature around five thousand degrees . . .*

She felt a horrifying urge to laugh. It didn't seem real—it couldn't be real. Ratua must've tuned in to some future-fic holo by mistake. It wasn't a real planet she was watching burn. No. Things like that just didn't happen.

Memah stared at the image. She could not look away.

SUPERLASER FIRE CONTROL, THETA SECTOR, DEATH STAR

Tenn looked at the images from the targeting cam. He still had his hand on the firing lever. He released it and stared, watching as the very air on the prison world caught fire in a runaway planetary holocaust. Seismographic sensors showed that massive groundquakes had begun, rumbling down into the bowels of the planet. Giant waves in the ocean, generated by the shifting of tectonic plates, rushed for the shores of the big continent. Volcanoes spewed lava. Clouds of steam and volcanic ash began to rapidly obscure the surface from view—but not fast enough.

He had just killed everything on the planet Despayre. If all life wasn't dead already, it would be soon.

The CO moved to look over his shoulder. He didn't congratulate Tenn on the shot; he just stood there.

"Stang," Tenn said.

The CO nodded. "Yeah."

COMMAND CENTER, OVERBRIDGE, DEATH STAR

Motti said, "Engineering says the capacitors will be recharged in an hour and thirteen minutes."

Tarkin watched the projection as the effects of the beam manifested on the planet. By the time the second pulse was ready for discharge, there wouldn't be anything alive on the world below them to care. The chain reaction was massive. And at only one-third of the power that would be available when it was fully operational.

Amazing.

"I hope you're right about this," Motti said. "Politically, I mean."

"Of course I am, Admiral. The population of that world consisted of condemned criminals sentenced to life imprisonment. They were never going back to civilization. It was a constant drain on Imperial resources to transport them and to maintain them. Those troops will now be freed up for service. Nobody will mourn the murderers or the filthy planet on which they lived."

"And where will the Empire send its major criminals now?"

Tarkin turned away from the images of carnage and looked directly at Motti. "Unless I am seriously mistaken, the death penalty will be used more frequently. Imperial justice is about to become swift and sure, Admiral."

He turned back to watch the image of the dying world.

G-12 BARRACKS, SECTOR N-SEVEN, DEATH STAR

Nova woke up screaming, beset with horror. The other sergeants watched him, but none of them approached. Bad idea to get too close to a martial arts expert coming out of a nightmare.

Nova tried to calm himself, to slow his breathing, but he had never felt anything like this before. It was as if he had heard a million people cry out, all at once, as they were killed.

He stepped from his cot, went to the refresher, and washed his face. He needed to see that doctor again. He was beyond caring what anyone thought. Something was definitely wrong with him, and he couldn't live like this.

56

SUPERLASER FIRE CONTROL, THETA SECTOR, DEATH STAR

An hour and fifteen minutes after the first beam, Tenn fired the second one.

The planet Despayre, already scorched lifeless and beset with cataclysmic groundquakes and volcanism, began to shake like some tormented creature in its death throes. Massive cracks, thousands of kilometers long and tens of klicks wide, striated the world. Mountains collapsed in one hemisphere as they jutted up and rose in another. It was impossible to see all this directly, of course, because of the cloud cover that had blanketed the surface, but the IR and VSI scopes showed everything all too clearly. The molten core of the globe, already venting through innumerable new volcanoes, oozed to the surface and produced oceans of lava that spread across the land. This was how the planet had been born, and this was how it was dying.

An hour and nineteen minutes later, when Tenn fired the third beam that blew the charred and burned-out cinder apart, shattering it into billions of pieces, it seemed almost pointless. Everybody and everything on it had already been roasted, scalded, or drowned. The system's gravity twisted as the planetary well ceased to exist. Shield sensors quietly recorded the thousands of fragments, from the size of pebbles to that of mountains, deflected from the station.

Sweet Queen Quinella. A whole planet, destroyed. Just like that.

No matter how tough you thought you were, that was hard to stomach.

Especially when you were the one who had pulled the lever.

ISD *DEVASTATOR,* APPROACHING DEATH STAR

Vader had felt the fabric of the Force tear even in hyperspace. Some vast and terrible event had taken place. When they'd dropped below lightspeed, it had taken but a few seconds for his sensor crew to determine the cause of that event.

The prison planet of Despayre was no more.

Vader nodded to himself as he looked at the magnified view of planetary debris. That should convince the military that they had developed the ultimate weapon. They were wrong, but they would believe it. They would be full of their pitiful dreams of power and glory, unable to comprehend the truth, certain that they were unbeatable.

That was not his worry. He had his orders, and he would carry them out. He would get the information he sought from the dissident Princess. They would find the Rebels' main base and destroy it. The war would be over, and Vader would finally be free to resume his studies of the dark side in earnest. He had much to learn and, with the Emperor no longer preoccupied with this petty conflict, he could resume his training.

That was what was important. That way lay real power.

MAIN CONFERENCE ROOM, COMMAND CENTER, DEATH STAR

Motti wanted to reach over and smash in General Tagge's face—the man was insufferable!

Tagge said, "Until this battle station is fully operational, we are vulnerable. The Rebel Alliance is too well equipped. They are more dangerous than you realize."

Motti could have pointed out that the vaunted Rebel Alliance had sent a huge carrier against the station and that unfortunate vessel had been blown out of existence by a single, low-powered pulse of the not-yet-fully-operational Death Star's main battery, from more than two thousand kilometers away. Which was nothing compared with the fact that an entire planet had just been destroyed with three partial-strength pulses, any one of which could blow an armada out of the galaxy.

But Tagge already knew this, of course. He was putting his objections into the record, covering his bets and his backside, just in case.

Two could play that game. Motti said, "Dangerous to your starfleet, Commander, not to this battle station."

Tagge was as thickheaded as a durasteel plate. He just kept prattling on: "The Rebellion will continue to gain support in the Imperial Senate as long as—" He stopped as Grand Moff Tarkin, followed closely by Darth Vader, strode into the conference room. As he entered, Tarkin cut in: "The Imperial Senate will no longer be of any concern to us. I've just received word that the Emperor has dissolved the council permanently. The last remnants of the Old Republic have been swept away."

Even that didn't shut Tagge up: "That's impossible! How will the Emperor maintain control without the bureaucracy?"

Tarkin said, "The regional governors now have direct control over their territories." He smiled, ever so slightly. "Fear will keep local systems in line—fear of this battle station."

"And what of the Rebellion?" Tagge kept on. The man was like a borrat with a bone: he wouldn't let it go. "If the Rebels have obtained a complete technical readout of this station, it is possible, however unlikely, that they might find a weakness and exploit it."

"The plans you refer to will soon be back in our hands." That from the deep-voiced Vader, who stood behind the now seated Tarkin.

Motti couldn't contain himself any longer. "Any attack made by the Rebels against this station would be a useless gesture, no matter what technical data they've obtained. This station is now the ultimate power in the universe. I suggest we use it."

Vader said, "Don't be too proud of this technological terror you've constructed. The ability to destroy a planet is insignificant next to the power of the Force."

Motti wanted to laugh. Vader had to be insane! How could he say that, especially with the rubble of Despayre still sweeping past the station? "Don't try to frighten us with your sorcerer's ways, Lord Vader," he said, feeling safe in the presence of witnesses. He was aware that Vader was moving toward him, but Motti was committed. Even knowing what a bad idea it was to bait the man in black, he continued: "Your sad devotion to that ancient religion has not helped you conjure up the stolen data tapes or given you clairvoyance enough to find the Rebels' hidden fort—*ukk!*"

Three meters away, Vader leaned forward and made a small motion with his hand, closing it into a fist.

Motti felt his throat clench and close up, as if it were being crushed by a steel clamp. He . . . couldn't . . . breathe . . . !

He dug his fingers into his collar, trying to remove what felt like an unbreakable band around his neck. It didn't work. The pressure was there, but there was nothing material around his throat to cause it.

"I find your lack of faith disturbing," Vader said.

Motti felt himself start to gray out. He wanted to scream, but he could not utter so much as a squeak as he slid toward the abyss of unconsciousness and death . . .

He barely heard Tarkin speak. "Enough of this. Vader—release him."

"As you wish," Vader said. He turned and strode away, and a moment later Motti fell forward onto the conference table, not feeling the impact. He could breathe again, however. The constriction was gone. He sat up, filled with rage, and glared at Vader. If only he had a blaster!

But, though he was not a cowardly man, his rage was tinged with fear. How had Vader done that? He had been three meters away.

Motti swallowed, his mouth dry, his throat sore.

Tarkin said, "This bickering is pointless. Lord Vader will provide us with the location of the Rebel fortress by the time this station is operational. We will then crush the Rebellion with one swift stroke!"

Motti believed that. But he also knew something else now, too. Vader had power, and it was real. Motti had felt it, and, if Tarkin had not intervened, he believed with every fiber of his being that he would be dead.

That was a sobering thought. What did it matter if you commanded a station that could destroy a world if you could be killed yourself by a freak waving a hand in the air?

Something would have to be done about Vader. But very, very carefully done.

57

PRISON BLOCK AA, DETENTION CENTER, DEATH STAR

Uli had just completed his rounds, which included a quick tour of a different prison block every cycle. Most of the prisoners were there for minor infractions, drunk-and-disorderlies and the like. He was in the corridor, heading to his office when he saw none other than Darth Vader coming from the other direction.

With him was a beautiful young woman.

It was such a surreal sight that he was momentarily tempted to question his senses. But it was real enough; he could see the fluorescents' distorted reflections slide along the black helmet as Vader walked, and could hear the regulated breathing of the man's respiratory apparatus. The sound of his boots against the floor grating was oddly soft for so large a man.

Vader had one hand clamped on the woman's upper arm, and even from ten meters away Uli could see by her expression of pain and anger that the grip was hard enough to be hurting her. Whoever she was, she was obviously not with Vader by choice.

The woman wore a white gown, and she looked somehow familiar, although he couldn't place her. Her dark brown hair was long, but rolled into tight circles against the sides of her head. Even through the discomfort and indignity of her situation, she seemed extraordinarily self-possessed.

The three of them were alone in the prison block corridor. As Uli drew near, Vader stopped. Paying no attention to the doctor, he opened one of the cells and pushed the woman unceremoniously inside. The hatch dropped shut behind her.

Uli had slowed and glanced back over his shoulder to watch as he passed. After incarcerating the woman, Vader turned, ebony cape flaring behind him. He looked back at Uli. Although no part of his face was visible, Uli somehow had no doubt that Vader was looking directly at him.

He set his gaze in front of him once more and continued walking. Just as he exited the block, three black-clad and helmeted technicians passed him. Behind them, floating on a cushion of repulsorlift energy, an interrogator droid followed.

Uli took the lift back to Medical, wondering who the woman was and what her crime had been. The lift doors opened and he started up the corridor, but stopped as C-4ME-O wheeled around the corner.

"Good after-midday, Dr. Divini."

"Not for everyone, it appears. I just saw Darth Vader, of all people, apparently intending to interrogate a young woman in the prison block. Do you know who she is?"

"Princess Leia Organa, a member of the Imperial Senate, from Alderaan. It is said that she is also a sympathizer with the Rebel Alliance. Apparently she has information the Empire wants, and thus her impending interrogation by Lord Vader."

Uli winced at the thought. Interrogation technology was imprecise, more brute force than finesse—intentionally so, for the most part. Many prisoners started talking a klick a minute at the first sight of one of those glossy-black ISB globes, bristling with archaic hypodermic syringes and electrodes. And woe to them if they didn't, because the term *interrogator droid* was just a euphemism for its real function. It was a torture device, purely and simply. Many who underwent examination by the probes were mentally or even physically damaged beyond repair.

A harsh fate for such a lovely and brave young woman as this Princess apparently was. He had seen only a hint of fear in her as she passed; that she was willing to resist Vader to the extent of requiring such extreme measures indicated a fortitude Uli doubted that he himself possessed.

He was outraged by the thought of such barbarism being practiced by the Empire, although not particularly surprised. But he knew there was nothing to be done about it. To protest the actions of the Emperor's whip would do her absolutely no good, and no doubt result in his own immediate imprisonment. He could finally get his discharge from the medical wing of the Imperial Navy, although it would likely be a discharge from this plane of existence as well. He shook his head and looked at 4ME-O. "Were you looking for me?"

"Indeed. Dr. Hotise wishes to discuss the overages in last month's supply budget with you."

Uli nearly groaned aloud, but the thought of the young woman in the cell made him feel somewhat ashamed of himself. She was facing far more than a bureaucratic upbraiding about expenditures.

He followed the droid around the corner. What a shame. She was so young, so lovely. She reminded him, somehow, of Barriss.

CELL 2187, BLOCK AA, DETENTION LEVEL, DEATH STAR

Vader, accompanied by three black-clad and helmeted technicians, entered the cell where Leia Organa was being held. He had hoped that she would have become more tractable after her capture. But she had remained silent. Her choice. She would regret it.

Behind him the interrogator droid followed. It was a crude tool, a blunt instrument compared with the subtlety and precision possible with the Force; however, Princess Leia's mind was too strong to easily manipulate, even with the power of the dark side at his beck and call. It was possible that he could wrest the knowledge from her, but he might end up destroying the very information he sought. She would force him to burn her brain to a husk before she would willingly part with the data—of that he had no doubt.

However, after being subjected to the tender mercies of the device floating behind him for a time, her mind should be a bit more . . . pliable.

Now and then, one had to make do with the tools available, however crude they might be.

The chamber's door slid up, revealing the Princess sitting on a platform in the mostly bare room. Vader and two of the techs entered. The third waited outside in the corridor.

"And now, Your Highness, we will discuss the location of your hidden Rebel base," Vader told her.

As the interrogator droid floated in behind him, Vader saw her defiant expression falter. He felt her fear as the machine approached her.

Good . . .

He heard the door slam down behind them.

But, after half an hour, despite the truth drugs, electrical shocks, and other inducements he had administered, it was evident that her resistance had not been lowered enough for him to probe her mind. That was surprising.

She was physically weakened and in considerable pain, but her mind remained shielded. She had revealed nothing.

Most unusual for anyone except a Jedi to have such control, he mused.

He kept his anger and frustration under tight rein, letting none of it show. He had other matters that required his attention—for now.

"We are not done here," he told her. To one of the technicians he said, "Have a medic attend to her."

The technician said, "But isn't she sentenced to die?"

"When I decide it is time," Vader said. "If she is not alive and well until that moment, I will hold you personally responsible."

The tech grew visibly paler. Vader swept by him and out of the chamber.

MEDCENTER, DEATH STAR

Uli couldn't stop thinking about the imprisoned Princess. Something about her touched him, somehow.

As he left Hotise's office, he told himself that there was no point in thinking about her. Most likely she was already dead by now, another casualty of war, like the millions of people destroyed along with the prison planet.

"You there!" a man's voice called loudly.

Uli turned and saw an interrogation tech standing down the hall. "Are you the medic on duty?"

"I'm Dr. Divini, yes."

"I have a patient for you. This way, quickly."

Uli followed the tech back up to the prison level. Vader was gone, along with the interrogation droid, but their work was evident. The Princess lay on the cell's platform in no small amount of distress.

Uli passed his hand over the cell's reader and said, "EM kit!"

The reader recognized his ID. A slot in the wall opened, and a drawer containing a full emergency medical kit extruded. He grabbed a handheld diagnoster from it and moved to the supine woman. He pressed the sensor against her bare shoulder and watched as the readout's infocrawl began.

Her eyelids fluttered, then opened. She gave him a faint smile. "Pardon me if I don't get up, Doctor. I'm feeling a bit tired."

He gave her an automatic smile back. "Sorry," he said. "I'll do what I can to help you."

"First time I've heard that in a while."

"Just relax and I'll take care of things."

"I've heard that one before, too."

Despite the gravity of the situation, Uli grinned. He had to admire the woman. Pumped full of chem and suffering from electrical shocks and who knew what else, and she was still able to joke. If she was an example of the Rebels' mettle, the Empire wasn't going to win this war anytime soon.

THE HARD HEART CANTINA, DEATH STAR

Generally, the atmosphere in the place was, at the least, festive. Today, however, the mood was subdued. Ratua sat at the bar watching Memah make drinks, and neither of them was happy. She went through the motions, but he knew her mind was not on her task. They had recently witnessed the death of a planet, an act committed by the huge weapon upon which they lived. Whatever one's politics, it had been a sobering, nightmarish sight. What kind of monster could order such an atrocity, could cause the destruction of an entire world?

A world that, had Ratua not managed to escape, would have taken him with it, along with the millions of other lives cut short in panic and agony.

They weren't the only ones who had seen it, and for something of this magnitude, word spread quickly. It was true that the Death Star had been built with the capability to commit such heinous acts, but he'd been given to understand, along with most of the station's population, that it was never actually going to have to use such destructive power. What had the man in charge—Tarkin, he remembered—said on one of the public comcasts? "Fear would keep the systems in line." Ratua could understand that—it made a skewed kind of sense. But to actually use the station's ability; to annihilate an inhabited world, even one populated by the hardest hard cases in the galaxy, not even as a demonstration, but purely to test . . .

That was something no sane man could grasp.

The war had just taken a very ugly turn, and Ratua feared it might get worse before it got better.

Commander Atour Riten, who was not given to much in the way of socializing, sat alone at a table, drinking a potent liquor distilled from some kind of tropical tuber on Ithor. It had quite a kick, and while he usually enjoyed the fiery taste, that wasn't the reason he was drinking it now.

How had it come to pass that the Empire was destroying entire worlds? Atour was an intelligent and sensible man; he might be apolitical, but he wasn't naïve. He was aware of the purpose for which this battle station had been built. The Death Star was a doomsday device, a weapon of such unimaginable horror that its very existence would, supposedly, prevent any insurrection, anywhere. Even the concept of war would become a thing of the past. And even if such ultimate power had to be demonstrated, there were plenty of uninhabited worlds floating out there; blow one of them to flinders and the message is delivered, loud and clear: *Your world could be next.*

He had been naïve, he realized. He'd let himself believe that there was a limit to inhumanity—that there could be such a thing as a weapon too powerful to use. But such was obviously not the case. There were, it appeared, no depths to which sentient beings could not sink. Build a blaster that could destroy a planet, and some bigger fool would build one that could extinguish a star. It would go on and on, insanity without end, because there's always a bigger blaster.

How could a being with any conscience remain politically neutral after such an event?

He took another swig from his glass. It was certainly enough to drive any sane being to drink.

Teela and Vil sat at a table, drinks before them, but neither bothered to pick up their glasses. They didn't speak.

She watched Vil stare moodily into his glass. He was a pilot, he was trained for war, he risked his life in fights—but even so, the destruction of Despayre had shaken him. Badly.

Teela was beyond shaken. She was appalled. Horrified. She could have been on that world—she *had* been on that world, and if not for an ability the Empire had decided it needed, she would have still been down there when Despayre was shattered.

She'd had nothing to do with the weapons aspect of building the station. She designed and built housing and recreation and living space. And she'd had no real choice, had she? After all, she was still a prisoner.

Right?

Her inner self could have a fine old time saying *I told you so* along about now, she knew. Instead, it was uncharacteristically silent.

58

THE HARD HEART CANTINA, DECK 69, DEATH STAR

Uli sat at the bar next to a humanoid with unbelievably bright green eyes, and thought about cantinas he had frequented during his time in the military. Some had been fun, some merely places to get lit; some had been dens of comrades-in-thrall—doctors, nurses, techs, all dragooned and forced to serve in a war that they all detested. The beings who had to patch up the wounded or cover the dead they couldn't save were generally less enthusiastic over the glory of war than most. After a thousand young people pass under your knife, torn and battered by the effects of blasters or shrapnel, it got old, and it made you weary to your depths. War was as stupid and antisurvivalist an action as a species could undertake, and if Uli could suddenly be made some kind of god, as his first act he would erase the knowledge and memory and ability to make war from the universe.

Now the Empire had a planet buster—and here he was, on the blasted thing. How much worse could things get?

"Hey, Doc."

Uli looked to his left and saw a sergeant arrive at the bar. It took a couple of seconds to place the man—he was a patient. The guy with the bad dreams and the midi-chlorians.

"Sergeant Stihl. How are you sleeping?"

"Truth is, hardly at all. Recently got worse. A lot worse." He sat on the stool.

"I understand. Pills didn't help?"

"Not really."

"Sorry."

"Me, too. I—" He stopped and looked past Uli at the green-eyed fellow on Uli's right. "Celot Ratua Dil?"

Has to be a Zelosian, with those eyes, Uli thought. One of the rare chlorophyllians in the galaxy. And he and the sarge obviously knew each other.

The plant man turned and stared, and Uli saw panic well briefly in those eyes. But then they resumed their slightly cynical outlook. "Well, blast," he said. "You changed your shift, didn't you, Stihl? I should've checked." He shook his head, shrugged, and grinned. "Oh, well."

"What are you doing here?" the sergeant asked. No sound of hostility that Uli could tell; nevertheless, he was starting to feel acutely uncomfortable sitting between them.

"Having a drink," Celot Ratua Dil said. "Wishing I were back on my homeworld. Things weren't so bad there, in retrospect. I could have had a pretty good life at home, but, no, I wanted to travel and see the galaxy. Stupid choice."

The tender drifted over, and Uli noticed that her right hand was under the bar, out of sight. He was feeling very uncomfortable now.

The tender, a Twi'lek, looked familiar, too. Where had he seen her? Ah, yes . . . just picture her naked. Another patient.

"Dr. Divini, nice to see you again." She looked at the fellow to Uli's right. "Everything okay here?"

The green-eyed man said, "Oh, yeah. Just renewing an old acquaintance. Been awhile."

Stihl looked at the tender. "Memah. You know this guy?"

She nodded. "I do."

Stihl looked at the Zelosian again. Uli felt a current of something uneasy passing back and forth, and he leaned back a bit to get out of the flow.

Stihl said, "How did—"

"I decided to leave," Celot Ratua Dil said.

Stihl didn't say anything for a moment. Then he looked at the

Twi'lek woman behind the bar. "You wouldn't have your hand on a stunner under there, would you, Memah?"

"I might."

Stihl nodded, as if to himself. He looked at the Zelosian, then back at the Twi'lek. His eyebrows arched. "So that's how it is?"

"That's how it is. And I do know who he is and where he came from."

There was a pregnant silence.

Uli said, "Pardon me for butting into what's probably not my business, but since I'm sitting in the middle of this conversation and we're all of a sudden talking about stunners, somebody want to tell me what's going on?"

The other three looked at one another.

The Zelosian said, "Sorry, Doctor, ah . . . Divini, is it? It's fairly straightforward. Before he was transferred here, Sergeant Stihl was a guard on Despayre—you know, that planet this station just blew to space dust? And I was, for a time, a resident there."

"He's an escaped prisoner," Stihl said. His voice was still quiet and calm, but it carried clearly to them. He looked at his hands, which were, Uli noticed, quite callused. He looked back at the Zelosian. "You were sentenced there for life."

"You mean 'death,' don't you, Sarge? Because when the powers-that-be on this station let go with that death ray, anybody who was on Despayre got cooked to ashes, and those ashes got blown all over the galaxy, if I recall recent history."

Stihl nodded. "Yeah."

"So now what?" the Twi'lek asked.

"Yeah," Celot Ratua Dil added. "You can't exactly send me back, can you, Sarge?"

Uli watched Stihl's face. He would probably be a good card player, because he wasn't giving anything away. "No," he finally said. "I guess I can't." He looked at Memah. "You really think he's worth pulling that stunner for?"

"I really do."

Another five seconds passed. Then: "How about a mug of Alarevi ale?" Stihl said. "And give the doc and Radish Boy here another of whatever they're drinking, on me."

Memah nodded and removed her hand from under the bar. She and her boyfriend seemed a bit relieved. Not that much, but then Uli would wager his eventual possible IMSLO discharge that nobody was spiking any sine waves tonight. Shock tended to have that effect on people.

He was aware that a potentially nasty situation had just been avoided, and it might be wise to let it lie, but he was curious. He said, "As I recall, Sergeant, aren't you some kind of martial artist?"

"I am."

"If the lady had pulled a stunner, couldn't you have defended yourself against it?"

"Probably. But she wasn't the problem."

"Oh?"

"Want to show him?" he said, looking over Uli's shoulder at the Zelosian.

"Sure. Where's your glass, Doc?"

Uli turned away from the sergeant and looked at the bar. His half-drunk glass of beer was . . .

Where was it?

He looked up at the Zelosian. There was a blur of motion—

His glass was back in front of him. The beer sloshed a bit but otherwise gave no indication that it hadn't been in front of him the whole time.

Stihl laughed softly. "Ratua's fast."

"I get that," Uli said. "So—if Memah had pulled her stunner, while you were dealing with her, Ratua could've clonked you one. If you'd gone after him first, she'd have stunned you."

"Not a high-percentage situation for me," Stihl said.

Uli blinked at him. "So just like that, you're okay with this? You're going to let it go?"

Stihl nodded as Memah drew a mug full of dark ale for him. "Why not? Not like he's going anywhere, and he's right—I can't send him back to a place that doesn't exist anymore." He took the ale, smiled, and sipped at it. "Ah. Thanks." He looked back at Uli again. "And compared with what the Empire just did, how much harm could a smuggler do? You want to turn him in?"

"Not particularly."

"Well, there you are, then."

The other drinks arrived, and the tender had poured one for herself.

Uli held up his glass. "To the end of the war," he said.

The others raised their glasses and echoed his words.

59

COMMAND CENTER, OVERBRIDGE, DEATH STAR

Tarkin looked at Vader, the unspoken question in his eyes. General Tagge stood there as well, still recovering, no doubt, from Tarkin's earlier revelations.

Vader said, "Her resistance to the mind-probe is considerable. It will be some time before we can extract any information from her."

Tarkin shook his head. Why was it always the small details that seemed to trip up the largest projects?

One of his staff officers arrived. Tarkin regarded him.

The man said, "The final checkout is completed. All systems are operational. What course shall we take?"

Excellent! If the superlaser was now fully functional, they could go anywhere. But they needed the location of that base, and—ah, wait. Tarkin rubbed at his chin. "Perhaps she would respond to an alternative form of persuasion."

"What do you mean?" Vader said.

"I think it's time we demonstrated the full power of this station." He looked back at his officer. "Set your course for Alderaan."

The man mumbled something and left, but Tarkin was already thinking ahead. If Princess Leia Organa was a thorn in the Empire's side, then Alderaan was a forest of thorns.

Well, it was time to purge that forest. With fire.

Tagge started to say something but apparently thought better of it. Tarkin smiled almost benignly and said, "I understand your concerns, General. Rest assured I've spoken with Emperor Palpatine recently about demonstrating his battle station's range and strength. He has assured me that I have full rein to do so." He looked at Vader. "You disapprove, Lord Vader?"

"Not at all, Governor."

CELL 2187, DETENTION LEVEL, DEATH STAR

Uli looked at the reads on his sensors. Princess Organa was doing as well as could be expected, given her unpleasant experience. If you didn't know what she had undergone, it would be hard to tell by looking at her.

They were alone in the room—he had made the tech wait outside.

"Thank you, Doctor . . . ? Sorry, I didn't get your name."

"Divini. Kornell Divini. My friends call me Uli."

"I appreciate your medical help, Dr. Divini, but I don't think we're going to be friends. I don't expect I'll be around much longer, and you are an Imperial officer, after all."

He shrugged. "Not by choice. I was drafted. And they aren't letting doctors muster out, as I am sure you're aware."

"You could have deserted."

He laughed. "Really? When? I haven't been anywhere I could have walked away from without being shot by both sides for my trouble. Besides, I'm not sure working for the Rebels would be any better."

She raised herself by one elbow off the examining couch. It took effort, he noted, but she did it, the better to look him in the eye. "You support the Emperor's agenda?"

"I have no clue what his agenda might be. And like I said, I'm not sure that the Alliance would be any better. Yes, they talk a good show, but so did Palpatine before he declared himself Emperor."

"The Senate will continue to oppose him," she said.

"You haven't heard? The Emperor has dissolved the Senate. You are out of a job, Princess."

She paled, and one of the sensors *ping*ed quietly, registering the momentary orthostasis. Uli put a hand on her shoulder and tried to push her gently back down, but she brushed his hand away. "When did this happen?"

He shrugged. "I don't know. I had a patient who works for someone who was in a high-level meeting. It was announced right after Vader arrived on the station with you."

She shook her head. "This is terrible news."

"All the news is terrible," Uli said. "It has been since this war began."

She looked up at him. "If there's ever going to be good news for any of us again, Uli, it has to start with us. We have to create it, not wait to read about it the next morning."

The door slid up. Uli looked up in annoyance and said, "I thought I told you to—" He stopped. It wasn't the tech.

It was Vader.

He entered, his cloak spreading like black ink against the eggshell white of the exam room's floor. "Doctor. I trust your patient is well?"

The words came out before Uli was aware of them. "Yes—no thanks to you."

Leia laughed.

Vader regarded him. "You are insubordinate, Doctor. But I have no time to show you the error of your thoughts." He gestured to Leia. "Come with me, Your Highness."

For a moment, Uli and the Princess locked gazes. Her eyes were brown, he noticed.

Barriss's eyes had been blue, he remembered.

If he'd had a weapon, he might have used it on Vader in that brief instant of time, to allow her a chance to escape. But he was a doctor, not a fighter. It was not his path.

"Good luck," he said to her.

She nodded. "And to you."

Vader ushered her through the door ahead of him with a gesture that was almost courtly. The panel dropped, and they were gone.

COMMAND CENTER, DEATH STAR

Motti entered the control room to report to Tarkin. "We've entered the Alderaan system."

It had been a quick trip, and all systems had performed flawlessly.

The station was as fast as any ship in the Imperial Navy, and faster than most. The jump to lightspeed had been smooth, the hyperspace lanes had been cleared by Imperial order, and it seemed that it had taken no time at all to reach the Alderaan system. The superlaser was charged to full capacity and ready to fire.

Tarkin nodded. He seemed about to speak when Vader entered, along with a couple of guards and the fetching Princess Leia Organa. *Gorgeous woman,* Motti thought. He wouldn't mind getting to know her better. Alas, she wasn't going to be with them much longer. A waste.

She was hustled up to Tarkin. It seemed obvious that Vader's tortures had had little or no effect, because her spirit was unbroken. "Governor Tarkin," she said. "I should have expected to find you holding Vader's leash. I recognized your foul stench when I was brought on board."

Motti suppressed a laugh. My, but she was a spitfire. A real shame she had to die.

Tarkin favored her with a smirk. "Charming to the last." He reached out and touched her chin. "You don't know how hard I found it signing the order to terminate your life."

She jerked her head back. "I'm surprised you had the courage to take the responsibility yourself."

Motti held his smile in check, but not without effort. She might be about to die, but she wasn't going to cringe in fear. You had to respect that in an enemy, even a woman. Maybe especially a woman.

"Princess Leia, before your execution, I would like you to be the guest at a ceremony that will make this battle station operational." Tarkin took a few steps, raised his hands to take in the vastness of the station, and turned to regard her again. "No star system will dare oppose the Emperor now."

She sneered at him. "The more your tighten your grip, Tarkin, the more star systems will slip through your fingers."

Tarkin walked back to her, pointing a finger for emphasis. "Not after we demonstrate the power of this station. In a way, you have determined the choice of the planet that will be destroyed first." He loomed over her, face-to-face. "Since you are reluctant to provide us with the location of the Rebel base, I have chosen to test this station's destructive power on your home planet of Alderaan."

That wiped the smirk from her face.

She said, "No! Alderaan is peaceful. We have no weapons! You can't possibly—"

"You would prefer another target?" Tarkin asked. "A military target? Then name the system!"

Motti watched as Tarkin crowded the Princess, giving her no space, no chance to regain her balance, either figuratively or literally. He leaned over her, nose-to-nose, backing her up. She was stopped by Vader standing behind her.

"I grow tired of asking this," Tarkin told her, "so it'll be the last time. Where is the Rebel base?"

Motti watched as she looked at the viewer. Alderaan was centered there, a beautiful green, white, and blue world, quite unaware of its impending danger.

"Dantooine," she said. Her voice was soft. Defeated. "They're on Dantooine." She lowered her gaze.

Tarkin looked up, pleased. "There, you see, Lord Vader, she can be reasonable." He looked at Motti. "Continue with the operation. You may fire when ready."

Leia looked up in shock. "*What?*"

Tarkin turned back to face her. "You're far too trusting. Dantooine is too remote to make an effective demonstration. But don't worry—we will deal with your Rebel friends soon enough."

"No!" She struggled, but Vader held her fast.

Motti smiled as he prepared to give the order. Tarkin was right. Fear was the key . . .

SUPERLASER FIRE CONTROL, DEATH STAR

Tenn heard the order crackle over the speaker. He couldn't believe it, but there it was:

"Commence primary ignition."

He hesitated a second. Could it be some bizarre kind of test? To see if he had what it took?

No, that was foolish. He had already killed the prison planet, hadn't he? They couldn't have any doubts about his loyalty, both to the Empire and to Governor Tarkin.

But in a way that made it worse—because it meant the order was real. He was about to destroy yet another world—and it wasn't a virulent jungle planet swarming with criminals this time.

This time it was a world all too similar to his own homeworld.

He was aware of his CO watching him. He reached up, grabbed the lever. All systems were green.

His crew once again performed their functions flawlessly, adjusting switches, checking readouts, balancing harmonics. All too soon, everything was in readiness. All systems were go.

Tenn felt sweat dripping down his neck, under that blasted helmet. He looked at the timer: 00:58:57.

He pulled the lever.

It would take a second or so for the tributary beams to coalesce. He wanted to look away from the monitor, but he couldn't.

The superlaser beam lanced from the focusing point above the dish.

The image of Alderaan on the screen was struck by the green ray.

It took no more than an instant. Tenn knew that the beam's total destructive power was much bigger than matter-energy conversions limited to realspace. At full charge, the hyper-matter reactor provided a superluminal "boost" that caused much of the planet's mass to be shifted immediately into hyperspace. As a result, Alderaan exploded into a fiery ball of eye-smiting light almost instantaneously, and a planar ring of energy reflux—the "shadow" of a hyperspatial ripple—spread rapidly outward.

The timer read: 00:59:10.

So little time. So much damage. It was incredible.

If, somehow, the Rebel Alliance were to win this war—not that Tenn Graneet could see how that would be possible, given what he had just witnessed, what he had just *done*—then surely this act would condemn his ashes to the deepest pit they could find after he was executed.

It was his job, and if he hadn't performed it, someone else would have, but his belly roiled with the enormity of what pulling that lever had caused.

Billions of lives snuffed out. Just like that.

There was no sense of triumph in it, none. He had not destroyed a Rebel base or a military target. Instead, a planet full of unarmed civilians had been . . . extinguished.

And he had done it.

It made him feel sick.

G-12 BARRACKS, SECTOR N-SEVEN, DEATH STAR

Nova was taking a sonic shower to relax before trying once again to sleep when he felt a roar in his head—soundless, but nevertheless so loud that it knocked him completely unconscious.

When he awoke, he was lying on the floor of the shower plate, the hum of the sonics still vibrating his body. His nose was bleeding, and his muscles tremored and shook as if he'd been hit by a stunner on maximum. He could barely stand.

Something had just happened. Something terrible.

60

MAIN CONFERENCE ROOM, COMMAND CENTER, DEATH STAR

The Imperial officer strode into the room, his boots echoing on the polished deck. Tarkin sat at the opposite end of the conference table, and Vader had taken a position near the wall to the left of the door. No one else was there save a pair of guards on the sides of the doorway.

The officer came to attention.

Tarkin looked at the man. "Yes?"

"Our scout ships have reached Dantooine. They found the remains of a Rebel base, but they estimate that it has been deserted for some time. They are now conducting an extensive search of the surrounding system."

Vader felt a small surge of triumph, even though the news was bad. He had expected this.

As the officer turned and marched away, Tarkin came to his feet, simmering with rage. "She lied! She lied to us!"

Vader was amused at Tarkin's outrage. Now who was too naïve and trusting? Aloud, he said, "I told you she would never consciously betray the Rebellion."

Tarkin took a few steps toward him. Vader could sense that the governor's anger had gotten the better of him. "Terminate her! Immediately!"

Unseen under his helmet, Vader's tight features formed a painful grin. He understood Tarkin's anger—after all, he himself was a master of anger—but Princess Leia Organa might better serve them alive. He would consider the matter. Tarkin could not order, only suggest various courses and actions to him, and he was not averse to going along with those suggestions most of the time, since they didn't really matter. But Darth Vader bowed to no one's wishes save those of his Master, the Dark Lord of the Sith. Should his Master's wishes and Tarkin's collide, Tarkin would be swept away with the rest of history's dust without a second's hesitation.

Nova hadn't really been surprised to be assigned as one of the guards for the conference room on the Command Level. It wasn't his normal duty, but he was a senior sergeant, and when one of the men normally at the post developed a sudden illness Nova had been tapped as a temporary replacement. He was the kind of guard they liked, adept with either weapons or his bare hands.

Mostly the room was empty the entire shift, and there was little to do but think; however, toward the end of the shift, Governor Tarkin and Darth Vader had arrived. Nova could not help but overhear, of course, as the two had a discussion that ranged across several topics—mostly concerned with the next target for the Death Star. It seemed that the Rebels' main fortress had been located, and they were awaiting reports from the scouts before spacing there to destroy that planet as well.

Nova was still reeling from the results of the most recent test. He had passed out in his sonic shower at precisely the instant that the superlaser had shattered the peaceful world of Alderaan, and he was certain this was no coincidence. The doctor's diagnosis about midi-chlorians had to be connected. He'd done research on it with the station archivist's help, and had come to the reluctant conclusion that he was somehow receptive to the pervasive energy field the Jedi had called the Force. A *Force-sensitive* was the term. It explained why he sometimes could anticipate the moves of his opponents, the skill he called Blink.

He wasn't sure what to do about this—he wasn't even sure that anything could be done. It had evidently been with him to a certain degree for his whole life; it wasn't just going to go away. Since he seemed to be stuck with it and the visions it brought, maybe there was something he could do with it besides just dodge incoming fists.

The door opened and a senior officer marched in, as stiff as if he had a durasteel rod for a spine.

The man gave his report, and Nova kept his face stolid as he listened.

So the girl that the doctor had spoken of in the cantina had given Tarkin and Vader a false lead. Brave, but not very smart, since Tarkin was now irritated enough to tell Vader to execute her.

Once upon a time, Nova would have shrugged that bit of news away. It wasn't his business how the higher-ups behaved; he just followed his orders and did his job, a good and loyal soldier. But if blowing up Despayre had been terrible, killing Alderaan was several orders of magnitude more horrifying. Billions of innocents had died there, not hardened and convicted criminals—billions of civilians of all ages—and how could you in good conscience serve somebody who thought that was the way to wage war?

It had rocked him to his core, maybe more because of the whole Force thing. But he hadn't been the only one. Sure, there were always some kill-'em-all types who said they must have deserved it, else it wouldn't have been done; but there were a lot of people on this battle station who couldn't accept these actions as things even to be contemplated in a sane and rational universe. It wasn't supposed to have gone this far. From everything he'd heard it was to be merely the *threat* of mundicide. Blowing up a planet—killing everything that lived on it—just to make a point?

This was his last tour, Nova decided; he wasn't going to stay in a military that would commit such atrocities. And if there was anything he could do to help prevent it from happening again, he ought to seriously consider it.

Killing civilian populations on a planetary scale was evil beyond comprehension. Nova could fight a room full of men straight-up, face-to-face, and if he had to kill half of them to survive, he'd do it. But he hadn't signed on to slaughter children asleep in their beds.

LIBRARY AND ARCHIVES, DECK 106, DEATH STAR

Atour Riten considered himself a man of the galaxy; he had traveled far and wide and seen much. He had toured the spice mines of Kessel, explored the ruins of Dantooine, and witnessed the death of stars in the Bi-Borran Cluster. Even though most of his working days had been within the walls of libraries and archives, he had also breathed the outside air of scores of worlds in the course of his years. And he had remained apolitical for all those years, going his own way, avoiding commitments to things he didn't think he could influence yea or nay.

But not anymore. Not after Alderaan.

The destruction of Despayre had been bad enough, as much for what it had portended as for the act itself. But Alderaan had been a peaceful world; its government had sympathized with the Rebels, true enough, but the Empire's reaction had been overkill in the most horrifyingly literal sense imaginable. The immensity of it overwhelmed him each time his imagination started down that killing road: mothers, babies, grandfathers, pets . . . all wiped out in a heartbeat.

He could not help but be reminded of the Mrlssi saying: *Evil compounds exponentially.* It was true. Such horrors inevitably fed upon themselves, mushrooming into the unthinkable in very short order. Atour could not stand to see this happen again. He was old, he had lived a long and full life, and he decided now that whatever days he had left, he would dedicate to defeating an Empire capable of such abominations.

"Persee, initiate a search for weak points in this battle station—those that might be most vulnerable to internal sabotage."

"That would be unwise, sir. Such a scan would almost certainly be detected, and Imperial intelligence operatives would undoubtedly wish to engage in conversation with the initiator of such a search. It would not be a pleasant conversation."

"Then I suggest you do it cautiously."

"Sir, I feel compelled to point out again that the risk of such a venture would be great."

"And I appreciate your concern," Atour said. He leaned back in his formfit chair and steepled his fingers. "Do it anyway."

The droid acknowledged this order and shuffled away to implement it. Atour sighed. He realized that P-RC3 was going to suffer a traumatic memory loss in the near future. That would be a shame—he'd actually become rather fond of the droid—but given the gravity of what the Empire had done and must be made to pay for, the price of a droid's memory—and one old man's life, come to that—was small enough.

CONFERENCE ROOM, COMMAND CENTER, DEATH STAR

The intercom cheeped, and Tarkin activated it. "Yes?"

The voice from the comm said, "We've captured a freighter entering the remains of the Alderaan system. Its markings match those of a ship that blasted its way out of Mos Eisley."

Tarkin frowned. Mos Eisley was on Tatooine, where the stolen battle station plans had, according to Vader, landed. Coincidence? Not likely. He looked at Vader, who said, "They must be trying to return the stolen plans to the Princess. She may yet be of some use to us."

Tarkin considered that. Yes. While his anger at her deception had not abated, there were more important things at stake here than one prisoner's life or death. Vader was right. She might be useful as a decoy.

"Best you go and personally deal with this, Lord Vader."

DOCKING BAY 2037, DEATH STAR

Vader stalked into the bay as a lieutenant and several stormtroopers exited the captured freighter. The lieutenant said, "There's no one on board, sir. According to the log, the crew abandoned ship right after takeoff. It must be a decoy, sir; several of the escape pods have been jettisoned."

Vader nodded. "Did you find any droids?"

"No, sir. If there were any on board, they must also have been jettisoned."

"Send a scanning crew aboard—I want every part of this ship checked."

"Yes, sir."

Vader was about to speak again when he felt a ripple in the Force. It was fleeting, too brief to grasp before it flitted away, but startling. Almost to himself, he said, "I sense something. A . . . presence I've not felt since—" He stopped. No. He must be mistaken. It could not be, after all these years . . .

Abruptly, he turned away. If the plans were on the ship, they would be found; if not, then the ship was of no importance. As for that tingle in the Force . . . well, if it was indeed generated by who he thought it might be, then no doubt the man responsible had sensed Vader as well.

If Obi-Wan Kenobi was really aboard the Death Star, then it was inevitable that they would meet. The Force would draw them together as surely as opposite particles in a vacuum.

61

LIBRARY AND ARCHIVES, DECK 106, DEATH STAR

"Odd," P-RC3 said.

Atour looked up. "What?"

The droid turned away from the monitor, its data display reflecting from its blue durasteel chassis. "Someone has just accessed the main computer in a forward bay command office."

"And this is unusual because . . . ?"

"The access is via droid interface plug."

"Which was put there for droids, if I am not mistaken," Atour said. "So?"

"The accessor is requesting information on the location of terminals controlling a tractor beam recently used to capture a ship suspected of being a Rebel freighter."

Atour frowned. "Who would do that? Is the tractor generator in need of repair?"

"Not that I can determine."

"And why are you bringing this to my attention?"

"I have flagged operating systems to report unusual events for your protection, sir."

"Hmm. Is there a security cam in that office?"

"Yes, sir."

"Can you access it?"

"Not without the security codes."

"Oh, those. Here." Atour tapped a ten-digit number into the computer console.

"Having that code is illegal," P-RC3 said. "You could be arrested for it."

"That would likely be the least of my crimes. Access the cam."

The droid turned back to the terminal. "I have visual only. No sound."

"A pixel is worth a thousand bytes—and isn't that a strange saying to be coming out of the mouth of an archivist?"

"Sir?"

"Never mind. The cam. Put it on my terminal."

The holo over Atour's desk lit. What he saw was the interior of a command office in which were standing two stormtroopers, their helmets removed. They seemed unremarkable, although their haircuts were a bit long for regulation status. There were others as well who were not so unremarkable: a golden protocol droid, an astromech unit, a Wookiee with a bowcaster, and a balding and bearded older human in a hooded cloak with the cowl pulled back. Atour realized with slight surprise that the old man was dressed in the vestments of a Jedi Knight.

There were also the bodies of two Imperial troopers lying on the deck.

It appeared from their attitude that the humans were listening to the protocol droid. Then after a moment, the humans started talking to each other.

"Persee, can you lip-read?"

"Certainly, sir."

"Tell me what they are saying."

Persee watched the image for a moment. "The oldest one just said to the younger of the stormtroopers, "Your destiny lies along a different path from mine. The Force will be with you, always."

The Force?

As Atour digested this, the command office door slid up and the old man exited. One of the stormtroopers and the Wookiee had a brief conversation.

"Sorry, sir, but I can't see the Wookiee clearly enough to read what he is saying. The older human male just said to the younger, 'Where did you dig up that old fossil?' "

Atour frowned, perplexed. What did that mean?

"The youngest one appears to be speaking now, but I can't see his face. The two humans appear agitated, judging by their body language."

Atour continued to watch as both men stopped arguing and looked at the droids.

"I surmise the droids are speaking," Persee said. "Now the older human has just said, 'Princess?'

" 'Where is she?' the younger one asks."

Princess? "Persee, check the main computer for information on 'Princess.' "

The droid tapped console controls as Atour continued to watch the image. The two men were talking now, both somewhat agitated. The younger one—no more than a boy, really—seemed to be trying to convince the older one of something.

"Sir, a human female, Princess Leia Organa, was recently brought aboard by Darth Vader. A Rebel, according to the files, and scheduled to be terminated."

Atour shook his head in incredulity. It seemed obvious that the two men he was watching were not stormtroopers, and that they were here due in some part to Princess Leia. He knew the name, of course. Bail Organa's daughter. Of the late planet Alderaan.

The protocol droid shuffled forward and handed the boy a pair of electronic stun cuffs. The boy moved toward the Wookiee and attempted to put the cuffs on him. The Wookiee did not seem at all pleased with the idea. The boy backed away quickly, turned to the older man—who wasn't really all that old himself—and gave him the binders.

"Persee? What are they saying?"

" '. . . Chewie, I think I know what he has in mind.' That from the older one."

The man put the cuffs on the Wookiee's wrists. "Ah," Atour said.

"Sir? I don't understand."

"They are apparently marching right into the nexu's den." He smiled. "They have come for the Princess."

"That hardly seems wise."

"No, it seems foolhardy in the extreme. How will they escape if they do find—aha!"

"I am still at a loss, sir."

"That's why they're investigating the tractor beam. They must mean to steal a ship. I'll wager that the old man—a Jedi, if I'm not mistaken—has gone to disable the device. Clever." Atour frowned. "Unlikely they will succeed, however."

The men and the stun-cuffed Wookiee exited the room, leaving the two droids alone in the office.

"I think we've seen enough of this," Atour said. "Where is the Princess being held?"

P-RC3 adjusted a control on the console. "Level Five, Detention Block AA-Twenty-three."

Atour nodded. He didn't fancy their chances of success, but he had to give them credit for bravery. He would have helped them, but he didn't see any way that he could. Detention cells were controlled locally; they couldn't be overridden by the central computer.

It occurred to him then that they would have to take a lift up to the Detention Level, and they would need the current code to reach that level. Perhaps they already had access to it, but he doubted it.

Well, he couldn't magically open cell doors for them, but finding the proper protocol for section egress and feeding it to the lift they would be taking was the work of only a few moments.

"Good luck," Atour said softly, after transmitting the code. "You'll need it."

As for himself, what he needed was a drink.

62

THE HARD HEART CANTINA, DEATH STAR

Memah had asked Rodo to remove the few patrons who were having too much fun, and what was left was a somber crowd; mostly people who kept their conversations to themselves or had conversations with themselves. Either way, they did it quietly.

Rodo and Nova Stihl sat at the bar, with Ratua. It was apparent that the bond he and Nova had formed on the prison planet was stronger than their differences as guard and prisoner. Memah was glad to see that.

There were a couple of Alderaanians in one corner, and they just sat there, not saying much, not drinking much; just staring into some personal distance.

One of the pilots and his companion—an architect, Memah had learned—also sat at the bar, talking quietly but intensely. Apparently the pilot was one of Nova's martial arts students, a double ace named Vil Dance. The woman was named Teela Kaarz.

An older man entered the cantina—Memah recognized him as having been in before, but she didn't know who he was. He walked to where Stihl and Rodo and Ratua sat, and was greeted by the sergeant.

For herself, Memah tended the bar, made drinks, and when there was a lull, drifted over to talk to Green-Eyes. It felt like a memorial service, and, in its own way, it was.

A pair of troopers entered and moved to a table near the Alderaanians. They ordered ales and seemed oblivious to the generally hushed mood in the cantina. Memah was considering having Rodo throw them out, too, when one of the two said something loud enough to carry to the bar:

"Guess the Rebel scum won't be giving us much trouble after Alderaan, hey?"

Rodo was already up and moving when one of the Alderaanians stood and stepped over to the soldiers' table.

"Rodo," Memah said.

He stopped, turned, and looked at her. She held up her hand in a *wait-a-second* gesture.

The soldier glanced up at the man standing next to him and probably wasn't impressed. The Alderaanian was slightly built, short, and hardly seemed a threat. "What can I—"

That was as far as he got. The smaller man swung a fist that was driven by grief and rage, and the soldier fell out of his chair and hit the deck, hard.

"Go," Memah said to Rodo.

Rodo was there before the second soldier could do more than get to his feet. He grabbed him by the neck. "Out," he said.

"The frip you say! Nobody punches a trooper and—"

Rodo tightened his grip on the man's neck. The trooper suddenly became very quiet.

"Out," Rodo repeated. "On your own or with my help. Get your buddy and get gone."

The second soldier was not a fool. He nodded, bent, and helped his dazed friend to his unsteady feet. They headed for the door.

The Alderaanian, fists still clenched in simmering rage, face red, stood there glaring at Rodo. Memah knew that even though he didn't have a prayer against the big bouncer, he would still swing on him if Rodo tried to evict him.

Rodo knew it also. He glanced at her.

She shook her head: *Leave him be.*

Rodo nodded, said something too soft to hear to the smaller man, and returned to the bar. After a moment, the Alderaanian, as if in a dream-like trance, shuffled back to his seat. His motions were stiff, droid-like, and he sat down heavily.

Rodo returned to the bar, and Memah moved to meet him. "What did you say to him?"

"I told him I was sorry. That his table was comped, and that if anybody else said anything that stupid, to let me handle it—I could hit harder than he could."

Next to him, Nova said, "I dunno. That was as good a punch as I've ever seen."

Nobody replied to that.

Nova indicated the older man and said, "This is Commander Riten. He runs the library."

Memah nodded. "Commander."

"Call me Atour," he said. "I don't much care for the rank or its associations right now."

Memah nodded. "I hear that."

She looked at the door and saw Dr. Divini come in. He came straight to the bar, where he was greeted by the group and introduced to the librarian and the young couple.

"Missing all the fun, Doc," Nova said. "That little Alderaanian in the corner just decked a soldier twice his size."

Uli nodded as Memah, unasked, put a stein of ale in front of him. "Rodo didn't throw him out?"

"Our sympathies do not lie with the Imperial military tonight," Memah said.

Uli nodded again. "Nor mine. I feel tainted just being on this station."

That got a chorus of agreement.

"There ought to be something we can do about this," Nova said.

Rodo said, "What'd you have in mind, Sarge? Challenging Darth Vader to a death match?"

"Maybe."

"That wouldn't help," Uli said. "The Imperial machine is too big. Nobody can stand against it. Witness Alderaan."

"So what does a person with any sense of justice do?" Memah asked. "Shrug it off and go on about his or her business?"

Riten, who had been quietly nursing his drink, shook his head. To Nova, he said, "As a martial arts expert, what do you do if you have an opponent who is bigger, stronger, faster, better trained, and armed—and who has many friends?"

Nova shrugged. "Haul your glutes away, fast."

"Precisely," Riten said.

They all turned to look at him.

"At the very least, you don't have to abet a murderous thug."

Dance, the TIE pilot, spoke up: "Refusing a direct order gets you sent to the detention cells. How's that going to do you or anybody else any good?"

"Well," Riten said, "you might not be part of the solution tucked away in a cell, but at least you won't be part of the problem."

"Some choice," Dance said.

"There are other choices," Riten said.

"Really? What?"

The archivist regarded his drink as if it were possible to read the future in it. "You could leave."

Dance laughed, and it was far more bitter than amused. "Yeah. And just how would you pull that off? Nobody leaves the Death Star without the express permission of the powers-that-be. Even pilots like me—you can't get far in a TIE fighter, unless you have one of the new hyperdrive-equipped x-ones I've been hearing about, and there aren't but a couple of those on the whole station. We have more weapons than a naval armada—tractor beams, turbolasers, and a bunch of bored, trigger-happy gunners who'd like nothing better than to shoot anything that moves. Leaving isn't exactly an option."

"But if it was? What if you could go? Would anybody here exercise that choice?"

There was a moment of silence. "We're talking hypothetically here, not real conspiracy to treason, right?" Nova said.

"Of course. Just a what-if conversation among friends."

"I'd go," Memah said.

They looked at her. "You aren't in the military," Ratua said. "You didn't have anything to do with blowing up Alderaan. You're a civilian. It's not like you pulled the lever."

"Imagine what that must feel like," Kaarz said.

"But I am here," Memah said, in answer to Ratua. "And I know what the Death Star can do—what it's already done. I serve drinks to people like that soldier the little guy knocked down, who not only think it's okay to kill planets full of innocents but actually take pride in it." She shook her head hard enough to swing her lekku. "I'd go in a heartbeat."

Kaarz nodded. "Me, too. Of course, I'm a prisoner, and when it all settles down, I doubt that the Empire will have much use for me."

"Assuming the Empire wins," Rodo said.

"Can't really assume anything else," Dance said. "We all know what this battle station can do. If they can build one, they can build more—maybe even bigger than this one. The Rebels don't have a chance."

"Perhaps," Riten said. "But wars are not won by technology alone. There's always a new version of the ultimate weapon being developed, and historically they've never been enough to put an end to war."

"Peace is found neither in hot blood nor in cold sweat," Nova said.

Riten looked at him in mild surprise. "*The Fallacy of War,* by Codus Romanthus. One doesn't often encounter a soldier who can quote obscure philosophers."

Nova drained the last of his ale. "I'm sensitive." He belched.

"I'd go," Uli said. "I'd have bailed a hundred times already if there had been any real opportunity."

"Me, too. What about you, Sarge?" That from Ratua.

"Yeah, count me in. Not just because my head nearly exploded when they burned Alderaan, but because it's wrong. People get killed in war, but it's one thing to shoot a guy shooting at you; it's another to go to his house and burn it down with his wife and kids inside."

Dance said, "Yeah. One on one against another pilot, I'm good. What the Empire did to Despayre and Alderaan? That's not right. Next planet might be one of our homeworlds—nobody's safe, anywhere."

"All very high-minded of us," Rodo said, "but we don't have that choice, do we?"

Riten said, "Maybe we do."

They all turned to look at him again.

"What are you talking about?" Nova asked.

Riten said, "I'm an archivist. Over the years I've learned ways to obtain all kinds of information that isn't supposed to be accessible."

"Yeah—so?" Ratua said.

"Knowledge is power," Riten said. "What if you knew the entry and takeoff codes for an Imperial shuttle that was fueled and ready to fly? What if you had the passcodes that would keep the station's gunners from firing on you when you left? Or the tractor beams from locking on to you?"

"Big what-ifs," Rodo said.

"Indeed. But—again, hypothetically and just for the sake of this discussion—suppose that I could lay hands on this information. Should I bother?"

The group was quiet for what seemed a long time. Finally, it was Nova who broke the silence.

"Yeah," he said. "Go ahead and bother."

63

CONFERENCE ROOM, COMMAND LEVEL, DEATH STAR

Vader stood at just inside the door, the guards flanking him, talking to a frankly incredulous Tarkin.

"He is here," he said.

"Obi-Wan Kenobi? What makes you think so?"

To anyone with a connection to the Force, the question would not need an answer or an explanation. Even though Vader had thought initially to brush it off—he had, for so many years, hoped to feel that presence that at first he thought he'd imagined it—he knew. He said, "A tremor in the Force. The last time I felt it was in the presence of my old Master."

Tarkin stood. "Surely he must be dead by now."

"Don't underestimate the Force," Vader said, though he knew it was pointless. The man could not understand.

"The Jedi are extinct. Their fire has gone out of the universe."

The intercom on the table chimed. Tarkin moved toward it, continuing to speak. "You, my friend, are all that's left of their religion."

No, Tarkin could not understand. He had no way of grasping the concept. It was like trying to explain color to someone blind from birth.

"Yes?" Tarkin said into the intercom.

The voice from the unit was terse: "We have an emergency alert in Detention Block AA-Twenty-three."

Tarkin frowned. He obviously knew the significance of that location. "The Princess? Put all sections on alert!"

Vader did not need the confirmation, but this new event might help convince Tarkin. He said, "Obi-Wan is here. The Force is with him."

Tarkin, always quick to shift stances when he realized it was necessary, said, "If you're right, he must not be allowed to escape."

It was a reasonable conclusion for someone who did not know their history. But wrong. "Escape is not his plan. I must face him. Alone."

Vader turned and strode out of the room. Now that he was certain his old Master was on this station, he would be able to find him. The Force was sometimes maddeningly inexact. There were times when, even knowing what he was, you could stand next to a Jedi Master and not feel his power; at other times you could sense him on the other side of a planet or halfway across a stellar system—distance was no barrier to the Force. The swirls of energy often hid as much as they revealed. But Vader knew Obi-Wan was here, and he knew he would be able to find him.

Find him and, after all these years of waiting, destroy him.

GUARD UNIT LOCKERS, DECK 17, DEATH STAR

Nova arrived for his shift only a few minutes late, still chewing on the conversation in the cantina. He had gotten most of his armor on—and why they had to wear that inside the battle station made no sense at all to him. The eighteen-piece suit was a pain to don, and it offered only limited protection against a regulation power blaster, anyway. But regs were regs.

The lieutenant suddenly turned from the comm board and yelled at him: "Sergeant Stihl, we have intruders! There's a breakout on Level Five, Detention Block AA-Twenty-three. Take a squad and get over there!"

Stihl stared at the lieutenant. Intruders? A breakout? How was that possible?

"Sergeant! Move out!"

"Copy, sir, on our way! Bretton, Zack, Dash, Alix, Kai, with me! Mahl, Cy, Dex, Nate, on point! Move out, people!"

The squad hustled out of the barracks and into the hall, the sound of their armor rattling as they moved. The corridors were strangely deserted, it seemed to Nova, which he chalked up to luck. Fewer people meant fewer civilian casualties.

"Who are we after, Sarge?" That from Dash.

Nova didn't know. Who were they after?

Well, kark it, he'd know them if he saw them.

"Just shoot who I tell you to," he told the trooper. Then he raised his voice to include the rest of the squad: "Double-time it, people!"

They ran through the gray-and-black halls, following the four guards on point, their sidearms held up, fingers outside the trigger guards, as per regulations. The ceilings and floors were covered with blaster-proof absorbital, so if somebody accidentally cooked off a round it wouldn't do any damage. If you carried your weapon pointed at the floor, however, there was a good chance in a crowd that you'd shoot somebody's foot off, and the walls and vent grates weren't all that sturdy, either.

The corridor branched ahead. As they approached, Nova desperately tried to remember which one led to D-Unit. Ahead, a blaster bolt sizzled through a cross corridor, and the four guards on point skidded to a stop, then moved ahead slowly toward the intersection to peer around it.

Nova suddenly realized that this was one of his dreams. It was as if he had been here before, seen the events that were now unfolding.

"*Aaahhhh!*" Somebody beyond the bend in the corridor screamed, and a moment later half a dozen troopers barreled around the corner of the hallway intersection, heading toward Nova.

They were being chased by a single man with a blaster, yelling like a berserker as he ran. The man—Nova saw that he was dressed like a down-on-his-luck spacer—stopped, realizing that there were suddenly overwhelming odds in front of him. Then he turned and ran back the other way, putting on a burst of speed as he disappeared around the corner.

"After him! Go!" Nova led the pursuit, followed by his squad and the others. Once around the bend, he saw that the fleeing spacer had been joined by a Wookiee, and both of them were now shooting back at their pursuers as they fled. They returned fire, but no one was hitting anything; the excited troopers were just spraying blasterfire.

They wouldn't hit the two. He was sure of it. But how could he know that?

They rounded a corner. "Close the blast doors!" somebody yelled.

The heavy durasteel panels ahead began to iris shut, but the running man and the Wookiee managed to leap through before they closed completely.

"Open the blast doors! Open the blast doors!" somebody was now shouting. It was almost comical. Since he was the closest, Nova reached for the controls.

But in that moment, he hesitated. He knew—felt it in a way that he couldn't explain but also could not deny—that the man and the Wookiee they were after had to escape. That somehow it would be, as the old archivist had said, part of the solution and not part of the problem.

How could he know this? Was it part of the connection to the Force that the doc had talked about? Nova didn't know . . . it seemed crazy, but he had to acknowledge what he felt.

One of the troopers said, "Sarge? You gonna open the doors?"

"I'm trying. The switch is jammed." He moved his armored hand over the controls, pretending to try to move them, knowing that none of his men could see what he was doing.

A few more seconds might make the difference. He could give them that much.

"Still not working," Nova said. He activated his comlink. "Blast Control, this is Sergeant Stihl, operating number four-three-nine-five-seven-zero-four-three-seven. I need an override on the blast doors, Level Five, Corridor Six. Open them."

"Manual controls appear to be functional on all doors in that corridor," came back the reply through his helmet's commset.

"And I'm telling you they aren't. You gonna open it or let the terrorists we're chasing escape?"

"Acknowledged."

The blast doors opened. "Let's go!" Nova said.

Ahead, the corridor branched. Again, he could not say how he knew, but he was sure the fugitives had taken the turn to port.

"Which way, Sarge?"

"To the right," Nova said, and led the charge.

There's your chance, friend, he thought. *I hope you make good use of it.*

64

CORRIDOR OUTSIDE DOCKING BAY 2037, DEATH STAR

There he was. After so much time and across so much space, the hooded figure of Obi-Wan Kenobi, his former Master and friend, stood right in front of him. He had aged; his face was lined, his beard white. It was impossible not to remember vividly the last time they had seen each other, when his Master had crippled him and left him to die on the fiery banks of a river of molten rock, light-years from here.

Now his anger smoldered in him like the banks of that coursing stream of lava. *You should have killed me then, Obi-Wan.*

Vader lit his lightsaber. The red beam crackled with power.

Obi-Wan had already known Vader was there, of course. The Force swirled about the two of them, forging a link impossible to miss.

Vader strode toward the old man. As he drew nearer, Obi-Wan ignited his own lightsaber. The blue gleam of the blade flashed brightly.

"I've been waiting for you, Obi-Wan. We meet again, at last. The circle is now complete."

Vader raised his weapon to attack, and Obi-Wan matched his pose.

"When I left you, I was but the learner; now I am the Master."

"Only a master of evil, Darth." With that, Obi-Wan stepped in and cut.

Vader blocked the attack easily. Obi-Wan attacked again, and again, Vader blocked each strike.

If the old man thought he could rattle him by attacking instead of defending, he was mistaken. Vader riposted, sped up his timing, and took the initiative, forcing the erstwhile Jedi to defend.

He still had some skill, his old Master did, but he was out of practice. Vader could feel it through the Force.

Obi-Wan twirled and blocked a slash, then wove a defensive pattern with his blade. The Force was still with the old Jedi; he was able to anticipate Vader's strikes and block or parry them. But after a quick exchange, Vader felt the energy shift in his favor. "Your powers are weak, old man."

There had always been in Vader a small bit of worry about this day. Not much; just a trace. He had been sure, in his youthful arrogance, that he had been stronger, had been better than the Jedi Knight who had been his teacher, and the memory of what Obi-Wan had done to him would never be erased. He had been a superior fighter even when he had been Anakin Skywalker, and yet Obi-Wan had defeated him.

Could he win now?

It was as if the old man could read his thoughts:

"You can't win, Darth. If you strike me down, I shall become more powerful than you can possibly imagine."

Vader knew that Obi-Wan was taunting him by using the Sith honorific, but he would not allow himself to be baited. Obi-Wan lunged again, attacking, but Vader was ready. Their sabers clashed, sparks spewed, the stink of ozone wafted over them, but Vader stood his ground. The blades slid along each other's length, then stopped, bound together in the magnetic handle guards, the men face-to-face.

Vader shoved, hard, and they broke the clash. Obi-Wan retreated a step.

Vader felt the fierce anticipation of victory pound in his heart. "You should not have come back," he told the old Jedi.

Another exchange—four, five, six attacks and blocks—and Vader knew the old man was weakening. The Force might be strong in Obi-Wan, but the dark side was stronger in Vader. It let him anticipate his adversary's strikes and counter them almost before they began.

Obi-Wan knew it, too. He began a retreat, backing away, his lightsaber itself seeming weaker as he moved.

Vader backed Obi-Wan past an open blast door leading to the forward dock where the Rebel freighter was being held under guard. The old man was obviously tiring.

You're mine, old man, Vader thought.

But just as he was ready to deliver the final strike, Obi-Wan managed a fast series of attacks, and Vader had to move quickly to avoid the strikes. Even as old and weak as Obi-Wan was, his technique was accomplished enough that a foolish move on Vader's part could still be fatal.

A group of stormtroopers standing in the dock became aware of them. Vader felt rather than saw them notice the strange duel, and sensed the troopers heading toward them.

He did not wish them to interfere, but even to warn them off would take concentration that he could not afford at the moment. Should his attention falter, Obi-Wan could kill him in the blink of an eye.

Vader heard someone call from the dock: "Ben?" It was a young man's voice. Still he could not risk a look in that direction.

But Obi-Wan glanced away, quickly, then looked back at Vader. Then he did the last thing Vader could have possibly imagined—

He smiled.

It was an expression not the least worried; almost beatific, in fact. Then, still smiling, Obi-Wan lifted his lightsaber so that the tip pointed straight up at the ceiling.

The action was so totally unexpected that Vader paused for an instant in shock. Not even the Force had lent him prescience concerning this. His former Master had left himself wide open. Was it a trap?

It didn't matter. If it was, Obi-Wan wasn't fast enough, or strong enough, to spring it in time. Vader shifted his lightsaber and cut from the right, hard, aiming for the neck—

His lightsaber sheared through the old man as if the latter were no denser than the air itself, and Obi-Wan collapsed.

Yes! Fierce, exultant joy coursed through the man who had been Anakin Skywalker. He had done it! He had slain Obi-Wan Kenobi! His revenge was complete!

From a distance he heard someone scream *"Nooo!"*—a cry of utter despair. But Vader paid it no heed. The dark side surged within him as powerfully as he had ever felt it—for an instant. But then it stopped.

What had just happened?

Vader looked down at the body. But there was no body. Only Obi-Wan's robes and cloak.

This was impossible! It could not be!

The squad of stormtroopers began firing at somebody in the docking bay, but Vader could not be bothered to look. He stepped forward, stared down in disbelief. An illusion of some kind? Some Jedi mind trick that the old man had never imparted to him?

Impossible! Obi-Wan had taught him everything Vader knew . . .

But, whispered a voice from within, *maybe not everything that* Obi-Wan *knew.*

Vader reached out with his boot to touch the corpse, but he only stirred the empty vestments, charred by the lightsaber's heat, with his questing foot.

Obi-Wan Kenobi was *gone.*

How could this be?

For the first time that he could remember, the dark side had no answer. And a great surge of unfamiliar emotion suddenly washed over him.

Darth Vader, the Dark Lord of the Sith's apprentice, one of the two most powerful beings in the galaxy, was afraid.

65

COMMAND CENTER, DEATH STAR

Tarkin watched the recording of Vader fighting the old man in a lightsaber duel, fascinated. Obi-Wan Kenobi had survived all these years. Who would have believed it?

That he was still able to make a fight of it against Darth Vader was even more impressive. The man looked old enough to be Vader's father, and then some. Amazing.

The sound was not the best quality, but Tarkin could hear some of the exchanges between the two fighters. One statement from Kenobi in particular struck him, something about becoming more powerful than his ex-student could possibly imagine if Vader struck him down.

How droll. Had Kenobi expected Vader to flee in superstitious terror by telling him such a thing?

The thought had barely crossed Tarkin's mind, however, when moments later Vader did indeed strike the old man down, and the former Jedi simply . . . *disappeared,* leaving nothing behind but his robes and cloak.

Tarkin stared at the image, his jaw dropping in disbelief. This was impossible—there had to be some trick at work. Nobody could survive decapitation by a lightsaber!

"Lord Vader is on his way in," came a voice from the intercom.

Tarkin nodded. He switched off the recording and changed to an external view of the starfield, which he stood regarding. After a moment, Vader entered the room and came to stand next to him.

"Are they away?" Tarkin asked.

"They have just made the jump into hyperspace."

"You're sure the homing beacon is secure aboard their ship? I'm taking an awful risk, Vader. This had better work."

It was indeed a risk, letting the Princess and her band of rogues "escape." If it didn't work, they would not only lose a high-level prisoner and a couple of Rebel spies—they would lose the Death Star plans as well. And even though Tarkin tended to agree with Motti that having the plans wouldn't really do the Alliance any good now that the battle station was operational, he wasn't interested in taking any risks with the ultimate weapon. But if the escapees fled to the main Rebel fortress, as Vader was certain they would, the war would be over sooner than expected.

Much sooner.

The plans, after all, would hardly survive the destruction of whatever planet they came to rest upon.

The Death Star was at last operational, and there was no place in the galaxy where a beat-up Corellian freighter could run that they could not follow.

LIBRARY AND ARCHIVES, DEATH STAR

Making good on his promise that he could retrieve classified information and use it was proving to be somewhat harder than Atour Riten had anticipated. While he had certain codes that would allow him to access restricted files, the nuts-and-bolts operation of a vessel as large as this one was not a simple matter. There were so many subsystems, so many backups and redundant programs, that winnowing out the precise details was time consuming in the extreme. Were it not for P-RC3, he would never have been able to manage it.

"What do we have so far?" he asked the droid. "And please skip the part where you warn me how dangerous it is."

P-RC3 said, "I have accessed the shuttle-craft codes. The vessel most likely to be of use is the E-Two-Tee Medical Shuttle, a small, fast ambulance craft. It is unarmed and clearly marked as a noncombat medical transport, and under normal circumstances neither the Rebel Alliance nor the Empire will fire on it. It also has limited hyperdrive capability. It generally carries a crew of six, with facilities to transport and maintain twice that many human-sized patients."

"Good, good, that gives us plenty of room. What about the tractor beam?"

"Recent misuse of tractor beam controls has resulted in increased security. However, surreptitious programming using an ouroboros routine will, with a proper activation signal, result in a temporary overload to the beam projector's circuit breaker in the sector from which the ship would, in theory, be departing. This will keep that particular projector offline for approximately thirty seconds before the automatic reset. A return to full power will require fifteen seconds more. A pilot of sufficient skill should be able to accelerate far enough during that time to be out of range; however, if he ventures into the path of any of the other sectors' beams, they could capture the ship."

"Excellent."

"I have not, however, been able to bypass bay door controls for egress. Those systems are not yet linked to the main computer."

"That's no good," Atour said. "If we can't get the shuttle launched, the rest doesn't matter."

"So it would seem."

Atour considered the problem. "What is the procedure for standard emergency medical transport launch?"

"The onboard crew sends a copy of its orders to Bay Door Control and requests permission to depart. The flight plan is checked via comlink to Flight Control and, if valid, the officer in charge gives the order to his technicians. A force field sufficient to retain atmosphere but permeable enough to allow vessels to penetrate is produced. The vessel exits, the doors are closed and sealed, the field is shut off."

Atour nodded. "So the only reasonable solution here is to have the doors opened by the BDC crew."

"Yes."

"Hmm. Can you produce a bogus flight plan and order for transmission?"

"I can, but I cannot insert that plan into the Flight Control systems, which are independent of the main computer. They will have no record of them."

"But you can jam or redirect communications if you have the op-chan frequencies?"

"Certainly, sir. Even you could do that."

Atour gave him a look. "So if the door crew sends a signal to the Flight Control crew and instead of getting to them it goes somewhere else, then whoever gets that call could verify the orders?"

"In theory," the droid said.

"Well, then that problem is solved. You'll just have it set up so that that call comes here."

The droid turned to regard him.

"Oh, don't look at me like that—I won't be here. You will take the call and verify it."

"That would be illegal, sir. I cannot knowingly violate Imperial law."

"But if I am on that shuttle and you don't confirm the order, then I'll be arrested, and possibly even executed."

"In that case, my primary programming, which is to protect you from harm, would allow such illegal activity."

Atour slapped P-RC3 on the back. "Good man. I knew I could count on you."

"Yes, sir."

"Set it up, Persee. I have a feeling we won't have a lot of time. Once this station comes out of hyperspace, things will get very active around here."

"Right away, sir."

"I'm going to pay a visit to the local cantina now. Let me know when you get everything done."

CONFERENCE ROOM, COMMAND CENTER, DEATH STAR

Vader was still attempting to come to terms with the disappearance of Obi-Wan. His moment of triumph as he'd cut the old man down had been short-lived. How ironic that he'd been constantly telling non-believers like Tarkin not to underestimate the power of the Force, and now he'd witnessed an event that made him realize he was guilty of just such heresy himself.

His Master had never spoken of Jedi just vanishing into nothingness. This bespoke a power that Vader had not yet seen, even in the dark side. But surely it must exist there. Perhaps it had something to do with the darksome hints that his Master had dropped, from time to time, about Darth Plagueis, the Sith Lord who had been Darth Sidious's Master. Plagueis had been, according to the Emperor, obsessed with the preservation of the immaterial ego after the physical death of the body. Vader determined to ask his Master about it as soon as this distracting foolishness with the Rebels was—

The intercom beeped. Tarkin answered it. "Yes?"

"We are approaching the planet Yavin," a tech said. "The Rebel base is on a moon on the far side. We are preparing to orbit the planet."

Tarkin smiled as he disconnected and looked at Vader. "Well, Lord Vader, it seems you were correct. We are almost in position to break the back of the Alliance. I am sure the Emperor will be pleased."

"If the station performs as it is supposed to," Vader said. He believed that it would, but Tarkin seemed a bit too smug and sure of himself. It served him to keep the man slightly on the defensive.

"Oh, it will," Tarkin said. "I guarantee it will."

66

THE HARD HEART CANTINA, DEATH STAR

Memah had closed the cantina again, this time ostensibly to repair a malfunctioning cooler unit.

Ratua came back to the bar, waving a small electronic device. "Sniffer says we're still clean. No listening devices have been brought in since we got here."

"That's good," Rodo said, "because if we weren't involved in a conspiracy that would get us all shot before, we sure are now."

Memah looked around at the others: Riten, the instigator; Dance, the TIE pilot; Kaarz, the architect; Stihl, the guard; Divini, the doctor; Rodo, Ratua, and herself. Eight of them, against the might of the Empire. *Not very good odds,* Memah thought. One misstep and they were all dead.

"Any questions?" Riten asked.

"It seems too easy," Rodo said.

"Not really," Nova said. "The station is designed to withstand massive attack from without, but nobody worries too much about security within. The place is full of stormtroopers, guards, army and navy personnel, even a few bounty hunters thrown in. Plus, the only ways in or out are well protected. And if you do manage to get out, there are enough guns to turn you into subatomic particles, and twenty-four tractor beam batteries to hold you still while they do it."

There was a small jolt. Everyone reacted uneasily. "What now?" Uli asked.

"Just came out of hyperspace," Vil observed. "Wherever we were going, we're probably there."

"The Yavin system," Riten said. "Three planets, the only one of which concerns us being Yavin Prime. A gas giant with a number of habitable moons."

"And why is this important?" Ratua asked.

"Remember the Rebel freighter that 'escaped'? The one with the doc's girlfriend on it?" Nova asked.

Uli shook his head. "Not my girlfriend, alas. Although she made Atour's point about not being part of the problem well enough to convince me to join this raggedy crew."

"Yeah, well, the scut in the guard shack is that the ship was bugged and let go so we could follow it. Tarkin thinks there's a Rebel base here somewhere."

"Bad for them if it's so," Rodo said.

"But perhaps not for us," Riten said. "If the navy is busy fighting off Rebel attack ships, it might make it easier for us to escape."

Nova said, "Nothing the Rebels have can get close enough to scratch the finish on the Death Star—anything bigger than a fighter'll get blown apart a thousand klicks out."

"Still, during a battle, ambulance ships sometimes get dispatched without causing undue concern."

Rodo shook his head. "I hope you and your droid got all this right," he said to the archivist. "Otherwise even an ambulance won't do us much good."

Teela said, "So what do we do now?"

"Go on back to your routine, keep your heads down, and don't cause any fuss. Set your personal comlink to the library's data channel—that's five-five-seven-point-nine. As soon as everything is in place, I'll call, and with any luck, that call will be very soon.

"You'll have thirty minutes to make it to the transport. If everything goes well, we'll be in deep space a couple of minutes after that—and free."

"*If* everything goes well," Vil said. His voice was dry.

LIBRARY AND ARCHIVES, DEATH STAR

Two black-clad security guards were waiting, flanking P-RC3, when Atour arrived.

Atour felt his insides freeze. "What's going on here?"

"Is this droid assigned to you, sir?"

Stay calm. "Yes."

"Apparently it is malfunctioning, Commander. Our computer security monitor detected it attempting to access restricted data."

"This must be a mistake. This droid has been performing in an exemplary manner. I couldn't be happier with—"

"That may be, sir, but our orders are to take the droid into custody and arrange for a memory scan."

Oh, dear. I'm sorry, Persee.

He tried, knowing that it was fruitless. "That may disrupt its ability to function. And it is a most valuable assistant."

"I'm sorry, sir, but we have our orders," the guard said. "Come along," he added to the droid.

P-RC3 said, "I'm sure it's a simple mistake, Commander Riten, and a scan will straighten it all out. Oh, by the way, I did finish those filing chores you asked me to do. I hope they will be of assistance to you."

"Good luck, Persee."

"And to you, sir."

The guards led the droid away.

Atour sighed in regret. Pretty soon P-RC3 was going to have a mental meltdown. Atour felt bad about it. Yes, the droid could be reprogrammed, but it wouldn't be the same. Sad. He had liked P-RC3, more than he did most people.

But there was a bigger problem to consider. If P-RC3 wasn't here to take the call to verify the medical transport's right to leave the station, it wouldn't be going anywhere. And P-RC3 was gone.

It seemed that somebody else would have to be here to take that call.

SUPERLASER FIRE CONTROL, DEATH STAR

"Ready to crank it up, Chief?"

Tenn Graneet looked steadily at his CO. "Absolutely, sir," he said.

It was a lie, of course. He was not ready. Not after Alderaan. The destruction of the prison planet had been gut wrenching enough, even though he'd known the place had been home to killers and spice dealers and other scum of the galaxy. He reminded himself of that often, trying to find comfort in it, trying not to think about the thousands of guards and other personnel stationed on Despayre, some of whom had been his friends, not to mention the considerable number who had been wrongfully convicted and exiled there, all of whom had also died in fire because he had thrown the lever. Try as he might, he couldn't justify their massacre simply as collateral damage.

And even if he could, there was still Alderaan. That hadn't been collateral damage. That had been genocide on a planetary scale, an entire world wiped away, and for what? Why did all those millions of people have to die?

As an object lesson. To show the galaxy that the Empire meant business, that Palpatine was not to be trifled with. To make sure that Tarkin's fear doctrine was taken seriously.

And to punish—no, to torture—a young noblewoman who was part of the Rebellion.

He'd heard the story from more than one source. There had been no Rebel force hidden on Alderaan—if he could have believed there had been, it might have helped. But there had been guards there when Tarkin had told Motti to drop the hammer. They had heard the truth.

And it had been Tenn who'd pulled the trigger. He had sent the beam that killed at least a billion people, maybe more; he didn't know what the planetary population had been. No doubt there was an up-to-date census in some datafile somewhere, but he wasn't going looking for it. He didn't want to know the figures. The bottom line was that he had done it.

That knowledge was worse than gut wrenching. Much worse. Tenn hadn't had a peaceful night's sleep since he'd done it, and he didn't see how he ever could again.

"Scut is we're on the trail of the Rebels," his CO said. "Just wanted to give you a head's-up. Stay frosty." He turned and descended the steep stairs—almost a ladder—back down to the deck, leaving Tenn alone in the control room.

Alone, he thought. If only. Tenn knew he would never be alone again.

Yes, he was a good soldier, a cog in the well-oiled machine that was the Empire. He followed orders. He did his job. But how could a man live with the knowledge that he, personally, had dropped the curtain on more people at once than anybody had ever done before?

How could he live with all those ghosts?

He, Master Chief Petty Officer Tenn Graneet, was the biggest mass murderer in galactic history. That was something to tell those hypothetical great-grandkids about, wasn't it?

And now he was about to add still more to the total. Hey, why not? What was a few hundred thousand, or even a million more, when you had already scragged the populations of two planets?

He didn't know if he could do it again. When the moment came to destroy the Rebel base, he wasn't sure he could.

He knew he didn't want to—of that he was certain.

But if he didn't, somebody else would, and he'd get tossed into detention for disobeying an order. Then he'd have plenty of time on his hands to think about that moment when he had put every vile dictator or madman who had ever committed genocide to shame. General Grievous, the Butcher of Montellian Serat, Grand Admiral Ishin Il-Raz . . . pikers, all of them. None of them had ever slain so many, so suddenly.

So easily . . .

There was an old proverb his grandfather had taught him when he'd been a boy: *Take care what you wish for, Tenn—you might get it.*

Now he understood exactly what that meant. He had wanted to fire the big gun, and he had gotten to do just that. The only man in the galaxy who had shot it for real, at real targets, and look what it had bought him:

Misery beyond his ugliest dreams.

Graneet, the planet killer. Two up, two down.

People were already looking at him funny. Someday this war would be over, and what he had done couldn't be kept a secret. Alderaan had been destroyed, and somebody had done it. The citizens of the Empire—or maybe even the Republic once again, though he didn't see how the Alliance stood a chance, now—they'd want to pore over the details of the action. And once they did, they'd find him. They'd hold him up to the light and decry his hideous aspect.

Graneet, the planet killer. Unique among men. Got a pest problem? Call the chief—guaranteed to get rid of 'em all.

He wouldn't be able to walk on a street on any civilized planet in the galaxy; people wouldn't be able to abide his presence.

Nor would he blame them.

He couldn't stop thinking about it. He didn't believe he would ever be able to stop thinking about it. The dead would haunt him, forever.

How could a man live with that?

67

COMMAND CENTER, DEATH STAR

Vader and Tarkin watched the schematic representation of Yavin Prime glowing in the air. The smaller image of the moon Yavin 4 behind the translucent gas giant moved in small increments toward the outer perimeter.

The voice from the comm said, "Orbiting the planet at maximum velocity. The moon with the Rebel base will be in range in thirty minutes."

The countdown flashed on the screen.

Vader had thought long and hard about his duel with Obi-Wan, and had come to a somewhat satisfying conclusion: whatever had happened to his body, his old teacher was no more. That was what mattered. Wherever his form had gone, whatever it had become, he would not be seen in this galaxy again. That was more important than anything else.

To Tarkin, he said, "This will be a day long remembered. It has seen the end of Kenobi. It will soon see the end of the Rebellion."

Tarkin glanced at Vader. The latter did not need the Force to sense the Grand Moff's pride—it shone from his face. The culmination of all his decades of work was about to take place. This had been his project from the beginning, and it was about to produce the result he had always said it would. How could he not feel proud?

"Sir," came the voice from the intercom, "we have picked up small Rebel ships leaving the moon and heading our way."

Tarkin smiled, a cruel expression.

"Shall we scramble TIEs to intercept?" the voice asked.

"That won't be necessary," Tarkin said into the intercom. "I believe our gunners can use the practice."

He turned back to Vader. "It will be like swatting flies."

LIBRARY AND ARCHIVES, DEATH STAR

Atour felt a faint vibration in the deck beneath his chair. Whatever it was, he hoped fervently that it wouldn't interfere with his work. He was almost finished with the final stage of the plan. He concentrated on programming, the monitor's flickering light painting his face with pallor. Almost there . . . almost . . .

Ah. He leaned back in satisfaction, feeling stiff back muscles protest. He had found the link in the comm system that P-RC3 had built for him, and had locked it down. A dedicated pipe for communications from the Door Control room.

He picked up his comlink.

TIE FIGHTER PILOT BARRACKS, DEATH STAR

Vil Dance felt the vibration through his boots as he passed the watch commander. "What's up, Commander?"

"That's what it feels like when the guns are locking and loading full power charges. We got company come to call."

"We scrambling?"

"Negative. I guess they think we hogged all the fun last time—they're letting the gunners deal with this. Too bad."

Vil's comlink chirped. "Oops, sorry, need to take that. New girlfriend is supposed to be cooking me dinner."

The watch commander grinned and made a kissing sound.

Vil grinned back. "I hope so," he said. He took a few steps away, pulled his comlink from his belt. "Yeah?"

"Go," Riten's voice said. "A little under thirty minutes."

"Copy. See you there."

There was a short pause. "Right."

Vil's mouth was suddenly dry. This was it. If he was going to change his mind, this was the time. He could still back out, stay the best pilot in the fleet, on the fast track for promotion.

No. He remembered blowing up that shuttle of escaped prisoners. He remembered the nightmares he'd had for weeks afterward. He remembered the slaughter of the attacking Rebel fighters. And of course, he remembered Despayre and Alderaan.

He didn't want to be on the side that performed such atrocities.

He was going.

THE HARD HEART CANTINA, DEATH STAR

Ratua's comm buzzed. He looked at Memah. Nobody had the number but her—and Riten, the archivist. She looked back at him, her lovely teal face expressionless.

He answered it. "Yeah?"

"Go."

"I have Memah and Rodo right here."

"Then I won't call them. Get to the rendezvous point."

"On our way."

ELECTRONICS CORRIDOR 7B, DEATH STAR

Nova was standing guard on a restricted corridor when his comlink cheeped. Since he was in duty black instead of whites, he was able to answer it without routing it through a helmet comm. "Stihl."

It was the archivist. "Time to take a walk, Sergeant."

"Copy."

Nova left his post and started toward the turbolifts.

"What's up, Sarge?" the guard at the lifts asked.

"Sudden call of nature," he said. "Those lamitos at the mess hall last night."

The guard laughed. "I hear that. I'll keep an eye on your hall till you get back."

"Thanks."

COMMAND CENTER CORRIDOR

As Vader strode down the hall, one of his own crew officers hurriedly approached.

"We count thirty Rebel ships, Lord Vader. But they're so small, they're avoiding our turbolasers."

Vader's burned face twisted into its unseen, stiff smile. Once again, Tarkin had been overconfident, so certain his beloved monster was proof against anything. A fly could sting you if you missed swatting it. He had his own personal wing of TIE fighters on board. He would lead them out, and they would deal with what Tarkin could not.

"We'll have to destroy them ship-to-ship. Get the crews to their fighters." His officer knew the command referred only to Vader's elite fliers. A squadron would be more than enough.

68

ARCHITECTURAL OFFICES, DEATH STAR

Somebody with access or clout or both had installed a first-rate holoprojector in the conference room that had access to external cams, and a small crowd had gathered around the images flashing across the screen.

Teela walked into the room. She said to one of the drafting droids, "What's going on?"

"The station is apparently under attack by Rebel fighters," the droid said. "And the station's gunners seem to be having little success hitting them."

She nodded. Of course. The turbolasers were designed and timed to track larger targets. She had seen the specs. "Why haven't they scrambled TIE fighters? That's what they're for, isn't it?"

The droid said, "That is beyond my capability to comment on. I do drawings, not military tactics."

As she watched, a pair of the attacking fighters, both X-wings, dived into one of the surface trenches, firing all the while.

One of the architects laughed. "They're wasting their ammunition. Their guns're too small to penetrate very far into the armor."

Teela frowned. That trench looked familiar . . .

She stepped out of the conference room and moved to her office. She tapped her computer console, waved her hand over the reader, and brought up a schematic.

Why would those fighters think they had a snowflake's chance in a supernova against the Death Star? If they had the plans, like she'd heard, they'd know the ship could withstand anything they could possibly fire at it without sustaining major structural damage—they could shoot themselves dry and whatever harm they did would be repaired in a couple of shifts as if it had never happened.

Something nagged at her, tugging at the edge of her memory. Let's see, that was the trench that led to the main heat exhaust vent, wasn't it? Of course that vent was heavily shielded by both plate and magnetics, so no fighter would be able to penetrate it.

So why would they try—if they had the plans, they'd know it would be futile, wouldn't they?

She blinked and looked closer. Oh.

Oh!

The secondary port, the unnecessary one that she'd tried to keep from being built! It was just beyond the main!

Teela Kaarz was an architect, and a good one, and she had an engineer's eye. That portal was small, only two meters or so. If you didn't know it was there, you'd never spot it. The ray shielding at the mouth was minimal, meant to stop stray particle beams. And even if one of those got through, it would be absorbed by the anisotropic walls of the tube before it traveled half a kilometer, so no problem there.

But if something like, say, a proton torpedo were to be fired directly into it . . .

Her comlink chirped. The sound's clarity surprised her, because it wasn't coming from her pocket, where she'd thought she'd put it. She felt a quick surge of panic upon the realization; what if one of her co-conspirators had tried to call? She looked about, spotted it on a shelf, grabbed it.

"Yes?"

It was Riten. He sounded very agitated. "I've been trying to reach you—why haven't you answered?"

"Sorry. I left the comlink in my office."

He hissed in exasperation. "It's past time to go, Teela!"

"In a few minutes. I have to—"

"You don't have a few minutes. You need to get to the rendezvous now!"

"Listen, the Rebel attack—I know what they're up to!"

"It doesn't matter what they're up to. Go!"

"You don't understand! They could destroy the station!"

There was a short pause, no more than a couple of heartbeats. Then: "So?"

Teela blinked, confused by his response. "Riten—"

"We live on a battle station called the Death Star, Teela. It's already killed billions of people, and you know it can and will do worse. Anybody who tries to stand against the Empire will feel its teeth. There's no limit to how many this abomination could slaughter."

"But—all the people on board—"

"Don't begin to approach the numbers who were on Alderaan. Go, Teela. Get off while you can. You don't want to be a part of this any further."

Her emotions warred with themselves. All her work. All the dead of Despayre and Alderaan, and all those who might yet die. All her friends and colleagues. Civilians. Prisoners. A thousand worlds within easy reach of the Death Star.

He was right.

"I—"

"Go, *now*!"

"All right," she said.

She left the images floating over her desk and hurried out into the corridor.

FLIGHT CORRIDOR SEVENTEEN, DEATH STAR

Vader strode down the hall, where he came upon a pair of his own pilots. It was time for him to take the field. These Rebels were up to something—he could feel it. To the pilots he said, "Several fighters have broken off from the main group. Come with me."

His TIE fighter was fueled and ready—it was always fueled and ready—and he would personally show the Rebels what happened when you went up against Darth Vader. His prototype craft was the Advanced x1—faster, better armed, and equipped with short-range hyperspace capabilities that the older models did not have.

Whatever the resistance upstarts had in mind, he was going to stop it.

Vader gestured, and the hatch to his fighter slid open as if by itself.

He climbed into the ship, fired up the engines, and, with his two wingmates, flew through the open bay doors and into the black coldness of space.

MEDCENTER, DEATH STAR

Uli, having just received the comm call from Riten, was in his office packing a small tote with the few mementos of a military life. Suddenly the door panel opened without buzzing first. Two military security officers, uniforms starched and creased, hair severely cut and wearing implacable frowns, stepped in.

"Captain Dr. Kornell Divini?" one of them asked.

Uli stared at them, feeling the hope that had burned in his heart for the last few hours flare and go out. It was over. They'd been discovered. All that was left to look forward to now was a speedy military trial and then a blasting squad.

He felt no fear for himself, oddly enough. What he felt was that he'd let two people down—two women who had made a big difference in his life: Princess Leia Organa and Jedi Barriss Offee.

"Yes," he said. No point in denying it; no point in denying anything anymore. "I'm Dr. Divini."

The other officer said, "You are under arrest for violation of Statute OB-CPO-One-One-Nine-Eight, illegal medical research."

"Come with us, please," the first one ordered.

Uli was too astonished to ask any questions, which was probably just as well. The two security officers marched him out of his office and down the passage toward the main conduit corridor. They fell in with the traffic flow of servicemen, civilian workers, and droids, most of whom gave Uli and his escorts a wide berth.

Uli was relieved that his friends and co-conspirators were evidently not in the same jam that he was. They apparently still stood a chance of escaping. At least he wasn't dragging them down with him.

But illegal medical research? What could he have possibly done that qualified as—

And then he remembered.

Sergeant Stihl's midi-chlorians. He'd put up an inquiry on the MedNet weeks ago concerning them. He'd never gotten a response, and, eventually, what with the workload and all, he'd forgotten about it. He remembered wondering at the time if posting the question had been a good idea.

Evidently not . . .

POLAR TRENCH TWELVE, DEATH STAR

Vader said to his two wingmates, "Stay in attack formation."

There were three Y-wings diving at the station, making for one of the trenches. Were they mad? They couldn't do any real damage even if they deliberately plowed into the hull. But they must have something in mind . . .

Vader switched to the Command Channel: "All guns in the D-Quadrant cease fire immediately."

Three Y-wings, and they'd obviously chosen some kind of target they deemed vulnerable. To his wingmates he said, "I'll take them myself. Cover me."

They acknowledged his order, but he wasn't listening.

The trio fell in behind the Y-wings. It was but the work of a few seconds to lock on to the rearmost fighter. Vader thumbed his firing buttons . . .

A hit.

The ship exploded into a fireball. He flew through it.

He lined up on the second fighter. He didn't even need to use the Force. There was no room for the fleeing Rebel pilot to maneuver.

Vader fired. Another one destroyed.

He lined up on the last Y-wing. Shot it. Another explosion.

Too easy.

Was this all they had?

UPPER DECK CORRIDOR, DEATH STAR

Uli walked with his two captors along the gently curving corridor. He'd often heard it said that once hope has been truly extinguished, once one realizes in one's heart that the race is over, there comes with the realization a feeling of serenity, of acceptance, of peace.

There's often even a sense of relief at having the terrible uncertainty that is life resolved by death's inevitability. He believed it; he'd stood at the side of too many deathbeds, watching the occupants' final moments, to think otherwise. It wasn't the way everyone died, of course. But of those who passed away at least semiconscious and reasonably in possession of their faculties, a surprising number reported, moments before breathing their last, that they had entered this state of grace.

Not Uli. He wasn't on his deathbed, but he certainly had reason to believe that his life had just ended. Maybe his value as a surgeon could save him, but he doubted it. His only chance at finally getting out of this lifelong insanity that was war had been snatched from him at the eleventh hour. Maybe it was because he was still in shock from the unexpected dashing of his escape plan, but what he was feeling certainly wasn't serenity. It was anger.

His life had gone wrong the moment he'd set foot on the pestilent dirt of Drongar two decades earlier, although he hadn't realized it at the time. His plan had been to do his tour and rotate out, then start in private practice. Big Zoo on Alderaan had been his first choice. He'd seen himself, at this age, mostly retired save for the occasional consulting job, with a wife and kids.

Instead his life had been one long series of bush assignments, frontline care, Republic and Imperial Mobile Surgical Units, and other work, most of it dangerous, wearisome, and thankless. And now, just when it looked like he might finally have the opportunity at last to change it, to be hoisted by an earlier attempt to do his job responsibly and morally, well . . .

There was much to be said for it if one was a fan of irony.

He might as well accept it—if such a thing as destiny existed, then his was obviously to be a military surgeon for the rest of his life—assuming said life wasn't cut short by blasterfire in the very near future. Perhaps it was only in resignation, in bowing to the inevitable, that he would find peace. Because it would take a miracle to rescue him now.

The sound of a muffled explosion, more felt than heard, rumbled around them. Several passersby reacted nervously.

"What was that?" Uli asked.

At first he thought he wasn't going to receive an answer, but then one of the officers said, "Rebel fighters bombing the surface, is my guess."

"Or going splat on it," the other suggested. This brought grim chuckles from both. Uli found the humor a little hard to appreciate.

"All the good it'll do 'em," the first officer said. "Lord Vader's out there with his elites—those Rebel scum are dead men flying."

"Let's take a lift down to Three-A," his partner suggested. "We can cut through Hydroponics and—"

The wall exploded.

Later Uli realized that it had to have been another bomb, or crash, on the surface just "above" them. At the time all he knew was that several nearby panels had erupted in a shower of sparks and shrapnel, causing panic among the nearby people. And in the smoke and general confusion, Uli found himself separated from his captors.

There were many different deities worshipped on many different worlds, all supposedly capable of miracles. Uli had no idea which of them, if any, might have been responsible for this one, but he wasn't taking the time to question it, that was for sure.

Better let them know I'm coming, he thought. He pulled his comlink from a pocket as he ran through the panicked crowd, fumbled it, and saw it vanish into the stampeding chaos.

According to his chrono he had less than fifteen minutes to reach the rendezvous point. No time to even think about looking for the comlink. He ran faster.

69

STORAGE ROOM 3181, DEATH STAR

Teela tapped the access code into the pad next to the door, which slid up to reveal the others, all dressed in medical transport grays. She wondered briefly how they'd ever found a size big enough for Rodo, and then Vil practically knocked her over when he hugged her. "Where have you been? I was worried sick! Get changed—hurry!"

The room had no other compartments, and this was hardly the time for modesty anyway. Teela stripped and quickly donned a set of pale gray coveralls. There were medical insignia on the sleeves and breast.

As she dressed, she looked at the others, doing a head count. Vil, Memah, Ratua, Rodo, Nova . . .

"We're light two people," she said.

"We've noticed," Ratua said. "We haven't heard from either the doc or the old man."

Teela pulled her comlink and was about to input Uli's code when the room's access panel whooshed up again. Uli, red-faced and breathing hard, entered.

"Cutting it kind of close, aren't we, Doc?" Nova asked.

Uli gave him a strange look, almost as if he blamed the sarge for his tardiness. But all he said was, "I've got to listen to the advice I give my patients, and exercise."

Teela's comlink cheeped. She thumbed it. "Riten?"

"You made it to the rendezvous?"

"I'm getting dressed now."

"The others?"

"They're all here. Except for you."

"Good, good. You have less than ten minutes to get from there to the ship."

"Where are you?"

A slight hesitation. "In my office."

"What?" Teela looked about, saw that the others were as shocked as she was. "But—you can't—"

"I'm afraid there has been a glitch in the plan," Riten's voice said. "My faithful droid was a bit clumsy in its research, and as a result, it won't be able to fulfill its part. Somebody has to be here to vet the call from the man who will open the door for you. That would be me."

"Can't you take the call on your comlink?"

"Alas, no. My droid set it up, and I'm not technically skilled enough with hard- and firmwire to jigger what it did. It doesn't matter. I did a check on that possibility you brought up, and I think you're right, Teela. If that happens, no one will be coming for me. If it doesn't happen, well, I've had a long and enjoyable ride. No regrets."

"Atour—"

"No, no, not now. You don't have time. Get moving. Have a good life, child. Now go—all of you."

He shut off the link from his end.

Nobody moved or spoke for a few seconds.

"Can't we go back for him?" Teela asked, fighting back tears. She knew the answer, of course, even before Memah said, "There's no time. All we can do is make sure his sacrifice isn't in vain."

"She's right," Rodo said. "Let's go."

Vil opened the door, and they moved into the corridor. "I really hope somebody knows where we're going," Ratua said.

"This way," Nova said. "The entrance to the dock staging area is just around the next corner." He took the lead. The corridor widened out, ending in a blast door guarded by a pair of stormtroopers in black uniforms.

Nova stepped up to one of them. "We've got an emergency medical flight."

"Your orders?" the trooper said.

"C'mon, Sarge, we're in a hurry. We got guys dying out there."

"And if I let you in without scanning your orders, I'm gonna be dying in here."

The fake orders were logged into the shuttle's computer. They didn't have any kind of flimsi or datachip on them. Nova said, "They didn't give us anything—the orders are on the ship."

"Fine. I'll have somebody download and check them."

Teela saw Nova glance at his chrono, then look at her. They had less than ten minutes before that tractor beam would be shut off, and it was only going to be offline for forty-five seconds.

They couldn't wait. Something had to be done, *now.*

CORRIDOR OUTSIDE MEDICAL BAY, DEATH STAR

Nova knew they were out of time. There was only one course left open to them. He glanced at the other guard, then at Rodo, and knew, by that kind of telepathy fighters can sometimes share, that the big man understood.

Nova turned back to the guard and shrugged. "Okay, you're in charge. Let me get you the comlink code—" and with that, he fired a punch into the guard's throat, flipped the man's helmet up with his free hand, then snapped an elbow to the now bare temple.

The guard dropped. He saw the second guard fall as Rodo swept his feet from under him, then followed him down to the deck to bounce the guard's head against the plate. Excellent—both taken out with a minimum of fuss.

"Let's go, people!" Nova opened the blast doors—

Just as three squads of black-suited guards came around the corner. Fifteen men, in all. Fifteen armed men.

The lieutenant in charge saw his two fallen comrades. "Hey, what the—"

Nova said, "These men have been poisoned. We were called to take care of them and contain the area."

That wouldn't work for long, he knew. Seven medics dispatched for just two guards? The lieutenant would have to be pretty challenged to buy that for more than a few seconds.

Nova looked at Rodo again. "Whaddya say, Rodo?"

Rodo nodded. He looked at the others, particularly at Memah. "Go," he said, softly.

Memah stared at him, shocked. "Rodo, *no*!"

Nova looked at Dance, jerked his thumb at the blast doors. "You're the only one who can do it, flyboy. Go!"

There was a long moment that seemed to stretch to infinity, and then the others started to move.

The lieutenant said, "Hold up there! Let me see your authorization." He approached, and his men followed.

Nova held up a hand. "You'll need respirators," he said. "These two were gassed. Nerve toxin—better not get too close. I've got some antitoxin ampoules here, if you'll let me inoculate you and your men—"

The guards were only a few meters away now. They showed no concern about any possible proximity to nerve gas.

"You gonna take the right side?" Rodo said out of the corner of his mouth.

"Yeah. Watch that little guy on the left—he's already got his hand on his blaster."

"Copy. Nice knowing you, Nova."

"You, too, Rodo."

70

CORRIDOR OUTSIDE MEDICAL BAY, DEATH STAR

Ratua saw the action begin as if the participants were moving in slow motion. He was no fighter, but as the guards and Stihl and Rodo tangled, he saw one of the guards draw a blaster, and he knew his old jailer and the bouncer wouldn't be able to stop the man in time.

But Celot Ratua Dil might.

He moved as fast as he had ever moved in his life.

The blaster came up, and the guard extended his arm. Ratua could see the man's finger begin to tighten, slowly, slowly . . .

Ratua slammed into him. There was no skill involved—it was just a body block—but his speed magnified the force with which he struck the trooper enough to knock the latter into the corridor's far wall. The blaster clattered to the floor, followed by the unconscious trooper.

Ratua was momentarily stunned himself, the impact having hit him just as hard, of course. But he'd been prepared for it. He reeled, but managed to stay on his feet until his head cleared.

The world resumed its normal speed. He saw other troopers going for their blasters, but Stihl and Rodo were among them now, too close for the guards to shoot without risking hits on their own people.

Time to leave.

Memah, Vil, Teela, and Doc Divini were just inside the doors. Ratua moved to join them, kicking in the afterburner again. He slapped the hatch control as he blurred by it.

The blast doors closed behind him and locked.

The bay was a small one, used primarily for berthing and launching medical vessels. And there was their ticket to freedom, the E-2T shuttle, sitting on the landing turntable.

As they approached, another officer came down the ramp. He eyed them suspiciously; Ratua was convinced that there was a certain rank of Imperial officers whose only job was to eye everything suspiciously.

The officer, a sergeant major, said, "What do you people want here?"

Uli stepped up. "I'm Dr. Divini," he said. "This is my team. We have a medical emergency we need to get to, stat. That's our ship."

"Your orders—"

"They're in the ship's computer. I'll transmit them from there once we've launched."

"Protocol—"

Uli stepped up close to the officer. "Shut it, man," he said in a low voice, "do you want to be responsible for the death of Admiral Daala?"

The officer's eyes went wide. "Admiral Daala?"

"Her ship has been hit by Rebel fire and we're detailed to collect her. You sure you want to be the man who held us up?"

The officer stepped aside.

"Let's go, people!" Uli said. "We've got a job to do."

They moved quickly up the ramp into the shuttle, Ratua thinking, *The doc's a pretty good con man. Who knew?*

Nova ducked a wild swing, caught the attacking guard's arm, and spun him into the trooper behind him. Both men fell, but he had no time to rejoice, because there were others coming for him, lots of others. He waded into a pair of guards and hit both at the same instant with a double punch, smashing their noses, then dropped and swept, upending another one, and before that one hit the deck he was up again firing a side kick into the belly of yet another—

Beside him, Rodo grabbed a guard by his front, lifted him off his feet, and head-butted the man, knocking his helmet off, then threw him into another trooper. He whirled and took out two more with a spin kick.

"We're having fun now, aren't we?" the big man said. He laughed.

Nova recognized his recurring nightmare, which had now become reality. He didn't know the how or the why of it. He only knew that they were going to lose.

Well, then—that was how it would be.

They'd taken out a goodly number of guards, but there were still seven or eight of them standing, and the only reason he and Rodo hadn't been roasted yet was because the fighting had been too close for the guards to use their blasters. That was about to change, however. They were backing away, going for their weapons. The game would soon be over.

Nova felt fear welling inside him. Not for himself; he knew he was a dead man fighting. Two against fifteen, the latter armed with blasters? A win was never in those cards. But it was vitally important that he prolong the fight as long as he could, to give the others time to escape.

This would be his last dance, and he wanted it to be the best he could manage. Going up against impossible odds, going down swinging, using what he knew.

There were a lot worse ways to check out.

Beside him, Rodo grabbed a guard's head in both massive hands and twisted. The guard dropped, his neck broken. But another trooper had come up behind the big man, and now he thrust his blaster into Rodo's back. Nova saw Rodo's midsection turn black and charred as the energy beam burned its way through, saw Rodo's look of shock as he fell . . .

He saw another trooper drawing down on him, saw the blaster's muzzle aimed at his head, and knew he could never reach it in time.

The world turned white hot, like the center of a star, and then icy black, colder than space.

71

E-2T MEDSHUTTLE 5537

Dance dropped into the pilot's seat and fired up the central processor. The heads-up display appeared.

"Sublight drive up," he reported. "Now, if someone'll just open the door . . ."

It took only a couple of seconds for Door Control to query over the comm: "E-Two-Tee Medical Shuttle Five-Five-Three-Seven, why are you powering up?"

Dance looked at Uli. Uli activated the comm.

"This is Dr. Kornell Divini, op number 504614575. We have an emergency pickup."

"Transmit your orders, Doctor."

Uli looked at Dance. "Do it, Vil."

Dance sent the file.

LIBRARY AND ARCHIVES, DEATH STAR

The hardwired comm line lit. Atour picked up the headset. "Flight Control," he said.

"Flight Control? The comm station must have given me the wrong connection. Sorry."

Atour blinked. "Who are you trying to contact?"

"The library. This is Lieutenant Esture. We just had a droid we were examining do a firmware meltdown and we need to talk to its supervisor."

"Sorry I can't help you, Lieutenant—we're kind of busy here."

"Right. Out."

Atour broke the connection and began to sweat. This was bad. They'd recheck the number and call again. If he didn't answer—and he had to answer, in case it was Bay Door Control—they'd know something was wrong, and they'd be sending somebody to have a little talk with him right away. Droids that suddenly went blank were rare enough that they'd suspect tampering. Add that to a comm number that was misconnected more than once, and even an Imperial officer could do the math.

How much time did he have? Minutes, if he was lucky. Seconds, more likely . . .

The comm lit again. Atour activated it. "Flight Control."

"Flight Control, this is Bay Door Control Five-Seven-Five-Four-One. We have orders for departure of an E-Two-Tee Medshuttle."

Atour tried to sound bored. "Order number?"

The tech read off the code. Atour counted slowly to three. "Ah, yeah, here it is. That's a valid number, Control. Let 'em go."

"Copy that, Flight Control."

Atour shut down the comm and leaned back in his chair. Now if P-RC3's programming continued to work, the ship would be away in a moment or two, and if anybody tried to stop it with the rigged tractor beam—which they might, because Tractor Beam Control wouldn't have a copy of the ship's order in its computer any more than the real Flight Control did—then, in theory, the beam wouldn't work and they should fly free.

In theory.

In any event, there was nothing else he could do now. He rose and stepped away from his desk. If Teela Kaarz's evaluation of the danger was correct, and if the Rebels could read the plans well enough to spot the design flaw—both entirely reasonable assumptions—then the Death Star might have only a few minutes more of existence left to it. If that indeed proved to be the case, he knew where he wanted to spend those last few minutes.

Atour walked into the stacks until he was surrounded by shelves of various data storage. Tapes, chips, disks, even books. As always, it comforted him to be encompassed by knowledge. He sat down on a bench.

A pity he would never write that book. The destruction of the Death Star would have made a powerful final chapter. Ah, well . . . perhaps someone else would put stylus to screen someday and tell the tale.

Atour smiled. He took a deep breath of the musty air.

He was content.

COMMAND CENTER CONTROL ROOM, DEATH STAR

Tarkin stood watching the planet/moon graphic as the orbit around the world came closer to being complete.

Vader had taken out his elite TIE squad and knocked off several of the Rebels, though that hadn't been necessary. They couldn't hurt this station. Nothing could.

An operations lieutenant approached. Tarkin looked at him. The man was obviously worried. He said, "We've analyzed their attack, sir, and there is a danger."

Danger? Impossible!

"Should I have your ship standing by?"

Tarkin stared at the man. "Evacuate? In our moment of triumph? I think you overestimate their chances." He turned back to watch the graphic.

Cut and run just as they were about to wipe out the head base of the Rebellion? Preposterous!

The voice from the speaker said, "Rebel base, three minutes and closing."

What harm could those last few fighters possibly do in that time? In less than three minutes, they would be orphans, easy pickings, and the war would effectively be won.

SUPERLASER FIRE CONTROL, DEATH STAR

Tenn Graneet watched the graphic on his screen. The target would be within range in another couple of minutes.

His mouth was as dry as desert sand, his belly churning like a heavy sea. He couldn't do this. He couldn't murder yet another world. But he couldn't stop it, either. Were he to stand down, another gunner would be up here to replace him in mere minutes, and he would be in the brig with a military death mark against him.

What was he going to do?

E-2T MEDSHUTTLE 5537, YAVIN SYSTEM, GORDIAN REACH

The bay doors opened, and Vil punched it. The little ship rocketed out. Now all he had to do was stay in the groove . . .

"E-Two-Tee Medical Shuttle Five-Five-Three-Seven, this is Flight Control. Where are you going?"

Vil said, "Flight Control, this is Lieutenant Fayknom. We have an emergency pickup."

"I show no record of your flight plan."

Stall, Vil! "Hey, that's not my problem. I just fly where I'm told. Check with Door Control, they vetted us."

"We are attempting to do that now, Lieutenant. Turn it around and return to the dock until we get it cleared up."

"Negative on that, Flight Control. This is a priority mission. We come back, it'll be too late to do our job."

The Flight Control officer was between a rock and a hard place, Vil knew. He had his protocols, and they weren't being met. But somebody had opened the doors and let the shuttle leave, so maybe it was a computer error. It wouldn't be the first one.

"This is TIE x-one," came a deep voice over the comm. "What is the nature of your mission, shuttle?"

Vil felt his insides freeze. Any starfighter pilot who knew a tractor from a pressor knew that designation. It was Vader himself on the comm.

Vil said, "An incoming Imperial ship has been damaged by Rebel fire. They have wounded."

"I know of no such Imperial arrivals," Vader said. "Return to the station."

"Copy, Lord Vader. We are returning to the station." He shut off the comm.

Ratua said, "What? Are you crazy?"

"Relax," Vil said. "We aren't going back. But if he thinks we are, that buys us a few more seconds to get clear. We're faster than he is, once we get moving. He won't be able to—uh-oh."

"What?" That from Teela.

"He's coming at us."

TIE X1

The instant he had seen that medical conveyance, Vader had felt something wrong, a clamor from the dark side. While he ordered the shuttle back to the station, all it took was a moment's probing with the Force for him to recognize a mind that was familiar.

There were several aboard, none of them weak-minded, but one . . . a woman . . . where had he felt her before?

Ah, he had it. On the station, when he had toured during construction. One of the builders, an architect, had shut him out of her thoughts, as if slamming a door in his face. He'd been impressed by her strength of mind and will.

What was an architect doing on a medical rescue ship?

And then he knew: deserters!

His anger surged. There were so many things about this project that he had not been able to control. Well, he could deal with this! The X-wings could wait a moment or two longer. He would take care of these traitors himself. They would learn that resisting Darth Vader was fatal . . .

As he and his wingmates bore in, the medical ship slewed into a tight, high-g turn. Vader felt the fabric of the Force shiver as he adjusted his path to intercept.

He opened the channel again. "Return to the station, shuttle, or I will fire on you," he said.

E-2T MEDSHUTTLE 5537

They were in deep trouble, Vil knew. They weren't even armed, and Darth Vader was the best fighter pilot in the galaxy. He remembered saying something once to the effect that he would probably just augur his ship in if he ever found himself in Vader's crosshairs—that way at least he got to choose when to die.

It wasn't just his life on the line now, though.

Desperate, Vil ran every trick he could think of through his mind. None of them was going to do the job. They were cooked.

Unless . . .

TIE X1

Vader bored in. The targeting computer narrowed the scan. He had a lock. Whatever they were up to—spies, perhaps?—it didn't matter. He would eliminate them, then return to the main task.

He thumbed the fire buttons.

72

E-2T MEDSHUTTLE 5537

Vil slapped the retrofire controls. The reverse thrusters all lit full-out. The ambulance didn't stop, but it slowed enough so that Vader and his two wingmates blew past as if the larger craft were standing still.

Vil punched the sublights back up to full and angled to starboard. No tricks now, just a straight run, a sprint—

TIE X1

Vader was angry with himself. They'd used such an obvious and simple avoidance ploy that he hadn't seen it coming, even through the Force. He toggled the comm channel. "Get a tractor beam on that medshuttle!"

The reply crackled through his headphones. "I'm sorry, Lord Vader, but the beam generator for that sector has tripped its breakers. We'll have it back online momentarily—"

Blast!

Vader swung around to follow the fleeing ship.

"Lord Vader," came the voice of one of his TIE pilots.

"What is it?"

"Another trio of X-wing fighters is making a run up the same trench."

Vader reached out with the dark side, seeking . . .

And immediately sensed a presence in whom the Force was powerful, as powerful as it would be in a Jedi Knight.

Vader realized immediately that this was by far the greater problem.

"Break off," he ordered his wingmates. "Back to the station to intercept the new attackers."

"What about the medshuttle?"

"Let it go. It's not important."

Vader led his pilots back toward the station. They arrowed down into the trench, their fighters screaming between the high walls.

There were the three X-wings. Vader and his wingmates followed, blasting them one by one. Again, no real effort was necessary. Were they all suicidal?

But, he realized, none of them was carrying the pilot with whom the Force had been riding. That one was still out here somewhere. Vader knew he had to find that one. He was a danger—perhaps the only real danger.

"I need locations on the remaining Rebel fighters," he said.

"At once, Lord Vader." There was a short pause. "There are only three more, my lord, and they have just entered—"

"—the same trench," Vader finished. Whatever the target, the Rebels were convinced it was worth every ship they had. He knew he had best finish the last three quickly.

E-2T MEDSHUTTLE 5537

Vil didn't know why Vader had broken off the pursuit, but he wasn't complaining. He tried to coax a little more juice out of the sublight engines. The encounter with Vader had lost them precious time; they still had to make it out of tractor beam range before—

He felt the ship lurch, even as Ratua asked, "Why are we slowing down?"

Vil shoved the feeder slide control to maximum, but the shuttle continued to slow. He said, "They've got the tractor beam working again."

"Can we break free?" Uli asked.

"I don't know. We should be right at the limits of its range. I'm locking in the auxiliary power . . ." He dialed up the rheostat, suiting action to words. The E-2T surged, then slowed again.

"Vil?" Teela said.

"We're still moving in the right direction," he said. "There's still a—"

The ambulance ship started to shudder; then, after a few more seconds, it stopped.

Then it began to move backward.

"Frag," Vil said, his voice quiet. "They got us."

The engines strained, but there was a definite increased speed sternward. The drive power dials started to move into the overload zones. "The engines'll blow if I don't shut them down," Vil said.

"Let them," Teela said. "Better to die trying than to let them capture and execute us. We owe Atour, Nova, and Rodo that much."

Vil looked around. The others all nodded. He reached for Teela's hand, held it.

73

COMMAND CENTER CONTROL ROOM, DEATH STAR

The officer said, "Less than a minute, sir."

Tarkin nodded. Seconds away from glory. At last. After the years of scheming, of work, now he would show them, show them all!

TIE X1 MERIDIAN TRENCH

Vader and his two wingmates flew the trench, the last three X-wings dead ahead.

His wingmate fired, hit one of the Rebels. The wounded ship pulled up, out of the fight.

"Let him go," Vader commanded. "Stay on the leader!"

One of the ships hung back, obviously trying to delay Vader and his pilots. He focused on it. Lined up.

Fired.

The ship exploded.

One left. Vader moved to engage him. "I'm on the leader," he announced.

The TIE x1 screamed down the length of the trench, hot on the X-wing's tail. Closer . . . almost there . . .

Vader felt energy coming from the pilot in almost palpable waves. "The Force is strong in this one," he said, more to himself than his wingmates.

Strong, but not strong enough to stop Vader. Not strong enough to prevent the man who killed Obi-Wan Kenobi from doing what had to be done.

Vader triggered his guns.

He hit the fighter's R2 unit, saw the smoke and flames erupt from the hit.

Good.

Now, he thought, *we finish this.*

COMMAND CENTER CONTROL ROOM, DEATH STAR

"Rebel base is in range," the voice from the comm said.

Elated, Tarkin turned to Motti. He kept his voice calm. "You may fire when ready."

TIE X1 MERIDIAN TRENCH

Slowly, Vader crept up on the last X-wing. The Force swirled about the mysterious pilot; eddies, clouds, a vortex of powerful energy. Who could this be? This was no Jedi, of that Vader was certain, but he was steeped in the Force like one.

The target danced back and forth across his screen. Then, finally, a lock!

"I have you now," Vader murmured. He moved to thumb the firing buttons. Then, suddenly—

His starboard wingmate's TIE exploded.

"*What?*" Vader twisted about, trying to see through the cockpit's transparisteel while simultaneously reaching out with the Force. Enemy fire was coming in from a totally unexpected direction. But how? There weren't any more enemy fighters in the vicinity!

Then he felt the attacker—approaching from above, to the port side. Vader couldn't see it, but his remaining wingmate could. He screamed, "*Look out—!*"

The port wingmate's TIE collided with Vader's ship and was knocked spinning, out of control. The x1 ricocheted off the wingmate, sending the latter to a fiery doom against a trench wall. Vader's ship was hurled out of the trench and sent, pitching and yawing, into an uncontrollable series of flips.

At one point, he caught a blurred glimpse of the unexpected attacker. He couldn't be sure, but it looked like the battered old Corellian freighter he'd investigated earlier, which had escaped just after his duel with Obi-Wan.

No time to wonder about that now. Vader fought to stabilize his craft, but the control surfaces were damaged. He had to use his drive pulses.

His TIE continued to spin, however, and he realized he was an easy target. He managed to get the spin under control and then ready the little ship for the jump to lightspeed. A second or two would be enough. A couple of light-seconds would put him more than half a million kilometers away and give him a chance to get the TIE under control.

But, he realized grimly, whatever that pilot who was one with the Force planned to shoot, he was now going to have a chance to hit it.

74

SUPERLASER FIRE CONTROL, DEATH STAR

Tenn heard the order as if he were at the bottom of a deep mine shaft. It echoed over him:

"Commence primary ignition."

His crew threw switches, adjusted rheostats, pushed buttons. The status reports came in one by one, like pronouncements of doom.

All too soon, it was down to him. Slowly, Tenn lifted the incredible tonnage of his right arm. His hand trembled on the lever. He saw his CO watching him through the smoked lens of the blast helmet. He could read the man's mind: *Shoot, Chief! Shoot!*

Tenn wasn't a believer in anything more than he could see and hear and touch, never had been. But now he prayed for a miracle—for something, anything, to deliver him from the burden of so many more deaths. For something to stop it, somehow. With his free hand he activated the comm. "Stand by," he said, hardly knowing why he was saying it, seeking only to delay the inevitable as long as possible.

"Stand by . . ."

COMMAND CENTER CONTROL ROOM, DEATH STAR

Motti yelled in the background: "They've fired proton torpedoes down an auxiliary heat shaft! Incoming! Incoming! The reactor will blow!"

Tarkin blinked. No. No, it wouldn't. He was calm. All would be well. This station was invulnerable. It was unbeatable. It was unthinkable that it could be beaten.

Unthinkable—

E-2T MEDSHUTTLE 5537

The shuttle suddenly leapt forward as if kicked by a giant's boot. The inertial dampeners kept them from being whiplashed, but they could see the starfield shift crazily about them.

"What the—" Ratua began. He stopped as he, and the rest of them, stared.

The rear viewer was focused on the Death Star, which had exploded in a silent, horrendous flare of red and orange and yellow. A hyperspatial reflux ring expanded outward.

"What . . . ?" Memah was shaking her head in disbelief.

"It blew up," Uli said. He sounded stunned. "The Death Star just . . . blew up."

"Everybody, hang on," Vil said. "The edge of the shock wave will hit us pretty fast—"

The ship jumped, shook suddenly, then began to tumble, a leaf in a gale.

"Kark!" Vil said, fighting to regain control of the ambulance. "I hope she doesn't break up!"

The tumble continued. There was a bad moment, another worse one—and then the battering stopped.

"What happened?" Teela asked.

"Shock wave passed us. We're still in one piece." Vil engaged the sublights. "Now if we can just stay ahead of the shrapnel we should be okay."

"Remind me to find out who made this ambulance," Ratua said. "I want to send them a testimonial. And if they make flitters, I want to buy one."

The others laughed—the relieved laughter of those narrowly delivered from death. All except Teela.

"Teela?" Vil said. "You okay?"

"Yeah. It's just that—the Death Star was a monster, no question about that. It was conceived by monsters and controlled by them. But not everyone on board was a monster."

Nobody said anything for a while.

"How did it happen?" Ratua asked. "Was it the Alliance, or did someone just push the wrong button?"

"We'll never know," Memah said.

"The superlaser must've misfired. That's the only explanation that makes any sense," Vil replied. "It couldn't have been anything the Rebels threw at it. Those X-wings were like buzz-beetles trying to take down a ronto."

"Don't be too sure," Teela said. She quickly explained about the unshielded vent.

Vil looked skeptical. "I'm not buying it. Even with the targeting computer, the chances of lobbing a proton torpedo down that shaft were a million to one."

Teela smiled. "What was it you told me once? Sometimes long odds are the only ones worth playing?"

There was another short silence.

"So what now?" Uli asked. He was tired, and he could see that the others were, too. They were all in fairly heavy shock. Watching two planets—or one planet and one battle station the size of a moon—blow up within the span of a cycle was just too much for the mind to encompass.

"We have pretty good star charts," Vil said. "And a decent cruising range. We can get to any of half a dozen systems. But there's a Rebel base on that moon right over there, and I'd guess they're pretty happy right now. Might be room for a few people willing to sign up."

"You'd do that?" Memah asked. "Join the Rebellion?"

Vil shrugged. "I'm a fighter pilot. It's what I do, and I'm good at it. More to the point, I'm a fighter pilot who's extremely disillusioned with the side I've been on. In addition to my piloting skills, I can take a TIE apart blindfolded and put it back together. I know a few secrets our new friends might be interested in."

"Not to mention," Memah said, "you're the man who outflew Darth Vader."

Vil grinned, then looked at Teela. "Of course, it depends on your plans."

"It does? Why might that be?"

Vil looked like he'd just swallowed a cup of too-hot caf. "Well," he said, "if you're agreeable, I thought we might get married."

"Interesting way to propose, flyboy," she said. "I'll think about it." But she grinned. Then her expression turned serious. "They'll need planners and designers, too," she said. "And I wouldn't be a prisoner, but a free woman. There are a lot of political prisoners still under the Empire's hand. I'd like to help them."

Memah said, "Not a bad idea. Maybe I'll tag along, try to find another cantina to run. Girl's got to eat, after all, and I'm guessing the Rebels don't mind lifting a glass now and then."

"I wouldn't worry about having to work if I were you," Ratua said to her.

"No offense, Green-Eyes, but as much fun as you are, I don't want to be a smuggler's woman. I'm done with the adventurous life for a while."

"Well, I was thinking of getting out of the smuggling business," he said. "Into legal ventures."

"Uh-huh."

Ratua grinned. "Probably should have mentioned that my family is, um, well fixed. I think they'd like to meet you. They always hoped I'd find a good woman and settle down, get into the family business."

"Which is?"

"They manage real estate. Own a few properties, here and there. Places like the Netaluma Tower on Imperial Center."

"Coruscant," Uli corrected him. He realized it was a measure of just how tired he was that Ratua's admission of wealth was hardly even surprising.

"My mistake. Anyway, my share of that alone would mean you wouldn't have to work if you didn't want to."

"Your share? And how much would that be?"

"Well . . ." He hesitated.

"Speak, or I'll twist your head off."

"Half a billion credits, give or take a couple of million."

She stared at him. "What? You're *rich*? Why'd you become a smuggler?"

Ratua shrugged. "I thought property management was boring. I was young and rebellious, and I wanted to do something more interesting. But I'm thinking maybe I've had enough excitement for one lifetime."

"I'm going to kill you," Memah said. "No, maybe I'll wait until after I meet your family. They'll probably want to help."

Teela looked at Uli. "What about you, Doc?"

What, indeed? Uli opened his mouth, fully intending to tell them that he planned to head for the farthest stars, to find a world somewhere way out in the Reach and open up a practice there. Someplace where neither the Empire nor the Alliance was known. He'd been working in unwilling servitude for just about all of his adult life, after all. Freedom—the ability to choose where he wanted to work, for how long, and for whom, if anyone, was a powerful lure.

But what he heard himself say was, "I'm with Vil. If the Rebellion will have me, I'll throw in my lot with theirs. I'm a pretty good battle surgeon—at least, I've had a lot of practice. And the Empire has to be stopped."

"Somebody made a pretty good start on that today," Memah said.

"So," Vil said, "since we're all in agreement, let's go see how the other half lives, shall we?"

75

TIE X1, INTERPLANETARY SPACE, YAVIN SYSTEM

Darth Vader had been safely out of danger when the Death Star had blown up. His ship was damaged, but still spaceworthy enough that, with a couple of careful jumps, he could reach a hidden Imperial naval base a few light-years away.

Despite the direness of the situation, he couldn't help another painful smile. The Death Star, with all its troops and weapons, the superlaser that could by itself destroy entire planets, trillions of credits' worth of labor and material—all of it was gone to incandescent dust in an instant.

He didn't know exactly how it had happened, but he knew it had something to do with the pilot of that tiny, insignificant X-wing. Somehow, he alone had taken out the battle station. Vader didn't need the dark side to tell him that, or that the pilot had survived the explosion.

One man had done what a fleet could not have managed.

The Force was indeed strong in this one.

Who was he? Not a Jedi—Vader was certain. He had felt no sense of the control that a Jedi would possess. In the final analysis, however, it really didn't matter. Be the mysterious stranger a Jedi or not, Vader knew that he and this other who was so permeated with the Force would meet again.

It was inevitable.

He checked his position and readied his small ship for the next insertion into hyperspace. He knew he would have to make his report to the Emperor immediately, even though he was certain that the Dark Lord of the Sith was already aware of what had happened to his pet project. He was not looking forward to the meeting. As he made the jump to lightspeed and beyond, Darth Vader was certain of one thing:

His Master would not be pleased.

About the Authors

Michael Reaves received an Emmy Award for his work on the *Batman* animated television series. He has worked for DreamWorks, among other studios, and has written fantasy novels and supernatural thrillers, including *InterWorld* (with Neil Gaiman). Reaves is the *New York Times* bestselling author of *Star Wars: Darth Maul: Shadow Hunter,* as well as the co-author (with Steve Perry) of the two *Star Wars: MedStar* novels, *Battle Surgeons* and *Jedi Healer.* He lives in the Los Angeles area.

Steve Perry was born and raised in the Deep South and has lived in Louisiana, California, Washington, and Oregon. He is currently the science fiction, fantasy, and horror book reviewer for *The Oregonian.* Perry has sold dozens of stories to magazines and anthologies, as well as a considerable number of novels, animated teleplays, nonfiction articles, reviews, and essays. He wrote for *Batman: The Animated Series* during its first Emmy Award–winning season, authored the *New York Times* bestseller *Star Wars: Shadows of the Empire,* and also did the bestselling novelization for the blockbuster movie *Men in Black.*

About the Type

This book was set in Sabon, a typeface designed by the well-known German typographer Jan Tschichold (1902–74). Sabon's design is based upon the original letterforms of Claude Garamond and was created specifically to be used for three sources: foundry type for hand composition, Linotype, and Monotype. Tschichold named his typeface for the famous Frankfurt typefounder Jacques Sabon, who died in 1580.